The Temperature of Me and You

Brian Zepka

HYPERION

LOS ANGELES • NEW YORK

First Edition, January 2022
10 9 8 7 6 5 4 3 2 1
FAC-021131-21344
Printed in the United States of America

This book is set in ITC Slimbach Std, Spectrum MT Pro/Monotype
Designed by Marci Senders

Library of Congress Control Number: 2021933792
ISBN 978-1-368-06471-2
Reinforced binding

Visit www.hyperionteens.com

For Gus, Finn, and JJ. May your childhoods be filled with adventure, hope, and affirmed first love.

one

I have four main takeaways from my Chemistry test today. First, the symbol on the periodic table for oxygen looks like the number of interesting things that happen in my life on a regular basis. The symbol for sodium, Na, represents my history of romance—not applicable. The symbol for radon, Rn, stands for my thoughts on when I want a boyfriend—right now. And the symbol for ununhexium, Uuh, is my response when people ask me if I am going to do something about it.

The most life-altering decision I've made in the past year is to proclaim that I prefer hard ice cream over soft serve as a Dairy Queen employee.

Speaking of which, another hour and tonight's shift will be over. My friends and I have been talking about Chemistry class while I pretend to wait for customers I not-so-secretly hope won't show up.

"The only answer I knew was hydrogen," Perry says, shoveling a spoonful of her large Reese's Peanut Butter Cup Blizzard into her mouth.

"Well, duh. The symbol for that one is literally just an *H*," I say.

"You got oxygen too, I hope, right?" Kirsten asks.

Perry rolls her eyes, digging deeper into her Blizzard. "Yeah, I think. I put *Ox* for that one."

Kirsten smiles and shakes her head. "It's an *O*. That's literally the easiest one."

"What? I thought *O* was for olerium."

"Olerium?" I ask, twitching my head. "Is that even a thing?"

"Of course it's a thing. But it wasn't on the test," Perry counters.

"Yeah, because it's definitely not a thing."

She laughs. "Are you serious?" Crushed Reese's Cups line her bottom row of teeth.

Kirsten reaches across the table and puts her hand over Perry's mouth. "Close this," she says, laughing. "No one wants to see that."

"I'm sorry," Perry says, grabbing a napkin and wiping the corners of her lips. "At this point, who cares? When will I ever need those elements in my actual life?"

"Um, this very second as you breathe them in," Kirsten answers.

"So technical."

Perry tries. She really does. And when I say tries, I mean tries everything she can to *not* do schoolwork and still pass. Like, when the three of us got together last night to complete the Chemistry worksheets for our test today, Kirsten and I actually did the work while Perry spent the night trying to find the answers on Google and replying to message boards that haven't been active in five years.

Unlike Kirsten, who is banking on her good grades for college, Perry Lyle is piling all her hopes into a cheerleading scholarship. She's on a regional all-star cheer team in addition to the school team.

I'm sure she could do both cheer squads *and* do well in school at the same time. But Perry says she would rather be amazing at one thing than average at a bunch of things. So she chooses cheer over school.

"Dylan, can you make my Blizzard now?" Kirsten asks, spinning around in her seat.

"Here, you can finish mine," Perry says, slamming her ice cream onto the table. Her chest rises as she holds in a burp.

Kirsten Lush is without a doubt the prettiest girl in the junior class. And, in my opinion, all of Falcon Crest High School. Me, a skinny gargoyle who is teetering on *okay* in the looks department, and Perry, a confused meerkat who is above average in the looks department but loses major points for her lack of any common sense and basic human functionality, are not who you'd expect Falcon Crest's own Elle Woods to associate with.

I lift my arms off the service counter and stand up straight. I push my hands into my lower back to stretch myself into a normal, upright human position.

My elbows are red from not moving once during my shift. To no one's surprise, I haven't had a single customer all night. It's January and twenty degrees in Falcon Crest. Even my manager knows how pointless staying open year-round is because he leaves as soon as I get here after school. Which, by the way, is probably illegal because I'm sixteen and operating a store by myself—but I don't ask questions. Perry and Kirsten don't count as customers because they come here whenever I am working to get free ice cream and keep me company.

"Perr, next time I'm making you a kid-size because you never finish what I give you," I say.

"How dare you," she says, squinting at me.

"What do you want, Kirsten?" I turn and walk toward the rattling ice-cream machines, staring at the colorful menu above me decorated with pictures of ice-cream cones and candy labels.

"Hey, did Jimmy escape out the back door or something?" Perry asks. She stands and looks down the hall to the bathrooms.

"I'll just finish Perry's ice cream," Kirsten replies, grabbing the cup from the table.

"He's in the bathroom," I say. Jimmy is an unfortunate soul from another school who's been directed here as a possible boyfriend candidate for me. But my thoughts about that are represented by the symbol for the element nobelium, No.

"Yeah, he's been in there for twenty minutes," Kirsten says. "He must really not be interested in you."

"Or dropping a big ole you-know-what," Perry says, crossing her arms and laughing to herself.

"Ew! Stop!" Kirsten shrieks. "I'm eating."

"I don't know why you brought him here," I whisper. "I told you I stalked his Instagram and I wasn't interested."

Perry shrugs. "Sometimes people are different in person. Savanna said he was single and looking, so I'm helping you out," she whispers back. "Plus, Kirsten and I agreed you guys would look cute together."

"First of all, I don't know why we would take a recommendation from Savanna Blatt. She is mean to all three of us and is most likely using this to screw us over somehow. He probably has an STD of the throat or something!"

"As I am sure you're well aware, nice boys are in short supply in this town. You take what you can get."

"It's too forced and awkward for me. I'm not in the mood for Perry Love Connections tonight."

"Every day is a day for a Perry Love Connection, my friend."

Perry has made it her personal mission to get me a boyfriend. But sometimes I would appreciate it if her mission had some standards attached to it.

"He's been rude this entire time."

"He really has," Kirsten says, nodding. "He hasn't even acknowledged me yet."

"See," I say, gesturing at Kirsten. "I can't date someone who doesn't acknowledge my overachieving best friend. If Kirsten can't get acknowledgment, then I have no chance."

"Ugh," Perry grunts. "How does it always end up you two against me? Let's just see how he is when he gets back."

"And how he smells," Kirsten says with a mouth full of ice cream. Perry and I roll our eyes in unison.

The bathroom door clicks, and Perry and Kirsten sit up as if they were misbehaving. Perry smirks at me while shimmying her shoulders.

"Watch . . . he won't talk to me," Kirsten blurts at the last second. Perry smacks her arm, shooting her a look.

Jimmy rounds the corner from the bathroom hallway and plants himself next to the service counter. I take a few steps away from him toward the other end. Perry smiles. It's quiet for a few seconds.

He's so out of place. Even if I did like him, he would never mesh well with the three of us. He looks like a church boy who just came from Sunday service or something. He's wearing thin, slip-on brown leather shoes that I swear my dad also owns, khaki pants, and a button-up shirt that's tucked in. Meanwhile, my shaggy, curly hair is reminiscent of a tumbleweed, and ice cream is splattered across the front of my shirt and arms. Kirsten's long brown hair rolls down her back in knotty waves. Perry's blond hair is tied on the top of her head into a baseball-size bun with a polka-dot scrunchy. They are both wearing leggings, sneakers, and their cheerleading hoodies.

"Did you want anything?" I ask, tapping my fingers on the counter. I want to fling a spoonful of hot fudge at Jimmy to mess up his clean-cut image.

"Nah, I'm good," he says. "Did I hear you guys talking about chemistry?"

I don't respond. Instead, I stare at Perry, raising my eyebrows, and wait for her to say something, since this is *her* guest, after all.

"We were," she says. "We had a test on the periodic table and had to match all the elements with their symbols and stuff. Dylan over here aced it. Didn't you, Dyl?" She smirks.

"We did that stuff, like, freshman year at my school," Jimmy says.

I resist the urge to roll my eyes again. "I thought it was fine," I say. "I don't know about acing it, but I didn't bomb."

"I aced it," Kirsten says.

"Nice, man!" Jimmy exclaims. I jerk my head back at his enthusiasm. "Right on." He extends his arm and puts his palm up. I scan it with my eyes, tracing the lines on his skin. He leaves it in the air for what I'm assuming is a high five.

I want to melt into a puddle like a vanilla ice-cream cone, be washed up with a mop, wrung out, and never be seen again. Kirsten's and Perry's lips curl in, ready to burst from laughter knowing I'm going to have to partake in this bro moment. I take a few steps toward him, because he's too far from me to reach, and lightly tap his palm with mine, inwardly cringing. My teeth are clenched.

"Thanks," I say, clearing my throat.

He inspects his palm, then wipes it on his pants. I must've left some sticky residue on his hand. At least the interaction wasn't a total waste.

Perry lets out her laughter in the form of a burping grunt.

"Yikes," Jimmy says to me. "Not hard to see why you did better on the test than those slobs." He laughs to himself, then taps my arm with the back of his hand.

"I said I aced it," Kirsten says, squinting at him. Jimmy ignores her comment.

I retreat into my phone, wondering how long this guy is going to stand here for.

"Oh!" Perry gasps. "Our newest paint-by-numbers kits just shipped."

"Yay!" Kirsten squeals. "Right on schedule."

We try to complete a new paint-by-numbers piece each season. We just completed our Christmas-themed canvases last week. But we finished past our deadline, or rather Kirsten's deadline, and didn't get to see the finished products before the holiday. As a result, Kirsten forced us to order our spring kits earlier than expected so we wouldn't fall behind again.

"You can't just paint on your own?" Jimmy asks. "You need little numbers to tell you were to put a color?" He laughs.

"No, actually, I don't need the numbers," Perry snaps. "It's just more relaxing that way. I'd like to see you try."

"Doesn't mean you're actually good at painting."

"What the—" Perry stands.

I clear my throat. "I need to start cleaning up to close the store," I lie. "Everyone should probably go." I exhale.

"What?" Perry asks. "But we—"

I slice my neck with my hand and glance at Jimmy.

She nods.

"Good idea. I can wait around after everyone leaves if you want?" Jimmy asks.

I blush. "Um, no, it's okay. Closing the store takes a while," I lie again. "You don't have to stand here that whole time."

He nods. "Here, take my number."

"Uh . . ." I start. I stare at him, my mouth hanging slightly open.

"Your phone?" He shakes his phone in his hand.

"Right."

I pull my phone from my pocket and punch in my code. He says his number for me to save, but I type 555-555-5555.

"Got it. I'll text you mine," I lie again.

"Sweet." He gives me a nod and walks past Kirsten and Perry without saying anything.

"Bye!" Kirsten screams. She turns her attention back to me. "What a rude boy."

"Well, I don't like him," Perry proclaims, throwing up her hands.

"I would hope not," I say, and fling a straw at her. "That was your pick. Thanks for putting us through that."

"You better have some self-respect and not text him," Kirsten says. "I've taught you better."

"I'm not going to. I didn't even type in his number."

"Oh, you're a player," Perry says, winking.

"Shut up. I can't deal with you guys anymore."

"His shoes were so weird," Kirsten says, crossing her legs. "If he was going for classic vintage, he completely missed the mark."

"Right? He looked like an old creeper," Perry says. She straightens her back. "Oh my gosh." Her eyes widen. "What if he is a creeper and gets mad when you don't ever text him and he stalks you and kills you? Remember that school assembly we had where the cop talked about that girl who was killed by the guy who found her through social media?"

"Are you kidding, Perry?" I ask. "Why would you say that?"

What if he is, though? It could totally happen. He knows where I work and go to school and could probably figure out where I live from my Instagram. Maybe I need to make my account private.

"Calm down. He's not," Kirsten says, dismissing the claim with a hand wave. "Savanna said she knows his family."

"Next time you see Savanna, tell her I'll handle my love life from now on," I say.

"What love life?" Perry asks.

"My *potential* love life."

"It has great potential," Kirsten says.

"Thanks, Kirsten. I think so too."

"I don't. You're ugly and smell bad!" Perry yells, smiling.

I laugh and scoop a pile of rainbow sprinkles into my hand, then chuck them at her. She screams and runs to the other side of the store. I keep throwing them as she tries to dodge. Kirsten remains seated. She wipes the sprinkles that landed on the table into her hand, escorting them carefully to the nearest trash can.

"Are you done?" Perry asks, brushing the sprinkles out of her hair.

"Yes, because I realize I have to clean this up now." I thrust my hands on my hips.

I get the dustpan and broom from the closet and sweep up the sprinkles.

Kirsten stands. She clears her throat before speaking while her facial expression morphs into a look of concern. "Dylan," she says in her announcer voice.

"Here we go," Perry mumbles.

Kirsten is dead set on being a news anchor or TV host of some sort in her future life. I've done more mock interviews for her than I can count.

"Many people would be hurt after another lost chance at love," she continues. Her tone drops two octaves. She enunciates each word slowly. "How are you coping right now?"

"By considering myself lucky I lost that chance," I say. Kirsten inhales. But before she can get out another word, I keep talking. "Can you guys go now for real?" I ask. "I want to finish cleaning and get out of here."

"Fine," Kirsten says, returning to her normal voice. Her shoulders dip. "Please text us when you're done." She pulls her keys from her hoodie's front pocket.

Kirsten is the only one out of the three of us who has her license, and I'm pretty sure she enjoys making everyone aware of it. Her car keys have enough key chains, rings, and bracelets to fill every accessories store in the Philadelphia area.

"See you tomorrow," I say.

They leave, and I finish sweeping the floor. I wipe the counters, tables, and the ice-cream machines. I refill the napkins, straws, spoons, syrups, and candies. I empty the register and put the money in a pencil case in the safe in my manager's office. The entire cleaning process only takes about ten minutes because there were no customers today. We close at 8:00 p.m. and it's 8:10 p.m. I'm ready to go, but as usual, my manager is nowhere to be found when it's time for him to lock up the store.

While I'm waiting, I start picking at a piece of the plastic counter that's chipping off. I think about how it's made of atoms and how atoms are made of protons and electrons. How do people even come up with this stuff?

My favorite elements we had to memorize were californium and americium. Mainly because they were super easy to remember, but also because the people naming them were so over it they just picked some obvious name. Like, what if I discovered an element here at Dairy Queen? My teacher said elements are everywhere. I could name it oreoanium. Although that kind of sounds like some weird sex thing people would rap about.

The door clicks open. My daydreaming is broken at the perfect time before my mind wanders any further into picturing various sex positions involving Oreos.

I look up, expecting to see my manager, but it's someone else.

two

"Are you still open?" a boy asks quietly. He pulls down his hood, revealing a head of thick brown hair. My eyes travel from his head to his feet *twice*. He has dark brown eyes and tan skin.

Correction—a cute boy.

His red hoodie has yellow lettering that says *Arizona State University*. He's wearing black jeans and black Vans. He looks my age, but I'm terrible at telling ages.

"Yeah," I say, swallowing and ignoring the fact we closed ten minutes ago.

He walks to the counter. I gaze into his eyes. He looks back at me, and I snap my head downward to stare at the floor.

"What do you want? Or—I mean...Sorry. That was rude. I meant, like, what can I get you?" I ask.

I suck.

I shift my eyeballs upward. He smiles, revealing big white teeth. My pulse intensifies. A layer of sweat coats my palms. I literally want to jump across the counter and lick this stranger's face. All my human abilities are failing. Inhibitions are dropping. What is happening? I pull my hands behind my back so I can't make any awkward hand gestures.

"Um . . ." he starts. He stares at the menu above my head. I stare at his perfectly messy hair. It's cut short on the sides but on top is a bird's nest of curly brown strands. If he wasn't close to me, I'd think it was black. But when he stands in the light, shades of brown shimmer along the curls.

He mumbles something I don't understand.

"What?" I ask, leaning toward him. I discreetly sniff but smell nothing. Which is better than an overwhelming cologne.

"Can I get one of those?" He points to the menu.

I follow his finger and there's no way I can tell what he's pointing at. If this were any other customer, I'd be super annoyed right now. But him not reading the menu and pointing is kind of adorable.

"One of what?" I ask with a laugh.

"The Blizzard thing."

"The Blizzard thing?" I raise my eyebrows. "You've never heard of a Blizzard before?"

"Not really."

"Okay?" I massage my eyebrows. "What do you want in it?"

"Vanilla ice cream and . . . Oreos." He taps his chin.

Such a simple, ordinary choice. I thought he'd choose something more interesting like chocolate ice cream with M&M's and Reese's Peanut Butter Cups. Or maybe I was *hoping* he would choose something more interesting. Everyone gets vanilla ice cream with Oreos.

All the old, boring people from this town just come in and get vanilla ice cream with Oreos. Every time. I'm hoping he's not like everyone.

I turn around and walk to the ice-cream machine. I grab a medium cup, even though I didn't ask him what size he wants, and fill it with vanilla soft serve. I'm not going to risk sounding stupid again to ask him what size.

But the three seconds of silence is too much for me to handle.

"Are you from Arizona?" I ask, watching the soft serve swirl into the empty cup.

"Yup," he says. His voice is deep but breathy. Almost as if he's afraid of talking too loudly.

"Do they not have Dairy Queens there? I've never been."

"I'm sure they do. But I'm from a small town north of Phoenix. We didn't have much of anything."

I nod. I attempt to put extra Oreos into his cup. My shaky hand spills half of them onto the clean counter. I glance over my shoulder, and he's smiling at me. I quickly look away, then blend the Blizzard. Is he, a good-looking boy my age in my town, actually into me? My body quivers at the thought.

"Anything else?" I ask, placing his order on the counter.

He shakes his head, then pulls some cash from his hoodie's front pocket.

"It's three dollars and seventy-five cents. Spoons are right there." I point to the basket of spoons and wait to see how many he picks up. Is he by himself? Or is someone waiting in the car to split the ice cream with him? A boyfriend? A girlfriend? His parents? His dog? That'd be cute if he was splitting it with his dog.

Then again, this has chocolate in it and chocolate is poisonous for dogs and a dog poisoner is not cute. Scratch the boy-next-door-with-his-dog fantasy.

He picks up one spoon. I sharply inhale.

"Do you have, like, a cup holder?" he asks, looking around and making a circle with his fingers.

"Um, we have those cardboard trays that hold four cups."

"That'll work. Can you put the cup in there?"

"What? You can't carry one cup of ice cream? Too heavy for you?" I joke.

His face flushes. He rubs the back of his neck but doesn't say anything. We stare at each other for a few moments until I realize he's serious.

"Oh, okay," I say.

I pull out one of the cardboard trays from a cabinet and place it on the counter.

"Are you here every night?" he asks.

I'm reaching for his ice cream when he asks the question.

"It feels like most."

My fingertips wrap around the cup. The outside is wet with condensation. My eyes are so distracted by his long, tan fingers spinning the spoon in front of me that the cup slips from my grip. It bounces on the counter, then spins toward the edge.

"Oh no. My bad," I say, diving over the counter to try and catch the falling cup.

He twitches, bends over, and grabs the cup before it slams into the floor. When his fingers grasp it there's a loud pop, like a firework.

I scream. The cup literally explodes. The ice cream bursts into a cloud of white liquid, then splashes onto the counter.

Thick droplets crash into my eyes.

"Ugh!" I groan.

I blink while wiping some of the milky water from my face. When I'm able to see again, the paper cup is melted around his fingers.

three

I back away from the counter. "What was that?" I ask. I spit
Oreo chunks from my lips.

"I...I'm..." he mutters. He inspects his hands like he's never
seen them before. Drops of ice cream run down the center of his
forehead between his eyebrows. His brown hair has white tips. A
creamy liquid covers the floor around his feet, as if someone dumped
a milk carton everywhere.

The front door swings open as my manager walks inside with
his longboard in hand. He stops after taking a few steps. "Whoa.
What happened here?" he asks. His eyes are bloodshot.

Arizona boy turns and bolts out of the store before I can say
anything.

"Hey!" I yell. "Where are you going?"

"Did that dude just make this mess?" my manager asks.

"I think so. . . . Kind of. . . . But so did I." I scratch the side of my
head.

"What?"

"I dropped the cup and it was ice cream before and then he grabbed it and then it all melted instantaneously and blew up in our faces."

"Are you high?"

"No."

"Okay, well, just clean this up, then."

"No, I have to go." I run to my manager's office, grab my parka and backpack, and race back to the front of the store.

"Are you serious, Dyl? You're not leaving this here." His feet slip and slide on the puddle of melted ice cream as he tries to grab my arm.

"I'm usually out of here at eight and it's eight twenty. You've been gone all night smoking. I have to go get this person. I'll explain later!"

I burst through the front door and scan the strip mall parking lot. There's only my manager's parked Jeep and a few cars in the Burger King drive-thru. I try to wipe the ice cream off my arms, but it clumps into my arm hair, becoming stickier and grosser.

To the left, there's no one in sight. Just the closed UPS Store. To the right, I see the boy's bright red hoodie in front of the Thai restaurant a few stores down.

"Hey!" I call out again.

He spins around, then breaks into a run when he sees me.

I dart after him. The textbooks in my backpack slam into my body with each stride. I pull on the straps to tighten the bag around my shoulders.

The boy turns the corner of the strip mall. I pick up my pace. Why is he running like this? How is it that serious?

I finally reach the corner of the mall where he disappeared and slide on some gravel as I make the sharp right turn. I place my hand on the tan cinder-block wall to stabilize myself against the momentum. There's a row of four green dumpsters along the side of the building. A six-foot-high fence cuts off the path behind the building and there are thick woods to the left. The boy's head swivels in front of the metal fence, searching for an escape route. Clouds of breath puff from his mouth into the freezing air.

I stop sprinting and slowly jog to the last dumpster, where he's standing. He takes a few steps toward the woods.

"I wouldn't go in there if I were you," I say, resting my hands on my knees. "I mean, unless you want to die. There's a steep drop-off over a cliff. You won't get far."

That's a lie. Well, not totally a lie. There's no cliff, but I wouldn't go in there. Kirsten's house is on the other side of those woods, and I've been among those trees many times. It's where I had my first kiss, with Kirsten, in sixth grade. But it's also where a guy beat me up in eighth grade after I decided I didn't like kissing girls. So I would say there's a steep drop—but not a physical one. A metaphorical drop-off into a weird time in my life that I'm not trying to relive right now.

"Why are you following me?" he asks. He puts his hands on his hips.

"Why are you running from me?" I ask. "I should be running from you. You just made ice cream blow up."

"No, I didn't."

"Well, that's what it looked like."

"You dropped it and it spilled everywhere."

I laugh. "Are you kidding? I've dropped Blizzards before. They don't spontaneously combust. Nice try."

"I don't get what you're trying to say." He runs his hand through his hair.

I shrug. "I'm not trying to say anything. Just looking for an explanation. It's not every day that happens. How did you do it? It was kind of cool, slash, also kind of scary. Do you have a firework up your sleeve?"

He shakes his head.

"Is that why you needed a cup holder? You couldn't touch the ice cream?"

He paces in silence. His face is tense.

"Okay, well, guess I'm seeing things, then."

A lightbulb buzzes on the wall behind him, casting a shadow over one side of his face. I slip off my backpack, put on my parka, and zip it to my neck.

"Well, I should say the real reason I came after you is because you forgot to pay. I'm going to need those four dollars from you to cover damages."

He thrusts his hands into his pockets, then fumbles around.

I sigh. "I'm joking. You really want to get rid of me, don't you?"

He takes a deep breath and clutches his hands. "Kind of. What's your name?" he asks.

I cross my arms. "That's not the smoothest subject change, but okay. It's Dylan. You?"

"Jordan."

"Nice to meet you, I guess."

He nods.

I bite my chapped lip. "If we're going to talk normally as if nothing weird happened back there, can we at least go somewhere else away from these dumpsters?" I say. "It smells like poop and sour milk."

"Are you done working?"

"Yeah, some random person came in and blew up a Blizzard, so I got to leave. Are you free to leave the premises?"

He smirks.

Finally. His smile melts me again.

"Yeah." He lifts his hoodie to wipe some of the ice cream off his hair, revealing his stomach. I gaze at the perfect lines diving into his underwear.

We walk to the front of the strip mall in silence. Red banners with the words *Happy Holidays* hang on the lampposts in the parking lot.

"Did you walk here?" I ask, searching for another car besides my manager's Jeep.

"Ran."

"Oh? It's fifteen degrees. Who runs to get ice cream in the winter?"

"Do you want to walk home with me?" He ignores my comment. "It's not far."

I look around, mulling over the decision and wondering why this mysterious person refuses to answer any of my questions. Maybe Jimmy wasn't the creeper Perry was talking about after all; maybe it's Jordan. And I'm about to walk through the streets with this stranger just because he's cute.

Why do I do this to myself? It's pitch-black outside and freezing, making perfect conditions for a murder. This is out of an episode of a true crime docuseries. Hopefully, the detectives will use my second-most-recent picture from Instagram as my missing-person photo. It had good lighting from the snow. Kirsten is in it, but it's an easy crop job.

"I can. Yeah," I answer, accepting my fate.

We walk past the Burger King to the sidewalk along the main road. There are no streetlights, so soon we're engulfed in the night's darkness.

"Aren't you freezing?" I ask. My ears sting. I pull my furry hood up over my head.

"Not really. I have a high tolerance for the cold."

"For real? That's weird since you're from Arizona. I thought people from the Southwest died when it got below fifty degrees or something. I'm from here, and I can barely function in this."

Leftover salt from the previous snowstorm crunches beneath our shoes as we walk.

He shrugs. "Yeah, maybe some people do."

"So, what are you doing in the Philly 'burbs?" I ask. He's not the greatest at conversation, but this is the most I've talked to a cute boy really ever. I lean closer to him. I notice a lone, long brown hair that has fallen from the top of his head and curls around his ear.

"I just moved here."

"How recent is 'just'?"

"Like, two weeks ago. For the new semester."

"That's very recent. Wait, do you go to Falcon Crest? Why haven't I seen you?"

"No, I go to St. Helena's."

"Yikes. I hear that place is a freaking prison."

"It's not too bad."

"Meet any of Helena's Hos yet?"

"Meet who?"

"Helena's Hos? It's, like, a joke that the girls that go to the Catholic school are wild because they hang with the nuns all day."

"Oh, no. I guess I haven't."

"Never mind. It's stupid local humor and you're not a local, so, duh." I tap my forehead.

He runs his hand through his hair again and clears his throat. I look back toward the shopping center and can no longer see it. Endless darkness stretches in both directions.

A semi drives toward us on the road. We both take a step to the side, away from the bright headlights, and continue to walk in long stretches of silence. Our shoulders brush against each other's. There's a shock every time, causing me to flinch.

I'm waiting for him to ask me any sort of question about my life—literally anything at all. But he seems pretty disinterested, and it's safe to say this is going nowhere fast.

"What neighborhood do you live in?" I ask. "I'm going to text my mom to pick me up."

Ask me to hang out more. Ask me to hang out more. Ask me to hang out more.

"I live in Smithson Hills. She can pick you up by the entrance. It's up here to the right."

FAILURE.

My shoulders slump.

He points in the direction of his house and his hand is lit up by a passing car. Dried pieces of blue-and-red paper from his melted Blizzard cup stick to his fingers.

"I'm sorry you didn't get your ice cream," I say. I'm not going to let this go.

"I didn't even really want it. Just had to get out of the house. It was the first place I saw. Kind of getting stir-crazy."

"Why?"

"Just . . . you know."

I shrug and raise my eyebrows.

He exhales. "New place, new home, new school. All that stuff. It sounds lame."

"I bet that sucks."

He laughs. "Thanks for your sympathy. Yeah, it does. I've basically just been alone in my room painting for three weeks."

I stop walking. "You paint?"

He smiles. "I try to paint. I'm not very good. My goal is to do a scene from each of the national parks out west. But I cheated and ordered a few of the kits that have you paint by the numbers on the canvas. Don't tell." He puts his finger to his lips.

My heart flutters. I assess his face, trying to comprehend how he's a piece of art in his own right.

"I do those too with my friends!"

"Stop."

"Yeah. I have a bunch in my room. I can show you sometime." My breath catches in my throat. "Erm," I grunt, awkwardly, realizing how forward that invitation was. I dig my fingernails into my palm.

"Yeah, could be cool."

"I'm curious, did you have braces? You have perfect teeth."

"No," he says.

"That's unusual. I had braces and my teeth aren't half as good as yours."

"I'm pretty unusual."

Yes. Yes, you are.

"Well, I will put my jealousy of your annoying teeth behind us and be your friend if—"

"If what?"

"If you tell me how you exploded—"

"I said nothing happened." He raises his voice and cuts the air with his hand. The smile disappears from his face. "You know what? I don't know why I asked you to walk with me. I'll go the rest of the way myself." He thrusts his hands into his pockets, then trudges ahead.

I laugh softly. "Are you serious? Relax, man. I was kidding."

He keeps his back to me.

I step into a light jog to catch up to him. "Hey, Jordan. It's fine. I'll let it go."

I grab his shoulder to get his attention, and it's like I've put my hand on the stovetop. I scream, pulling my hand from his body. The pain is so intense it brings me to my knees. I grab my wrist with my other hand and study my burning palm. It's beet red and throbbing. It tingles as if it's being stabbed with one million needles. I squeeze my eyelids shut. Tears run out of the sides.

"Dude." I breathe heavily. "What is going on with you?" I ask. My voice trembles. There's no response. I push my hand into a mound of snow. A sudden coolness courses through my body. I exhale.

I look up and I'm alone on the dark road.

four

I'm staring at the ceiling when my alarm goes off the next morning. My eyes are scratchy. I was up all night thinking about Jordan—and also because I had to put an ice pack on my burning hand, and it was super uncomfortable and made me feel like I had to pee.

After completing a thorough analysis of Jordan's incident for exactly seven and a half hours until the alarm went off, I determined that, yes, the interaction with Jordan was real and did take place in my actual life. I have also determined that he is one of three things: a boy with a really high fever, one of those creepy kids who are obsessed with fireworks and pyrotechnics and torturing squirrels, or a younger version of the Human Torch from the Fantastic Four. What scares me is that he could be none of those things.

Sidenote: I hope he's the Human Torch because, like . . . body. Spoiler alert: He's probably the pyro who chugs three Mountain Dews for breakfast and then proceeds to burn scars onto his arms at lunch in front of the entire cafeteria. I don't even know why I tease myself.

My phone lights up with texts from Kirsten, complaining about how she's been waiting outside my house for more than thirty seconds and how we're going to be late for school.

I wonder if she's mad because I didn't text her or Perry last night. But I didn't want to get into a conversation about what went down and somehow try to explain Jordan. I didn't think they would believe me through text messages.

I put on jeans and a hoodie and run through my silent house to grab a Pop-Tart in the kitchen.

My parents commute to the city for work, so they always leave before I do at some absurd hour I can't even comprehend waking up at. Mom is an admissions counselor at the University of Pennsylvania, and Dad works at some financial company doing something only people with money can understand.

My sister is in sixth grade and takes an earlier bus because she is a mini Kirsten in training and has band practice before school. She participates in a different extracurricular activity every day. I'm already annoyed with her overachieving status. It's hard to keep up with her schedule. She's one of those kids who lays it all out for everyone to see, and you know just by looking at her that she's going to be a monumental success.

I am more of a slowly developing gift. Many people look at me and think, *Should I approach this earthling?* Those who invest their time are fortunate enough to thrive in my presence. Those who don't are one less person annoying me.

Luckily, I'm going to be away at college by the time my sister reaches high school and becomes class president, varsity field hockey captain, lead soloist in the choir, first chair in the concert band, all-state freestyle swimmer, and homecoming queen. I swear Mom is priming her for an easy admission to Penn. I think if Mom looked at my application to Penn without knowing it was mine, she'd probably reject it.

This means I get ready for school every day by myself, which also means I am a saint because I could easily skip every day. But I don't because school is cool and I got dreams beyond these suburbs, you know? Without my high school diploma, how am I EVER going to move into my managerial position at Dairy Queen?

I run down my driveway to Kirsten's car and hop into the back seat. Perry is in the passenger seat. Kirsten's car is a small navy-blue sedan from the early 2000s. We call it the go-kart because it is a literal go-kart zooming around the streets. The sides of the car are an inch thick and there's no doubt we'd be dead in two seconds if we ever got into a car wreck. But one nice thing about it is that the engine shakes the entire car, so you get a thorough massage if you sit in either of the two front seats. I also have a theory that if one of the skinny tires ran over your foot, it wouldn't hurt. But no one wants to try it out with me.

"Why are you running?" Perry groans. Her head rests on the window.

"I have major, major news," I say.

Kirsten puts the car in park. They both turn around.

"Wait. Pause. You didn't hook up with Jimmy, did you?" Kirsten asks.

"What? No." I shake my head. "I forgot about him already. I met someone last night at Dairy Queen."

"Jimmy?"

"No! Screw Jimmy. I'm not talking about him. After you guys left, this boy came in to get ice cream and things got super weird."

They raise their eyebrows.

"No, not like that. We didn't hook up or anything. Although I would've liked to because he was really hot."

"So why didn't you?" Perry asks.

"Because he blew up his ice cream."

"Blew up?"

"He threw it?"

"No, like, kaboom!" I circle my hands in the air.

"With, like, a bomb?" Perry asks.

"No, with his hand."

Kirsten rolls her eyes, then faces front. "We don't have time for semantics this early in the morning, Dylan."

"You lost me," Perry says.

Kirsten puts the car back in drive and pulls away from my house. "I'm sure he was holding something and was pulling a prank on you."

"That's what I thought, but he wouldn't tell me how he did it. Then I touched him, and he was so hot."

"You told us that," Kirsten says.

"No, like physically hot."

"What's the difference?"

"Hot as in temperature. He was both attractive and hot to touch. I burned my hand!" I hold it up to their faces.

"Are you high?" Perry asks.

"No! Why does everyone keep asking me that? I don't even smoke. I knew you guys wouldn't believe me. Hence the radio silence last night." I sit back in the seat and cross my arms.

"I was wondering why you weren't texting the group. I thought you were mad at me because we brought Jimmy to Dairy Queen," Perry says.

"You did deserve the silent treatment for that. But no."

"Did you get his number? I want a picture. I need proof and I'll believe you."

Perry grabs my phone from my lap. I snatch it back.

"Hey! Can you two stop?" Kirsten interrupts. "You're going to cause me to get into an accident."

"I don't have a pic and I didn't get his number." I swat her arm away from me.

"Did you search for him on Instagram?"

"Duh, the second I got home."

"And?"

"And nothing."

"Then how are you going to date this hot, hot-as-in-temperature mystery boy?"

"Well, I'm actually not even sure if he's gay," I say.

"Dylan! You're slacking. Does he go to Falcon Crest? Do I know him?" Perry asks. "I always have to do everything for you."

"No, St. Helena's."

"Private school?" Perry asks, while exchanging a glance with Kirsten. "Seems like drama."

"I say move on to the next one," Kirsten says, waving her hand in the air. "I don't want to have to worry about your boyfriend lighting me and my ice cream up when we hang out. It seems like the risks outweigh the benefits of this person joining our group."

"It wasn't just that." I sigh. "He paints too and was damn near perfect."

"Dyl, relax," Perry says, talking to the window. Her breath fogs the glass. "We believe you met a hot, *hot* as in *attractive*, guy last night. I don't see where this temperature thing is going."

"There's no correlation to me," Kirsten adds.

"Me neither." I collapse to the side and lie across the back seat, using my backpack as a pillow.

"I hope we get our Chemistry grades today," Kirsten says, moving on.

I shut my eyes. Maybe I am making no sense. The Blizzard blowing up can be explained. It's a stretch, but weird stuff happens with food all the time—like how Mentos in a Pepsi make the bottle explode. But the way he burned my hand when I touched him is really throwing me off. And he didn't stay to help me. That means he wasn't surprised by what happened.

Jordan knew he was untouchable.

five

The school day drags along because my throbbing hand doesn't let me write anything down, nor does it let me forget about Jordan for one second. My list of questions for him has grown by the dozen. How does he even go to school if he burns people when they touch him? How does he hold a pencil? Wouldn't it just incinerate? How does he deal with paper? Does he even go to St. Helena's? Was everything he said last night a lie? Why am I obsessed with this person?

Something flops on my injured hand and I gasp.

"Better, Mr. Highmark," my Chemistry teacher says.

"Let me see," Perry says, tapping my shoulder from behind immediately after the test hits my desk. I cringe at the facedown paper. Perry and I are in Track 2 Chemistry, so we get to commiserate together without Kirsten, who is in Honors Science, blasting her three-digit scores in our faces every chance she gets.

"So nosy," I say. "Let's guess."

"Fine. Seventy—"

"Wait, what did you get? If my grade is higher than yours, you have to buy me a print from one of the galleries this weekend."

She grunts. "Maybe if they're cheap enough."

Every month, Falcon Crest's town center has Second Saturdays, where on the second Saturday of the month all the art galleries stay open through the night and serve free appetizers and wine. Perry, Kirsten, and I go every month, and we're usually the youngest ones there by about ten years. Sometimes we can sneak a glass or two of wine. But most of the time we just go for the cheese and crackers and shrimp cocktail.

She flips her paper over, with her other hand over her eyes. She peeks through the cracks between her fingers.

"Seventy-nine," she mumbles.

"C-plus!"

"Oh my gosh! I'll probably be moving to Honors Chemistry next week." She claps her hands to her cheeks.

"How did he mark your made-up element olerium?"

She scans the page and laughs. "He put an *X* and a question mark next to it."

"I'm dying. He was probably like, 'What is this girl on?'"

"You got a seventy-six," she guesses with a smirk.

"I hope not."

"You wish you could get a seventy-six. It would be ten times better than the thirty-eight you got last semester."

"Shut it! That's in the past. I'm a changed person now."

She's right. I did get a thirty-eight on my Chemistry midterm last semester. When I checked Grade Connect online, I thought it was a mistake and marched up to Dr. Brio the next day all cocky and asked him what my real grade was. He said it wasn't a mistake and I nearly collapsed. I thought I was going to be sent to the alternative school in the basement. It wasn't totally my fault, though. Dr. Brio didn't include the equations on the test and expected us to memorize them all. Pure deceit, if you ask me.

"Well, flip the test over, Jaime Lannister, and let's see. Or do you need my assistance with your one hand and all?"

"Ha! You could never be my Brienne of Tarth."

I flip the paper over and a seventy-seven is in a red circle at the top.

"Ugh!" I grunt.

A smile grows across Perry's face. "Ha! I win."

"That's not fair."

"Karma comes back around," she says.

"No, karma would be me getting a better grade than you because I put in the work with Kirsten. I studied all week."

"No, karma is me getting a better grade than you because you and Kirsten put me down, and don't value the fact that I simply have a different way of acquiring knowledge."

"Acquire this." I scratch my nose with my middle finger.

She laughs.

The speaker above our classroom door squeaks. Everyone's faces turn to the sound. A familiar throat clearing echoes through the room.

"Hi, everyone!" Kirsten shrieks. "Happy end of eighth period! Please listen carefully to the following announcements. The junior varsity and varsity cheerleading practices have been canceled for today due to HVAC maintenance in the gymnasium. However, the freshman squad will still hold practice in the auxiliary gym at three o'clock. Varsity girls, don't forget we have practice this Saturday and Sunday to go over our routine for Nationals. 'Kay, thanks, everyone!"

Finally, something goes my way today. I'm not a cheerleader, but since practice is canceled that means I don't have to waste an hour in the library picking my fingernails and waiting for Kirsten to drive me home.

The class bell rings. I slam my hand on Perry's desk. "Off to the car!"

I stand, but a hand on my shoulder pushes me back into my seat. "Not so fast, my wenches."

The shrill voice of Savanna Blatt pierces my skull. Her long fingernail slides along my back. I spin around. Her head cocks to the side with her usual aggressive, bright pink-lipped smile beaming at me. Her white-blond hair is pulled up in a tight ponytail. Long fake eyelashes curve from her eyelids to the ceiling. She smells like the cotton-candy Blizzard from Dairy Queen.

"What do you want?" I grunt.

"You're always so pleasant, Dylan."

"Hi, Savanna," Perry says. Savanna turns and gives Perry a tight-lipped smile.

"I spoke with Jimmy after your little meet-up last night," Savanna says. Her pink fingernails tap the textbook in her arms.

"And?"

"And he said you were quiet, awkward, and smelled like sour milk."

"Oh, perfect. That's what I was trying to project."

She narrows her eyes. "He also said you haven't texted him yet. Your explanation?"

"Also a deliberate move on my end."

She huffs and drops her textbook on the desk. It slams. I jump at the sound. She leans toward me. "You know, Jimmy is ten leagues above you! You're lucky I allowed Kirsten and Perry to set you up with him." Her voice drops to a whisper. "I don't know how you're even brave enough to come to school looking the way you do." Her eyes travel up and down my body, slowly. They laser in on my chewed-up fingernails and study my mud-covered shoes. I curl my fingers into my palm. "If I saw that face in the mirror every morning, I'd keep it under the bedcover where it belongs."

I stand and brush off the front of my jeans. Perry pulls her lips closed and looks out the window.

"Thanks, Savanna," I say. "I really do appreciate the recommendation, but your prep squad friends who are birthed from an L.L.Bean catalog every morning are not my type."

"Better than whatever you got birthed from," she snarls.

I shrug. "You're probably right."

"Well, fine. That's the last time I'm ever charitable and do a nice thing for you two. Why does Kirsten even hang out with you?" She flips her long ponytail at us as she turns and struts out the door.

"I see Savanna is in her full Cruella de Vil form today," I say.

Savanna's white hair, tall and skinny frame, bright lipstick, and long fingers with perpetually red-and-pink-painted nails helped earn her that nickname throughout the school. Oh, and the fact that she'll bark at you for no reason—like what just happened.

"I want to know what eats at her," Perry says after Savanna disappears.

"I don't know why you're even nice to her sometimes. The only reason she talks to you is because you're Kirsten's best friend, and she needs you to get close to her."

"Overanalyze much? It's just easier to let that stuff go."

"Whatever. At least no more setups from her."

"For now."

I nod. "For now."

We walk straight to the parking lot without stopping at our lockers. There's no need to pick up any books. We both know we won't be doing an ounce of homework over the next few days. Our brains need a rest after all our intellectual power was spent on our recent Chemistry test.

Outside, Kirsten skips down a parking lot aisle toward us. Everyone stops what they're doing to admire. Her voluminous brown hair shimmers as it bounces in the afternoon sun. Savanna Blatt is right about one thing—questioning why Kirsten would hang out with Perry and me.

Yet Kirsten's loyalty is what I admire most about her. She could jump ship and join any other group at school since she has a connection to every club and sports team, or go off and serial-date the gross boys who gawk at her all day, but she's chosen us since kindergarten and that's the level of realness we should all strive toward.

"Dyl Pickle, what's the four-one-one?" she shouts in her announcer voice.

"Thanks, Kirsten! I'm coming at you live from Falcon Crest High with a witness of the day. Ma'am, what happened here today?" I stick my iPhone in Perry's face, circling her.

"Literally nothing exciting, so you both can stop," Perry says. We laugh.

"If you're accepting feedback, Kirsten, your announcer voice was a little too perky today," I say.

"Thanks! But I'm actually not accepting sexist feedback at this time," Kirsten says.

"You got to be more serious, like the tone of entertainment news shows when they report on a celebrity going missing or something and they have the dark music humming in the background and they're shaking their heads."

"I'm going more for respectable broadcast news anchor, thank you very much."

"Hmm. That could work."

"Do you want to sit in the front seat?" Perry asks me.

"Sure." I spin my body to open the door with my good hand.

"Why are you being awkward?" Kirsten asks.

"His arm is injured from the hot Dairy Queen boy," Perry says, sighing.

Kirsten rolls her eyes. "My feedback for you is to find that boy and figure out what happened."

"And how do you suggest I do that with no intel?"

"You have plenty of intel!"

"Such as?"

"Hot guy . . . lives near Dairy Queen," Perry says.

"Are you serious right now?"

"You said he's from Arizona, right?" Kirsten asks. "Go into his neighborhood and look for cars with Arizona license plates. There can't be that many."

"Oh wow, she's onto something," Perry says.

"What would we do without you, Kirsten?" I ask.

"Die," Perry says. "We would be dead, Dylan. But wait, wouldn't that be stalking?"

"Yeah, are you trying to get me arrested?"

"No, it's most certainly not stalking," Kirsten says. "Just go for a fake run or something and then if you see an Arizona car, knock on the door."

"And if it's the wrong house?" I ask.

Perry laughs.

"See! It is creepy." I smile.

"If what you say about him is true, then you need to figure it out," Kirsten says. "He hurt you."

My smile disappears.

"Plus, it could be my big break." She brushes her hair behind her shoulder. "I'll report on it. I can give you some of the advertising royalties from my article if you wish."

"Wait, stop. You're scaring me now," I say. I clutch my hand to my chest. "I'm stressed. I need to think on it." I exhale.

"Well, you are in luck because the paint-by-numbers kits just arrived on my doorstep," Perry says, reading her email. "Should we de-stress while we paint? I don't think I am comfortable leaving Dylan to his own devices yet anyway. We can't have him blow this shot at love too."

"Depends on what our theme is," I say. "I forget what we ordered. If it has to do with love, I'm not emotionally ready yet. How could I add color to a heart when mine is jet-black?"

Kirsten laughs.

"Oh God," Perry says, sighing. "We ordered from the flower collection for spring, which perfectly symbolizes new beginnings, if you ask me. Kirsten, please reroute to my house before we drown in Dylan's self-pity."

The painting kits make us feel more legit when we go to the art galleries in town, even though they take no skill set or artistic eye whatsoever.

One time, a man struck up a conversation with Kirsten at one of the galleries, and she told him she had her own garage art studio— which was a lie. He ended up being the owner of the gallery and asked to see some of her art. She had nothing to share except her beet-red face. Afterward, Kirsten insisted on us needing to build an art portfolio to prevent future faux pas. It's been one of her best ideas. And, besides the bonding time, it's a great excuse for Perry and me to get out of doing homework.

Honestly, matching the number on the paint to the number on the canvas is the most difficult part. And staring at the canvas with a million different numbers splattered across it reminds me of math class, which is not something I enjoy remembering or go into confidently. Once we get through that headache, our masterpieces come together like how my love life unwinds—quickly.

My Christmas painting was the first piece where I was upset with the outcome. I painted Father Christmas, Perry painted a white horse in the snow, and Kirsten painted a winter forest scene. The canvas told me where to put each skin-color blotch. But even with guidance, Father Christmas's face looked like Freddy Krueger. Mom wanted to hang it above the mantel in the living room, but I hid it in my closet and said, "Maybe we'll hang it up next year. How about that?"

We unwrap our new kits at Perry's kitchen table. The paintings are similar blue, pink, and yellow flower bouquets set in different vases. I choose the blue bouquet, then line up my paint colors with their coordinating numbers.

Perry runs to her bedroom and returns with her laptop. She opens it on the table. Her fingers start typing wildly.

"What are you doing?" I ask. "I thought we were de-stressing while painting."

"*You* are de-stressing while painting," she says. "I'm not stressed. In fact, I am excited." She smiles, bouncing her shoulders.

"And why's that?"

"I texted Emily Huntsville on the way home. She's from my all-star cheer team and goes to St. Helena's. She knows who Jordan is. I'm talking to her now."

My stomach flips. "You did what?"

Kirsten drops her paints. She sprints across the table to peer over Perry's shoulder. "Excellent use of resources," she says.

"Perry Love Connections is back in business," Perry squeals. She gives Kirsten a high five.

"This is the furthest thing from okay," I say.

"Exactly right," Perry says. "It's more than okay, it's smart."

"It's genius," Kirsten says.

"This way, we don't have to waste another night at Dairy Queen on a deadbeat. We'll know everything we need to know beforehand."

"What did you say?" I ask.

Perry spins the computer on the table so the screen faces me. I read the first few messages.

Perry

Hey, Em. Have you heard anything about the new design for the uniforms slash I have a random request. Do you know a boy named Jordan at your school? He's in your grade and supposedly new this semester. Don't say I asked.

Emily

Yes! Check your email. Coach forwarded us some looks from the design team. Did you not get it?

And yeah. Jordan Ator? He's super cute. What's up with him?

Perry grabs the computer before I can read more. "I guess that's not too bad," I say.

"Just paint and let me handle this," Perry says, typing another message.

"You know I can't focus on anything else right now."

"Emily is typing," Perry says, waving me back to my painting. Our eyes meet. I organize a few more of my paints. Perry bites her pinkie fingernail. Kirsten brushes her hair from her left shoulder to her right shoulder.

"Okay, so—" Perry starts reading.

"What?!" Kirsten and I shout.

"Emily says he just arrived this semester. . . . Okay, duh, I said that, Em."

"Just read it word for word," I command.

"Okay, fine. . . . *He's super quiet but not in a weird way.*" We all look at one another. Perry shrugs. *"I haven't spoken to him, but I see him all the time in the hall and my math class. He's hot. Are you trying to hook up with him?"*

"I swear if you end up with Jordan after all this," I say, shaking my head.

Perry laughs. "I would never."

She clears her throat. *"His overall vibe is chill. He was invited to one of the Helena's parties last weekend and never showed. But there's drama. He's always leaving in the middle of classes to go to the nurse or guidance counselor. He's prob already missed four days of school out of his first two weeks. I heard drug problems. That might explain why he's always late. Or some people were saying he just got released from juvie and has to check in with a parole officer. But my friend Hannah Montour is friends with Rachael Hill. Rachael has a hard-core crush on Jordan, so she talked to Jani Allen, who is Jordan's orientation buddy—"*

"Orientation buddy?" Kirsten interrupts. "We don't have that. It sounds like a good policy to implement at Falcon—"

"Kirsten, shhh!" Perry says. "We're fixing Dylan's life right now, not Falcon." She brings her finger to the screen and continues to read.

"Jani said he has special medical permission to leave class whenever he wants. Don't say I told you that. Could be bad asthma or something like anxiety. I don't know. Just guessing. He seems nice, though. What other info do you want? I can text Jani."

Perry pauses. "That's it," she says.

I sit. "Interesting," I say.

"Very," Kirsten says.

Perry bites her lip. "So, I think our takeaways from Emily are that he's very attractive, chill, and nice," she says. "The rest is just . . . I mean . . . who can say for sure?"

"Apparently Jani Allen can," Kirsten says.

"Can I just tell her why we're asking?" Perry asks. "It would make this easier."

"No," I say. "I told you he seemed flighty when we met. If he finds out I'm asking about him, he'll run for sure."

"Can I say I have a friend interested, then?" Perry types a few more messages. "Okay, I just said that."

I flip my hands.

"Oh, awesome. She's responding super fast. She says, *Who?! I can try to set something up. I would tell her not to get her hopes up though. I texted Jani before you responded, and she said he's only here for the spring semester. He's planning to leave after this school year. Going back to New Mexico or something. No one needs to get into trouble if the dude is only going to be here for a couple months.*"

I sigh, running my hand through my hair. "Of course. I wish we never asked."

"I'm sorry." Perry pulls her lips inward. She shuts her laptop, then drags her canvas across the table to the space in front of her.

"It's okay, Dyl," Kirsten says. She turns to Perry. "Maybe we should relax with the love connections for a bit."

I groan. "Why do I get my hopes up after one meeting? What is wrong with me?"

"Nothing," Perry says. "Like I said before, every day is a day for a Perry Love Connection. Just because this day didn't work out—"

"Or the last," Kirsten adds.

"Yes, or the last. Doesn't mean one day it won't work."

I open one of my blue paints. I swirl my brush around the container until some of the blue liquid splashes over the sides. My teeth clench. "Let's just paint some flowers," I say.

The girls nod.

I match the blue to its corresponding number on the canvas. My brush runs along the outer edge of a flower petal, adding a royal hue to the bland white rectangle. The flowers begin to come alive in hopeful, romantic waves. As I bring more color to the canvas with each stroke, I wonder when my life will be touched by even just a piece of the beauty I put into my paintings, or when my life will be worth hanging on the wall for people to admire. I've never received flowers or captured someone's heart. I've painted them, though.

My other paintings are stacked under my bed. Each one reminds me of a time, place, and thing that I love. Some of the pictures are four years old, some are just one. But they sit on the floor as permanent, untouched splendor.

I have a lot of ideas for my own paintings that aren't by the number or prescribed by a box. But right now, I kind of feel the same way Kirsten did when that art gallery owner asked to see her work—embarrassed with nothing to show.

six

Yesterday's de-stressing event turned into a depressing event. I only managed to paint for an hour before packing up my things and heading home. I spent the night reviewing my incorrect Chemistry test answers, hoping I could turn my grades around and use them to get into a college far, far away from Falcon Crest.

This morning, I am midway through the funeral fantasy for my Jordan crush, right before I deliver my eulogy and bury my romantic hopes six feet under, when my bedroom door bangs. It slams against the wall as it swings open. I rip my covers off from over my eyes and my sister, Cody, is standing in the doorway, carrying a pink backpack that is wider than her body.

"You know, knocking is the polite way to enter a room that has a closed door," I say.

"Well, well, well," Cody says, ignoring my comment. She crosses her arms. "Look who decided to show up."

I raise an eyebrow. "Show up? This is my room."

"Which you've been in since six o'clock last night."

"And?"

"*Andddd?*" She enunciates the *d*.

"What do you have in there? A body?" I point to her bag.

"Yes. A body of art, history, and intellect."

I roll my eyes. "You can give it a rest here. You really don't impress me with that."

She unzips the pink bag, then flashes three textbooks: American History, English Literature, and Biological Sciences.

"Why aren't you at school yet? Don't you have band?"

"No. Tonight is the spelling bee competition in the city. I'm off and Mom is taking me to Penn's library to study. Want to come?"

"I'm busy," I say, scrolling through Instagram on my phone.

"Busy doing what?"

"Reading."

"Reading your phone?"

I sit up in my bed. "I know you don't listen to me often, but if there's one thing you should listen to me about, it's that being smart isn't just reading and memorizing those books. It's reading them and then questioning them."

"But you never read," she says.

"I know. I'm more on the questioning side. And you're on the reading side. This is why we're siblings. We balance each other out."

"Mom and Dad are always yelling at you about your grades. Questioning gets you Cs. Reading gets me As."

"But questioning is a letter in LGBTQ and that's all that matters. Don't you want to be questioning, Cody?"

"No!" She holds up her hand. "Please don't tell Mom and Dad that. I have enough going on. I don't have time to take off from my obligations for a Coming Out Week like you get every year."

I laugh. "You're such an old lady."

"Think what you must, but I have books to read and a competition to win." She pulls her backpack straps tight over her shoulders and marches to the stairs. "Have a nice day!" she shouts from the hall.

It's pretty amazing that the reason she wouldn't want to be gay is because she's afraid of too much support from Mom and Dad.

I came out to Mom and Dad in the fall of eighth grade after a particularly bad Halloween experience. Identical twins in my grade, Caleb and Carter Horizon, were hosting a Halloween party. I went dressed as a goth, mainly because I wanted to wear eyeliner and black nail polish. I slicked my hair back, put in fake facial piercings, stuck fake tattoos on my arms, and ripped up a black T-shirt and pair of black jeans. Mom was pissed I ruined my clothes, but otherwise she liked my costume.

Mom was the parent driver for the party. We picked up Perry and Kirsten on the way. Kirsten dressed as Ariel from *The Little Mermaid* like most years, and Perry wore a dead cheerleader costume.

The party entertained me in the beginning. The Horizons' house was huge and decorated better than most haunted houses I've ever been to. There was punch in a cauldron, strobe lights, spiderwebs at every turn, the theme song from the *Halloween* movie blasting from a set of speakers, a photo booth, and fifty horny eighth-graders—the scariest part of all.

It was only a matter of time before the Halloween spirits took ahold of the party's hosts, and when the clock struck ten, the spirits did just that. We stood in the basement and the lights went off. Carter Horizon held a flashlight to his face and announced that we were going to be playing Spin the Flashlight. He commanded everyone to form a circle. We listened, and I followed everyone to the center of the room.

The rules for the first round were that you had to hug whoever the flashlight beam landed on. We played that for ten minutes, but everyone got bored really quickly. So Carter made the announcement that we were moving on to round two, where we had to kiss whoever the flashlight pointed to on the cheek. He instructed that "if the flashlight lands on a guy and you're a guy, spin again. Same goes for girls."

Of course, I spun the flashlight and the first person it landed on was Carter Horizon. Everyone laughed. I quickly spun again, and it landed on Kirsten. I gave her a second-long peck on the cheek and returned to the circle, sitting cross-legged. My face burned.

We played round two a little longer than round one, but by round three I decided to quit the game. It was time for full-on making out, and I wasn't feeling it.

I texted Mom and told her I didn't feel good and wanted to leave. Kirsten's mom was scheduled to take us home, so I didn't feel bad leaving her and Perry behind.

In hindsight, I was so lucky I chose to wear my black goth costume because I was able to sneak up the stairs and out the front door without anyone saying a word to me.

When I got home, I walked straight into the kitchen and sat at the island. I didn't change my outfit or go to the bathroom or anything. The heaviness in my chest was unbearable that night.

I wanted my parents to ask me what was wrong. I couldn't bring it up myself. I don't know if it was fear or that I just didn't know how to verbalize what I was feeling, but I needed them to bring it up first.

I sat there and chipped the nail polish off my fingers. I remember everything so distinctly, more so than any other night of my life. Dad sat in the living room reading a *Sports Illustrated* magazine. His reading glasses were perched on the tip of his nose. CNN played on the television in the background. Mom was in the dining room sorting through the leftover candy that no trick-or-treaters claimed. It was mostly Smarties and Sprees, two candies that could not be less interesting to me.

Mom came into the kitchen and placed the candy bowl in the pantry.

"Dylan, you're making a mess," she said, staring at my nail polish chippings all over the counter. "Do you need nail polish remover?"

I didn't say anything and scratched the black polish off harder.

"Dylan?" she repeated. She came up behind me and placed her hand on my back. I flinched.

"Honey, your hands are shaking. Is everything okay? Were you drinking at the party?"

I shook my head.

"You weren't drinking?"

"No," I said. My voice cracked. "I wasn't drinking, and everything's not okay."

I turned and looked up at her. My vision clouded, and I wiped my eyes. Black mascara smeared on my fingers.

"I..." I swallowed. My throat thickened and itched like I was having an allergic reaction to something. The straight ghost of Dylan Highmark's past snipped at my vocal cords, trying to shut me up. I seriously needed to EpiPen him back to the weeds of the earth where he came from.

"What's wrong?" Mom asked. She sat on the stool next to me and leaned in. Dad stood up from the couch and walked into the kitchen. Mom shot him a concerned glare.

"I'm...I'm gay and I can't not be anymore."

It came out a little messy. I missed a few words in that sentence. But the event numbed my jaw, and I couldn't really speak.

My parents got the idea and from that point forward the Highmark house turned into the Highmark Haus of Gay Pride.

We ended up having the best night of my life. Mom told me how proud she was of me thirty-one times. Thirty-one is an estimate because I only counted twenty-four. But she said it a few times before I decided it was funny enough to start keeping track.

Dad was clueless and told me he could've sworn I was dating Perry Lyle. I agreed—about the clueless part—and told him that if he was going to voice that out loud, he could have at least guessed my one girl friend I actually kissed, Kirsten.

Halloween was on a Friday that year, and the next morning, I went downstairs, and Mom thrust a rainbow cake in my face with the words *Free to Be Me* written on it in white icing.

Over the next week, a rainbow flag appeared outside our house, a *Gay Is Good* magnet was placed on our fridge, rainbow pins were on my parents' work outfits, Mom suddenly had multiple pairs of rainbow yoga pants for her evening workouts, and every night my parents were trying to find queer movies to watch with me.

By the end of the week, I told them it was a little too much gay for me all at once. They apologized and said they just wanted to be sure home was a safe space for me. I told them it was the safest place I had, and Mom burst into tears.

Every year on Halloween before I go out to a party or trick-or-treating, my parents cut a rainbow cake in honor of my coming out. Mom marked that day as my second birthday, or "rebirth" as she calls it. Each cake has had a different gay slogan on it: *Love Wins*, *Born This Way*, and most notably this past year's—*Out of the closet and into the streets!* It was the first cake slogan Dad chose. I told them this was too far and that my gay birthday had to stop after high school. Mom agreed, reluctantly.

And it was so much gay that it apparently made Cody scared of being gay. Which I just *love*.

I might not know a romantic love yet, but I know of a love from and for Mom and Dad. Love has to have an impact, and every day I'm grateful for the direction their love has pushed me in. They made sure I knew that other people don't always get to make the rules and that I can pick up the flashlight and shine it on whoever I want.

I think back over the last two days, realizing other people took ahold of the flashlight again. Savanna and a random group of girls from St. Helena's pointed me in the wrong direction. And I let them.

But I'm going to spin again. Mom and Dad are right. Like Perry said, who can know for sure if that gossip about Jordan is true? We also don't know if, maybe, Jordan's light is shining on me.

After school, I meet Perry and Kirsten in the lobby. They're wearing their cheerleading practice uniforms—gold shorts and maroon T-shirts with high white socks. Their hair is sweaty. Kirsten's cheeks are flushed. Perry has her arms crossed.

"Hey, Dyl," Kirsten says. "How was your day? I figured we could stop for ice cream on the way home." She shrugs.

"Yeah," Perry agrees. "Sorry again for killing your vibe last night."

I greet them with a smile. "My vibe is alive and well, actually."

They exchange a glance.

"Huh?" Perry mutters.

"There's no time for ice cream. I have plans."

"Spill," Kirsten orders, stepping forward.

"Operation License Plate is underway." I smirk.

Their eyes go wide.

"What a turn of events!"

"You know, if you'd just listened to us yesterday and gone then, the operation could nearly be complete," Perry says.

"Quiet," I say, holding my hand up. I march toward the exit doors.

"We can look for him with you," Perry suggests, chasing after me.

I shake my head. "No, that'll just make it awkward if I do see him. You guys don't know what happened the other night."

"Is it safe?" Kirsten asks. "With the heat thing you described and now his potential criminality, I'm quite nervous."

I push open the doors. A gush of cool air blasts my face. "It'll be fine. Emily said no one knows him. It's all rumors. They said he's going back to New Mexico and he's from Arizona."

"Good point," Perry says.

"Well, text us this time if you see him and you need rescuing," Kirsten says.

"And then," Perry starts. She grabs my shoulders, bringing me to a stop in the parking lot. She places her hand on my thigh. "Just pretend to slip your hand on his leg and be like, 'Oops, sorry.' Then he'll be like, 'No, it's okay.' Then you know he's into you and make your move!"

I laugh. "It doesn't work like that."

"Well, make it work." She waves her hand.

"Drop me off at my house. I'm getting my bike."

When I get home, I toss my backpack in the living room, then head for my family's container of winter attire in the hallway closet. I know what to expect now with this boy, so I'm going prepared. I dig through the gloves and hats, grabbing a pair of thick ski gloves for extra padding to protect my hands if I touch Jordan again. I pull a beanie over my head and swirl a scarf around my neck so I look classy and attractive. Who says you can't look cute while wearing protection! Smithson Hills beckons me.

On my bike, I hang a sharp turn into his neighborhood, taking one foot off the pedal and sliding it along the street.

I know who lives in the first house, so I pedal past it. There's a woman unloading her kids from an SUV in the driveway of the next house, so that's definitely not it. The driveway of the next house is empty, and I'm realizing how stupid this plan is because what if the cars are in the garage where people keep their cars in the winter?

The next house has a few cars out front. Winning! My first lead. But on closer inspection I realize they have Pennsylvania license plates. I pedal onward.

The garage door of the next house is closing. I speed up, trying to get a quick peek before it closes all the way, but it's too dark inside to see the license plates.

A light flicks on in the house. My eyes shift to a woman walking into the house's kitchen from the garage. I watch her through the window. She puts a grocery bag on the counter and begins to unload it. She pulls out tin foil, sandwich bags, and a loaf of bread.

My stomach rises into my throat a bit, and I pull my beanie over my face. I'm embarrassed for myself. This was the creepiest idea ever. I spin my bike around toward home to end this adventure of grade-A lurking.

"Dylan," someone says.

I smash the pedals backward, skidding my bike to a stop. I turn around, and Jordan is standing on the curb next to the mailbox of the house I was stalking. He's wearing a St. Helena's uniform—a maroon cardigan, white button-up with a tie, and gray dress pants. I don't think I've ever seen a perfect boy in real life before, but I'm pretty sure that just changed.

He looks adorable, and I feel bad because he was clearly telling the truth about his life—at least parts of it.

"Oh, hey," I say.

"What're you doing here?"

I shrug and look around. "Just, like, biking." I reach under my scarf and scratch my neck.

"How did you know I lived here?" He points back at the house.

"I didn't. I mean, I don't."

"Oh. It looked like you were staring."

He jumps down from the curb and walks over to me. I inch my bike back as he approaches.

"Well, actually, if you want to talk about it," I say, lightly laughing, "I might have been staring."

His face flickers.

"I wanted to see you again...after everything that happened the other night," I continue.

His eyes snap toward the ground. "I'm sorry...but what exactly do you think happened?"

This time, I laugh loudly at his response. I point my finger at him and wave it in the air. "You're not going to do that. You saw the ice cream explode and know your skin was steaming hot. Actually, I know you were steaming hot because I felt it."

He crosses his arms, then mumbles something under his breath.

I shake my head. "Sorry I came by. This is stupid. Maybe Emily was right, and you aren't worth the time." I clench my teeth when I let the words slip. But after a second passes, I'm glad I said something because he looks me in the eye for the first time all night.

"Who was right? Emily? Emily Huntsville? You asked her about me? What did she tell you?"

I raise an eyebrow. "What does it matter?"

"It all matters!" he screams, raising his arms. They nearly hit me across the face. As they pass, a subtle gush of heat kisses my cheek. I jump and almost fall off my bike.

"What the hell, man? Can you cut it with that?" I demand.

He doesn't smile. "Please, don't be scared of me, Dylan."

My face scrunches. "Should I be?"

I can answer that question and it's a resounding yes.

Jordan looks up and down the street.

"I have to do this," he says. He reaches for me.

"Do what?" I put my feet on the pedals, eyeing the road and ready to *fly* out of here.

"Because you're not going to leave me alone. Trust me."

"Wait." I raise my arms, shielding myself. "Are you hot? Stop!"

He grabs my shoulders and a wave of heat travels down my body, fading everything to black.

seven

I snap my eyelids open, and all I see is a white wall. I'm in captivity.

My tailbone is throbbing, and my butt is asleep. There's a freezing, wet towel on my head. I'm shivering. Goose bumps cover my skin.

I extend my legs. They hit another wall. Am I really trapped in a white box an inch big? I force my body to roll over onto my back, then I'm staring up at a shower head. I'm in a bathtub. I grab my crotch, feeling pants. I exhale.

I sit up. The towel falls off my head and flops onto my lap. My ski gloves are still on my hands. I rip them off and toss them to the floor. My palms are sweaty.

The shower curtain is pulled back. The tub ledge is empty except for a bottle of Old Spice 2-in-1 shampoo/conditioner—meaning I'm in a random person's tub. What I would give to see some pink loofahs, Dove lavender body wash, and Pantene moisturizing shampoo. Then I'd know I'm with Perry and Kirsten. But they didn't save me. They left me to die again.

My captor is probably off getting the acid to disintegrate my body in this tub like in *Breaking Bad*. I have to get out of here. I let out a few dramatic coughs.

I grab the ledge and pull myself up. Then the bathroom door swings open.

"Ah, let me go! I'll do anything!" I shout before seeing who it is.

Jordan stands in the doorway. He changed outfits. He's wearing a white undershirt and black Adidas shorts. He somehow looks cuter than before.

"Shhh!" he hisses, putting his finger over his lips.

"You!" I shout louder than I screamed. "What do you mean, shhh? What are you going to do to me?"

"I'm going to explain everything," he says.

"Thanks. But a little late for explanations. Hard pass for me."

I stand and step out of the tub. My legs wobble. He grabs my forearm. I glance at his hand, and then we stare at each other for a moment as I feel nothing but a normal human hand. Our noses are almost touching. Our lips, inches apart. "How are you doing this and not burning me?" I ask. "Why did you knock me out?"

He bites his lip, then looks to the floor. "Because I like you, okay? And I want to get to know you," he says, his voice steady. "But I couldn't once you found out my secret."

Ding, ding, ding. I knew he had a secret. But wait, more importantly, he just said he likes me. I almost want to ask him to repeat himself in case I misheard, but I don't want to give him the chance to correct himself if it was a mistake.

"And what's that?" I say.

"Sit back in the tub."

"What? No." I rip my arm from his hand.

"You have to for me to properly show you."

"This is weird."

"Do you want to know?"

"Yes, fine. Fine." I rub my hand through my hair.

I get back in the tub. He gets in and sits across from me cross-legged. I take a deep breath. He smells like a fresh blast of deodorant. My head swivels, taking in the bathroom decor, or rather lack thereof. A painting sits on the vanity counter, leaning against the wall. Red cliffs cover the canvas. The words *Zion National Park* are etched across the bottom.

I nod in its direction. "That one of your paintings?" I ask.

He turns. "Yeah," he says. "Not by the numbers. I did that one freehand. Can you tell?"

"That's really good." My hands are shaking. I clutch them against my stomach.

"What do you paint?" he asks.

"We don't really have a theme. It's all over the place. Which is kind of fitting. We're painting flowers now."

"Do you ever paint by yourself?"

I look to the ceiling. "No, actually. It's always been a group activity."

"Maybe we could paint together sometime."

I swallow. "That would be awesome."

We fall into silence. Water drips from the sink. The house's heat kicks on and rattles a vent in the ceiling above us as the air pushes its way through the metal cracks.

"So, what did you want to show me?" I ask.

"Promise to stay calm?" he asks. He holds out his hand, with his palm facing the ceiling.

"I will." I poke his finger and it feels normal. "Okay?"

"Shut up. Just wait." He closes his eyes.

I tap my fingers on my knees.

Suddenly, a blue flame bursts into the air from his hand. The heat nearly incinerates my face. I scream. My eyebrows better not be gone.

I jump and dive from the tub. The white shower curtain wraps around my body as the rod comes crashing to the floor.

"Holy shit!" I yell.

The flame swirls back into his palm and disappears.

"You're actually, like, the Human Torch? I thought I was joking with myself."

Do I call nine-one-one? What does someone do in this situation? If he wanted to kill me, he could have scorched me while I was asleep, right? My film studies education from every streaming service flashes through my mind, thinking of what my peers have done during events like this.

Thor. I just watched *Thor.* Natalie Portman was scared of Thor at first, but then she embraced him. But Thor is Chris Hemsworth. Who would turn away a magical Chris Hemsworth? I'd let him scorch me. When those kids from *Stranger Things* found out Eleven had powers, they thought it was cool and fed her waffles. If twelve-year-olds can handle this, so can I.

"Stop. You're being too loud. My aunt and uncle are downstairs. You're not supposed to be here." He grabs ahold of the shower curtain around my waist, trying to untwist me.

"I mean, sorry. Next time a human shoots flames from their body I'll try to act more casual," I say. "Wait." I stop moving. "Aunt and uncle? I thought you moved here with your parents?"

"If you would hold on for a second, I'm trying to tell you." His teeth clench.

I stand with the shower curtain wrapped around my body like a dress.

"No. I'm calling the shots. What's your real name?" I ask, breathing heavy. I sidestep toward the door.

He rolls his eyes. "Jordan."

"Last name?"

"Ator."

"How old are you?" I grab a brush from the bathroom counter and hold it out in front of me.

"Seriously?" He shakes his head. "I'm seventeen and a junior at St. Helena's."

"Did you move here two weeks ago from Arizona?"

"Yes."

"Where are your parents?"

"Dead."

Chills erupt on my arms. My throat gets thick.

"Oh . . . my bad."

I lower the brush. I slowly pull the shower curtain off my legs, then sit on the floor, leaning against a wall. He follows my lead and sits across from me. He leans over the tub ledge, resting his chin on his forearm. I stare at the side of his face. His jaw muscle flexes.

"I'm sorry," I say.

"No, it's okay. This is confusing for you. I get it."

"Yeah, a little." I pick at the skin around my thumbnails.

"Last time I did that with the flame, I set my bed comforter on fire and almost burned the house down. I just assumed you would've been creeped out if I tried to randomly coerce you into my bathroom, so kidnapping you was the only option."

"Really? I probably would have thought you were making a move on me and gone along with it."

He doesn't smile or laugh.

"I'm joking."

"Anyway, so back to my parents," he says. "It's part of the story."

"Right."

"So, what happened is . . ." He sighs heavily, puffing his lips. "My dad worked for HydroPro. Have you heard of it?"

"Um, maybe. It sounds familiar."

"Well, it's a hydrogen fuel company in Arizona. They make hydrogen-powered vehicles and other machines. They were testing out this new battery thing. I don't even know what it was. But it was for powering cars. And they gave my dad one." His voice cracks. "Sorry. You're actually the first person I'm telling this to." His body rocks back and forth.

"You don't have to right now if you don't—"

"No. I just put you through all that. I want you to know. I want somebody to know. I *need* somebody else to know." He grits his teeth.

"Okay, I'm listening." I scooch my butt closer to him.

"It'll probably be easier if I show you?"

"More flames?"

He cracks a smile. "No. Wait here."

He exits the bathroom. I ignore his directions and quickly follow him, hoping to move this conversation to a more normal location than inside a bathtub surrounded by wet washcloths.

I step into Jordan Ator's room and it is pristine. There isn't a piece of clothing on the hardwood floor. His bed has a black frame. There's a wrinkle-free gray comforter on it and four pillows perfectly positioned equidistant from one another. At the foot of his bed is a black desk with nothing on it. The walls are bare, except for a black-and-white poster of the band the 1975 above his black dresser and a poster of Jon Snow on the back of his door. Floor-length black curtains frame two windows. The only area somewhat out of order is a stack of books on a window seat.

Outside, it's dark. It suddenly hits me that I have no idea what time or day it is. I pat my thighs and reach in my pockets, searching for my phone. There's nothing.

"Here," Jordan says. He's rummaging through one of the desk drawers when he pulls out a piece of paper. He extends it to me. I grab it and place it on the desk to read. He switches on an overhead light. It's a newspaper titled the *Local Valley Courier*. He moves behind me. His chest presses into my upper back. His body is so warm. The headline reads: "Area's First Starbucks Set to Bring Record Crowds to Sun Valley Shopping Center."

I glance at him. "I don't get it," I say. "What does this have to do with your parents?"

"Down here," he says, tapping on the bottom right corner of the paper. A much, much smaller headline above a tiny little paragraph reads: "HydroPro Director and Wife Killed in Fiery Inferno."

"Oh, Jordan . . . this is horrible. I'm so sorry."

"Keep reading."

On July 9, HydroPro senior director Gregory Ator and wife, Jennifer Ator, were killed in a motor vehicle accident off Lenape Road. Their sixteen-year-old son, Jordan Ator, was rushed to the hospital from the scene and is currently in critical condition. No other vehicles were involved in the crash. Police are investigating and, based on the the extent of the fire damage, believe the accident may have been fueled by a malfunction of a HydroPro-engineered hydrogen engine. HydroPro has given no comment.

"But how does this explain—"

"This?" Jordan says, shooting a flame from his index finger.

"Yes." I swallow and step back. "That."

"The article isn't entirely true. I wasn't taken to a hospital. I found out later HydroPro arrived at the accident first and took me back to their headquarters. I was in a coma for six weeks. Something weird happened to me during the—"

"Wait, Jordan, this is nuts. Why wasn't this national news? Was it? And did I miss it? Is this your medical condition? Who cares about this stupid Starbucks?"

"What medical condition? I wouldn't call it that. It wasn't news. Thanks to HydroPro. But it's better that way. You can't say anything. You're the only one who knows."

I tap my head to make sure I just heard him correctly. "Me? I am? Why me?"

There's a knock on the door. Our heads snap to the sound.

"Jordan?" a woman says. "We're going to bed. We'll see you in the morning, okay?"

"Okay," Jordan says. "Good night."

We stand in silence while we watch her shadow disappear from the crack beneath the door.

"Was that your aunt? What time is it?" I ask.

Jordan pulls his phone from his pocket. "Eight forty-six," he says.

"Shoot. I have to go. Can you tell me more later?"

"Of course."

I grab his phone and start typing. "Here's my number. Text me." He nods. "And where's my stuff?"

"Your phone and scarf and everything are over there on the dresser."

"And my bike?"

"It's on the side of my house."

I have four missed calls from my mom, two missed calls from my dad, and seventy-three unread texts from my group chat with Perry and Kirsten.

"Oh no," I mumble under my breath.

"What's wrong?"

"Nothing. Just have to get home." I shove my phone in my pocket.

"Sorry for keeping you out late."

"Don't be. I'm happy you told me. Everything kind of makes more sense now. But not really."

"Let me walk you out."

He cracks open his door and peeks into the hallway. It's clear, and he waves me along. We lightly walk down the stairs, then out the front door. The bitter, cold air stings my face the moment I step outside.

"Are you sure you're going to be okay riding your bike home?" he asks.

"I mean, I don't really have another choice. We humans have learned to manage without fire abilities."

He laughs.

"I didn't mean that to be offensive. . . . If it was . . . I don't know . . . I didn't mean you're not human."

He shakes his head. "It's fine. No offense taken."

"Bye," I say, and extend my arms for a hug.

"Oh, right," he says, stepping into my embrace.

"You're so warm."

"A steady one hundred ten degrees Fahrenheit."

"I'm a measly ninety-eight point six."

"Such a weakling."

I laugh and push myself out of the hug. "Don't get too comfortable with me now."

"What's that mean?"

"I'm just kidding. I'll see you soon?"

"Yeah."

I take a few steps off the porch but then stop. "Wait. What do I tell my friends?" I ask.

"What do you mean what do you tell your friends? You tell them nothing."

"But I kind of said how I met you the other night and you were—"

"You can't say anything, Dylan. People finding out about me is the reason I came here. No one can know. It gets too dangerous."

"It gets what?"

After I ask my last question, Jordan's eyes dart past my head to the street. I look in their direction. A silver car with tinted windows idles in front of a neighboring house. Clouds of smoke rise through the sky from its exhaust pipe. It lingers for a moment. Then the red brake lights flash on, and it speeds away down the snowy street.

"Jordan, are you outside?" his aunt asks from the house. Jordan closes the door behind him and grabs my shoulders.

"Come with me," he says.

"What's happening?"

"Just go."

He pushes me to the side of his house. We walk swiftly until he pulls my bike from the bushes. I take ahold of the handlebars and start wheeling it through his front yard. But Jordan grabs it and turns the bike around, toward the back.

"You have to go this way." His voice is panicked. His eyes search every direction. We cut through a few other yards before emerging onto a street I don't recognize. I mount my bike. He waves me along.

"Jordan, what's happening?"

"Nothing. We'll talk more tomorrow." He looks up and down the street several times. "You should be fine. Get home safe."

"Fine from *what*?"

"You'll be fine," he repeats.

He nods, then darts back toward his house through the trees without another word. I gaze into the darkness for a few moments, wondering if he will come back. The evergreen trees rustle from a light breeze. He doesn't return, so I decide to pedal down the hill. The cold air forces tears from my eyes as I pick up speed.

Earlier today, I was excited about the idea of being the only person who knew of Jordan's secret. But now that I know for a fact that

A. he has a secret and B. I *am* the only person who knows about it, I want to pass out in the middle of this street. Why would he tell me this if it's too dangerous that I know? And who was in that car outside his house? Like, come to think of it, what a mean thing to say: *What I just told you is going to put your life at risk, but have a nice night anyway. Go ride your bike home alone on an arctic January night.* Who does that?

It looks like I'm going to be a damsel in distress like Jane Foster from *Thor* after all. Fortunately, I'm in good company—Mary Jane Watson, Lois Lane, Pepper Potts. All lady baes and no gays. I'll be setting records even in my time of plight. I hope Jordan has a good reason for telling me this. Otherwise, I'll settle for Jimmy.

eight

I pull up to my house and every single light is on. I drop my bike in the driveway, then head for the front door. But before I reach it, someone opens it for me.

"Dylan!" Mom says from the doorway. Her long hair blows back from the resultant gust of air. She's wearing her robe and slippers. "Cam, he's here," she shouts back in the house to Dad.

"Hey," I say.

"Hey? Where have you been? You couldn't answer our calls? Our texts?"

"I'm sorry. I was at a friend's house and left my phone in another room."

"What friend? I called Perry's and Kirsten's parents, and they said you weren't there. The girls said they didn't know where you were either." She clutches her arms.

"Well, you'll be glad to hear I'm branching out and making new friends."

"Get inside." She points to the foyer.

I slink past her. She shuts the door behind me.

"This isn't funny, Dyl," Dad says, walking down the stairs. "Your sister was sitting outside on the porch when we came home."

I grunt. "Is today Thursday? I forgot it was my day." I put my hands to my temples.

"You can't forget. She's ten."

My parents thought it'd be a good idea for my sister to have Thursday nights off from her extracurriculars and chores, so she could take a break and do schoolwork. I can't imagine what it must be like to have just one day off a week. I have six and it's honestly still strenuous. My one shift a week at Dairy Queen makes me feel like I've been crushed by a stampede of elephants and rhinoceroses and the people from school aren't even there. I think the people in high school suck the life from you. My theory isn't proven, but it reminds me of the movie *Jumanji*. We're all playing the game, trying to get ahead. But in the end, we get sucked into an alternate dimension and forget who we are.

"I'm sorry. There's just a lot going on and there's this new person and I had to meet up to help him out—"

"New where? At school?" Mom asks.

"The area."

"Hm." She pouts. "That's nice of you."

"Didn't take you for the type to show around the new kids," Dad says, smirking while patting me on the back.

"Gee, thanks."

"No, really, that's great, Dyl. Just remember Thursdays. It's the only day we ask you to help out."

"I know. Won't happen again."

"Now get to bed."

"I will. I need some water. I'm a little parched."

I watch them walk up the stairs, then I head to the kitchen. I fill a glass with water and listen carefully until their bedroom door closes. Once it clicks, I race to the basement.

My upstairs bedroom is directly adjacent to my parent's bedroom. I swear this house was made from cardboard or something because you can hear all conversations through the walls. Therefore my covert calls with Perry and Kirsten must happen in the basement.

I plug in a set of Christmas lights twisted around bare wooden studs and the bulbs illuminate the cement-gray room. I pull my phone from my pocket, then fall back on a beanbag chair.

"Not so fast," a blanket-covered lump on the green beanbag chair next to me says. I shriek. The blanket flings itself to the side. My sister jumps up, bulging my eyes from my head. She's wearing bright pink pajamas.

"What're you doing, you weirdo?" I yell in a hushed scream. "Shouldn't you be in bed?"

"What're *you* doing is the better question." She stands and crosses her arms.

"None of your business. Go to bed, Cody."

"Ugh." She sighs and fake faints back onto the beanbag chair. The back of her hand rests on her forehead. "I was abandoned and left freezing and starved this afternoon and you still can't be nice to me." She coughs. "I still haven't warmed up yet. So cold." Her voice softens. She fakes a shiver.

I tickle her bare feet. "Well, maybe you should put on some socks, then!" She giggles and kicks me away.

"I'm sorry I left you on the curb like a trash bin," I say, and pull her close for a hug.

"As you should be."

"It won't happen again."

"As it shouldn't."

"Now go to bed before Mom and Dad realize you're down here and get mad at both of us."

"I will. But first, you have to tell me where you were."

"I was just with a friend."

"A boy friend or girl friend?"

"Boy."

"A boy you kiss or a boy you play video games with?"

Good question. In my ideal world, a boy I could kiss while playing video games would be a dream.

"I'm not sure yet."

"Not sure? If you're going to forget about me, next time be sure."

Out of nowhere, a parade of fire engine and ambulance sirens interrupt the basement stillness. The red-and-blue lights flash in the thin basement windows at the top of the walls.

"Do you hear that?" I ask. "They're coming for you because you're not in bed."

"Stop!" Cody yells. She runs up the wooden steps, then exits through the basement door.

I rub my hands down my face and sigh. If I have to play twenty questions with one more person about Jordan, this relationship is not worth it. No one is ever interested in my life and now I have something interesting going on and people are interested? Funny how that works.

I didn't ask for this and I don't know how to handle it.

My phone rings, and I jump. Kirsten is facetiming me. I glance at the time and it's nearly ten p.m. *I'm* supposed to be facetiming *her*. What could she possibly have to tell me now? Nothing could be more interesting than my life currently. I swipe to answer.

An orange glow covers the screen. Smoke billows from Kirsten's mouth. *Whoa.*

"Kirsten? Are you outside? Are you okay?" I ask.

She moves her mouth, but sirens overpower her voice. I lower the volume.

"Kirsten? Hello?"

I stand and pace across the room.

"Dylan?" She puts the phone to her mouth. The closeness of her face turns the screen black. "I can't hear you! Where have you been?"

"I can't hear you either. I was successfully sleuthing. I have to fill you in."

"What?" she shouts.

"This doesn't seem like the best place for you to be facetiming. Can you text me?"

"I can't hear you!"

I groan and pull on my shirt collar.

"You have to see this," she says. "Come outside to the woods by my house. The new town houses they were building are on fire. It's insane!"

"What?" I ask. "All right. Stay there. I'm going to come."

"I will!"

I take a deep breath to soak up the last bit of warmth before I head back into the southeastern Pennsylvania tundra. I slip out the basement's sliding glass door and run to the front of my house, where I dropped my bike. The ground feels like a concrete pathway. The frozen grass crunches beneath my boots like gravel.

The weather people said some polar vortex system has been hanging over us for the past few weeks, and as a result it's been negative one hundred degrees—negative one-fifty, if you factor in the wind chill. I can already see myself frozen outside in a bush later tonight, killed by the elements in the style of Jack Nicholson in *The Shining*.

Everything is bone-dry, and I'm sure that's not helping this town-house fire. It's definitely not helping my lips, which are splitting at this very moment. Come to think of it, I haven't ever really had to take care of my lips for someone else. I brush my finger across my bottom lip to feel the torn skin. My skin is almost as white as the snow. I wonder if Jordan was disgusted by me. I'm disgusted by me. I'll have to make a trip to the pharmacy tomorrow to get some supplies to make myself look like a functioning human and not an extra from *The Walking Dead*.

In the distance, the sky by Kirsten's house flickers orange. Scraps of paper, or wood, or *something* dance around in the glowing air. I pedal out of my neighborhood, past Dairy Queen, and on to the town-house development. Two fire trucks pass me on my way. They stream additional cold air in my face.

When I arrive at the scene, a crowd of about fifty people observe the blaze. A line of police cars blocks them from getting any closer to the raging inferno. Flames cover a row of five town houses. The orange-yellow waves twirl four stories high toward the black sky. The wooden frames of the neighboring homes are inches away from catching fire. A dozen Blatt Builders signs hang on the chain-link fence around the construction site.

I scan the crowd and recognize the pink pom-pom on top of Kirsten's winter hat. Campfire scent wafts through the air.

I grab her shoulder. She yelps.

"Hey," I say. "Is everyone okay?"

"I think. They were under construction, so no one was in them, but the firemen are putting out the fire."

"How did it start?"

"No one knows. But you could feel the heat at my house."

"Yikes." I squint, putting my hand in front of my face.

"Did you find Jordan? I am assuming the answer is yes since you were ignoring our texts. How was it?"

I scratch my head. "Good," I say.

She frowns. "Good? After all that it was just good?"

"Yeah, it was good. We just met. It's not like we're getting married."

"Well, what did you talk about?"

"He just told me about school and stuff."

"Okay? You're being weird. Did you make out or something?" She smiles.

"No!" I blush. "It was just uneventful. Maybe I don't like him as much as I thought I did."

She studies me, telling me with her eyebrows that she knows I'm lying.

I look around, avoiding eye contact with her. I rub my arms for warmth.

Across the crowd, Savanna Blatt watches the blaze with her dad. The long white hair down her back nearly blends in with the snow. Her head twists in my direction. We make eye contact before I can turn away. She beelines toward me.

"Savanna is coming from our right," I whisper.

Savanna reaches us. She strikes a pose, crossing her arms and extending her right leg. "What're you doing here?" she asks, looking at me.

"Kirsten told me about it. I thought I'd come to see if she's okay."

"This isn't a show. Do you know how much money my dad is losing from this?"

"I'm sorry about this, Savanna," Kirsten says.

"Thanks, Kirsten." Her voice softens. "This is the second property to go up in flames in two weeks. It's been really hard on the family."

"Second time?" I ask.

"Yes, Dylan. Do you pay attention to anything? Please don't tell me there's not a brain in your unfortunately shaped head." I grunt. "The model home over at the new development on Liberty Pike got torched two weeks ago. They think it's arson now." She purses her lips.

Savanna's dad and older brother come up from behind her with two cops at their side. Her dad is a tall guy with a huge stomach. If you only saw him from behind, you'd think he was skinny.

"Who are these kids?" he asks.

"People I know from school," Savanna answers.

"When did you arrive at the scene?" one of the cops asks, stepping forward.

Kirsten and I exchange a glance.

"Um, twenty minutes ago," Kirsten says. "I live right down the street. I've been home all night. You can check with my parents. I'm sorry if I'm not supposed to be here—"

The cop holds up his hand. "It's okay. Thank you. And you?" He turns to me.

"Um, five minutes ago," I say.

"Which way did you come from, son?"

"That way." I look and point in the direction of my house. My jaw falls open.

Down the street, the silver car that was outside Jordan's house pulls up to the scene. This time, it isn't alone. Two more silver cars pull up behind it. They park along the curb. A group of people exit the cars and congregate in a circle. One makes a phone call, one writes something on a piece of paper, one texts, and the other leans against a car with his arms folded. I hold up my phone and take pictures of them to show Jordan.

"Hey, kid," the cop says, tapping my arm. "I asked you a question."

I snap back to my conversation. "Wait, what? Sorry. What did you ask?"

"I said we have a few witnesses saying they saw a teenage boy fleeing the scene right after the flames started picking up. Have any idea what that's about?"

"No...no." I shake my head. "I was also at home with my parents. You can ask them."

The cop writes something on a notepad.

"Know any other boys your age out tonight?"

"You're wasting your time," Savanna says, stepping forward. "Dylan doesn't have any guy friends."

"Thank you, Savanna, for clarifying," I say. "I think that point you just made will really enhance the investigation."

"Of course. You two don't have anything against the Blatt family, do you?" Her nostrils flare.

"Thanks, miss," the cop says. "We can handle it from here."

The cops nod. They walk away with Savanna's dad and brother in tow to another group of onlookers.

"Savanna, you don't think we had anything to do with this?" Kirsten asks. "I would never do something like arson."

"Not unless you have something to tell me." She quickens her rate of blinking.

"What? Absolutely not."

"Good. Didn't think so."

"Savanna!" Mr. Blatt yells. He points his finger at the ground in front of him.

Savanna brushes a loose hair behind her ear. "I guess I'll see you in school tomorrow..." She glances at me. "Unfortunately." She takes a step toward her dad and purposefully slams her shoulder into mine as she passes.

"What is wrong with you?" I ask, rubbing my shoulder.

"You should be asking yourself that question, not me," she says.

I turn to Kirsten. "She's such a bitch sometimes," I say.

"I mean, this is a stressful situation for her. Anyone going through something like this is bound to lash out with atypical behaviors."

"Can't you just agree with me?"

"Arson is pretty scary, though," she says, ignoring my comment. "My house is right here."

"Yeah, but it looks like there's a theme to the fires if there's been two of them. So I think you're good."

"The theme being?"

"Blatt *de*-struction." I giggle.

Kirsten holds back a smile.

"Get it? Like, since it's a construction company—"

"Yes, I get it. But you never know what could happen. This fire is huge. It's also scary to think about someone doing this to the Blatts or there being a criminal in our town. What could someone possibly have against them that they have to do *this*? Seems like an investigation is needed." She gestures to the flames.

"I mean, I can think of a lot of reasons to hate the Blatts."

Kirsten slaps my arm. "Don't be so hateful. It isn't a good look."

"Ouch. It was a joke. Chill."

The flames die down from the relentless spray of water, revealing black skeletons of what used to be houses. The power of the flames took them out in less than thirty minutes and I met a boy who can control those same flames with his fingertips. I check my phone for any messages from him. There's nothing. It's probably not my smartest move to try to get closer to him—or the safest. But I can't ignore him. Not after tonight. Not after he opened up to me like that.

I look back to where the silver cars were parked. They're gone.

Kirsten and I turn away from the scene. We lose the warmth of the fire. I immediately think of wanting to touch Jordan. To feel the heat again. To feel the warmth of his chest against my back.

And this is where I redefine thirsty. Even though he used his powers to knock me out, I want to touch him again.

I have a new crush on a boy. Someone send help.

nine

There are a few reasons why I have never had a boyfriend. Some are circumstantial and are definitely changing for the better. Others, like my noodle arms, are just facts of life and don't do me any favors. Technically, they could be changed. But who has the time? I've calculated how many hours I would need to spend in the gym to even begin to pop a bicep, but by the time that happens I'd be out of high school and on to the next phase of this so-called life. So why would I waste my time in a gym with creepy lighting?

I pretended to be straight in middle school and have written those years off. No boys could've dated me if they thought I liked girls. During freshman year of high school, I had my first exploratory period and made out with two boys in one month! But it should be noted that neither of them was in my grade or from my school. My choices quickly dried up, and there haven't been any left to date. The drought has been severe, to say the least.

And now it looks like things won't be picking up speed anytime soon. It's been almost two days and Jordan hasn't texted me. He was supposed to text me his name, at the bare minimum, so I could at least save his number to my phone. I can't even text him now if I wanted to. What an annoying little—

My phone lights up as the thought crosses my mind. It's not Perry or Kirsten because I have the length and emojis of their message ribbons memorized. It's a Snapchat add from jay_ordan10. There are two flames after the username. He has to be joking. I sit up in my bed and add him back.

Two seconds later he snaps a selfie of himself. He's lying in bed. He's sticking out his tongue with his left eyebrow raised. A blanket covers most of his body, but his shoulders are exposed. He's shirtless. His collarbone pops from his skin above his chest muscles. I gasp. I recognize the long black curtains from his room in the background.

The picture disappears in five seconds. I message back because I don't have time for games.

Dylan
Oh hi?
Jordan
Good morning
Dylan
Where have you been?
Jordan
School
Dylan
Praying?

Jordan

Lol basically

We learn sometimes too

Dylan

Interesting

Jordan

V

Dylan

What're you doing today?

Jordan

I have to go downtown

Dylan

Downtown? To the city?

Jordan

Yeah

Dylan

That's random. For what?

Jordan

Stuff

Dylan

Oh. Sounds interesting

Thanks for the details

Jordan

Lol. It's stuff related to the accident.

I see a doctor

Dylan

Ugh. That's twice now. I'm sorry.

Jordan

One strike left

Jk

What're you doing?

Dylan

Art galleries

Jordan

Fancy

Dylan

So are you going to text me so I can have your number? Or are we just going to do the Snapchat thing

Jordan

Maybe if I get pic

A picture? What? Am I about to sext with Jordan? I guess it's only fair that I snap him back a picture since he sent me one. I exit from chat and the camera pops up. I tap the screen twice so it faces me.

There's a massive yellow eye booger in the corner of my right eye and white, dried drool crusted in the corner of my lips. I grunt. I toss my phone, then dart to the bathroom to cleanse myself from my fourteen-hour sleeping stupor. I jostle my hair as I jog back into my bedroom. I twist open the blinds for better lighting, dive on my bed, grab my phone, snap a selfie, swipe once for the brighter filter, and send to jay_ordan10.

It takes about one minute for him to respond. Hopefully, he didn't lose interest in talking to me during that time period. But who knows with this guy.

Jordan

Cute

I smile and run my hand through my hair.

Dylan

Thanks

So a fair trade?

Jordan

Pushy

Dylan

Says the guy who has literally pushed and burned me to the ground twice

Jordan

Fair. I'm just trying to figure this all out.

I'm really sorry

Dylan

I know

He reads my last message and doesn't reply. I sigh. Point taken that anything related to his abilities, abnormalities, powers—I don't know what to call them—is a sore subject.

He texts me his number five minutes later with the words *my number.* I get the hint he isn't in the mood to talk anymore.

I wonder why he would tell me probably the most secret thing about himself and then ghost me. In my personal psychology textbook of dating, I have a whole chapter devoted to ghosting. There's no physical copy of this book. It simply exists within my mind.

Although one day I should publish it with all the knowledge I've acquired from my hypothetical relationships. First, in order to be ghosted the dude has to show an interest. If he never shows an interest and stops talking to me, then he was just never into me. I get it. But what I can't stand is when someone shows an interest in me and then vanishes. No texts. No calls. Gone. Adios. Bye-bye. It's more infuriating than the fact that my sister is smarter at the age of ten than I'll ever be.

Like when I made out with Ryan Bonchetti at Maddie Leostopoulos's sweet sixteen party last year. Sophomore year of high school was ridiculous for many reasons, but one of the top reasons was how there was a sweet sixteen party every other weekend, and I was somehow invited to 50 percent of them. Maddie's best friend made an announcement early in the night that half of the invitees were only invited so Maddie could say she had one of the biggest sweet sixteens of the year—making this party more salty than sweet.

Ryan went to the neighboring high school, so I had seen him around before. He was tall, lanky, and always wearing sweatpants. He also had a buzz cut.

He approached me, and we started talking, which somehow led to making out. I didn't really like it. Not because he wasn't a good kisser. I had only made out with a few people before him, so I didn't have much of a baseline to compare it to.

I didn't like it because Perry had stolen a bottle of Salted Caramel Bailey's Irish Cream from her mom's liquor cabinet, and we threw it back in a matter of five minutes before the party. I told her I didn't think this was the kind of liquor people drank alone without mixing it with something else. Perry asked if I had a mixer. I didn't. So we drank it alone. At one point I burped mid-kiss and almost threw up in Ryan's mouth.

He ended up having a decent personality and asked for my number at the end of the party. I gave him my real number, and we texted the rest of the night and for a few days after. The following weekend, I texted him asking if he wanted to hang out again, and the dude left me on read. I texted him a question mark three days later, and my poor little question mark floated all alone in its blue bubble in the message feed for the rest of time—GHOSTED.

It was a different story when I made out with Marshall Andrews the summer after freshman year. He was about to be a senior and was the only other out person at my school. I was staying with Perry and her mom at their vacation home in Ocean City, New Jersey, for the week. Perry knew Marshall from her all-star cheer team, and it turned out he was down the shore with a friend that same week. Perry invited them over one night, and we played card games on the deck. After the game, we ended up running to the beach at midnight.

Things got hot on the beach with Marshall quick. And when I mean hot, I mean really hot. He had facial hair and actual muscles and was the first person I was kissing after publicly coming out. There was even dry humping. I couldn't believe it. I was quaking in my pants.

After we finished, he said, "I'm not looking for anything serious. Just so you know."

I thought it was the weirdest response to a make-out session ever. Like, *Chill, I don't want to marry you either.* But I appreciated his honesty, and we went our separate ways.

I saw him at school in the fall and asked if he wanted to get together sometime. And it wasn't because I wanted to date him. I wasn't a stalker and ignoring his intentions, but I thought maybe we could have been friends. I had no gay friends and hadn't made a new friend since Perry and Kirsten in kindergarten, so I thought I could try to make an effort. He said he would let me know but never did. I didn't consider this ghosting because he told me up front that he didn't want my ugly self, and so it didn't take up any of my mental space.

Either way, ghosting has happened to me for one of two reasons. Either because the guy found someone else, or he wasn't ready to commit to anything.

For Jordan, I'm leaning toward the idea that he isn't ready to commit to our friendship. I'll give him his space and let him cool down after his big reveal. I guess cooling down will take longer than usual, if it's even possible, since he's made of fire. I totally should've screenshotted his shirtless selfie, though. I pull my covers over my head and moan.

I stare at the Received symbol of my last snap to him, over-thinking his nonresponse. Jordan vanished from Arizona without a trace. His life revolves around hiding from HydroPro. He's basically a professional ghoster.

I google Jordan and his family. There's no mention of the accident. I pair Jordan's name with HydroPro in the search box. Zero relevant results emerge. But when I search HydroPro alone, there's plenty of information to digest. I don't need to scroll far before an article grabs my attention. It's titled "HydroPro Expands Footprint in Philadelphia Area." I sit up.

I copy the address of the new Philadelphia facility. I paste it into

Google Maps, click street view, and swivel around the structure. I repeatedly tap the screen to move closer to the building, but the street view stops near the parking lot. It doesn't matter, though. I've seen enough. I drop my phone onto my cover. I run my hands through my hair as I study the picture.

The same silver cars from the other night are parked in the lot. I'm beginning to think it's not a coincidence that Jordan and those cars have come into my life at the same time.

ten

I sloth around the house until four p.m. when Perry and Kirsten's cheerleading practice is over. I stand by the front door and watch the go-kart pull into my driveway. Perry's and Kirsten's shoulders bounce side to side as the car climbs over the curb. I sprint from my doorway to keep my bare skin from being exposed to the elements for too long.

"It's freezing," I say as I dive into the car, rubbing my hands together. The high ponytails of the girls reach above their headrests. They each have a white ribbon tied in their hair.

"How was practice?" I ask. "Are you going to win Nationals?"

They exchange a glance.

Kirsten's lip curls. "No, because the one stunt group falls every time. It's very frustrating," she says.

"It's so annoying," Perry echoes.

"Who is it?"

"Kara Bynum is the flyer," Perry says. "She's the skinniest girl on the squad, and she can't stand in the air for more than two seconds without falling."

"We've gone over the routine dozens of times. She has the best back spot too, so we know it's not that," Kirsten adds with a grunt.

She reverses out of my driveway, and we take off to the Chili's in town. I don't even need to ask where we're going. It's what we do before Second Saturdays.

"What is it, then?" I ask.

Kirsten shrugs. "Lack of discipline."

"Weak ankles," Perry says.

"Don't make fun of the thin jointed," I say. "Have you seen my wrists?" I thrust my arm between the two front seats and spin my hand. My wrist cracks.

"Well, you're not on the cheer squad," Perry says.

"You should get looked at for protein deficiency," Kirsten says.

And it's a good thing I'm not the squad. My self-esteem would take a big hit. And there's barely a target to hit as it is.

"How does one acquire strong ankles?" I ask.

"Milk and stuff. I don't know. Ask Popeye," Perry says.

"Who?"

"That cartoon sailor with the lazy eye who eats spinach."

"I don't recall him." I shake my head. "Maybe she needs a strong set of cankles. Slip her a weight-gain nutrient bar à la *Mean Girls* and get 'em nice and stout."

"Then she'll be too heavy to lift," Kirsten says. "You need to think these things through. Where do you even get those bars?"

"I'm joking, obviously. You seem to have unrealistic expectations for Kara. Let her live with her thin, weak ankles!"

"Ugh, we just don't want her to fall!"

"Speaking of falling." I fake-flick my hair to the side. "I think someone's falling for me."

"Ah, Jordan?" Perry asks, spinning in her seat to face me. "Are we finally going to get some details?"

I laugh and nod.

"Stop!" Kirsten shrieks.

"He's not falling for me. I was kidding," I say. "I think he hates me. But he did give me his phone number."

"I would say that's a positive move, Dylan," Kirsten says.

"Yeah, if he hated you, he would pull what you did to Jimmy and five-five-five you," Perry says.

"Fair."

"Did you check for his Instagram now that he's in your contacts?" Perry asks.

I gasp. "Oh no. I didn't."

I open Instagram and tap Settings to see the suggested people to follow from my phone's contacts. He's the first one. I tap his page.

"It's private!"

"Well, follow him. You're friends. It's not like it's creepy."

I laugh. "True." I keep forgetting I know this person more than anyone on the entire planet, which is *so* crazy. "Look how cute. I can show you guys a picture now."

I can't see his other pictures yet, but in his profile photo he covers half his face with his hand. His white smile sparkles like he's from a toothpaste commercial. I turn my phone to show Perry and Kirsten.

"He only has seventy-seven followers," Perry says.

I roll my eyes. "That's your first comment?"

"He's very handsome!" Kirsten says.

"He really is."

"Let me see again," Perry says.

I show her again. "He only has six posts too," I say. "He just moved here and said he's trying to start over, so he probably made a new page. Don't judge, Perr. He's had it pretty rough. He already has those St. Helena's girls spreading rumors. He doesn't need your negativity too."

I wonder if he has any pictures of himself on fire or shooting flames. That would be one way to quickly gain new followers.

"I'm not. It was just an observation. I never said anything negative."

"It was your tone."

"Okay, Mom."

"Anyway," Kirsten interjects. "Invite him to my house after the galleries tonight."

"I could. What're we doing?"

"I don't know. Hanging out."

I shrug. "I'll ask."

I'll text him. But I don't know if I necessarily want him to come. Every time I see him, those cars appear. It seems like a bad move to give up Kirsten's location. It also doesn't seem like he entirely knows how to control his powers when he gets upset. The last thing I need is for him to burn Kirsten's wrist right before Nationals.

We get to Chili's and build our Triple Dipper appetizer with boneless buffalo wings, chicken nachos, and southwest egg rolls. Usually we get crispy cheddar cheese bites or fried pickles, but Kirsten and

Perry are on a muscle-building, all-protein diet for Florida. Or so they say. I make my case for the cheese bites by telling them they've been eating Blizzards all week so what difference does it make? But it's two against one and I lose.

It would be nice to have Jordan in situations like this to even the playing field. He could potentially alter the Triple Dipper appetizer sampler forever. And to be honest, that might be a bigger change in my life than getting a boyfriend. My relationship with my Chili's appetizers has been going steady for years.

"Any headway on the cheering front for next year?" I ask Perry, dipping a buffalo wing into blue cheese.

"No, I don't want to cause any issues before Nationals," she says.

"You should do it soon before spring tryouts," Kirsten says.

Perry rolls her eyes. "Well aware."

Perry and Kirsten are BFFs for sure. But there has always been this underlying tension between them around cheerleading. Basically, Perry is the better cheerleader, but Kirsten gets all the accolades—at least for the Falcon Crest cheer squad.

It all stems from their bitter head coach, Ms. Gurbsterter. Her elbows would probably snap if she even attempted a handstand.

She's big on loyalty to the school—or so the story goes. I mean, anyone would probably be loyal to a school they've spent forty years of their life inside. But someone who spends forty years of their life in one place is obviously seeking some sort of validation, so we can't take her too seriously anyway.

If someone ever tries to correct her on something about the school, her go-to line is: "I've been here since Reagan. You think I don't know?"

Like, duh, the reason you don't know is that you've been here since Reagan. Your brain is oatmeal.

Perry made the school's varsity squad freshman year but then quit the school team sophomore year to focus on her all-star regional team. She tried out again for the school team this year because she missed her friends and cheering at the football games. And that's where Perry's shining cheerleading career for the Falcon Crest High School Explorers took a turn for the worse. Because Ms. Gurbsterter saw her as a traitor and put her on the junior varsity squad out of spite, while Kirsten became captain of the varsity squad.

After the other members of the junior varsity squad continued to land their back handsprings on their faces and Perry did standing double fulls and pikes over their limp bodies, Ms. Gurbsterter finally moved her to varsity for this spring semester. I told her it was because of her talent, but Perry thought the principal influenced the decision because he wanted good press for the athletic department after the athletic director, older than Ms. Gurbsterter, croaked and a mismanagement of funds was discovered.

Ms. Gurbsterter didn't make Perry a captain, or even a co-captain. Her stunt team doesn't get to participate in individual competitions either, which Perry wants for college. Ms. Gurbsterter gets off on the misery she causes Perry, but pretty soon I'm about to stage a protest against that woman.

"This dinner is dead. Let's get out of here," Perry says.

The first gallery is only a five-minute walk from the restaurant. Flurries float through the gray, clouded sky. We link arms and walk along the brick sidewalk in a horizontal line. Kirsten and Perry try to catch snowflakes on their tongues. My eyes lock on every passing car, watching for silver ones.

"Welcome back to the Ellis Contemporary Art Gallery," a man says at the entrance of our first stop. It's our first stop every time. Most of the staff recognize us and we recognize them. We don't ever try to sneak a glass of wine here.

The gallery is full of couples wearing pea coats and scarfs, holding hands and smiling at the art. A man kisses a woman on the cheek in front of me as they regard a picture of a heart that's more shades of yellow than I ever knew existed. I check my phone to see if there is a message from Jordan. There's nothing. I crack my knuckles.

Our stomachs are full as we take in the art. We decide not to eat or drink anything at the galleries, so we move quicker than usual. Perry buys a copy of the yellow heart at the first stop. Kirsten buys a copy of a painting of London at the third gallery.

Most of the galleries change their collections for Second Saturdays so there is always something new to look at. Except for the sculpture gallery, which has had the same sculptures for years. We still go inside, though.

One time we got kicked out after Perry tried to take a selfie making out with one of the naked man statues. Now we try to see how many poses we can grab with the statue before getting death glares from the staff. Tonight, we barely take two steps before the eyes of all three gallery attendants force us out.

"Do you want to do one more?" I ask. "I want to see if I can buy something . . . perhaps a piece with warm colors."

Perry nods.

"Yeah, one more," Kirsten says, rubbing her hands together. "Let's go this way."

The last gallery we enter is one we haven't been to before. It's located at the end of the main street. When we step inside, it smells like my winter jacket after Mom unpacks it from the attic in November.

"Did we just enter an episode of *Hoarders*?" Perry asks.

I gulp. "It appears so."

This place looks nothing like the other galleries, which have white walls, hardwood floors, and pictures hung ten feet apart from each other. It has a beige carpet with an assortment of stains. Vases, books, flowers, and old furniture are strewn among the crooked paintings hanging from the walls and ceiling. Long aisles separated by towering bookshelves run from the front to the back. We're the only people in the gallery. I stop at a painting.

It's a picture of three men. Two are up front with their arms around each other. Their hair is gold and their smiles big. Their lips reach for the other's. They are standing underneath a streetlamp that brightens their end of the canvas. Behind them is another man looking their way where the canvas darkens. His hair is dark and his face pale. His expression of envy is so distinct it almost makes him appear to be at the front of the painting. I've never seen a picture like this at all the other galleries.

An older man with an apron walks beside me. "Excuse me, sir," I say. "Do you have any prints for sale of this one?"

He looks at the painting and shakes his head. "No, I'm sorry," he says. His voice is raspy. "We don't do those here."

I sigh. I look back at the painting. My mind races. A heaviness fills my chest as I make up dozens of scenarios in my head for what that painting is trying to depict. I worry that I'll never be like the men in the front—golden, shining, and happily in love. Everyone is so pristine like those men and I'm not. I'm easy to forget about. I'm an in-the-moment kind of guy. A stepping-stone to the more polished love interest. An I-don't-want-anything-serious-with-you kind of guy. It's hard to think of a future where I don't end up like the guy in the background, alone and wondering what could've been with a guy who never even thought about what we were.

I take a step toward the exit but freeze when I see someone blocking the doorway. A large man stares at me with his arms folded. It's the same man who was leaning against one of the cars at the fire. His speckled black-and-white hair lies flat against his head. His long, oval face sits on a thin skeleton. He wears a black coat. He doesn't move.

I look around the empty gallery, then take a step back. My feet trip over an antique lantern on the floor. It crashes to its side and the handle disconnects from the base.

"Kirsten?" I mutter. My eyes search for my friends. My hands wildly try to fix the lantern, but the pieces are clunky and no longer seem to want to go together. I toss them aside. They clank against the side of a shelf.

The man in the doorway takes a step forward. "Dylan," he says. "Just wait." His voice is groggy and deep, as if a snore could talk.

I gasp. A surge of adrenaline is injected into my chest. My heart tries to escape my body through my throat.

I race down one of the aisles of bookshelves toward the back of the gallery. My shoulders clip book spines and the corners of paintings as I move. I reach the back wall, then investigate the areas to my left and right. I look back down the aisle. The man is gone from my sight. My breaths are heavy.

"Perry," I whisper. "Kirsten." No one responds.

The floor creaks behind me. A shock travels down my spine. I turn, but the space is empty.

I drop to my butt. I press my hands into my temples. I let my head slide back and rest against the wall. As my eyes travel upward, the man appears in my line of sight across the room at the top of a metal spiral staircase. He watches me from a loft. I let out a whimper. I turn to crawl away but career into a pile of books. They spill across the floor. I manage to get to my feet. My boots slide on book covers along the floor. My eyes lock on the exit, then I make a run for it.

I leap through the doorway like I'm trying to clear a track hurdle. Outside, my body slams into Kirsten's back. She tumbles into a snowbank from the force.

"Oh my gosh, Dylan," she groans.

"What's wrong?" Perry asks. "We were looking for you."

"Let's get out of here," I say. I help Kirsten up, then drag her down the sidewalk.

"Are you okay?" Her lip curls.

They continue to press me for answers. I say I'm just cold. But really, I'm terrified.

eleven

Jordan

What time are you getting to Kirsten's house?

I receive that text from Jordan the second we pull up to Kirsten's house. He's either checking in or asking what time he should come over. My heart rate just started returning to normal levels after HydroPro unexpectedly crashed the one event I attend each month, but it's speeding up again as I read over his text.

Rather than speaking on the ride home, I inspected every car that pulled up behind us. I wasn't sure if I wanted Jordan to come over before, but now I am 100 percent sure I need him here because I also need answers.

Dylan

Now

Jordan

Should I come?

Dylan

Yes

Jordan

Are your friends nice?

Dylan

Yeah

If they like you

Flirting isn't my strong suit. Flirting while being pursued by a Liam Neeson look-alike isn't even an option in my skill set. Usually, I'd be thinking about trying to not act excited about the thought of him coming so I wouldn't seem desperate. But right now, I can't even think twice about it.

Jordan

Lol. Let's hope they do

And why's that? Does he want to stick around for a while?

Jordan

What's her address?

My throat tingles. I text him the address and shift in the back seat. I tuck my phone into my hoodie's front pocket.

Kirsten parks along the curb outside her house. She pulls down the sun-visor mirror and fixes her eyelashes before getting out of the car. We bounce down the grassy hill in front of her house to the front door. The windows are black, so her parents must be asleep.

I look up and down the street. There's one parked car in front of a neighbor's house, but it's a blue SUV.

I clear my throat.

"How do I look?" I ask.

Kirsten fumbles around in her bag for her house keys. "What do you mean how do you look?" she asks, swinging her head to flick her ponytail out of her face.

"Like, do I look clean or dirty or tired or anything bad?"

Perry scrunches her face. "You're so weird, Dylan." She crosses her arms. "Hurry up, Kirsten. It's freezing out here."

I huff. "Jordan's coming, so I'm trying to get a sense of my aesthetic. Gosh."

"No way! He is?" Kirsten asks. "Why didn't you say anything? I don't understand why you refuse to speak these days." She yanks her keys from her bag and twists them in the bolt, pushing open the door. "You look horrible. Let's go." She grabs my hand and pulls me up the stairs to her bedroom.

"Ugh," Perry grunts as we walk into Kirsten's room. Kirsten switches on the light and tosses her bag on the floor. "I look haggard," Perry says. "I'm sweaty from cheer. This should've been planned better. I don't want to give off an ugly first impression." She pulls the ribbon from her hair. It swirls to her feet. Her blond hair falls past her shoulders.

"You asked me to invite him."

"I know but . . . you have to admit, did any of us think he'd actually come?"

We shrug while shaking our heads.

Out of the three of ours, Kirsten's bedroom is my favorite. There's a hot-pink accent wall behind her bed, not to mention her bed is king-size and fits the three of us perfectly. We always have plenty of space to snuggle at the beginning of the night and then separate once our creases start sweating. I've had enough sweaty boobs on me to make any straight guy jealous. On top of her desk are a dozen ring lights she uses for her mock news-anchor videos. The lights also come in handy for our self-timed group photos.

But the best part is her six-foot-tall Princess Ariel wall sticker. It's been there since elementary school. Kirsten can't remove it now because she claims she and Ariel are good friends. I support this decision.

In my room, I still have a twin bed like a third-grader, and I question its impact on my psyche. If my body is used to sleeping alone every night, how could I ever make room for another person? My mind would subconsciously push them away to keep the bed to myself—like a survival-of-the-fittest thing. At least if I had a double bed my brain would know that there's a possibility someone could eventually sleep next to me. Hopefully.

I sit on the edge of Kirsten's bed. They examine me.

"What can we do with this mess?" Perry asks, tapping her index finger on her chin. She grabs my face, turning my head side to side. "Such an ugly specimen. Don't you think?"

I push her hand off my cheek. "Okay, enough. You are dumb."

"Dylan, this is a pivotal moment for your high school career," Kirsten says. "You look better than you did at Dairy Queen, so there's nowhere to go from here but up. Just a few minor touches are needed. I'll be right back."

She leaves, then comes back with a jar of pomade and her

toothbrush. She unscrews the cap from the pomade, then squishes her fingers into the cream.

"No," I say, and put my hand in front of my face. "My hair is too long for that. It's going to look greasy."

"No, it won't," Kirsten says. "Your hair is one of your best features. Let it be highlighted."

"It'll add a little shine," Perry says, shrugging. "Kirsten looks good for a reason. She knows what she's doing. And it'll get rid of some of these crazy flyaways." She plucks a hair from my head.

"Ow!" I yelp. "Do you want me to be bald?"

"Far from it," Kirsten says, and smooshes the pomade through my hair. My scalp tugs back. She pats the sides of my head, then takes a step away from me. She inspects her work.

"So much better."

"Oh wow, it's like you're a model now, Dyl," Perry says.

Kirsten extends her toothbrush. "And this," she says.

"I feel like my breath is fine." I lick my hand and sniff it.

"You just ate chicken fingers, buffalo wings, and dip. I'm quite certain it's far from fine."

I grab her toothbrush. "Is this even clean?"

"Yeah, it's mine."

"So?"

"So, what? What're you saying?"

I guess if I ever had to use someone else's toothbrush, I would choose Kirsten's. I head to the bathroom to brush my teeth. I tuck a few pieces of loose hair behind my ears and smile in the mirror. I turn off the vanity lights because they're too bright and make me look ugly, and I look at myself in the mirror in the dim overhead lighting alone to provide myself with a false sense of confidence and altered perception of how I actually look in real life. I tug on my hoodie's shoulders, then walk back to the bedroom.

"Is he here yet?" Perry asks. She is sitting on the bed scrolling through her phone. I check my phone. There's nothing.

"No," I answer.

"What do you think we should do tonight?" Perry asks, biting her lip. "I guess we can't just watch TV like we usually do."

"Why not?"

"That's boring. We don't want to seem boring."

"What do we want to seem like?"

She tilts her head to the ceiling. "I don't know."

Randomly, one of the ring lights on Kirsten's desk pops on like a photography flash, illuminating the room. I'm nearly blinded. Kirsten appears on the edge of the bed next to me. She crosses her legs before speaking.

"Dylan, as Jordan embarks on his journey across town to see you, what are you most hoping to get out of this next interaction?" she asks in her announcer voice.

"You know, that's a great question, Kirsten, thank you for asking," I say, playing along. If I were to be completely frank, my answer would be to find out who is driving the silver cars and to make them scram. But I'm sworn to secrecy.

"I've been reflecting a lot on my past and I believe I often overthink relationships. With this next interaction, I am just going to let myself have no plans or expectations."

"That's a healthy mindset to have."

"Indeed."

"Now, when you say your past, what particular incidents come to mind?"

My phone lights up on the bed. Jordan texts that he's outside.

I gasp.

"What's wrong?" Perry asks.

"He's here."

"Where?" Kirsten asks, returning to her normal voice.

"Outside."

"Like, pulling up or at the door?"

"I don't know."

Perry leaps off the bed. She sprints down the steps to the window beside the front door, then presses her face against the glass.

"Perry!" I yell in a hushed scream. "Let me get the door."

"No, I'll get it," Kirsten says.

"What? No. Why would you get it?"

"It's my house."

"You don't know him. That's awkward."

"It would be rude of me not to greet a guest at my own house." Kirsten smirks and her shoulders bounce. She swings open the door.

Jordan is standing at the doorway. His arm is raised, about to knock.

"Oh!" Kirsten says.

"Oh," Jordan says, deeper.

I stare blankly. Perry freezes. Kirsten turns to me and nods, and I realize that we greeted him like a trio of robots. We don't know how to interact with a fourth. It's throwing off our dynamic.

"Hey," I say, exhaling.

He smiles. And I can't *not* smile back at his smile. My muscles relax. He's literally wearing the same outfit he had on at Dairy Queen the night we met, except instead of black jeans he's wearing blue jeans. His hair is naturally messy and there's no shine. I can't believe I let Kirsten put this gel in my hair like I was going to prom.

"Can I come in?" he asks.

"Oh, yeah, definitely. Sorry," Kirsten says, scurrying to the side.

"Yeah, get out of the doorway, Kirsten," Perry says.

"Please," I say.

I check the street as he steps in the house. It's still empty.

Jordan immediately opens his arms for a hug. It takes me aback. He was so afraid of touching me before.

I lean into his open arms. My hands float above his back for a few milliseconds before I squeeze him tight. He's warm, but nothing out of the ordinary. He releases me, and I scratch the back of my head.

"Hi, I'm Kirsten. This is my house." She flips her palms to the ceiling.

"And I'm Perry. Dylan's best friend." She interlocks her arm with Kirsten's and rests her head on Kirsten's shoulder.

Kirsten's mouth falls open.

"What? No," I say, blushing. "Equal best friends." I wave my hand between them.

I watch Jordan closely, waiting to see if he hugs them. I'm trying to figure out how this heat thing works. Does he only burn people the first time he meets them? Or, like, can he control it sometimes? Does he only burn boys and not girls?

If he gets hot when meeting people for the first time, then *please* don't let him hug Perry and Kirsten. I'll never be able to see Jordan again if he does to them what he did to me on the street the other night.

He stays put in his current position and waves. It's awkward, but I take a few calming breaths.

"Thanks for inviting me," he says to Kirsten.

"Of course! Shall we proceed farther inside?" She extends her arms toward the kitchen and starts walking down the hallway. Jordan follows her. After he takes a few steps, Perry smacks my butt. I grab her wrist and push her away. She giggles next to me as we poke each other's sides walking to the kitchen.

"So, Dylan tells us you're new in town," Kirsten says. She jumps to sit on the kitchen island. "What are your initial thoughts of Ye Olde Pennsylvania?" She raises her eyebrows.

My eyes narrow. "Ye Olde? We're not, like, the Amish. Stop being weird."

Jordan throws his head back. "It's definitely different."

I pull out my phone and it's lighting up.

Perry
Omg so hot
I can't
Kirsten
Seriously

I lock it and put it facedown on the counter because it's obvious we're texting each other. I avoid Perry's and Kirsten's eyes.

"Is it the boys?" Perry asks, poking me.

Jordan laughs, shrugging. "Maybe. You see more of them in Arizona for sure."

"There's more boys in Arizona?"

"No." He smirks. "I meant, like, you see more of them because it's hotter, so less clothing."

Perry's eyes go wide.

He's only ever seen me in my parka, hoodies, and jeans. Last time I was wearing ski gloves and a beanie. Ugh. He's, like, basically only ever seen my chin exposed. It's a fine chin at that, but I need to stop being such a hermit and show a little more skin to meet his expectations. I'll wear a T-shirt next time and flash the forearms first. I set a reminder on my phone to do twenty-five push-ups tomorrow.

"You'll have to check the census for actual demographic data," Jordan says.

"Yeah, she's not doing that," I say.

"At least not for a week," Perry says. "I'm still on my homework leave of absence."

"I thought of what we can do!" Kirsten shouts from the pantry. She bites into a soft pretzel. "Does anyone want one of these?" She holds up a brown bag of pretzels. Perry grabs one.

"We should do winter activities for Jordan. You've never done that, right?" Kirsten asks.

"The removal of clothing can come later," Perry says with a piece of pretzel in her cheek.

I clear my throat. Kirsten rinses the pretzel salt from her fingers at the sink. Her reflection in the window smiles.

Jordan shrugs and looks at me.

"No one knows what you mean by *winter activities*," I say, specifically putting the focus on the winter stuff and not the other activity Perry mentioned.

"A winter activity is doing nothing because it's miserable out," Perry says.

"We can go ice skating out back! The pond will be frozen."

"Kirsten, it's freezing," I say.

"Not with a little special liquid inside our bodies," Perry says, and points her finger to the sky and shimmies.

My face flushes. I know what she means. I don't know if Jordan does. If I knew this was going to be a drinking event, I probably wouldn't have invited Jordan. The last thing I need to do is ruin everything with another Ryan Bonchetti experience.

"Perry, I don't know if that's such a good idea with someone we just met," Kirsten says sternly.

"Oh c'mon, Kirsten," Perry says, waving her hand. "We don't need to act so goody-goody. There's always stuff downstairs. I'm sure Jordan wants to have fun."

"Are you talking about alcohol?" Jordan asks.

"No, crystal meth. You in?" Perry asks.

"Shut up," I say, slapping her arm.

"Yes, she means alcohol," Kirsten says. "Do you drink? You don't have to if you don't want to. Peer pressure–free zone here." She makes an X with her arms. "We can wear jackets if it gets too cold."

"Sure," he says. "No peer pressure felt."

"Excellent," Perry says, smiling.

Kirsten's basement is its own house entirely. A flat-screen TV hangs on the wall in front of a large couch with one of those comfy long seats on the end you can stretch out on. Behind the couch is a fully stocked bar. It's basically a ranch-style house underneath her real house. No one needs it. But everyone wants it.

We walk to the bar. Every time I'm down here I question her parents' life choices. It's some grade-F parenting putting an open bar in the same room your kids hang out in. It's stocked with more liquor than just Bailey's Irish Cream. But if I had a daughter like Kirsten, I would trust her too, so it only makes sense.

"How much do you want?" Kirsten asks, inspecting a bottle of some clear liquor.

"Not that much if we're going to be spinning around on the pond," I say. "I'll throw up for sure."

"You throw up?" Jordan asks, stepping away from me.

"Sorry, no." I laugh and grab his arm and pull him back closer to me. My smile fades and my breath catches. I glare at my hand on his arm. I don't know who I am. My mind quickly wanders back to my train of thought. "I've gotten nauseous a few times before, but never actually sick. That's Perry's go-to move."

"Um, not true," Perry says. "I threw up once from drinking, and it doesn't even count because it was after I ate a funny burger from McDonald's that wasn't cooked."

"Still blaming it on the burger," Kirsten says, shaking her head. "You were just irresponsible." She grabs four shot glasses from the cabinet and places them on the bar.

"People throw up more than once from food poisoning," I say.

"I took a Pepto tablet, duh. Cured myself," Perry says.

"Jordan," Kirsten interrupts, smiling. "What is your drink of choice? You're the guest, after all. You pick."

"Um, I don't really like the taste of any of it. I usually just drink what's in front of me."

"Fair enough. How about rum or vodka?" Kirsten asks.

"Rum," I say.

"Are you Jordan?"

"No, but I'm overruling him. I've had vodka too many times."

"Rum it is!" Perry shouts. Kirsten pulls a bottle of brown liquid from a cabinet underneath the bar and slams it on the counter.

"Oh no. Not the dark one," Perry says. "Isn't there a clear one?"

Kirsten rolls her eyes. "You are annoying."

Kirsten finds a clear rum, and we each take three shots. I chug a yellow Gatorade after the last one to remove the taste of death from my tongue.

Kirsten and Perry run back upstairs to get their coats, leaving Jordan and me alone in the basement.

"Can I have a sip of this?" he asks, reaching for my Gatorade.

"Yeah," I say.

His Adam's apple bounces as he gulps the liquid. He places the bottle back on the bar. His lips are wet, slightly parted.

"What are you staring at?" he asks. His eyes flicker down to my chest, avoiding eye contact.

I'm staring at his full pink lips. I'm staring at the bottoms of his two front teeth peeking out from behind his top lip. I'm staring at the faint shadow of dark facial hair circling his mouth.

"Nothing," I say. "I'm happy you came tonight."

"So am I." He looks around the room. "This is fun."

He's sitting on a barstool, and I'm standing in front of him. I want to sit on his lap, but I don't think we're at that level yet. Although the alcohol is already telling me we're beyond that level.

I hold up my hand and spread my fingers in the air. He's right. This is fun. I don't want to ruin the moment by bringing up the silver cars. But with the girls gone, now seems like the only time.

"When are you going to tell me how it works?" I ask.

"How what works?" he asks. I watch as he raises his hand and pushes his palm against mine. There's another shock. Heat transfers from him to me, but I'm not burned. "You said you're in Chem, right?"

"Depends on what you're about to say."

The corner of his mouth curves up.

"You know how your body is mostly made up of oxygen?"

"Stop asking rhetorical questions or whatever. The answer is most likely no. Just tell me." I bite my lip, looking to the stairs.

"The human body is made up of a few main elements, like oxygen, carbon, hydrogen, and nitrogen. Your body is mostly oxygen, like everyone else. Something around seventy percent. But mine is mostly—"

"Hydrogen."

"Yeah." He sighs. "The accident changed mine all around. Or so they told me after I woke up from my coma."

"Who is *they*? How do you control it?"

"HydroPro." He studies our hands, still touching, and starts rotating his back and forth.

"Is that who is in the silver cars? Are they after you?"

"Can we go out next week? Just us." He presses his palm harder into mine. "I'll tell you. I'm nervous about saying anything with the others here."

I don't know if I can wait until next week. He keeps pushing his hand into mine. I counter the force. His palm heats up, sending chills down my spine. It starts to sting. I gasp and pull my hand from his. My fingers brush against his knee and he jumps.

The basement door opens, and Perry and Kirsten stomp down

the steps in their parkas. Jordan spins the barstool away from me and chugs more Gatorade.

"Here," Kirsten says, tossing us a pair of coats. "Jordan, you can use my brother's coat."

I slip my arms through the sleeves and hoist the coat over my shoulders.

"Thanks," Jordan says, putting the coat on the bar. "I should be fine, though."

Perry and Kirsten laugh.

"Jordan, it's very cold outside," Kirsten says.

"Yeah, you can't be that drunk yet," Perry says. "Although I think I might be."

"What?" Kirsten and I say in unison.

"Later, losers." Perry smiles and slinks out the back door.

"Did she take extra?" Kirsten asks. "That's not fair."

I shrug.

"Guess you'll learn about the cold weather the hard way, Jordan," Kirsten says. "C'mon, boys, let's hurry up and follow Perry. She's probably frozen in a ditch somewhere already."

"You guys do know there are parts of Arizona that get snow and stuff?" Jordan questions. "We also have an NHL team."

"Tell me more outside," Kirsten says.

We open the back door, and I cross my arms when the cool air hits me. Breath puffs from our mouths as we walk to the edge of the woods. The four of us are in a straight line. Jordan's breath is heavier than the rest of ours.

Every time I walk through these trees, a pang reverberates in my chest. It's impossible not to think about reason number one why

I dislike the Blatts. The same reason why I didn't want to come in here the night I met Jordan.

It happened in eighth grade right after I evolved from cute, closeted, gay Charmander to openly out and brooding gay Charmeleon. I was still high off the injection of confidence and possibility that coursed through me after telling people I was gay. But Savanna stole it out from under me, and I sobered up real quick.

I was swinging on Kirsten's backyard swing set after soccer practice. I was still wearing my pinny, cleats, and shin guards. Kirsten was lying on the blue plastic slide in her cheerleading uniform, and Perry was leaning against one of the wooden posts spinning a dried leaf.

Kirsten's older brother, Trever, burst out of the basement door with Savanna's older brother, Miles, close behind. Our heads turned and we stared.

Kirsten's and Savanna's parents were friends growing up, which put Kirsten and Savanna into a prescribed friendship. The presence of Savanna or her brothers or her parents was always a potential risk factor for misery going over to Kirsten's house.

Before I came out of the closet, I overestimated how much the people I knew were going to care about it, and I underestimated how much random people were suddenly going to be interested in my life. Once I was out, I discovered Savanna's older brother was one of those random people.

"I didn't know the gay kid was so close with your sister," Miles said loud enough for me to hear. I swear the guy never even knew I existed before. We had been at Kirsten's house together dozens of times, and he'd never said a word to me. But suddenly I was surrounded by a glowing rainbow that always needed a comment.

"Shouldn't you be in a cheerleading skirt too?" he asked.

"Shut up, Miles!" Kirsten yelled.

I stopped swinging and focused on the muddy ground.

"He's not going to get any boys hanging out with girls all day!"

"Trever, tell him to shut up!" Kirsten yelled again to her brother.

Trever mumbled something and slapped Miles's arm.

"Let's get out of here, Dylan."

The three of us jumped off the swing set and walked to the woods. My body went rigid as we approached the other boys in the middle of the yard. When we passed them, Miles made sure to clip my shoulder with his.

"Ow, dude," I said, gritting my teeth in an attempt to maintain a neutral expression. Miles was a senior then, and my arms were like dental floss. My frame was fragile at best.

"Aw, my bad, man. Did that hurt? I thought they tell us not to stereotype now and that all gays aren't sissies," Miles said. He brought his hand to the air, pretending to slap me, but stopped a few inches from my face.

I flinched. My vision clouded. I looked to Perry and Kirsten. They gripped a tree trunk near the edge of the woods, frowning. Miles stood between us. I clenched my fists and cleated him in his inner thigh. I was aiming for his balls, but my legs were heavy from practice, so I missed. It ended up being a fatal mistake because he was able to grab me right after I turned to run and got in two punches to my face before Trever, Perry, and Kirsten pulled him off me.

At school the next day, Savanna asked me how my face felt. I thought she was being nice. But after I said it felt better, she told me to be less annoying and maybe her brother wouldn't need to punch me.

twelve

We finally reach the frozen pond. There are no clouds in the sky, and the ice glows from the direct moonlight. My chest is warm from the alcohol, and my head is starting to feel heavy.

"Have you skated before?" Perry asks.

"No," Jordan says. "How are we going to skate with no skates?"

"Well, this is, like, makeshift amateur skating. We slide around on our shoes and push ourselves with sticks."

Kirsten steps onto the pond with a stick in her hands. She shoves it into the solid ground and pushes off. She glides to the center of the frozen circle. She comes to a stop, then does a 360-degree spin and puts her hands in the air.

"Now you're going to win the Winter Olympics too?" Perry shouts.

Jordan and I clap.

She laughs. "Get out here," she says, waving us onto the ice.

"I'm going to shimmy," Perry says. "These sticks are muddy and disgusting." She steps onto the ice and moves her feet back and forth as fast as she can. She's basically running in place and barely moving an inch per minute.

"Do you want to try?" I ask Jordan.

"Only if you come on the ice with me."

My chest expands as my heart flutters inside it. "It's the only reason I came out here, to be honest."

He laughs.

"Get a stick, though," I say. "Unless you want to struggle like Perry."

"I heard that!" she shouts from the same place on the ice where she started. She's pumping her arms now but still can't seem to pick up any traction.

Jordan grabs a stick and puts one foot on the ice, leaving his other foot on the grass. His foot on the ice starts sliding, and he slowly lowers into a split.

"Oh man," he says, laughing. "It's so slippery."

I drop a few sticks that are too short and run over to him. I step onto the ice, extending my arms for balance. He's sitting now with his knees awkwardly bent. I put my hands in his armpits and hoist him up.

"Thank you." He exhales and brushes off his hands.

Both our feet are on the ice. Our stomachs touch. It's the closest we've ever been. His hot breath warms my face.

"Now what?" he asks.

I swallow. "It's harder than it looks," I say.

"I guess we're going to have to make this work with one stick." He holds out the stick in his hands.

I take it from him. "Let me do this since you clearly have no idea what you're doing."

He slides behind me. Without asking, he wraps his arms around my waist. A tingle of anticipation spreads across my legs.

"Ready?" I ask.

I push the stick into the frozen ground, and we glide across the ice, away from the shoreline. We don't go far, because I lack the strength to push two bodies to the center of the ice, but we go far enough to pass Perry. Kirsten is in her own world, spinning in the far corner of the pond with her arms over her head like a majestic Olympian.

We only move for a few seconds, but gliding backward across a frozen pond with a boy wrapped around my waist in the middle of the night is probably one of the most magical things I've ever done. I look at the moon and think about how weird life is—that one place can hold one of my worst memories, but somehow there's still room in it for a new moment to become one of my best memories.

I spin around to see his face and grab his waist. My thumb touches his bare skin underneath his hoodie. I stare at his lips.

He smiles, then pushes off me, moving backward across the ice. "Bye," he says, waving.

Such a tease. I reach for him and swipe at air.

"Come back," I yell.

"Guys," Kirsten says, her voice high-pitched.

I look over my shoulder in her direction. She's still. Her knees are slightly bent, and her arms are extended out in front of her. Her face is expressionless.

"What?" I ask.

Jordan stops himself from sliding any farther and looks at Kirsten, wide-eyed.

"The ice is cracking over here," Kirsten says.

"Are you kidding?" Perry asks. She stops shuffling and slips. Her arms flail.

"No! I'm not kidding." Her voice shakes. "There's a huge crack between my legs."

"Um, well, don't move," I say. I scan the ice around my feet for any cracks.

"Do I look like I'm moving?"

"Can you push yourself away from the crack?"

"How? I tossed my stick when I was spinning. What do I do?"

The night is so quiet without any of us moving or talking. We're spread apart at the four corners of the pond. A slight breeze grazes my cheeks. The tall trees sway above us. I swallow hard.

Perry is the closest to her. Kirsten takes a step. The ice murmurs beneath her. "Help," she says. Her voice quivers.

"Here," I yell. "I'm going to slide my stick to you. Use it to push to the shore." I slowly bend down and get on my knees. I lay the stick on the ice and point it in her direction. Using my best aim, I slide it to her. I leave my arm extended in the air, watching the stick rattle along the ice like I'm one of those Olympic curlers.

The stick bounces off a few bumps in the ice, but it hits Kirsten's feet and stops beneath her body.

Kirsten lets out a sharp breath. She tucks her hair behind her ears and then lowers her left arm.

"Slow," I say.

She nods. She leans down and reaches for the stick. Her fingers hover a few inches above it.

Then there's a sharp crack and she disappears beneath the ice. My stomach drops.

"Kirsten!" Perry shouts.

Water splashes into the air where Kirsten stood.

Kirsten's hand suddenly shoots up from the hole and slaps the ice. She gets ahold of the ledge, but it crumbles from her weight. She disappears again.

The cracks in the ice spiderweb across the pond. Perry gets on all fours and crawls toward Kirsten.

"Perry, be careful!" I yell.

"We have to get her!"

There's another sound, like an ice tray twisting. Perry's right arm plunges through the ice as she gets closer to the hole. She collapses onto her chest. Her chin bounces off the hard surface. She pulls her hand out of the water and her sleeve is dripping.

I wipe snow and dried leaves from the ice, looking for Kirsten floating beneath the surface. My breath comes out in short bursts.

I look across the pond, and Perry is moving again. She makes it a few more feet, but then her right knee goes through the ice. She whimpers. She pushes herself back up and the entire front side of her body is soaking wet.

"You need to get to shore!" I yell.

She nods and studies the surface. Her hair hangs in front of her face. She lies flat and, rather than crawling, rolls to the shoreline in a few seconds. It's the smartest thing she's ever done. She vaults up and races to the shoreline closest to Kirsten.

"Should I call nine-one-one?" she asks. "Oh no, my phone is all wet." She frantically wipes her phone with her shirt.

I keep searching for Kirsten, swiping the ice with both hands. But I can't for much longer. My hands are freezing. My fingertips are numb.

"Kirsten!" I yell.

Then I realize it's the first time my hands have been freezing all night—and I remember why. I whip my head toward Jordan.

"Jordan," I say, breathing heavily. "You have to help."

He shakes his head and slides away from me.

"This is my best friend," I say through gritted teeth. "You can do something."

"I . . . I can't," he says.

I pound the ice. My knuckles start to bleed.

"No one can know," he says. "If I make a scene, HydroPro will know where I am. They'll come after—"

"What?" I throw my hands up. "No one is going to—" I begin, but cut myself off. I spin around. "Perry, go get help! Go get Kirsten's parents." I point to the woods.

"I'm not going to leave!" she shouts back.

"Just go!"

"I'm not going to—"

"If you get help, someone can get her! We'll be here. Go."

She grunts, turns, and disappears into the trees.

"Now, Jordan," I say. "No one is here. You can get her. No one will know. Please." Spit flies from my mouth.

He looks behind him. His lips tighten. Kirsten hasn't popped back up again.

"Get off the ice," he says flatly. He clenches his fists.

I nod and crawl away as fast as I can. I slip a few times as I make my way to solid ground. When I'm there, I scramble to my feet and brush off my knees. Jordan stands alone in the middle of the pond.

"What are you waiting for?" I shout.

He doesn't move. He's looking at his feet. It's silent. I walk along the pond perimeter. Dried leaves crunch underneath my shoes.

"Jordan!"

"Shut up, Dylan!"

I stop walking and pull my hand to my chest.

Then he puts his hands to the side of his head. His mouth opens, and he lets out a guttural scream. I yelp and fall back at the sound. My eyes go wide. My chest heaves. Black birds erupt from the tree branches above us and dive up and down through the sky. Thick veins burst from his neck.

An orange halo develops around his body. I squint and smack my hand to my forehead. The air rushes toward him like a vacuum. The bitter gush of wind bites into the back of my exposed neck and sends a shiver down my spine. Dead leaves and sticks are pulled onto the frozen pond. They crackle as they get closer to him.

There's a pop and Jordan explodes into a ball of fire. A wall of light smacks my face. It's so bright, it forces my eyes closed.

thirteen

When I open my eyes, the ice is gone. And so is Jordan.

Waves rise and fall from the center of the pond. The water laps ashore like someone did the biggest cannonball. Splashing water echoes through the woods.

It's hard to see anything without the white glow from the ice reflecting the moonlight.

"Jordan?" I whisper.

I slowly stand. My knees crack. My stomach turns. I don't know what I was expecting to happen, but this definitely isn't it.

When I asked Jordan to help, I was thinking more along the lines of him simply jumping into the same hole Kirsten fell through and bringing her to the surface. I didn't think it was too much to ask him to swim through the freezing water to save a life when it wouldn't affect him at all. But he actually went AWOL and blew himself up. Let me add that to his list of powers—create heat, shoot flames, make inanimate objects combust, make *humans* combust.

Clearly he thought more drastic measures were needed. I just hope the dramatics were enough to bring back Kirsten.

The birds settle on the trees above me. I'm the only human around the pond. There should be three. There needs to be two more. I begin to pace. I extend my head as far as I can over the water. It's black.

"Kirsten?" I whisper.

How long has it even been since she fell in the water? A couple minutes? How long does it take for someone to freeze to death? There's a loud crack in the woods behind me. I spin around.

What will I say to Perry when she gets here with help? How am I going to explain two dead kids while I'm standing on the shore completely dry? The frozen pond explanation isn't going to work without ice.

There's a loud splash, and I turn back to face the pond. A mound of water grows into the air and Kirsten's head breaks the surface. When her mouth clears, she gasps for oxygen. She sounds like a Dementor about to suck out someone's soul—and she looks like one too.

I run into the shallow waters to help bring her to land. The freezing water quickly fills my shoes and my legs become heavy to move. My toes sting and my balls get sucked up into my stomach. Kirsten's arms flail above her head.

"Kirsten!" I yell. "I'm here."

"Dylan," she mutters. Water gurgles in the back of her throat.

When I get close, she springs from the water and dives into my arms. She pants as she tries to catch a breath and her body convulses.

I'm suddenly transported to the final scenes of a gender-swapped *Titanic*. Her skin is purple, and her hair is stuck to the front of her face. My hands slide along her wet, frozen arms as I try to get a good grip.

"I'm so cold," she whispers. Water spits from her lips.

I dig my fingers around her biceps and pull her to shore. Her waterlogged clothes make her ten times heavier than she normally is and my frozen limbs make me ten times weaker than I normally am, but I keep pulling.

"I have you," I say. "Almost to shore." I grunt. I step on a rock beneath the water and my ankle falters. My mouth puffs steam like a chimney in the middle of the night. Hers does too, which I take as a good sign.

With a final, long step, I bring my boots out of the water. Kirsten's upper body is in my arms, but her legs are still floating in the pond. Jordan bursts from the water by her feet like an orca preying on a seal. I jump and fall on my butt.

"Dude," I say. I twitch my head and shake off the scare. "Help me." I point to her legs. He grabs them and together we carry her away from the pond, sidestepping. We gently lay her on her back.

Her eyes are closed. "Kirsten?" I shake her shoulders. Her eyelids flutter, but there are no other movements.

"Get out of the way," Jordan says, tugging on my arm.

"What?"

"Take a few steps back."

I listen. He puts his hands on her shoulders and within a second, it's like her body deflates. The faint slither of steam swirling from her mouth turns into a thick, billowing gray cloud. Her muscles relax, and her purple skin fades back to her normal flesh color. Her chest rises and falls at a quickening pace.

I kneel beside her, and she rolls into my body. I pull her into my arms and rest her head against my inner shoulder.

"Kirsten!" a deep voice calls out from the woods. *Mr. Lush*. Twigs snap in the distance.

Jordan's eyes look over my shoulder to the sound. "I should go," he says.

"What? No. You don't have to," I say. "No one can tell what happened."

He stands and takes a step away from me and Kirsten. "You don't understand, Dylan."

"Please, just stay."

"I can't." He shakes his head. "I hope Kirsten is all right." He turns and jogs to the other end of the pond.

"You don't have to disappear every time something happens!" I call out after him. "Are you going to come back?"

He stops running but keeps his back to me. He stands motionless for a few seconds.

"I'm not disappearing," he says. "I just can't be with you."

Then he starts running again, fading into the black trees.

My chest feels like I'm sinking even though I'm finally on land. I want him so badly, but he keeps running away from me. They always run away from me. How can I get it across to him that I don't care about his powers? Well, I do care. He's extraordinary. The good kind. But I'm not going to judge. I'm not like the people from Arizona who want to hurt him or scare him. I'm just a boy with a really bad crush who wants to get to know him.

"Kirsten! Oh my god," Mrs. Lush shrieks as she, Mr. Lush, and Perry emerge from the woods. Mrs. Lush wears a pink robe and gray sweatpants. The backs of her feet crush the heels of a pair of running shoes she must've slipped on in a hurry. Mr. Lush is in a T-shirt and plaid pajama pants. He pushes me aside and lifts Kirsten into his arms.

"What happened here?" he asks. But he doesn't wait for a response. He darts back into the woods toward their house. Kirsten flops in his arms.

"Dylan, sweetie, are you okay?" Mrs. Lush asks. I nod, trying to wrap my mind around the flurry of events happening around me. She grabs my cheek. "You're freezing."

"The ice?" Perry asks, scanning the pond.

I rub the back of my neck. I'm tempted to just explain everything. Tell her what happened with Jordan. But Mrs. Lush is right here. If Jordan is going to trust me eventually, I have to give him a reason.

"It all started crumbling after you left . . . and sank," I say.

It's the best I've got.

She stares at me, eyebrows pressed together. I don't know if she believes me. I wouldn't believe me. There isn't a single piece of ice left on the pond. If this were to happen naturally, I feel like there would be some tiny pieces still floating on the surface. Or even some frozen ice at the edge of the shoreline. But there's nothing. The pond looks the same way it does in the summer when the water is warm and we use it for swimming.

But Perry isn't typically one for questioning. And I am hoping tonight isn't the night she decides to turn a new leaf and become a critical thinker.

"Where's Jordan?" she asks.

"He went to get help too."

Confusion is painted across her face.

"Perry, let's go," Mrs. Lush says and grabs her arm. "I need you to help me get some of Kirsten's things. We need to take her to the hospital." Her tone is sharp.

"Right. Of course," Perry says, nodding. "C'mon, Dylan."

I look across the pond. "I . . . I think I'll go get Jordan and let him know we got her," I say.

"Are you sure?"

"Yeah. I don't want him to run around in the cold for longer than he has to. Just go." I wave her after Mrs. Lush.

They scramble back into the woods. Mrs. Lush's feet pop in and out of her shoes.

They're gone in a hot second, and I'm alone by the pond.

A wave of exhaustion hits me. I realize my face has been tense for a straight fifteen minutes. I let my muscles relax and my shoulders dip. My arms are sore from heaving Kirsten's motionless body through the water. I spread my fingers and my joints crack. Some of the wounds from punching the ice reopen and blood spreads across the back of my hand. I shake my hands, hoping to get rid of the pain.

There's nothing more I can do for Kirsten. I know she'll be safe after Jordan's touch. Her dad probably has her in the car off to the hospital by now. And I can't be around Perry for further questioning. I can't explain. At least not yet. There's nothing I can do for her either. So I turn and decide to go after what I can do something about.

I chase after Jordan.

fourteen

I follow his path for as long as I saw him run. Just like the night we met, I'm taking things into my own hands. It's a new position for me, and it's only been getting me in trouble so far. I'm used to waiting for something to happen to me. I'm not the guy to send the first text, to like the first photo, or to make the first move. But I am pulled to Jordan like a magnet. The men who are after me must know something. They think I shouldn't be with Jordan. And sometimes when outside forces are trying to keep you apart, it means you're meant to be together. I can't sit this one out.

The first night we met, I thought he was going to be a guy I put into one of my hypothetical relationships, someone I stalk online for days and then ask myself how could he be so perfect and how I could get a boyfriend like that.

That was my safe space. The hypothetical relationships weren't real, but my heart was never broken. But I don't want to wonder with Jordan. I want to *know*.

I trip over a fallen tree and slide through a pile of leaves.

"Jordan!" I yell. I wipe dirt from my lips. I'm at the lowest point I've ever been after drinking and I'm not even drunk. My coat is soaking wet and Jordan's nowhere to be found to keep me warm.

Something snaps beside me. I spring up. "Jordan?"

A shadowy figure darts through a row of trees a few yards ahead of me. My feet are rooted to the ground. "Hello?" My voice shakes.

The figure appears again, and this time the bright red Arizona State University hoodie of Jordan Ator flashes in the corner of my eye. My pulse starts hammering the inner wall of my chest.

"Jordan!" I take off after him.

This is the most running I think I've done since, like, my last soccer game in eighth grade, and I am paying for it. Maybe if soccer involved chasing after a cute boy, I would've been somewhat decent at it.

I can't see Jordan anymore, but I'm following his sounds. He's not stealth, which I think is an overarching problem of his. He's terrible at keeping his "secret" a secret. But right now, his inability to be quiet is playing in my favor. I know he knows I'm here, because otherwise he wouldn't still be running. I lick my lips and squeeze between two trees.

A light grows ahead and I regain my bearings. We're coming out the other end of the woods near the Blatt construction site of those new town houses. The streetlamps shine down on us.

I burst through the last line of trees into the clearing. Jordan scales the chain-link fence of the construction site. His butt is in the air. His feet kick a Blatt Builders sign from the metal as he prepares to launch himself over the fence to the other side.

"Jordan, why are you going in there?" I take a deep breath. "Just talk to me."

He looks back at me, and his eyes go wide. He falls from the top of the fence and lands on his back.

I reach the fence and there are missing links where he climbed up. The gray metal links have morphed into solid drips, like they melted. Handprints are squeezed into the top metal bar. A thin orange outline simmers at the edge of the melted metal.

He stands and wipes his chin with his arm. I wrap my fingers around the fence and stare at him.

"You again," he says, breathing heavily.

"Me again," I say.

He takes a step back. "You need to listen to me, Dylan."

"Listen to you about what? I don't get it."

"You should be afraid—"

He screams and hunches over, grabbing his stomach.

"Are you okay?"

"You should be afraid of me."

A flame shoots from his free hand, scorching the ground. The green grass turns black.

"Oh no," he mutters. He screams again like he's in pain. He squeezes his eyes shut so hard the creases run from the corners of his eyes to his hairline. Another flame shoots from his hand, and this time blasts the ground an inch from my feet. I hop away.

"You need to go," he grunts.

"What's happening? Do you need help?"

"No." He shakes his head aggressively. "I need you to go."

He looks at me one last time. His eyes are orange-gold. A light blue circle appears around his pupils. A halo starts to glow around him again. He sidesteps toward the town house. His back lurches as he moves away. "Don't follow me. Whatever you do."

"That's not fair." I shake the fence.

He limps toward the closest row of empty homes. A blue tarp flaps in the wind over the roofs of the wooden structures. Jordan's left foot drags along the ground as he hops on his right. He clutches both arms over his stomach. A sporadic flame shoots from his body every few seconds.

I read the sign next to me that says *Construction Zone: Do Not Enter*, and it all clicks. *No.* Not another one. Not this soon.

I start to climb the fence. He's nearly at the doorway. "Don't go in there!"

I fling myself over the top and awkwardly slide down the other side. My jacket gets caught on one of the melted, jagged edges of the fence. I tug the fabric and it rips. I fly a few steps backward from the force.

I turn, and Jordan has disappeared into the house. Flame light flickers through the square window openings. I run to the house and burst through the door, but it's too late.

The stairwell is on fire and a line of flames slowly crawls across the ceiling. The heat is unbearable.

Sweat droplets quickly form on my forehead. I strip off my jacket and throw my winter hat.

Jordan is standing in the hallway literally on fire.

"Is this what you wanted to know?" he asks, throwing up his hands. "This is how it works!" His bottom lip quivers.

I look around at the site and swallow. "I don't know what I wanted to know. How are your clothes not burning? Can't you make it stop?"

He shakes his head. "This is how it works. The clothes are from them. Everything is from them. I don't know how to control it." A beam falls from the ceiling behind him and crashes to the floor, erupting in a flock of orange sparks that disperse through the air like lightning bugs. "I'm made up of hydrogen, so I get all the properties of hydrogen. And you know what they are?"

Another rhetorical question. But this one I know the answer to. "Flammable."

"And combustible and explosive and everything else."

"Did you do this to the other Blatt houses?" We're yelling, but I don't think it's because we're mad at each other. At least, I'm not mad at him. The crackling fire around us is so loud.

He nods. "What else was I supposed to do? Where else could I go? I don't want to hurt anyone, so I come to these empty houses." His voice cracks. "I have to let it burn out. It happens when I get over-whelmed or something." He taps his hands against his chest. "It's like a crappy symptom of anxiety. That's what happened at Dairy Queen. I was so nervous around you that the heat blew up that cup."

My chest tightens. I take a deep breath but inhale smoke. I cough, and my eyes water.

"So two weeks ago the model home on Liberty Pike—"

"Was me. Because I just moved here and had no friends and didn't want to be here."

"And a few nights ago, the town house next door—"

"Was me. Because I met you."

Mic drop. I get chills in a burning house. Did he just say he was overwhelmed by meeting me? Now I know I'm not the only one feeling the heat. I want to race across the room and hug him. But I can't without bursting into flames and dying. The words he just spoke have already killed me, though.

I swallow. The roof of my mouth is dry. "And tonight?"

"I don't know. Being pressured to save a dying girl is pretty overwhelming." He looks over his shoulder as another wooden stud crashes to the floor from above us. The flame light casts a shadow above his cheeks. His eyes look like sunken black holes. A few of the flames around his shoulders flicker out.

"Well, when you put it like that."

There's a crack and his feet fall through the wooden floor. His legs disappear up to his knees. I gasp. I take a few steps closer.

"We need to get you out of here," I say.

"No, you go." He waves me away. "You can't survive this. I can."

"I don't think you can survive a house falling on top of you. Or can you do that too?"

He looks up at me. My face is reflected in his glassy eyes. "Not quite," he says.

He climbs out of the hole, then sits on the floor. Most of the flames around his body are gone.

Then the sirens. I was waiting for them the second we reached the construction site. It sounds like multiple cop cars and at least one fire truck. The smoke is probably visible across town.

I kneel beside him. "Before we go, you have to tell me who is after you. Because now they're after me."

"The silver cars?" he asks, then nods. "I didn't want to admit it to myself. But when I saw the car the other night at my house, I knew they knew."

"Knew what?"

"My location. It's HydroPro. They've been spying on me. I came here to get away from them. But they want to take me back because of all this." He waves at the flames. "They want to continue their experiments on me. I know they do. When they had me in Arizona after the accident, they were always poking me to test my blood and cutting off pieces of my skin and making me cold, then hot, then cold again. That's why I couldn't be around you. But it's too late."

The sirens arrive just outside the front door.

"Okay, now we really need to go." I extend my hand. Our faces sparkle with sweat. It runs into my eyes, stinging them.

He studies my hand. "You know I can't touch you right now."

"Do you, though? You said you didn't know how it worked. We can find out as we go."

He taps my leg with his foot. Testing me out.

The sirens grow louder.

"If you come with me, I'll buy you a Blizzard and feed it to you, so you can actually eat it this time," I say. "If the only thing you get out of our friendship is tasting a Blizzard, then I'll consider it a success."

He laughs and shakes his head. His orange eyes morph back to their natural shade of dark brown.

"What?" I ask.

"You're entirely overwhelming and completely calming all at the same time. I thought you didn't have powers."

I bite my lip. "Who knows? I could. But they're probably under-developed, like most things in my life."

He raises his eyebrows.

"That came out differently than it sounded in my head. I'm not underdeveloped, like, anatomically . . . or even emotionally. Actually, come to think of it, I might be underdeveloped emotionally. I'm still figuring that one—"

"Dylan," Jordan says. He smacks his hand on mine. There's nothing extraordinary about it. His palm is coarse and cool. Our fingers interlock and our eyes meet. "I'll come with you if you promise we can start over next week. Can we go on a normal date? No flames. No combustion."

"You, like, literally don't even have to ask me that."

"Is that a yes?"

"Yes!"

"Let's go, then."

I help him to his feet. For a few seconds there, I forgot we were in a burning home. We head for the door. Through the flames, blue-and-red lights approach us.

"We can't go that way," I say, pulling him back.

He lets go of my hand and grabs my coat from the floor. "Here. Wrap this around you."

I take it from him and throw it over my shoulders. He pulls it tight across my chest.

"We're going to run through the back door," he instructs. I look toward it. The opening isn't really an opening. It's dancing flames.

"Um, are you sure?"

"Yes. If we run fast enough, nothing will happen. It's science."

"Right, cool. Love science."

"Ready? I'll count to three."

"Just say go."

"Go!"

We sprint to the door. His arm wraps around my shoulder. I grip the inside of my coat so it stays closed and my arms aren't exposed to the flames. I close my eyes, and we jump through the fire.

Our feet hit the dirt and we crumple. We roll down a hill and slow to a stop, unscathed. I'm on top of him, and our chests touch as we breathe in the warm air. Sweat drips from my nose onto his chin, but he doesn't show that he cares.

"Science worked," I say.

"It always does."

Cops pull up to the front of the house with an armada of silver cars like the one outside Jordan's house the other night, and the ones at the other fire. Humans emerge from the doors. The tall, slender man from the art gallery rises above the rest.

They click their flashlights on to scan the property. Jordan pushes me up, his warm hands flat against my chest. I wish we didn't have to leave this position, but the last thing I want is this moment ruined by the Blatts and HydroPro. We take off into the night, hand in hand.

I wonder where our date will be? And *he* called it a date.

Every time I hang out with him my heart feels a little fuller.

fifteen

I've never been in love. I've never yearned to be with someone for long stretches of time and then melted into a moody stupor when they were gone. I enjoy my small circle of friends and the time to myself outside school. It's hard for me to imagine a stranger coming along and changing that.

People in this town get married after dating each other for one or two years. I've known Perry and Kirsten for ten years, and I'm still finding out new things about them every day. I don't understand how you're expected to select a stranger for life partnership after such a short period of time. I'm genuinely curious to know what happens in those few years. Does everyone do it because they're supposed to? Or is romantic love different from the love I have for Perry and Kirsten, and there's a magical switch? I get there's physical stuff involved that's different than a friendship. And I've had crushes for sure. But love, actual love, is something I've been trying to figure out for years. When does a crush turn into love? What must happen?

During sophomore year, Perry dated Keaton Cyrus for eight

months and at month two they were saying they loved each other. It was a little quick for me, but it wasn't my relationship, so I didn't judge.

He was gone by summer and I appreciated that, because I got Perry to myself again. But Perry was happy with him, and the breakup was a little upsetting for her. I was curious as to how he built a relationship in two months that was just as special as the one Perry and I had built over the course of a decade.

Keaton is one of the better-looking boys at school. He's six feet tall and has dark facial features. He plays soccer in the fall and runs track in the spring, so he's got hot, toned legs. But what's so great about Keaton is that he's just really nice.

Throughout their whole relationship, he was always making an effort to be my friend. For my birthday last year, he bought me a thirty-four-dollar Regal Cinemas gift card. I asked him why such a random number, and he said he calculated how much it would cost for me to get two tickets and a small popcorn. My jaw dropped when he told me this. I don't think my own friends had ever put that much thought into a gift for me.

For Christmas that same year, he gave me a painting that he won off eBay. The painting is a terrible mismatch of geometric shapes over the outline of a cat. Sometimes I get secondhand embarrassment thinking about him actually believing it was good, but gems like that for me don't come out of Falcon Crest High all that often, so I cherish them when I can. I have the painting propped up on my desk.

At the Spring Fling dance, Perry went with Keaton and Kirsten went with a senior on the baseball team. There was no one else to go with, so I went by myself. I danced alongside Perry and Kirsten and their dates the whole night—which was fine. I was used to being a fifth wheel. Around nine thirty p.m. the DJ announced the dance was wrapping up in a half hour, and he was going to slow it down one last time. I nodded to the group and retreated to the bleachers as I usually did during the slow dances.

A minute later Perry ran over and asked me to dance.

"Why aren't you dancing with Keaton?" I asked. Perry grabbed my hand and pulled me to the dance floor. Keaton walked past us and said, "You guys be dates the rest of the night."

And it wasn't in a creepy, *I'm giving you permission* kind of way. It was in a nice Keaton way. He knew what Perry and I had, and knew Perry's night would be better if she had this moment. I asked her if she wanted to be my date for the final act of Spring Fling and she accepted.

I could see why Keaton was so lovable and why Perry said she loved him after only two months. This got me thinking that one ingredient for love might be when the person you are with starts loving the people in your life who came before them.

I asked Perry how she knew she loved him, and she said, "You know when you're away for a long time on vacation and everything is foreign and then you come home and sit on your bed and there's that overwhelming feeling of comfort and ease? That's what it feels like when I'm with him. And it's not just for that day. It's all the time."

It was abstract but honest.

"What's, like, the physical feeling?" I pressed.

"I don't know," she said. "Have you ever used one of those weighted, heated blankets? That's what it feels like. Like you're being kept warm and safe in the arms of someone else."

I had never used one of those blankets. But I went to Target the next day and bought a thirty-dollar heated blanket to experience love. I brought it home to my bedroom, plugged it in, turned the setting to high, and watched *The Conjuring 2*.

I didn't feel love—just an underwhelming sense that I was missing out on something. I had the heated blanket over me for only thirty minutes because my feet got sweaty, so maybe I didn't give it a chance to bestow its full effects. Combined with the movie's influence, it was that moment I decided love must be different for everyone else. It had to be. If that was love for everyone, I didn't want it.

I'm most afraid of love becoming a routine. A word that's just said to people you're supposed to be close with. Can you love someone just because you're supposed to? I think that's a love that has no reason to be called love. If it's presumed or expected based on probability, like making out with the only other out boy in school, I don't want it. It wasn't created from a feeling. I think that's the kind of love I want. I want there to be a push and a pull. I want my first love to be fought for, not granted to me by circumstance. I want to build new love with someone who's unexpected so that every time I say it, I mean it. So that every time I say it, I can taste the Spring Flings, the Second Saturdays, the movies, the kisses, and the art it's made of.

Perry honks the go-kart in my driveway. I look closely to see if Kirsten is in the front. She hasn't been at school since before the accident. But she granted Perry access to driving the car this week, so I've been co-captain. And it looks like I'm getting the passenger seat again today, because it's still empty.

I've been lying on the couch in my living room, contemplating whether I'm going to take a mental health day. I've been running a hundred-degree fever for days.

On Sunday, my throat closed up by nightfall. I went to the bathroom, inspected my mouth in the mirror, and it looked like the kraken that Johnny Depp got sucked into at the end of *Pirates of the Caribbean: Dead Man's Chest*. There were white bumps and red sores and swollen gums. Something was going to jump out at me fast. I ran back to my bed and didn't move for the rest of the night.

I think I might have been lovesick these past few days. It's no better this morning. I wonder what the school office would say if I gave them a sick note midday saying I was "lovesick." Would they send me to the nurse or the psychologist?

"Hi," I say, getting into the car.

"Hi," Perry says.

"Still no Kirsten?" I clear my throat. "Have you talked to her today?"

"No. But she's totally fine. We facetimed last night. She wants to use the day to catch up on all the work she missed and relax."

"Ugh, jealous."

"Of?"

"Her being fine. I'm, like, over here dying."

"From what?"

"Hypothermia or some flu sickness."

"Dylan, please. If she didn't have hypothermia, then you definitely don't have hypothermia."

Kirsten went to the ER Saturday night but left before noon on Sunday. They said she was fine and had no signs or symptoms of hypothermia. That would have been impossible to believe if you saw her on Saturday when she jumped from the water. But the only person who saw her in that moment was me. After that, Jordan wiped everything clean. Convenient for her, terrible for me. I was partly in the ice water too and didn't think about getting sick. I'm even more excited to see Jordan now. I hope he can send a wave of heat down my body and cure me too.

Perry and Kirsten are in the same homeroom because their last names both start with *L*. That means their lockers are next to each other, which also means they get to see each other a lot throughout the day. I'm always jealous. I hate when we get to school and I have to turn down the *A* through *K* hallway by myself. The people with last names that start in the second half of the alphabet get to have all the fun because their lockers are in the back of the school away from the front offices.

The *A* through *K* hallway, where my locker lives, has a hundred-yard wall display of our "hometown heroes." It's essentially portraits of everyone from our school who has either joined some branch of the military or went on to play college sports. Behind my locker are three portraits of Savanna's older brothers, who have played college football at Penn State, Louisiana State, and the University of Florida. I get to look at their faces when I pack up every day. Today, their faces are more punchable than usual. It's hard to see how Savanna is going to follow in their footsteps and end up as a "hometown hero." Maybe she knows it too and acts out because she can't handle the truth.

"Dylan! Hey! Oh my gosh," a squeaky voice says. I jump. I turn, and Darlene Houchowitz smiles up at me. I take my history book from my locker and start walking.

"Hey, Darlene," I say.

Everyone calls her Lena, but Darlene is *such* a good name that I refuse to call her anything else. When I think of the name Darlene, I picture a gray-haired, seventy-five-year-old woman, but our Darlene is the complete opposite. She's five feet one and always emphasizes the inch. She has an angled bob cut and wears black combat boots and bright short skirts that sit high above her waist. Every day she wears a new pair of mirrored sunglasses with a different colored tint. Today, my purple reflection stares at me while I talk to her. It makes my head spin.

"I've been looking for you," she says.

"Have you? What's the occasion?"

"Well, don't freak out, because I know how you get, but I need you for something."

I stop walking and pull my backpack straps tighter over my shoulders. The heat inside my body is intensifying, and I am also 100 percent positive my fever is higher now. I wipe sweat from my forehead.

"You're scaring me," I say.

She rolls her eyes. "Dylan, it's not scary." She pauses and purses her lips. "I want to know if you would like to join your school's very own GSA." She claps her hands together and lets out a beaming smile.

"GSA?"

Her eyes tighten and she flips her hand. "The Gay–Straight Alliance."

"We have one of those?"

"Of course we do. But not for much longer unless we do something. We only have three members and our faculty sponsor is retiring at the end of the year."

I wrinkle my nose. "Who's in this thing?"

"It's yours truly"—she pulls the sides of her skirt out and curtsies—"Maddie Leostopoulos, and Brenton Riley."

"Who the hell is Brenton Riley?"

"A freshman passionate about social change."

"That's the randomest assemblage of people I have ever heard of. Is Brenton gay?"

"No, but you don't have to be gay to be in the Gay–Straight Alliance."

"Clearly."

"This is why we need you, Dylan!"

I start walking again. Darlene follows.

"So?" she asks, dodging a few students to keep up with me.

"You know I don't do extracurriculars."

"Well, if there was one extracurricular you were going to do, wouldn't this be it?"

"Why? Because I'm gay?"

"Yes! Precisely because you're gay. We haven't had a gay member since Marshall Andrews graduated two years ago and the GSA guidelines from the Gay, Lesbian, and Straight Education Network, aka GLSEN, say our group should be inclusive and composed of diverse identities."

"You know your stuff."

"I don't half-ass things, Highmark."

"Have you tried recruiting anyone else yet?" My eyes dart up and down the hall trying to locate the nearest bathroom. A lump grows in my throat. Saliva pools in the back of my mouth.

She sighs and puts her hand on her hip. "No."

"Well, maybe you'll have better luck than you think, and it all won't hinge on my participation." I grab a boy by the shoulder as he walks by us.

"Hey," I say. "Do you want to join the GSA?"

"The GS-what?" he asks, and continues walking. I shake my head.

Kara Bynum from cheerleading is standing by her locker. Maybe I'll have better luck with her because she knows of my existence. I run up behind her and tap her back.

"Kara!"

"Hey, Dylan," she says.

"Quick question. Do you want to join the GSA?"

"What's that?"

"The Gay–Straight Alliance."

She purses her lips. "When does it meet?"

"Good question." I turn to Darlene.

"It meets every other Monday after school, and we have a few events on the weekends here and there," Darlene says.

"Oh, sorry," Kara says, frowning. "I have cheerleading after school and Nationals are coming up, so I probably can't. Sorry."

When she closes her locker door, Savanna comes into view.

"Should we try?" I ask Darlene. I know Savanna won't join. But I can't pass up an opportunity to make her uncomfortable. I also need to end this interaction fast because I am going to puke any second now. Talking to Savanna is the best way to kill any kind of situation—at least for me.

"What? No!" Darlene says through gritted teeth. I take a few steps forward and she grabs my arm. "Dylan, I don't want her in the—"

"Savanna, how are you this morning?" I ask.

She takes a few books from her locker and places them in her bag. She doesn't say anything. I'm talking to the side of her face.

"Darlene and I are recruiting for the Gay–Straight Alliance and were wondering if you wanted to join."

Her head turns. She looks Darlene up and down, swishing gum in her mouth. "Why would I want to be associated with that freak show?" she asks.

"Gee, I don't know. Maybe I thought you had a nice bone somewhere in your body."

"I'm busy after school doing things that actually matter."

I lurch forward and gag. Savanna takes a step back. "Ew. What the hell is wrong with you?"

I swallow hard, then prop my hand on the locker next to hers. I clutch my throat. "Nothing. I'm fine."

"You're sweaty and disgusting. I said I am busy after school, so go away before you get us all sick."

Darlene clears her throat and raises a finger. "Um, if I may add something?" she asks. Savanna's eyes go from me to Darlene, but her head doesn't move. Darlene swallows. "The GSA actually has a pretty impressive impact outside of school," she starts. "Last year, we volunteered at nearly twenty events and during the holiday season we led a donation drive for—"

Savanna puts her hand to Darlene's face. "Lena, the fact that you even thought to consider me for this group is insulting enough," Savanna says. "But your squat presence around me is making my stomach sick. As you're the school's resident toad, I know the only way you can make friends is by starting a group for other friendless creatures to congregate. I get it. But here's a news flash for you since you probably can't see through those idiotic rainbow sunglasses you wear every day: I am *not* one of those creatures. So scram."

Darlene takes a step back. She clutches her arms over her stomach. Her fingernails dig into her skin, turning it bright red. She bites her bottom lip and remains silent.

"Why would you say that to her?" I ask, stepping in front of Darlene. "What do you even do after school? Mock trial?"

"Yeah, exactly that. And volleyball and tennis."

"They call it *mock* trial for a reason. It's fake, acting, and no one cares."

"There are tryouts for my sports and a twenty-person waitlist for mock trial. I think people care." She squints at me. "Your group, which no one knows exists, is obviously desperate for members. I saw everyone in this hallway already turned you down. That must suck. I have to use my influence elsewhere."

I laugh through my nausea. "Please. What influence?"

"I can't really explain it. Maybe if you weren't so 'woe is me I'm the only gay kid in school' all the time, you could gain some and understand it better."

"Right." I tap my fingers on the locker and hang my head. The bell rings for first period. "Better get to woodshop," I snap.

"We don't even have that class, weirdo."

"Well, maybe you and your dad can start one."

"Maybe he will! Right after he finds the idiots burning down his buildings. Whoever is responsible for the fires should be very afraid. Missing out on woodshop will be the least of their concerns."

I snarl at her. She spins and struts down the hall. Her ponytail sways from side to side.

"I'm so sorry about that, Darlene," I say, tugging my shirt from my chest to cool myself. She's staring at the floor. Her face is paler than mine.

"I . . ." she starts. "I never really had an interaction with her before and I heard she was mean, but I didn't know she was mean to your face like that. She thinks we're a freak show?"

I roll my head in a circle. "I'm sorry. I shouldn't have asked her. We have a long history, so just ignore that."

The warning bell rings, meaning we have a minute to get to class.

"I have to go. Can I let you know about the club?" I ask.

"I guess. Why won't you join? If Perry Lyle and Kirsten Lush were in it, would you come then?"

I shrug. "I mean yeah, probably." I don't lie. "Why do you care so much if I'm in it?"

"I don't know. High school is hard enough. I can't imagine having to go through it all by myself like you have to."

I let out a long sigh. That's twice in a minute people feel the need to tell me how lonely I am.

"Well, maybe it shouldn't be up to me to fix it, then." I throw my hand up. "Do you talk about that in the club? Why should the one gay guy have to make the school better for everyone else?"

My voice cracks when I finish my rant. My hands suddenly go

numb. My feet rise a few inches off the ground, and my back slams against the lockers as if I am swept away by a gust of wind. My body crumples to the floor.

My head spins. I can't even process what just happened because I'm intensely staring at one of the brown marks in the speckled tile floor to stabilize the room. Was there an earthquake or did I explode in my pants and the force threw me? Wouldn't be surprised at this point if it was the second option.

I finally look up and Darlene's eyes are wide. We stare at each other for a few seconds in silence.

Her chin trembles and she crosses her arms. "What was that?" She looks up and down the hall.

I shake my head.

She yelps at my slight movement. "Don't do that."

"Do what?" I ask.

"Move."

I shrug.

She yelps again and slaps her hand over her mouth. "You moved."

"Darlene..."

She backs away from me. Her eyes glisten. "I don't know what this is, but I do know you're mean, Dylan. I was just trying to be nice and include you."

"Wait," I mumble. I reach for her. "Darlene, I'm sorry. I have a lot going on and I—"

She swats my arm away. "I said don't move!" she screams. "You're just like Savanna." She bursts down the hall without helping me to my feet.

A group of boys walking by me cut her off from my line of sight. "Cruella get to you again, Highmark?" one asks. The group laughs. He kicks my history book, and it slides down the hall. I roll my eyes. "Toughen up, man. She sucks."

I ignore them as they enter Dr. Brio's classroom. I stand and brush off my knees.

"Don't you have somewhere to be, Mr. Highmark?" Dr. Brio asks, emerging from his room. I look up and down the hall and I'm the only one here.

"I do," I say. "And I think it's home."

sixteen

I went to the nurse after I collapsed in front of Darlene, and she recorded a fever of 101 degrees. Mom had to leave work to pick me up from school. When I got home, I slept off and on for fifteen hours, no exaggeration.

Yesterday, I responded to a good-morning text from Jordan at 12:30 p.m. and told him I was sick. He couldn't text back because he was at school and replied at 3:15 p.m. I was asleep at that time, so I replied to his second message around 7 p.m. Then he eventually responded to my second message at 10 p.m. saying he was going to bed. It wasn't how I envisioned the conversation leading up to our first official date to go.

"Dylan!" Mom yells from the kitchen. "You need to come and eat something. It'll be good if you move around a little bit."

"I disagree!" I yell back. I can't feel my legs. How does she expect me to walk down a flight of stairs?

Suddenly, stomping sounds erupt in the hallway. "Oh no," I mumble. My doorknob twists and Mom bursts into my room.

"Give me this," she says, plodding toward my bed. She swipes my phone from my bedside table.

"Hey!" I shout. I roll toward the edge of my bed, in slow motion. I reach for my phone, but Mom is already back in the hallway by the time my hand grazes the empty surface.

"If your hands have enough energy to scroll on this all day, then you can make your way to the kitchen. Let's go." She points down the hall.

"Ugh," I grunt. "Give me a few minutes."

I lie in my bed for more than a few minutes—more like a half hour—but I can only sit in my room staring at the ceiling for so long after my phone was illegally confiscated.

I get up to pee and decide I can use this momentum to make my way to the kitchen. I slide down the stairs on my butt, clutching my bed pillow in my arms. I rest my head against it because my neck can't support the weight of my skull on its own.

I prop my hands against the walls as I slowly step to the kitchen table. My ankles wobble with each step. I plop into a seat. The wooden legs creak as if they are going to snap. I picture the chair falling apart beneath me, the wood legs splintering and stabbing my body as I fall to the ground. I get more nauseous.

Mom rips the pillow from my lap and throws it into the family room. She shoves a plate of strawberries, eggs, and toast in front of me. Then she pours an entire jar of honey into a mug of hot tea and places it in my shaking hands.

"Enough with the dramatics, Dylan," Mom says.

"I'm not being dramatic," I say. "I'm sick. Why are you in such a bad mood?"

She puts her hands on the counter, hanging her head. She sighs. "I'm sorry. I'm not in a bad mood. Just worried is all."

"About what?"

I take a bite of the food and hunger hits me like a wave. I realize I haven't eaten anything in almost a day. I shovel every crumb into my mouth.

"Well, I can't help but think you are sick because you were out late last weekend." She throws her hand up. "And then missing Cody's night...You know, there's nothing wrong with the quiet, sweet Dylan you are now. I hope this new friend isn't something—"

I sigh. "I was with Perry and Kirsten last weekend doing the same stuff I always do."

"I know...I know."

My stomach gurgles like rolling thunder. Mom's eyes go wide. I think my brain's hunger receptors are satisfied, but my body is most certainly not pleased. I grab my stomach. The kraken in my throat is preparing itself to be unleashed.

I launch myself from the table and *almost* make it to the downstairs bathroom toilet before my soul leaves my body. A yellow-red liquid explodes from my mouth. Half makes it into the toilet; the other half is on the bathroom door frame and the hallway floor.

Mom comes rushing in behind me. "Oh my goodness. Dylan, what are you doing?"

"You think I'm doing this on purpose?" I heave. Vomit spits from my lips.

She helps me to my feet, and together we walk upstairs to my bedroom. She puts my phone back on my dresser, then apologizes for making me do too much.

I muster up enough energy to text Jordan and ask if we can reschedule our date, but somehow I don't have enough energy to care that I am canceling. I chalk this one up to my usual luck, karma for being dismissive of Darlene, Savanna's voodoo doll she has of me in her room, and all the other forces in the universe acting against me.

Jordan replies with a sad face, deflating my chest. I am just happy my pillow made it out alive sans egg chunks. It's fresh and clean, and I immediately pass out on its fluffy support.

The next morning, my bed is a literal kiddie pool. I'm floating in my own sweat. It looks more like a Slip 'N Slide with my blue sheets, but it's not slippery at all. It's warm, sticky, and smells bad, so exactly like a kiddie pool in the middle of July. Who knows? There could even be feces here too for the full kiddie-pool effect. I wouldn't say there was a zero percent chance I pooped myself last night.

But even though this is gross, it's good. Right? I think this means I broke my fever or something. My body fought the sickness and pushed it from my pores! I'm glad my body can fight a rare swine flu but can't solve a routine acne crisis on my forehead.

I sit up and rainbow circles appear in the corners of my eyes. My vision goes black but then my room quickly comes back into focus. Jordan texted me a few times last night saying, *I hope you feel better* and *I wish we were together right now.* But I'm feeling better, so I'm optimistic I can salvage our relationship this weekend.

Mom bursts through my bedroom door. I rapidly swipe out of my messages and pull my comforter over my bare chest.

"Whoa," I say. I realize this is the first time I've muttered a word in days without it feeling like a cactus is spinning in my throat. "No one knocks here?"

Mom tilts her head. "Sorry," she says. "I have to get your sister to school and was waiting until you woke up to check on you. I heard you shuffling around, so I thought it was okay." She picks up clothes from my floor and shoves them in my dresser as she walks to my bed.

"Shuffling?" I question. "I literally haven't moved."

She sits on the edge of my bed and pulls a thermometer from her pocket. "Oh dear," she sighs, staring at my bed. "We need to wash these and get rid of the germs." She grabs at my sheets. I pull them back.

"You can wash them when you get back from work today. You're going to make me throw up again."

"Here." She shoves the thermometer down my throat. I gag.

She goes back to cleaning the clothes from my floor. She rearranges my deodorant, retainer case, and face lotion on my dresser. Then she closes a few schoolbooks and stacks them on my desk.

I hum, while tapping my fingers on my knee as I wait for the thermometer to get a reading. It beeps, and Mom grabs it from my lips.

"Hm," she grunts, staring at the white handle. She shakes it in her hand.

"What's wrong?"

"It has three lines across the screen. I don't know if the battery is dead."

"I mean, I think I'm fine. I sweated out the fever."

"Oh, you know what?" She stands, puts her finger in the air, and walks out of my room.

Cody appears in my doorway with her arms crossed.

"Well, look at you," I say.

"Well, look at *you*," she says. "Your room smells like feet."

I slide my foot out from my covers and thrust it into the air.

"Ew." She turns her nose up.

Mom stomps back down the hall and pushes Cody to the side. "Use this one," she says. She hands me an old-timey thermometer that looks like a glass ruler with that red line down the middle.

"What is this? From the sixties?"

"Just use it. Always more reliable."

I stick it in my mouth, but then quickly pull it back out. "Wait, doesn't this have mercury inside it?"

"Yeah, that's how it gets the reading."

I scrunch my face. "Isn't that poisonous?"

Mom scratches her head. "If you eat pure mercury, yes. But it's inside the glass. They wouldn't make people use something that poisoned them. Come on. I have to get going."

I'm into chemistry these days but can't say why.

"Are we almost ready, Mom?" Cody asks. "We're going to be late."

"Yes, Cody. Just go downstairs and wait. We're almost done."

"I thought they used to put mercury in old people's teeth and that's why the baby boomers are all turning against us now and trying to destroy the earth," I say.

"You're being ridiculous."

I stick it under my tongue and wait.

"Oh, good. It's moving fast," Mom says.

She grabs it after a few seconds. She looks at the glass tube and throws up her hands. "Today is not my day."

"What?" I reach for the thermometer and pull it from her fingers. The red line reaches the notches at the last number—110.

I swallow. My heart rate intensifies. I start counting the beats, but in a few seconds the blood beats through my heart at a rate too fast for me to count and the numbers jumble together in my head.

Mom feels my cheek. "You're still so warm, though."

"Is that right?" I ask. I rub my palms on my knees.

"No, honey. I think you'd be dead if your body temperature was 110 degrees. Maybe you're right and this thing is too old. We've had this since before you two were born."

I nod. The heat of my body becomes more apparent. Beads of sweat form on my forehead and a drop slides down the back of my neck. I run my hands through my hair and my hairline is soaked.

"Are you sure you feel fine?" Mom asks. "You seem better."

"Yeah. I should be good." I lick my lips. "I'm going to go to the bathroom." I get out of my bed and my knees wobble.

"Okay, well, Dad is going to work from home today. So just let him know if you need anything."

"Right." I walk past her and enter the hallway bathroom. I rest my head on the door as I shut it behind me, my hand gripping the doorknob. "Um, what is happening?" I mutter. My sweaty palm slides off the knob.

I think I would be able to easily dismiss the thermometer reading as *wrong* like Mom if I hadn't been hanging out with someone who has that exact body temperature. I splash cold water on my face. I take a towel and rub it across my forehead and through my hair. My hands are shaking. I clasp them together to keep them steady. I close my eyes and take a few deep breaths.

When the front door closes, I walk to the hallway linen closet. I dig through tiny white baskets of extra toiletries in search of the mercury thermometer.

Let's test the reliability and validity of this instrument. Dr. Brio would be so proud that I even remember those words. But I can't really remember what they mean. I'm not sure which outcome I want. If it's reliable, then I think that means it'll give me the same reading over and over again. So, a steady 110 degrees means we have a reliable thermometer. But how do I know if it's right? Or valid? I think I'm screwed either way. I might need to go stick it in Dad's mouth to see what temperature I get.

The thermometer is next to a box of Band-Aids. I stick it back in my mouth and walk into the bathroom. I watch the red line rise in the mirror. It quickly reaches 110 degrees, and I pull it from between my lips. "Oh no."

I hold it for a few seconds and the red line lowers. I pop it back under my tongue one last time, and it slides back to 110 in seconds.

I turn on the cold water and shove the thermometer underneath the stream. The red line plunges to the 30-degree mark. Then I twist the hot water handle on. Water blasts from the faucet. The red line shoots to the top of thermometer and the glass shatters. I gasp.

I drop the tiny shard of glass still between my fingers into the sink and slap the faucet handles off. I take a step back and clap my hand over my mouth. I peer over the counter, and there's little shiny gray blobs of mercury jiggling in the white sink.

Well, I guess now I'll never know if that thing was right or not.

Back in my room, I sit at my desk chair and examine my hands. They seem whiter than usual. Or maybe that's in my head. I bounce my knee and pick up my phone to call Jordan. I don't know what else to do. He doesn't answer.

I pace my room. I stop in front of the mirror hanging on the back of my door. Orange-gold eyes are staring back at me. I scream, clapping my hands over my mouth. There's an ice-blue halo around my pupils. I pull my lower eyelids downward for an inspection. A flame flickers from my finger. The shock catapults me backward, and I tumble onto the floor.

I look up and suddenly feel like an intruder in my own room. Staring at what used to bring me comfort, like my fluffy bedcover and paintings, has no effect on me. I grab a bath towel hanging from my bedframe and position it on the floor beneath me, trying to prevent any burn marks from forming on the hardwood. I curl into the fetal position, then squeeze my eyelids shut so I no longer see the orange-gold eyes of a stranger staring back at me.

Mom is right. There's nothing wrong with quiet, sweet Dylan. But I think that boy is gone.

seventeen

I wake up and prepare for school the next day without uttering a single word. My skin is perpetually layered with sweat. I change my outfit twice before accepting the wet stains across my shirt.

"Are you finally feeling better?" Perry asks as we drive to school.

"Yeah," I say.

"Good. You're falling behind on the spring paint-by-numbers collection. Kirsten came over to paint last night, and we are pretty much halfway finished."

"Okay." I rub my forehead.

"Did you pick a place for your date with Jordan yet?" It's such a normal question for such an unusual time.

"No, not yet."

"Well, get on it! Don't let him slip away."

"I mean, I've been unable to move. Pretty sure he understands." I cross my arms.

"Okay?" Perry presses her eyebrows. "Do you have any ideas?" She elongates the *s*.

"We mentioned Starbucks before."

Starbucks might actually be the best bet now because it's the most controlled environment I can think of. If he—or I, I guess—blow up at a restaurant or something, we're stuck there because of the check. At Starbucks, we can escape at any moment.

"That's boring."

"How is that boring?"

"I don't know. Go to the movies or something fun."

"I'm not going to take him to the movies and sit next to him for two hours and not be able to speak. That's not a date."

"Okay, cranky." Perry wrinkles her nose. "Maybe you should just stay home again."

"Whatever." I shift in my seat, turning away from her. My head pounds. I can't attempt to hold a conversation any longer.

"Apparently, there was another fire last night," Perry says.

I shift back toward her. "Wait, really?"

I start scrolling through my Twitter feed. I skim about fifty tweets from the middle of the night but stop when I get to the ones from this morning. Random local news accounts are retweeted onto my feed. I don't recognize any of them. They require my attention. I read.

LOCAL AUTHORITIES ARE ASKING FOR YOUR HELP IN IDENTIFYING TWO MALES RESPONSIBLE FOR NIGHTTIME TERROR

#BREAKING: Local police confirm arson in string of blazes

Blatt Builders Co. offering $10,000 reward for any tips in identifying arsonists. Unease sweeps across the area as police confirm recent fires were arson.

"Oh no," I mutter. My body sinks into the seat as I think of the added pressure this is going to put on Jordan. Not only is this going to help confirm any of HydroPro's suspicions about him being here, but the police are going to be after him too as an arsonist.

"What's wrong?" Perry asks.

I lock my phone, then put it in my pocket.

"Nothing," I say. "I saw someone tweet about an assignment I forgot to do."

"Which assignment? Did I not do it either?"

I shake my head. "It's for history. You're not in that class."

"Oh, good." Perry exhales. "I'm trying to stretch this homework leave of absence for as long as I can. It's really improved my quality of life, you know?"

"Yeah. I know."

I don't like how I just lied to her. I can't remember the last time I wasn't honest with her, and it's upsetting how fast the lie rolled off my tongue. It was an innocent lie. Nothing *is* wrong with me if no one knows who caused the fires . . . or what Jordan is . . . or what I am.

Perry and I get to school. I climb out of the car and shut the door, hastily scrolling through Twitter. I don't understand how they saw Jordan and me at the fire site. We made sure we left without a trace.

I read all the replies to the local news tweets about the fires and people are going crazy. One person blames it on the loss of Christ in our lives. Another person claims kids need to be in school for longer hours so they don't act out. A third says the criminals deserve life sentences in prison.

I tap my foot. This whole situation is getting a bit out of hand.

The replies to tweets from the Blatt Builders account make no sense. Everyone is saying how beloved a company they are in the area, and that their thoughts and prayers are with them. I don't remember the last time Falcon Crest cared about something as much as this. The Blatts build a few cheap cookie-cutter homes and people don't know how we're going to continue our lives without them? They're not saving the world. Children are starving and they're using up resources and cutting down trees.

I text Jordan, asking if he's seen any of the news. The police must have done an investigation earlier this week or something because this wasn't in the media before today.

As I watch for Jordan's response, Kirsten messages Perry and me a video. I click Play. The image is black-and-white. It's grainy. I pull my phone closer to my face, squinting to decipher the picture. Suddenly, a shadowy figure appears in the frame from the left side. They're running toward a fence or barrier in the center of the frame. When they reach it, they jump over it, sending sparks into the sky. I gasp, then realize what I am watching. I appear in the frame a few seconds later, chasing after the shadowy figure—chasing after Jordan.

Kirsten

On my way to the Pulitzer! Set up a camera in the trees and snagged this. Can you believe it? Going to set up more cameras later today.

"You've got to be kidding me," I mumble. I lock my phone and shove it into my pocket.

Why would she send that to the news? She must not think anything of it. But why would she? She doesn't know about Jordan. If the news can figure out who is in that video, then Jordan will be gone, our relationship will be over, and I'll be in jail.

"See you in Chemistry," Perry says, and we split in the hall. I glare at Perry's phone in her butt pocket as she walks away from me. I somehow resist the urge to grab it and snap it in half before she can see the video. I grab my throat instead, keeping the vomit moving in my stomach from rising any higher. I manage a step toward my locker.

As I turn, I notice everyone down the hallway is staring at me. Most are laughing. A group of girls point at me. I gasp. I look myself up and down, patting my body. There are no flames. I open Snapchat's front-facing camera to look at my eyes, and they're their normal shade of gray.

"What?" I ask to no one in particular. A few people scurry away. I mean, yeah, there are still sweat stains splattered across my shirt, but I didn't realize sweating could be so funny. No one knows what I'm up to. Maybe I worked out before school. These lazy bums should take a hint.

Darlene approaches me. Green sunglasses hang from a string around her neck. She clutches her books tightly to her chest. Her eyes don't leave the floor.

"Hey, Darlene," I say.

She ignores me.

I extend my arm to wave, but she lets out a scream before I even spread my fingers. She flinches, dropping her books and stumbling into the lockers. "Don't come near me! You stay over there." She's breathing rapidly. "I don't know what I saw the other day, but I don't want to find out."

I swallow while looking at the others around us. "I can explain. That was nothing." I scratch the back of my head. Giggles from my other classmates surround me. They grow in frequency and volume.

She shakes her head while collecting her books. "Was it?"

I no longer just have sweat stains. My shirt is drenched. The room starts spinning. Cackling faces, white teeth, and pointing fingers encircle me.

"What are you all laughing at?" I yell, clenching a fist.

"Also, don't expect a follow from me," she says, then jogs down the hall.

"A follow? What are you talking about?"

Once she's gone, I notice a paper stuck to one of the lockers behind where she stood. My name jumps out at me from the page.

"What the?" I snatch the paper and read.

Attention Falcon Crest! As many of you know, I paint in my spare time, and I think I'm getting really good. A lot of you have been asking me where you can see my work, so I've decided to start my own Instagram page! You can follow me @DylanHighmarkPaintings. I mostly paint my favorite things that make me warm and fuzzy inside. You can see samples of my work in the screenshot below. Hope to get your follow soon! —Dylan Highmark.

The paper shakes in my hands as I finish reading its text. The screenshot at the bottom of the flyer is of the Dylan Highmark Paintings Instagram page, which I did not create. Someone posted six pictures of random paintings. They are all at elementary-school-level quality and must have been filtered to look like paintings. The first one is of a teddy bear. The others are of an eggplant, a peach, a naked self-portrait that is my head photoshopped on a random body, a picture of Jordan with a bubble heart that says *my crush*, and a picture of me spoon-feeding ice cream into Jordan's mouth while he's covered in rainbow sprinkles. I look up. Everyone is watching me.

"You sleep with that teddy?" a boy asks as he walks by.

"You might want to reevaluate what *really good* means," another says, laughing.

"This obviously isn't me," I bark. My face flushes. I crumple up the paper, then throw it down the hall. The class bell rings. The crowds start dispersing. But as they shut their lockers, the flyer appears taped on every locker door.

"Who's the crush?" a girl asks.

"This is creepy as hell, man," a boy says. He shoves the flyer into my chest, knocking the wind out of me.

My crushes and paintings are two things I've always tried to keep hidden from Falcon Crest. They are the two things I want to keep to myself for myself. I don't even take art classes at school because I don't want to open myself up to the criticism. I don't need the others here telling me how much I suck. And I don't need everyone picking apart my crush after they have picked me apart by myself for years.

But now my hidden art hobby and relationship don't belong to me anymore. They're free game.

I collapse to my knees. My eyes begin to water. Through my blurred vision, I see the skin beneath my fingernails turn orange. I quickly wipe my eyes and stand, thrusting my hands into my pockets. The blood rushes from my brain, and I adjust my footing to keep balanced. My head begins to spin. My mouth fills with saliva. I turn and run into the bathroom.

I dive into the first stall as vomit forces its way from my mouth. I hold my hair to the side for what feels like an hour as my stomach empties itself. I sit on the floor, resting the back of my head against the stall. The bathroom door swings open and closed. An endless stampede of shoes stomp and squeak along the floor. I listen as the boys laugh and talk about me.

I bite my fingernails as I search for the fake Instagram page on my phone. It's real. Someone actually went out of their way to make this page. I cover my ears, banging my head against the stall.

When the bathroom falls into silence, I check for any lingering pairs of shoes. It's empty. I close my eyes, take a deep breath, and exit the stall. I wipe my face and swish water in my mouth at the sink. My eyelids are heavy.

I reach into my pocket for my phone, but my hands go through two huge holes. I turn the fabric inside out and the edges of the holes are singed. Blackened fabric turns to dust between my fingers. It sprinkles across the floor like a pepper shaker. I turn around, and my phone sits on the floor in the stall. I stare at my hands. The skin pulsates. Purple veins have grown around my knuckles like a wild vine. This prank made me forget how I've changed for a moment. I grab my phone, then dart out of the bathroom.

When I exit, Savanna stands in the middle of the hallway with her arms crossed. Her lips and nails are purple. Her white hair is braided into long pigtails that jut from the sides of her head and fall across her chest.

"I heard from a friend of mine named Jimmy that you liked to paint," she says, laughing. "But I didn't know you were so good." She places her long thumbnail between her teeth and smiles.

I scowl at her, my shoulders undulating up and down with each heavy breath.

"I mean . . . the detail on this bear is something else." She holds up the flyer. "And the self-portrait? Kind of weird to paint yourself naked, though."

"You?" I ask. "Why would you do this?"

"It was me," she says in a high-pitched voice, then flashes a tight-lipped smile. She pulls her phone from her pocket and scrolls. "Let's see . . . Your new page has . . . Wow! Seven followers. It looks like no one cares about this, just like the rest of your life."

"Just leave me alone, Savanna!" I shout, walking past her.

"I'm asking the same of you. Make the mistake of thinking we're friends or that I would want to be in your stupid group again, and I'll take you down with more than pictures of teddy bears and produce."

I give her the middle finger.

"Trash," she mumbles as she spins off in the opposite direction.

The hallway is empty. I stomp on the flyers as I trudge through the school, thinking of Savanna's face every time my shoe sole hits the floor. I rip the papers from each locker door, one by one. I've never retaliated against Savanna. I've always been able to let her antics slide. But this time, it's itching under my skin. She picked the wrong day to mess with me.

Dozens of revenge scenarios flash through my mind. I could rub poison ivy on her lipstick . . . fill her nail polish with jalapeño pepper juice . . . pay someone to cut off her hair when she isn't paying attention . . . flatten the tires on her car. My pace quickens to a jog, and I'm suddenly holding a pile of the flyers in my arms.

The scent of burning wood begins to ascend into my nostrils. I look down and realize it's coming from the collected flyers. They're on fire. I drop them, watching them glide through the air while I pat down my stomach to extinguish the embers stuck to my clothing.

"Oh no, oh no, oh no," I mumble. I prance across the hallway to put out scattered flames. But as I step on the flyers, my movement sends embers spiraling toward the other papers. Small fires erupt on the pages spread throughout the hallway.

I need to get rid of all the fuel. This hallway is basically like a tinderbox. I rip each flyer from the lockers next to me. The metal surface beneath them is cold but quickly warms from my skin. I read the humiliating note again as I move down the lockers.

136

135

134

133

A fresh fit of anger grows inside my stomach. It's almost as if I feel a surge of fuel move through my veins when five tiny flames pop from my fingertips. They ignite the clump of newly collected flyers in my arms. I scream, then toss them into the air as I stomp my feet out of frustration. They disperse downward like a weeping-willow firecracker.

The smell of smoke overwhelms the hallway, and I'm right in the middle of it. I can't smother this fire alone. Aborting mission.

I run to the fire alarm, pull the lever, then dart as far away from it as I can before the beeping ensues. The sprinklers kick on with a spitting sound. My hair is soaked in seconds. The ink on the papers beneath me bleeds from its lines, making the note illegible. The corner of my mouth curls up just slightly at the unintended outcome.

I head for the exit. Students and teachers begin spilling from the classrooms amid shouts and groans. People hold textbooks over their heads. A few students slip and fall to the ground as they run out. Girls, mouths agape and eyes wide, cover their now see-through shirts with binders. I hold my hand over my face to keep myself out of view.

Before leaving, I turn and peek through my fingers at the madness one last time. Savanna darts through the nearest hallway intersection, shielding her face. Her wet braids cling to her back. I'm sure she has waterproof makeup on, but I pretend she doesn't and picture her foundation smudged across her cheeks beneath smeared eyeliner. I leave the building. As I'm watching my steps, I take the deepest breath of my life.

eighteen

I run from FCHS. The sizzling embers beneath my skin keep me warm for the journey through the freezing air. I ignore the unending messages from Perry and Kirsten asking me if I am okay. My revenge smile turns to a frown after a few minutes. Not only am I alone on the side of the road, but the entire Falcon student body has labeled me as a joke, my mom thinks I am heading down the wrong path, Kirsten is investigating me for arson, Savanna still hates me, Darlene is scared of me, and my body is turning against me.

When I get home, Dad is getting out of his car in the driveway. I check my phone and it's eleven a.m. I look back down the street, contemplating if I should make a run for it, but my shoes crack pieces of salt on the sidewalk and Dad's head snaps in my direction.

"Dyl?" he asks.

"Dad?" I ask.

"Why aren't you at school?"

"Why aren't you at work?"

He shakes his head. "Cut the crap, son." He pulls his messenger bag over his shoulder. "I had an interview at a new company and am working from home the rest of the day."

I scratch my head.

"You don't look well," he says. "Are you still sick?"

I nod. I hang my head and take a few steps toward the house.

Dad sighs. A cloud of steam fills the air around his head. "This is getting ridiculous. Get in the car. I'm going to take you to urgent care. I told your mother we should have done this before." He tosses his bag onto the driver's seat.

I swallow. My heart rate picks up speed.

"No, I'll be fine," I say with a light laugh. I walk faster to the front door.

"You're not fine. Let's go." His car keys jingle in his hand. "You're missing too much school."

"Mom took my temperature and I was better. I just came home to get a little more rest."

"That's not normal. You need bloodwork. This could be viral with how long it's lasting."

Bloodwork? What would that even show? Is my blood still red? I picture it now more as a neon-lime-green color, a high-octane fuel ready to combust at my brain's command. It would probably melt those little tubes, or worse, the nurse's hand.

The tests would document me, put my vitals on record. The body temperature, the blood—everything HydroPro is looking for. They would have it all on paper with my name and address.

I keep walking toward the door. I step off the driveway into the front yard so I don't pass too close by Dad.

"Dylan, I am not messing around. I have about an hour before I need to get back to work."

I ignore his words. My back faces him now. I put my hand on the knob and turn.

"Dylan!"

"I'm just going to sleep it off! I'll talk to you later."

His yell reverberates through my chest as I spin through the entrance. I slam the door closed behind me, then run up the steps as if I'm being chased by a monster.

In my room, I push all the pillows from my bed to the floor and rip my sheets off the mattress. I hoist the pile of sweaty linens into my arms and carry them down the hallway to the washer. The blue sheets tangle around my ankles. After I fill the washer with my sheets, I strip off my clothes and throw them in there too. I turn on the bulky cycle and walk to the bathroom naked.

I take an ice-cold shower. My head rests against the tile on the wall, and I let the water run down my back for a good fifteen minutes.

Once I'm dry, I put on a hoodie and pair of sweatpants and then put away the last remaining pieces of clothing Mom missed from the floor. I make my bed with clean sheets, throw a few empty water bottles into the bathroom trash can, and cleanse my room of anything else associated with my sickness of the past few days.

I need Jordan's help. I tap my phone every three minutes to see how much closer I am to three o'clock, when Jordan gets out of school.

My room is the cleanest it has ever been since probably when it was last used as my nursery. I race down the hall and start cleaning

Cody's room. It helps me pass a few more minutes of time because there are literally only two pieces of clothing on the floor and one book out of place. I look out Cody's window and decide to go for a run.

Later, I wake up on my bed at four p.m., well past the time I was planning on calling Jordan. I roll over and hit his name in my contact list. It rings three times before he picks up.

"Hey," Jordan says. His voice is groggy.

"Hey," I say. "Sorry, did I wake you up?" I'm biting my fingernails.

He yawns through the phone. "No. I was just lying down after school." He laughs. "But it's cool. How are you feeling? I texted you last night."

"Yeah, I saw." I tap my fingers against the wall. "Hey, do you want to come over?"

He clears his throat. "Yeah, is everything okay? You sound, like, stressed or something."

"I'm good. Just feel bad about canceling everything from the past week." I let out a laugh.

He blows air through his nose. "Don't feel bad."

"When will you be here?"

"Oh, you meant now? Um, can you give me like an hour-ish?"

"Yeah. Come over whenever." I hang up and text him my address.

This can't be happening? Can it?

Jordan texts me *here* an hour and twenty minutes after our phone call. I jump up, run down the stairs, and walk to the kitchen. I peer into the family room, and Dad is sitting on the couch watching basketball with his laptop next to him. He doesn't notice me. Mom and Cody are at gymnastics or something. I walk to the front door and open it.

The cool air meets my face, erupting goose bumps on every corner of my skin. Jordan wears a yellow beanie, navy parka, dark jeans, and brown boots. He looks like he popped out of a fashion magazine. There's a loose strand of hair falling out of the side of his beanie. He's holding a brown bag in his left hand. He smiles.

"Hey," I say, exhaling.

"Hey," he says. "I changed because I didn't know if you wanted to go out to Starbucks or anything tonight." He steps inside. I quickly close the door behind him. "Are you sure everything is okay?"

I nod toward my room. "Let's go upstairs."

"Are your parents home? Should I go say hi?"

I shake my head. "What's in the bag?"

"You'll see." He bounces the small brown paper bag.

"Okay?" I laugh.

We walk upstairs and into my room. I sit on the edge of my bed and watch him put the bag on my dresser. He slowly pulls off his parka. He's wearing a dark green flannel underneath. The sleeves are rolled up to his mid-forearms. I follow two thick veins from the edge of his sleeve to his wrist. He smiles and dives onto the mattress. I bounce into the air like when the hammer sends that metal ball to the top of the tower at the carnival. Except rather than a bell ringing, it's my heart. He turns over on his back and scans the walls.

"This is nice." He nods.

"Oh, wait. This is your first time at my house, isn't it?"

I'm also realizing this is the first time I've ever had another boy in my room before. I think I should be more excited, but I can't stop thinking about Jordan's internal body temperature. And Jordan's human body composition. And if mine is the same as it was last week. And if it's the same as his now.

"It is. Your room is way more decorated than mine."

"Yeah, well, this has been my room for sixteen years. Your room has been yours for what? A month?"

"Are those all your paintings?" He points to the wall beside my bed.

"Those are all my favorite prints from the art galleries I go to with Kirsten and Perry." The prints are lined up in even columns from the floor to the ceiling.

"So artistic. I love it. Where are the ones you paint?"

"Here." I reach under my bed and pull out a stack of dusty canvases.

He laughs. "Why there?"

"Because the real paintings are better."

He picks up an Appalachian Mountains landscape I painted last summer and examines it. "How isn't this one real?"

I take it from his hands. "It doesn't matter. They're stupid anyway."

I scan my room. I thought it looked clean before, but as I watch Jordan take in everything on the walls, I begin to feel myself shrinking. Maybe I need to take some of this stuff down. Or I could group the paintings by subject, like landscapes and portraits.

But enough of this small talk. I'm scratching my arm so hard I think it's going to start bleeding soon.

I stand and walk to my dresser. I pick up the brown bag. "What's in here?"

He jumps over to me and rips it from my hand. "Hey, no peeking. It's a special treat."

"That sounds creepy. What is it? The bag is all wet."

"Oh no. It's probably melting." He opens it and reaches inside. "It's Dilly Bars from Dairy Queen! Cold stuff for your throat."

He extends one out to me and places it in my fingers. I grip the wooden Popsicle stick. A drop of vanilla ice cream slides down the stick from the chocolate-covered soft serve. My mind flashes back to the night we met.

The Blizzard. The explosion. The street. The lake. The house fires.

Every heat-infused moment erupts in my mind and forces my eyes to cross. The Dilly Bar goes blurry.

"Dylan, your hands are shaking," Jordan says.

"What?" I twitch and the Dilly Bar slides from my fingers. It falls through the air, splattering onto the floor.

"My bad," I mutter. I bend down and pick up the Popsicle stick, but it pops out of the smashed ice cream. "Ugh."

"What's up with you?" Jordan asks. He kneels across from me and places his hand on my shoulder. "I'm sorry if last weekend was too much." He sighs. "I should probably go. This isn't right of me."

"No!" I yell. It comes out louder than I intended. I toss the Popsicle stick across my room. It clacks against the wall. Jordan lifts his hand and slides away from me.

"There's something wrong with me . . . or not wrong with me, because there's nothing wrong with you. But this sickness..." I run my hands down my face. "I don't think it's a normal sickness."

Jordan shakes his head. "I don't get it."

I reach for him and cup his hands in mine. His eyes go wide.

"You're so—"

"Warm. My mom took my temperature this morning and it was a hundred ten degrees."

He rips his hand away and steps back.

"No," he says. He paces the room. "That doesn't make any sense."

"Well, that's what I was hoping you would know."

"It doesn't work like that. It can't work like that." He cuts his hand through the air.

"It can't pass to another person?"

"No! HydroPro would have told me if it could. I feel like they would have made me pass the powers to other people so they could do more experiments. Have there been any flames?"

"No," I lie. "I just learned of this temperature thing a few hours ago."

"Then I'm sure you're fine." He rubs his eyes and sits on my bed. "Maybe the thermometer was broken."

"It wasn't. What about that doctor you see? Can we just ask them? I'm kind of freaking out."

"You weren't in the accident. Nothing happened to you."

I let out a hard sigh. "Okay, well, I don't get why *you* are freaking out. You happened to me."

"Because, Dylan."

He covers his face with his hands and starts full-on sobbing. I walk over to my bed and sit next to him. I pull his arm to my chest.

"What haven't you told me?" I ask.

He shakes his head. His chin trembles.

"I'm freaking out because...because..." He sharply inhales between words. "Because I'm dying from this. And if you're like me, it means you are too."

nineteen

Dying? The word hangs in the hydrogen between us.

One time, during the summer after freshman year, Perry and I thought we were cool and took surfing lessons at the beach in Wildwood Crest, New Jersey. We mainly did it to get some sick pictures of us surfing, but also because earlier that summer we bought liquid Sun In from the pharmacy and sprayed it in our hair and were running around like two bleached-blond Swedish supermodels—or at least we thought we were. I was more of an Irish ginger hybrid because my hair was too dark to go completely blond. It ended up more orange. Perry killed it, though. Either way, surfing fit our theme for the season.

The instructor said the longboard was easier for first-timers to control than the shortboard, so based off my history of athleticism I chose the shortboard. We paddled out to the middle of the ocean, and I rode the first wave in to shore lying on my stomach like a champion. I paddled back out, and for the second wave I thought I'd stand up. Well, I stood up and flew off the board in two seconds. I sank beneath the surface, and the crashing wave slammed the surfboard into the back of my head. I was seeing stars and nothing else in the opaque Jersey Shore water.

My head was throbbing, I couldn't find air, and I was about to let myself sink to the bottom.

That's how I feel right now, staring at this boy. My heart stops beating for a few seconds. This boy, who I like so much, is apparently dying. And there's probably nothing I can do about it.

"What do you mean *dying*?" I ask. I push his arm away.

"It's exactly what I mean."

"Can you please be more specific for once in your life?"

"I don't know the specifics! The air on Earth can't sustain my body. Like I tried to explain to you before. You're made up mostly of oxygen. I'm hydrogen. Earth's atmosphere is slowly eating me or something. That's why I go see that doctor every Saturday. I sit in a big glass chamber that gets pumped with hydrogen and brings my body back to the levels of whatever the hell the doctor thinks is best."

"What kind of doctor is that?" I ask.

"Obviously not a regular one." He laughs through tears. "Her name is Dr. Ivan. She was with HydroPro before but then helped me escape. She left the corporation and has been trying to keep me alive since."

I stare at the side of his face. His eyes are on the floor.

"Happy now?" he asks. "I'm a science experiment. That's why I kept running."

My chest burns. I press my hand against it, and my palm only intensifies the sensation. I take a deep breath before speaking again.

"I'm happy you told me. I'm not happy you're dying, obviously."

My voice cracks. There's a pit in my stomach. I miss him already and he's still right here in front of me. The Dilly Bar has completely melted into a white puddle in the middle of my room.

Jordan turns to me. A tear runs down his cheek.

"I'm sorry, Dylan. I've just been so lonely. I needed a friend... a person. I should have never let us get close."

"Stop. Don't say stuff like that. You didn't, like, force yourself on me. We don't even know if I'm actually like you."

He swallows hard. His fingertips are orange, giving the skin beneath his nails a fluorescent glow. He rubs his hands up and down his thighs.

"I don't feel well," he says. He grabs my leg and then falls to the floor.

"Jordan!" I kneel beside him. His body shakes. Moaning sounds erupt from the back of his throat.

"Calm down," I say. "Just breathe." I grab his hand and rub his back with my other hand. I don't feel any kind of heat. There's no discomfort.

He takes a few deep breaths, but then his breath gets shallow. A thin cloud of smoke rises from his shoulder. An orange speck appears on his flannel shirt, and then grows into a large circle, revealing his skin. More tiny holes burn through his shirt all over his torso. He looks at me and his eyes are blank.

"Jordan, stop. You can't do this here." I grab his cheeks and pull his face an inch from mine. "You need to relax. Stop thinking about what I said. Pretend I never said it." I push him away from my wooden bedframe.

Singed pieces of his shirt fall off his body. They hit the floor and turn to black ash. I blow them into the air, hoping to stop the eruption of any flames.

"Why are your clothes burning? I thought they were fireproof!"

"Not these. I thought...I thought I was in control," he mumbles. "Bathroom." His eyes have morphed into the blue-and-orange fireballs again. He scratches his chest and his shirt basically disintegrates in his hand.

"What?"

"The bathroom tub. Now."

"Right." I nod.

I put his arm over my shoulder and pull him toward my bedroom door. His feet drag along the floor. I turn and notice a charred black streak along the hardwood. I hoist him into my arms. We limp down the hallway and into the bathroom, keeping the flames on his shoulders a safe distance from the hall's picture frames. He pushes off my body and dives to the floor. I shut the door and lock it behind us.

He crawls toward the tub, grabs the ledge, and heaves himself up. I push on his back and finish lifting him into the white porcelain tub.

His shirt is a tattered rag. Tiny orange flames flicker along the patterned stripes. He rips it completely off his body and throws it to the floor.

I gasp. I jump onto his shirt and stomp on the flames until they disappear.

Jordan's veins are a deep purple and protrude from his skin. His ab muscles are tight and contract with every shallow breath he takes.

He lurches his body forward and slaps the shower on. He screams and then pulls his feet to his chest. He rests his head on his knees and rocks back and forth. A line of fire squiggles down his spine. The water rains down on him from above.

I reach for him. He slaps my arm away. When we collide, my skin ignites in flames.

I shout. I stumble backward and fall into the wall, knocking down a framed picture. The glass shatters at my feet as it hits the floor.

"Oh no," Jordan says.

I wave my hand through the air, trying to get rid of the flames, but they only grow as I fuel them with oxygen. I turn on the sink faucet, letting the water run across my skin. I grab a towel and tightly wrap it around my hand until the flames die down.

Then my feet lift off the ground and my body rises toward the ceiling.

"Jordan?" I ask.

He's staring at me, eyes wide.

"Is this part of it? What's happening?"

I drop the towel and grip the edge of the sink. My body inverts and my feet hit the ceiling. I'm doing a handstand in the middle of the air. Blood rushes to my face. My pulse pounds in my neck.

"Jordan, what is going on?"

"I can't even," he starts. He wipes his face aggressively. "It must be a different level of manifestation. Dr. Ivan said this could happen to me eventually. But it hasn't yet."

Jordan stands in the tub. His jeans are soaked. The shower water pounds the back of his head and runs down his body over his chest muscles. Even in this moment, I can't help but think how good he looks.

The random force pulling me to the sky is overwhelming. My hands are shaking and my finger muscles, which I don't think have ever been worked out in my entire lifetime, can't hold on for much longer. I let go of the sink and fly across the bathroom. My back slams into the ceiling.

"I don't know what you're talking about with manifestations and Dr. Whoever-the-hell, but how do I get down?!"

There's a knock on the door. We both turn toward the noise. Jordan whips his head around so fast his wet hair splatters a line of water across the wall.

"Hey, Dyl?" Dad asks. "Is everything okay in there?"

I swallow. "Yes. Just showering." I wince at my obvious response.

"Who are you talking to?"

I try to lower my arm, but the reverse gravity force slams it back into the ceiling.

"No one. It's a podcast. What do you want?"

"Listen, I'm sorry I yelled earlier. I'm just concerned is all."

"It's okay."

"I'm going to run to Wawa to get some hoagies for dinner. Do you want anything?"

"No. Can't really eat right now. Still a little off."

"Okay. I'll be back in a little."

"Okay."

There's a minute of silence before we speak again.

"What is a hoagie?" Jordan asks.

"A kind of sandwich. Is that really important right now?"

He shrugs.

I reach for him, and he grabs my hand before it floats back to the ceiling. Our forearm muscles flex.

"You're not like me," Jordan says. "You're a different kind of me. It's manifesting in you differently."

"What is?"

"The hydrogen. The body composition. It's the lightest element. You're not combusting . . . you're floating."

"Well, how do I un-float?"

"Think of something else. Center yourself. The same way I get rid of my flames. You have to think of something else to bring your body back into your control. Close your eyes and see yourself there."

A flame shoots from his shoulder. I turn and watch it swirl through the air to make sure it doesn't set the bathroom on fire and lead to the destruction of my home.

I let go of his hand. "If I'm going to do that, I can't look at you."

He nods and sits back in the tub. He pushes his hair out of his face. "You have to breathe, Dylan. Just breathe."

I close my eyes. The hum of the shower water blasting from the faucet soothes my mind. I can't look at Jordan to bring myself back to center, but I have to think about him. I haven't been able to think about anything or anyone else lately. Between Chemistry class, my family, Dairy Queen, and burning homes, Jordan's arms are the only place I've wanted to be the past couple weeks.

I think about our normal moments together. I hear the Dairy Queen door opening right before I saw him for the first time. I smell the cool air of the woods as we skated across the frozen pond. I wonder what normal will be for us now.

I think about his red Arizona State hoodie and all the places it's been with him. I'm somehow jealous of a hoodie. I think about the three pairs of jeans he's rotated through—black, light blue, and dark blue. I'm waiting for the day I get to pull those jeans off his legs. I'm hoping that day will be soon. I'm hoping there will be more days together after today. But I don't know how much time we have left.

My heart rate slows. My body sinks.

I picture all the future days I wanted with Jordan. All the moments that could've turned into works of art.

He's sitting at my kitchen table with Mom, Dad, and Cody. There's a big bowl of spaghetti in front of us. Mom is smiling while she listens to Jordan tell a story about running into a snake on a hike in Arizona and how he fought it off.

I know Mom wonders if I'm happy. I know she questions whether she's being supportive and loving enough.

I wanted Jordan to be there at the table just once for me and for Mom, so she knows I think home is a safe place. I know that's all she wants. I wanted to show her this is the person I'm shining the flashlight on. But now I can only think, *Should this be the person I'm shining the flashlight on?*

My fingers wrap around the edge of the sink. My legs drop and the bottoms of my feet land softly against the floor. I open my eyes, and my reflection stares back at me in the mirror.

"What did you think about?" Jordan asks. He's sitting cross-legged in the tub.

"You."

His face flickers.

I rub my eyes. I walk over to the tub and step inside. I pull my hoodie off and sit in front of him. I grab his bright orange hands. The falling water feels lukewarm against my skin. I take a deep breath.

"What's going to happen to me?" I ask quietly. "Am I dying?"

"I don't know," he says flatly. "It looks like it's affecting you differently. So maybe not." He squeezes my fingers.

"Can I hug you?"

He looks down, shaking his head.

"Please?"

"Dylan." He wipes his forehead. His arm hair sticks flat against his skin. "I don't want to hurt you. I don't know what I did to you."

I dive forward and wrap my arms around the back of his neck. He pushes his forehead against mine, hard. He grunts.

"I should go," he says. He stands and takes a step out of the tub.

I grab his arm. "No, Jordan!"

"You shouldn't be around me anymore! Look what I've done to you."

"So you want me to do this alone, then?"

His head wobbles from side to side. "No. Of course not." He sits again. "I can't do what you want me to do." He's squinting as shower water runs over his eyes. "I don't know how it worked the first time."

"I know."

We sit for five minutes without speaking. I don't know what's going to happen when we get out of this tub. I don't know who's waiting for us out in the world. Jordan said there were bad people who tried to hurt him. It's why he left Arizona. Am I going to have to leave?

I clear my throat.

He sniffs. His eyes are bloodshot. He might be crying. Or it might be shower water. He scoots forward and rubs his tan torso against mine. He flips my hair back onto the top of my head.

I thought I was beginning to learn who he was. But now he's even harder to understand. Or maybe because I've changed, it won't make sense now.

I'm breathing in a different kind of breath, and nothing is going to be the same.

twenty

I suck at navigating life with my new body. I keep forgetting who or what I am. I feel like I'm going through puberty again and am getting random boners throughout the day that I have to hide from everyone around me. Every time someone looks at me, the same kind of panic rips through my body as if I was just caught masturbating. My constant cowering in public settings is moving beyond the point of embarrassment. One would think having these abilities would make me stronger, but I just feel meek and powerless.

Mom officially thinks I'm on drugs. The bags under my eyes are like a pair of face boobs. I haven't been able to sleep all week. Mostly because I've been stressing about my impending doom, but also because I've been floating to the ceiling in the middle of the night like I've been possessed by a demon. Of all the manifestations or whatever that could've happened to me, I got *floating*? What good does that do? All it does is make me look creepy. I already had that power before my body decided to play musical chairs with the elements of the earth and turn my blood into hot sauce.

Cody came into my room one morning and jumped on me when I was sleeping. Admittedly, I was having a dream about Jordan, and my temperature must've been higher than usual. I didn't wake up to the force of Cody's body on me, but to the high-pitched shriek of her scream after she touched my skin and I burned her.

It's on my list to ask Jordan how to control my temperature when I'm asleep and can't forcibly think about something else.

Now Cody is afraid to touch me. Mom and Dad want to touch me, but I refuse to get close to them. I haven't hugged Mom in three days, and every morning when she leaves, I swear she's fighting back tears. If this new body temperature doesn't kill me, then that definitely will.

I have been out of school for a week. And I called out of my shift at Dairy Queen last Tuesday. I don't see how I'm going to exist at those places without making a scene. If I start thinking about how to make it all work, the next thing I know I'm up against the ceiling.

Kirsten and Perry haven't caught on to anything yet—*luckily*. I texted them that I still wasn't feeling well, and would let them know when I was better and would need Kirsten to drive me to school again. They've been messaging in our group chat nonstop all week. I've been pretending that I'm not seeing the messages and sending a meme here and there to let them know I am alive. But the flu story is only believable for so long. I don't know what I'm going to do in a few days. I have to tell them eventually—whether Jordan likes it or not.

My parents think I'm taking the bus to school, but really, I ride my bike past my bus stop and head straight for Jordan's house. He meets me at the corner of the Smithson Hills development after pretending to leave for school too, and we circle back to his house. We've been spending each day in his room, going over what I can and can't do, what I can and can't say, and who I can and can't see.

Trying to talk to the people from HydroPro? That's a no.

Telling Perry, Kirsten, or my family about this? That's a no.

Having an outburst with flames or floating in public? The biggest no.

That's been the only silver lining to come from this whole situation. I get to see Jordan more than usual. And despite everything, he's sticking around.

"Can we do something different tomorrow?" I ask, sitting on Jordan's bed.

"Like what?" Jordan asks.

"Maybe pick up where we left off last week and have our date at Starbucks? I'm tired of doomsday prepping."

"It's not doomsday prepping. It's survival. It's important."

"Well, yeah. But so is living. We can't stay in here forever. We might as well test out leaving at some point. We can call it prepping for reintegration to society." I grin.

He smiles. "Fine. I guess Starbucks is a low-risk setting anyway. If anything happens, we can just leave."

The next day, I decide to ride my bike to Jordan's house and pick him up like a true gentleman. It's a little past five p.m. and the sun is halfway beneath the ground. The cold gripping Falcon Crest has finally let up a bit, but it's not like it matters. I'm always warm now regardless of the weather.

Thin gray clouds streak across the orange-blue sky like jet smoke. I turn in to Smithson Hills and pedal past the rows of identical boxes.

This is my first real date, and I think I'm ready. My previous interactions with boys have come from drunken party nights or ended with the kiss of death. I'm happy Jordan and I have taken it slow—at least with the romantic side of our relationship. The other stuff has been a blur. We've hung out a handful of times and there's been no kissing. Usually if I kiss boys the first time we hang out, they disappear—hence the kiss of death. Then again, those interactions have been with normal human boys. Maybe this will go differently.

He's waiting for me at the end of his driveway. The sun has set, and his face is lit up by the streetlamp next to his mailbox. His hands are folded at his waist like a schoolboy. I grin at the sight of him.

I skid my bike to a stop. "Hey," he says, and rubs his hand through his hair. My heart flutters. I jump off the pedals and lay my bike on the street. I've seen him every day for the past week and somehow still miss him.

I step onto the curb. The backs of my feet are in the air while my toes balance on the thin block of concrete. We wrap our arms around each other and hold it for our longest hug yet. When I let go, his puffy winter jacket has an imprint of my chest.

"Ready for coffee?" he asks.

"Absolutely," I say. I resist making a joke here about us feeling nervous or anxious and blowing up a Starbucks barista. I don't even want him to think about it. But it's literally all I can think about.

"Where's the passenger seat?" he asks, scanning my bike.

"You're definitely too big for the handlebars. Can you stand on the pegs?"

He smiles, sticking the tip of his tongue out between his teeth, and nods. I want to tackle him onto the grass and put my tongue between his teeth too. I want to hug him without the layers between us.

He stands on the pegs and rests his hands on my shoulders. A wave of heat travels down my arms. It soothes my muscles. I turn and look up at him. His dark eyes flick downward beyond his defined chin.

"Well, I can't keep you warm all night," he says. "Let's go before you freeze."

Oh, but you could, Jordan. You totally could.

I push down on the pedals and at first, I have trouble keeping the handlebars steady. Jordan is significantly heavier than Kirsten, Perry, or Cody, the only other people I've ever biked with on my pegs. But once we pick up speed, we glide through town toward the Starbucks.

We don't speak a word during the trip, and it's a beautiful silence. The wind rushes by my ears on the main road. I'm at ease with my town for once. I notice the star-filled sky beyond the stale Burger King and gas station price signs jutting into the air. Jordan's hands are heavy on my shoulders. It's nice to finally feel something new among all the routine.

By the time we pull into the Starbucks my knuckles are white from gripping the handlebars. I lock up my bike, and we head inside.

"Hey there," the barista says. "What can I get started for you?"

I step up to the counter. "Can I get a grande vanilla latte?" I say.

"Sure. And for you?" She turns to Jordan.

"Can I have a venti black iced coffee?" he says.

I laugh, fidgeting with a few of the granola bars in front of the register. "Iced coffee? It's freezing out."

I look up, and he's staring at me. My smile fades, and I stare back. "Oh," I hum. I realize my joke doesn't make sense for us now because we're perpetually hot. Iced coffee will always be appropriate.

At the table, I wrap my hands around my warm coffee. Water droplets slide down the side of his iced coffee. So far, the night is blissfully uneventful.

I'm taking in his looks again as we sit here, and my obsession with his face hasn't subsided in the slightest. Either the lighting is brighter in here or I never noticed, but he has a few brown freckles across the bridge of his nose. He slouches over the table, just slightly, emitting a cool and relaxed energy. His finger traces a circle around a bubble of water on the wooden table. The black hairs on his fingers above his knuckles scatter in every direction. His black arm hair makes his sun-kissed white skin appear tanner than the other areas of his body. The ends of his fingernails are jagged, like he bites them.

"So, I talked to Dr. Ivan this morning," Jordan says before sipping his coffee.

"Saying what?" I raise my eyebrows. "Did you tell her about me?"

"Yeah. I had to."

"I thought the plan was to not say anything? I have a feeling my powers—or manifestation or whatever—will go away in a few days. Why didn't you tell me?"

"It *was* the plan. But I don't know. I'm nervous. I feel like they did a lot of things to stabilize me in the beginning and they might need to do it to you too."

I sip my latte and swallow. "Stabilize?"

He nods. "There's a lot happening inside you."

"Well aware. But it's different for me. I wasn't in the accident, like you said." My mental health strategy is to keep saying that it's going to be different until it's true. "It could be something that happens to people once you start hanging out with them, then goes away."

"I'm not so sure. She wants to see you."

"When?"

"Soon. She's going to find a day for both of us to come. You could come along with me for my regular visit. It won't be more than a few hours."

I've somehow managed to be invited into some underground society of good HydroPro people versus bad HydroPro people. I know from Jordan that getting involved with HydroPro includes leaving your home state, weekly visits to a glass chamber, pursuit from scary-looking men, dead parents, and an overall sense of dread and misery.

If I get involved, I'll have to tell my parents and friends about Jordan and HydroPro, and they will most likely call the police. But if I'm not like Jordan and this is all going to go away, at least eventually, then it's best I don't tell them. For now, hiding this is better than putting it out in the open. Honestly, extreme stress has been a more common occurrence than shooting flames the past few days. Maybe this whole thing is already starting to fade.

"Let's just pick up where we left off," I say. "We're at Starbucks. . . . We're with other people. . . . Everything is fine."

He runs his hand down his face. "As fine as it can be," he says. "I won't rush things, then, but will you promise me that you will come along for my next visit? Just to be safe."

"Pinkie promise." I extend my pinkie. He smiles. He wraps his pinkie around mine. There's the smallest shock.

"Has this ever happened to someone else you know?"

He presses his eyebrows together. "I thought we were going with the thought that this wasn't because of me." His tone is sharp.

"Oh." I sit up.

His head bobbles. "I'm sorry. I'm kidding. I just wish it wasn't because of me." He turns and looks through the windows. The glass reflects the inside of the Starbucks against the black night sky. A layer of water glistens across his eyes.

I clear my throat. "So, I must ask. Why the Jon Snow poster in your room? Is he your favorite Stark?"

He laughs and wipes his eyes. "I got to go," he says.

"What?" My face flushes. Is he mad now that I changed the subject? I can't win.

"He's not a Stark, you noob. Remember the whole bit about everyone hiding his true parents so he wasn't murdered?"

"Ugh. I already messed up. How could I forget?"

"Don't do it again. And I don't know. He's not my favorite. I think I just identify with him the most."

"I could see that. You're both the cutest."

He blushes and takes a sip of his iced coffee. "That's not my reasoning. But I have a tendency to make you feel bad, so I'll let you figure out the reason on your own time."

"The parents. I'm sorry."

He smiles. "You don't have to apologize every time. Who's your favorite?"

I tap my chin. "Hm, I think I admire Arya the most. Her sword-wielding abilities are on point. Pun intended. Also, I too have a list of people I want wiped from the planet. Mine might be longer than hers, though."

"Hard-core."

Jordan's deep brown eyes stare through me, green straw between his perfect teeth.

Customers walk in and out of the Starbucks. Everyone looks at Jordan. Literally everyone. Whether it's a full-stop five-second stare or a quick glance of the eyes, no one can walk in or out the door without taking in his beauty. I wonder what it must be like to command that kind of attention, to be a can't-miss-him kind of guy. I don't know if he notices. His eyes haven't left me since we got here.

A group of four older women are gathered around a table in the corner, sitting on the booth seats with the comfy cushions. I would have preferred if Jordan and I were sitting over there, but they're taking up all the space. Every three minutes or so they break out into a synchronized, screeching laugh.

Beside them are two older men that I swear I've seen before. One has a coffee, the other one doesn't—which is curious to me. The one without a coffee pulls a notepad from his bag and starts scribbling. His back is to me. He turns and looks at the ceiling. I gasp when I see his profile. He's the same man from the night I met Jordan and at the art gallery. His wandering eyes are set deep into his long face beneath thick black brows, like they're in caves.

A ball of heat forms in my chest and then spreads to my shoulders and down my arms. My legs go numb. I grip the table to keep myself from rising into the air. I glance at Jordan to see if he recognizes them. He's playing with the paper straw wrapping.

Jordan nods in their direction. "What do you think is going on over there?"

"Who?" I ask, my voice a few pitches higher the normal.

"Those loud ladies." He smiles.

I exhale. He doesn't notice anything suspicious about the other table.

"I don't know." I look at the two men one last time and then focus back on Jordan. I grimace while stretching my neck. If I want to keep things normal, I have to act like everything is normal. "Book club maybe."

"There are no books."

"My mom has a book club, and there are never books. I think she uses it as an excuse to get my dad out of the house and drink wine with her friends."

"You should probably look into that."

"I probably should." My fingernails turn orange as I think about HydroPro's eyes peering over my shoulders. Beads of sweat sprout across my face. I lick my lips and taste the salty liquid. I'm not going to let them ruin this date.

"You're thinking in the wrong direction," Jordan continues. "Starbucks isn't someplace moms would come to have a night out.

Starbucks is for, like, serious-yet-casual business meetings. This is definitely a local moms' meeting for a neighborhood association that's taken a turn toward husband bashing. Look at the pen and paper. They're plotting."

They let out another howling group laugh.

"I want to be a part of it," I say, my throat nearly closed.

"Right? How do I get Linda's blond bombshell look?"

Linda, as she's been assigned, has a lion's mane of blond hair around her face. She has a slight streak of gray down her middle part and bangs that are also parted. For all the hair she has, it's still thin and looks like a tumbleweed. If we got too close to her, her hair would evaporate without question.

"Well, if you want that look, just throw out your conditioner," I say. He laughs. It eases me for a moment. I glance at the men again. "Like, none for a year. Just shampoo that mess every day and blow-dry on high heat."

"Maybe I'll go for the Deborah look, then."

"The brunette?" I ask. Three of the women have dried-up blonder hair. One woman has long, straight brown hair. She's more poised than the rest, wearing a chic cardigan and black skinny pants. I notice that Linda is wearing Uggs. One of the other women has a black wrist wrap around her arm.

"Yeah."

"Oh, no. That's Valerie. She was a party girl back in the day and went to graduate school in New York City. She had her children in her late thirties. She's wondering why she's back here with the local deadbeats from her high school discussing why Monday is better than Tuesday for recycling pick-up."

Jordan sips the last of his coffee. He twirls the cup and the ice jingles. "Poor Valerie."

"I'm afraid of being Valerie," I say. I forgot my coffee was in front of me. I take my second sip. My hands quiver as I bring the cup to my mouth.

"Are you okay?" he asks.

"Yeah...Yeah...Totally fine." I take another sip of my coffee. I want to tell him who's right next to us, but I shouldn't. He seems completely relaxed for the first time, like, ever and he deserves that after everything he's done to protect me. I'm going to take this one for the team.

"Okay." I can tell he doesn't believe me. "Where do you want to go to graduate school?"

I choke on the liquid sliding down my throat. "Graduate school?" I cough. "I haven't even thought about regular college. Do you have a ten-year plan or something?"

He shrugs.

"Of course you do. What's it involve?"

"I'm not really sure. I want to do urban planning and when I google it, most of the websites say you need to go to graduate school."

"Oh, cool. Like designing cities?"

He nods.

"I'm really good at *SimCity*, you know," I say.

"I've never played."

"Get on that. Although they really limited my creativity when my city could only be a couple square miles."

"What kind of city is that?"

"My thoughts exactly."

He shifts in his seat and sits on his hands. "You really haven't thought about it?"

"I mean, I'm not good at much."

"You're good at *SimCity*, apparently. And painting."

"Yeah, but I can't do that now. I'll be copying you. Thanks for killing my only career path before I even knew it existed."

He hangs his head. "Always killing your vibe."

"I want to go to school out west." I hold up my hand. "Not because of you."

"Like California?"

"No. That'd be too clichéd for me. I'm thinking more like Arizona, Colorado, Utah, or someplace like that. I've never been, and the mountains and stuff look really cool."

"Are you outdoorsy?"

"I think I would be if I were exposed to it. There's nowhere to hike around here. The pharmacies on every corner aren't really all that scenic."

"I'm sure there is. I'll look into it for the next time we hang out."

I pull my lips in. *Next time.* So this must be going well. I sit up straight and adjust my posture. *Next time. Next time. Next time.* I can't stop thinking about the next time when it's a date and not flame-thrower training.

"Dylan!" Jordan yells in a whisper.

It startles me and I jostle my coffee. "What?"

"Your hair." He holds up his phone screen to my face. My shaggy hair sticks straight up in the self-facing camera, reaching for the ceiling.

"Uhhh..." I mutter. I reach for my hair and run my fingers

through the floating strands, pressing down. As I let go of the table, my butt rises from the seat. My thighs crash into the bottom of the table. Jordan's eyes go wide. He steps on my shoes, pushing my feet back to the floor to ground me.

"Relax," he whispers. "Think of something that calms you."

I close my eyes and grip the edge of the table again, harder. I can't think of anything but this. I look at the two men following us out of the corner of my eye to see if they've noticed anything. They're sitting in silence. I clench my teeth so hard I can hear them grinding together.

The neighborhood association gets up from their table and heads to the exit. They make a scene as they leave, cackling out the doorway. It's distracting enough. I blink a few times and bring myself back to the present, exhaling. The tension leaves my arms.

Linda throws her coffee cup at the trash can but misses. It bounces off the counter and onto the floor. She attempts to pick it up but struggles, grabbing her lower back. The barista dashes over to assist.

"I think now might be a good time to leave with our ladies," Jordan says.

My heart sinks. Maybe this isn't going as well as I thought. I lost control and ruined everything. What's funny is that I chose Starbucks as a potential safe place so that he wouldn't combust, but now I am the one having an episode. Of course, that was before everything changed. I didn't think about choosing a safe place for me. I still don't even know where that would be. Is there a safe place with HydroPro following us everywhere?

We haven't even been here for an hour, and he already wants

to call it a night. It's probably not from nearly floating away to the low-lit wall decor. I shouldn't have brought up my *SimCity* skills. He definitely thinks I'm a nerd who sits in bed all day with my laptop on my crotch playing computer games and eating Cool Ranch Doritos. He wouldn't be wrong, though. That's exactly what I did before I met him.

"Oh." I huff and squirm in my seat. "Sure. Can I finish my coffee?" I spin the full cup around with the tips of my fingers. I don't take a sip in hopes to delay our exit for as long as possible.

"Yeah," he says. "We can probably go back to my place when you're done."

When he finishes his sentence, I bring my coffee to my mouth and chug it faster than my favorite three-a.m. water bottle after a long midnight marathon of *SimCity*.

"Ready," I say.

As I stand, the two men from HydroPro stand simultaneously. My eyes go wide. I quickly push my phone off the table.

"Oh, oops," I say. I kneel on the floor and search for my phone, slowly. I watch the men's legs. They don't move. I huff. I grab my phone, then stand.

"I forgot I wanted to show you something," I say. I pull Jordan's arm back to the table.

"What?" he asks.

I open my notes app to type as much information about the men as I can. I end the paragraph telling him not to look in their direction. "On my phone. There's this funny video." I sit back at the table, then show him my screen. As he reads, his mouth falls open, but he quickly snaps it shut.

The men linger for a few more minutes before realizing the awkwardness of their looming presence. We watch them leave, then drive off in their silver car. The barista is the only person left with us inside. Jordan gasps for air.

"They are—" I start.

"HydroPro? Yes," Jordan says. "Let's get out of here."

I follow him on our way out. He walks through the door and holds it open for me. The wind pushes his hair flat against his head.

I kneel next to my bike, then quickly turn the numbers in the lock to free it from the post, sliding the four into place to unlock my high-security bike code of one-two-three-four. Jordan's black boots rub against my maroon Vans as he peers over me. The lock clicks, and I pull the black wire from the tire spokes. The tips of my fingers sting.

"Have your friends brought up what happened to me the other night at the lake?" Jordan asks randomly. His eyes scan the parking lot.

"Um, no. They asked just the one time the day after like I told you, but I think everyone kind of got caught up in the craziness of it all. They still must believe I pulled Kirsten from the water."

"That's good they haven't questioned it." He grabs my shoulders, then hoists himself onto the back pegs.

"Why?"

"I'm trying to figure out why they're following me . . . and getting so close."

"They're following us," I say, swallowing.

He nods, then looks to the ground. "I'm really not supposed to use it like that. I messed up." He curses under his breath, then bites his lip.

"Use what?" I start rolling us through the parking lot.

"The heat. The flames. I'm not supposed to use it as a power to, like, help people. Or hurt them. Dr. Ivan said she will protect me as long as I don't act out. She can't help me if I'm working against her and making myself seen. Or so she says. But she doesn't seem to be doing a good job with the protecting part."

"Actually, now that I think about it again, I don't think I ever thanked you for that night." I turn and look at him. "Thank you. Like, so much. You saved my friend's life."

He shrugs. "I almost didn't because I was too scared."

"But you did. You risked everything for me."

"Yeah," he mutters. "I guess it's not really a risk, though, when I'm already halfway in the grave. . . . It's just accelerating the inevitable."

I put my feet on the ground to stop us from moving any farther. I crane my neck back. We look each other over. A streetlamp blasts a halo around his head.

"Isn't Dr. Ivan helping you get better?" I ask.

"Depends on how you define better. I sometimes wonder if it would be better if I stopped seeing her. I don't know if all the trouble I'm causing is worth it."

I swallow and grip his arm. "I'm not hanging out with you just because of this," I say.

"I know," Jordan says. He takes a deep breath.

"Like, you can trust me."

"I do."

"And I don't think you should stop seeing her."

"Okay."

"Because the feeling you're causing inside me is definitely not trouble, but I know it's worth it."

He smiles. "Okay, then."

He wraps his arms around my neck and rests his chin on my shoulder. I bring my feet back to the pedals. I'm not going to push him for answers or force him to make a plan to shake our followers. When I do that, he stops talking to me. I'll let him reveal things on his own time, like he's been doing. I just hope he lets me know stuff before anything can hurt me too.

My thighs flex as I drive the bike forward. I glide us back to his house, overcaffeinated and crushing on Jordan Ator more than the night we met. Even if he didn't literally glow, he'd be the brightest light among all the lights in this sleepy suburb.

twenty-one

We reach Jordan's house. It's lit up by white spotlights placed evenly across the grass. Jordan jumps off my pegs into his driveway. He jogs a few yards as he slows down from forward momentum. I let my bike fall onto the front lawn, then we follow the cement walkway to his front door.

"Are your aunt and uncle okay with this?"

"Yeah." He laughs. "You don't have friends over to your house? What do you think is going to happen?"

I swallow. I don't know. Maybe an aggressive make-out session that would be super awkward if his aunt and uncle walked in on us.

"Nothing." I giggle. "Did you text them so they're not confused when some stranger walks in their home?"

"Yeah, Dyl. You're such a worrier."

Not a worrier—a questioner. But more importantly, he just called me Dyl for the first time. A ping hits my chest. My knees go a little weak as we approach the door.

Relationship: LEVEL UP.

He opens the door, and the house is different than I remember. Or maybe I'm just actually able to look around this time and take it all in because I'm not running from my one-time kidnapper.

The foyer smells like cleaning products, and there's a round table a few feet in front of the doorway with a green vase full of colorful flowers. The staircase has a wrought-iron banister and curves up to the second floor. We walk around the table and past the staircase toward the kitchen.

Along the hallway, there are three portraits of three pretty girls, who I assume are his cousins. They all have dark brown hair and hold an identical white rose to their shoulders.

I'm expecting to see his aunt and uncle when we enter the kitchen, but the room is empty. It's mostly dark except for the dim glow from two lights, one over the sink and one above the stove. The stove light shines on a glass tray full of something that looks like lasagna. There's a spatula sticking out of it.

"Is anybody home?" I ask.

"Yeah," Jordan says. "They're probably upstairs."

"Am I ever going to see your aunt's and uncle's faces? They're always just lurking in the shadows."

He laughs. "I guess they tend to do that, don't they?"

He walks over to the dish on the stove, squishes his finger into a piece, and then sucks the red sauce from the tip of his finger.

"Mmm," he moans. "Do you want any of this?" he asks, licking his lips.

"What is it?"

"Eggplant lasagna. It's so good."

"I'm not really hungry."

"Okay, let's go to the basement." He nods to a door behind me. He picks up the lasagna from the stove and carries it to the basement door. "I'm going to bring this down. Do you care?"

"Not at all."

I open the door for him, and we walk down the basement steps. The temperature drops, like, twenty degrees when we get downstairs. The basement is finished, just like at Kirsten's house. There's a pool table behind the couch and a dartboard in the far corner. There's a long shelf along the back wall that holds more than one hundred tiny golden trophies. The three girls from the upstairs hallway appear again. This time, there are portraits of them above the trophy shelf kneeling with soccer balls on their hips, awkwardly holding basketballs in the shooting position and grinning menacingly at me with metal bats over their shoulders.

Jordan places the lasagna on the coffee table. I plop onto the couch. The cushions let out a gush of air, like they're deflating. Jordan sits on the cushion next to me. He tucks his one leg underneath the other. There's about a foot of empty couch space between us. He grabs the Apple TV remote.

"What do you want to watch?" he asks.

I bite my lip, staring at the side of his face. His hair sticks straight up from the bike ride just like mine when I freaked out at Starbucks. His extra-volumized curls are probably from the wind, but I'm enjoying the thought that he's having an incident with his powers because he likes me so much. My eyes follow his defined jawline from his ear to the corner of his mouth. There's a piece of red sauce stuck in the crevice of his lips. I sit up and scooch across the couch next to him. Our thighs press together. He turns his face, and his full lips are an inch from mine.

"You have eggplant lasagna sauce on your mouth," I say. I lean in and wipe it away with my thumb. I don't lean back. If I'm going to make this happen, it has to be now. I know myself too well, and I won't be able to lean in to kiss him without there being an excuse other than just wanting to kiss him. I wipe my thumb on my thigh and press my lips against his.

Oops. Combustion.

I hold them there for a few seconds. His lips are soft and warm. I pull away, and our eyelids snap open. Our eye contact steadies. Then he drops his head and rests his forehead against mine. We laugh into each other's mouths, and it's all the assurance I need.

I kiss his lips again and this time, I let my body fall into him. My weight pushes him onto his back. I climb on top of him. My hair falls onto his face. I taste the venti black iced coffee in his mouth. He lets the Apple TV remote slide from his hand onto the floor and then runs his fingers through my hair.

My chest rests on his and my heart pounds against it. I feel his heart beating, trying to catch up with the pace of mine. My heart is bursting from its cage, telling me to go faster. Faster. Faster. Faster. The feelings I have for Jordan are spilling up from my heart, through my throat, and onto my lips. I'm giving them all to him. No more kisses of death. This is the kiss of my life.

I fall to my side and put my hand against his cheek. I pull his face harder into mine. He grips the back of my neck. Our mouths are opening, wider and wider. Our noses blast hot air onto our faces.

I pull away, in need of oxygen.

"I'm so happy I let you into Dairy Queen after we closed," I say, breathing heavily.

He bites my bottom lip and pulls it before he speaks. "You lied? You said you were open."

"I did. But it was the best kind of lie."

He laughs and pushes a piece of my hair behind my right ear.

"Are you feeling overwhelmed?" I ask.

"Very. But it's the best kind of overwhelmed."

He grabs my neck and pulls our faces together again. His hand travels down the side of my body. He pulls me in tighter. I press my hand into his chest. His fingers tug up on the bottom of my shirt.

"Is this okay?" he asks into my mouth.

"Yes," I say. I bring my arms up over my head as he pulls my shirt off. He tosses it to the floor. He kneels over me, crosses his arms, and slides his shirt off. I push him down onto another cushion and lie on top of him, our bare torsos up against one another. I trace my fingers along his arms. I close my eyes to focus on the touch. There's more muscle than I expected. I feel his triceps and then his shoulders. His body warms up. The heat is almost too much for my fingertips.

And then suddenly—we're rising. I open my eyes and watch the couch move away from us. Jordan is heavy in my arms. I spin our bodies midair so that he's resting on top of me. The floating force helps carry him upward.

"Well, this is awesome," he says with a laugh.

I don't know what to say because this is more than awesome, and I can't think of a better word.

Our lips come together again, and I don't want them to separate.

I want to taste every element Jordan Ator is made of. I want to feel all 110 degrees. I wrap my legs around his hips. We spin in the air and melt into each other.

I'm blacked out on the bike ride home—mentally, physically, emotionally, metaphorically, literally, anecdotally.

I'm in my garage watching the door close over Dad's SUV when I snap back into reality. I don't even remember if I kissed Jordan goodbye when I left his house. I step inside and Mom, Dad, and Cody are sitting at the kitchen table. Their heads turn quickly in my direction as I let the door slam closed. Cody lifts a forkful of pasta into her mouth, but freezes when she sees me. The spaghetti noodles slowly slide off her fork and plop back onto her plate.

"What happened to you?" Cody asks, her top lip curling.

"What do you mean what happened to me?" I'm smiling as I pull my shoes off.

"Honey," Mom says. Her shoulders drop. "You look awful."

I laugh. "I do?"

"Why are you so smiley?" Cody asks.

Dad stares at me as he continues to eat his pasta. "I told you we should've taken him to the doctor," he says. "I don't know why this is a fight."

I quickly walk across the kitchen to a mirror in the family room and view a much uglier version of myself. I look like a cracked-out weasel. My nose is bright red. The skin around my lips is chapped. I rub my chin, and white flakes disintegrate onto my hand. My eyes are bloodshot and watering.

"Oh, wow," I mumble, taking a step back.

Mom appears beside me with a box of tissues. She rips one from the top and holds it by my face. "You overdid it today." She touches my cheek, then sighs.

"In, like, the best way, though."

She cocks her head back. "Where were you just now? You need to come eat something. You weren't with that new friend, were you? I've had about enough of this."

I follow her back into the kitchen. "I was."

"Where?" Dad asks sternly. He looks through the window over his shoulder. "It's freezing outside. What are you up to?"

"Probably making out again," Cody says. She sticks her tongue out. "Was this with the boy you ditched me for?"

"What boy?" Mom asks. "When did you ditch your sister?"

"Dylan, I thought we discussed this," Dad says.

I roll my eyes. "That was that same one time last month when I forgot about her. We already discussed it."

"Who's this boy?" Mom presses.

"Just someone I'm hanging out with."

"You're grounded." Mom points at me. "Dishonesty won't be accepted in this house."

"Oh, relax," Cody says. "He just has a boyfriend he doesn't want to tell you about. He better be cute."

"Not a boyfriend. But he is cuter than me."

"What about hygiene?"

The muscles in Mom's face relax. "You're seeing someone and you didn't say anything?" Mom asks. "I hope you weren't kissing tonight with this sickness you're carrying."

I step back from the table and blow my nose. "I'm not seeing someone! And I'm not hungry. I'll tell you about him tomorrow." I toss the tissue in the trash can, then quickly fill a glass with water. I take a sip as I head for the stairs.

Mom throws up her hands. "So you are seeing someone?"

Dad rubs his eyebrows.

"What's his name?" Cody shouts from the kitchen.

"I'm not telling you! Get off social media, you miniature lurker," I shout over the banister.

I step into my room and close the door behind me. I flop onto my bed, face-first. My body goes rigid as I suddenly feel every muscle. If only I had this happen to me during my muscular systems test in Anatomy and Physiology class last year, I wouldn't be in track two science.

My phone lights up with a text from Jordan saying *Hey.*

I smile and reply with a blushing emoji. Then I text, *Hey.*

Is this how dating works? Because I like it. Am I dating?

I've never actually seen two guys dating in person before. I see it on television and social media and in my hypothetical relationships in my head, but not in this town. Not here where it's the same identical four-person families living in identical houses, just with different-colored window shutters. Not in front of my own eyes. I don't know what it looks like. What are the rules? I guess there are none in Falcon Crest. Which is terrifying, but mostly cool. For the first time I'm going to get to see myself living not only in my head, but out in the real world.

I wonder if he can come to junior prom with me. I'll have to check the school policy. I'm sure he can. But if Ms. Gurbsterter had her hand in the policy, I doubt it. Why am I thinking about prom? Are we boyfriends? Not yet. I'm getting ahead of myself. I think we are still in that phase of stress-inducing euphoria where you have no clue what the heck is going on but it's fun, you guess.

I pop my headphones in my ears and turn on my favorite Adele album because my insides are currently a powerful British female vocalist belting at the top of her lungs. The first song comes on, and I crash.

twenty-two

I'm back at school the following week, assimilating into normal life as Falcon Crest's first floating student. My kiss with Jordan has helped ground me because our relationship is all I can think about. It's pushed thoughts about my body temperature, flames, and possible death to the side, at least for the moment.

I'm still getting occasional stares from people for the Instagram debacle. Though I've learned that staring back at them directly in their eyes scares them off, and they never look at me again. It's a great new tool and at the current stare rate, the entire school should be afraid of looking at me by the end of the month.

I am also realizing how much I hate couples. Actually, let me be specific. I hate couples at Falcon Crest High School. It's unfair that they get to see each other all day every day. They get to kiss before homeroom, hug at the end of second period, sit next to each other at lunch, and then make out in the parking lot after school. You would think they might show some respect for people whose crushes don't go to the same school as them. Long distance isn't easy.

I don't actually hate people. I'm just so distracted today. I saw Jordan again yesterday because the Starbucks night was too hot to not have an immediate follow-up date or hangout or whatever he wants to call it.

I went to his house again and I didn't see his aunt and uncle again, because they were at his grandmother's house installing a new Wi-Fi router, and we went into the basement again and he grabbed the Apple TV remote again—but this time we started and finished an entire movie.

We watched M. Night Shyamalan's *The Village*. Jordan had never seen an M. Night Shyamalan movie before. He was confused as to why I had to say *M. Night Shyamalan* every time I said the movie title. I got confused as well after I said *M. Night Shyamalan* for the fifth time in two minutes.

"I don't know. It's just the way it is," I said. "It's not anyone's *Village*. It's M. Night Shyamalan's *Village*."

I told Jordan that M. Night Shyamalan was from Philadelphia and lived twenty minutes from where we were sitting. That seemed to distract him from all his questions about Shyamalan's film ownership. We watched it with kisses throughout.

And now I have RLS, more commonly known as Restless Leg Syndrome. In history class, my teacher came up to me and asked if I needed to use the restroom because my knees had been bouncing for forty minutes. I miss Jordan and it's scaring me. As an introvert, I can usually hang out with new people for around two hours before I require them to leave me alone. But I hung out with Jordan for exactly five hours yesterday, and it wasn't enough.

I'm scanning the cafeteria and it's like every couple holding hands is staring at me, trying to make me jealous. I am jealous. I am jealous that they still have the option of forever. Jordan and I potentially don't have forever. We could have a year, five years, or ten years. I don't know how fast hydrogen eats away at a human body. So every moment I am away from him feels like time is being wasted.

"I see that the meat in the chicken patties is still gray," Kirsten says, cutting her circular, breaded chicken patty with a white plastic knife.

"If you were expecting school policy change to happen while you were gone, then I think that time under the water did mess with your head after all," I say. "Our food is still outsourced from New Jersey."

"Ugh." Kirsten takes a bite and chews the chicken like it's made of rubber. "I don't even know why I bothered preparing that one-page policy brief about better environmental practices for food procurement, if they're not going to use the information."

"'Sup," Perry says, emerging from the hallway. She sits on the bench next to me. She slides her bag from her shoulder, then tosses it on the table.

"Wow, it looks like the three of us are finally back together," Kirsten says. "I feel like it's been years."

"Where have you been?" I ask. "Lunch started, like, twenty minutes ago."

"Ms. Gurbsterter wanted to have a meeting with me about Nationals."

"She told me she was going to do that," Kirsten says. "How did it go?"

"Where was my heads-up?"

"Sorry. She told me two weeks ago after practice. Then I almost died. I forgot about it."

"You're the worst."

"Would you rather have me die next time, then?"

"Um, hi," I say, waving. "I'm not on the cheerleading team. What was this meeting about? Was it about next year?"

Perry shifts in her seat. "No. She asked if it was okay if she gives me more responsibilities at Nationals even though I'm not a captain."

"That's a strange thing to ask."

"This meat is truly disgusting," Kirsten says. Her face scrunches. "I really can't." She picks up a napkin and spits a chewed-up piece of chicken into it. The sight destroys my appetite.

"Can you not leave this here in front of me?" I say, flicking away the lumpy napkin. Kirsten pokes it toward Perry, who freaks and reaches for the ball of napkin-chicken and hurls it across the cafeteria. It splatters against a vending machine and falls to the floor.

"You're an animal," I say.

"I have a low tolerance for disgusting things right now! Ms. Gurbsterter was heating up a Lean Cuisine in her office during our meeting, and I seriously wanted to puke. I'm still nauseous."

"Not the Lean Cuisines."

She nods. "It was a shrimp one too."

Kirsten and I gasp.

"Is that one of your responsibilities at Nationals? To pack her Lean Cuisines?" I ask.

Perry rests her head on her bag. "No. She wants me to be a hallway monitor at the hotel one of the nights, and keep track of some of the equipment."

"You should've said no until she gave you your recognition."

"I honestly just said yes as quick as I could to get the hell out of there. Her microwave was broken or something because those seven minutes were the longest of my life."

"It wasn't seven minutes in heaven?"

"Don't make me picture that."

"Those things don't even make you lean. It's so dumb," I say. I open my blueberry yogurt and stir it with a plastic spoon.

"She said to me once that someone told her she was 'anti-aging' and it was about a month after she started her Lean Cuisine diet," Kirsten says. "She swears by them now."

"Oh wow," I say, nodding. "Kirsten, this is your next big story. Lean Cuisines as the fountain of youth."

I repeatedly check my phone even though I know there won't be any texts from Jordan. He told me his school has a strict no-cell-phone policy. Jordan said they confiscate your phone and give it back to you the next day. He reasoned with me that we would have to go a whole night without texting if he got caught. I told him not to text me because I didn't want to risk it.

"You're in your phone a lot these days," Kirsten says, smirking. "Are you sure you *just* made out with Jordan this weekend?"

I blush. "Yes. Do you really think I would do anything else and not tell you guys?"

"We don't know. You haven't been talking to us a whole lot lately. Plus, you've never done anything else before, so who knows what you'll do if it happens," Perry says.

"*When* it happens," Kirsten corrects her.

"Let's not jump to conclusions," I say.

"I jumped to conclusions three weeks ago when you got in Kirsten's car with a hard-on," Perry says. "I ran off the building and flung my body over the ledge to my conclusions. I have fallen one hundred stories and am lying in my conclusions. I am so comfy in my conclusions—"

"Okay, well, you need three body paragraphs to come before the conclusion, so calm yourself," I say.

"And one body paragraph was written this weekend. Was it not?"

I smile. "It was."

"And the second can be written this Saturday at my party because I just confirmed last night that my parents are going to be out of town!" Kirsten squeals. She stomps her feet underneath our lunch table.

"I forgot you were trying to have that," I say.

"Dylan, you can't forget," Kirsten says. "If you read our messages from the past week, you would have seen it was mentioned ten times. Put it in your calendar. It will be our send-off to Nationals. If you don't come, it will be bad luck."

"I'll ask Jordan to come too, for sure."

"If he can't come, you still need to be there," Perry says. "No ditching now that you have a boy. Otherwise my conclusions are revoked."

"All right, all right." I hold my hands in the air. "I'm going to be there. Is this the last time I'm seeing you before you go? When do you leave?"

"Most likely," Kirsten says. "We're flying to Florida on Monday and coming back Saturday."

"Is this, like, an us party or a school party? I'm assuming a school party."

"School party."

"So I can expect Savanna and the rest of the junior class to be there?"

"Duh. Savanna is obsessed with Kirsten," Perry says.

"Please." Kirsten sighs. "We're not in the fifth grade anymore. She and I have moved on from that friendship."

Perry rolls her eyes. "Maybe you did, but she didn't."

"You're going to invite her after what she did to me?" I ask.

"I'm not going to personally invite her, but I'm sure she'll show. She will only lash out at you more if I say she can't come specifically. Also, I have to keep things civil because of our parents. You know this. The Blatts are powerful in the community. I can't ruin those connections."

I like Jordan as my secret. Well, I should say in-person secret. Everyone knows he exists thanks to Savanna's prank. But I'm happy he's a safe physical distance away from Falcon Crest and Savanna and everything else here. Our world is Starbucks, ice cream, kissing, movies . . . and fire and floating. It's sweet, cool, and hot all at the same time. And it's just ours.

I would love to have him at school to kiss and touch between class periods, but he's so much better off not knowing this part of my life. I don't know if I want to merge the two, especially with everything going on with the Blatts. If Savanna gets a whiff that something is up with the fires or catches us in a lie, she'll never leave us alone.

On my way to sixth-period English class, I spot Darlene walking toward me from the other end of the hallway. She's hard to see, hidden among the crowd of much taller people. Her head is buried behind a stack of books in her arms. She's wearing a high-waisted forest-green skirt with black leggings and her black combat boots. A burgundy beanie covers her short hair. I sidestep across the hall to make sure we run into each other. She sidesteps and twists around me without saying anything.

I spin on my heel and follow her to her locker. She flings open the maroon door and almost smacks it into my face. I snap my head back. There's a rainbow sticker on the inside of her locker door that says *I am an ally*. Beneath it is a picture of Shawn Mendes that I kind of want to steal.

"Hey, Darlene," I say, rubbing the back of my neck. Last time we spoke, I almost burned her, and before that I floated across the hallway, so I'm trying really hard to be normal. Although it's having the opposite effect. My feet are already numb, and the tingling sensation is slowly traveling up my legs. I give myself one minute before I shoot through the panels of the drop ceiling above us.

"Hi, Dylan," she says. Her voice is high-pitched and more positive-sounding than I was expecting.

"Listen, I want to apologize for the other day. I put you in an awkward position and you were just—"

"It's totally fine," she says into her locker. She pulls out a crumpled pink Post-it note and throws it to the floor.

"It is?"

"You don't want to be in the group. I get it. Like, I really don't care."

Crap. It's totally not fine.

"I didn't say I didn't want to be in it. I said I was thinking about it."

"Again, totally fine." She closes her locker and spins the black lock three times. "I have to go. I have study hall and I need to plan tonight's GSA meeting." She turns. "Have a good week."

"But—" I hang my head and stare at the floor. *Have a good week?* More like, *Please don't attempt to speak to me again in the next five days.* Ugh. She freaking hates me.

Someone slaps my shoulder, and my head pops back to an upright position.

"Hey," Kirsten says. "Since when are you friends with Lena Houchowitz?"

"I'm not." We start walking. "She tried to be my friend, but I eternally suck at making new friends and ruined it by being rude."

"I feel like you're never actually mean. Were you joking and she didn't get it?"

"Savanna was a bully, and I lashed out at Lena because I'm twelve."

"Ahh, I see," Kirsten says. "Anyway," she continues. "I wanted to ask you about something earlier but didn't want to do it in front of Perry."

I come to an abrupt halt. My shoes squeak against the linoleum floor.

"Nope. I don't like this already. No secrets among us!" I cut my hands through the air.

She circles back to me, locks her arm with mine, and pulls me down the hallway.

"It's not a secret of any kind. I want to get your feedback on a situation."

"You're not dating Keaton Cyrus, are you? I don't think that will go over well."

She slaps my arm, laughing. "No! Listen. The news station is having a contest this spring for high school students, and I kind of want to do it."

She shoves her iPhone in my face. I only have time to read the title of the internet page before she rips the screen away.

"One winner gets a cash prize and an internship this summer."

"Oh, that's so exciting."

"I think it would be perfect for me."

"Well, yeah, I agree. I don't think there could be anything more perfect."

"Ah, me too. I hope I get to go on camera live. How cool would that be?"

"So cool. Why can't Perry know about this?"

"She can. I just didn't want to bring it up at lunch because she always gets so weird when either of us brings up summer plans because her cheer plans are messed up. I didn't want her to get sad. This is really cool for me."

"That's not true at all because one: I don't have summer plans, so I've never brought anything up. And two: You tell her what to do like a mom. Obviously, she's going to get mad at you every time."

Kirsten shakes her head. "I just present options."

"Options she doesn't want."

"She'll be thankful in the end."

"Negative."

"So, do you think I should apply to this or not?"

"Of course!" I nudge her with my elbow, and we stare at each other.

"See what I did there? I'm encouraging you. That's what friends do. I didn't tell you to maybe go apply to make the newsletter for the local senior center instead."

"Ugh, Dylan. Fine, I'll be more encouraging to Perry."

"This is what you get for trying to be a sneak."

She laughs. "Will you read over my application idea if I send it to you tonight?"

I nod. "I mean, I'm sure I can't write anything better than what you're going to write but of course. What is the contest, exactly?"

"Well, you can pick any topic you want. I am going to focus on the Blatt arsons!"

My insides empty through my butt and splatter on the floor. My life is a joke. My hands shake. I search the hallway for the nearest exit.

"Wait, *what*? Why that?" I lick my lips. I spot a water fountain and walk to it. My feet start hovering every other step. Kirsten follows me.

"Why *not*? It's one of the biggest stories ever in this town. It's making national news. If you get picked, they link you with one of the journalists handling the topics related to your case and you help investigate and create an article with your findings. I think they judge the final article. I'm not sure. They posted it today, and I skimmed the details before lunch. I might take an environmental angle and talk about the carbon dioxide emissions from the fires. I already have that video, which will give me an advantage." She taps her chin.

I grip the edge of the water fountain and squeeze my fingers around it. My body is light as a feather. A familiar upward force pulls me to the ceiling. The fountain is the only thing keeping my feet on the ground.

"Aren't there other topics?" I ask.

Kirsten squints and inspects me. "Yeah, but...what are you doing right now?" She tries to look behind me.

"Nothing," I blurt. "Nothing." My hands are slipping. "Don't you think that could get a little messy with Savanna and all? I'm sure there are other good ones."

What I really want to say is, *Don't you think that could get a little messy with JORDAN AND ME?* I'm genuinely surprised she doesn't recognize me from that video. But I wouldn't put it past her to find some video rendering technology with advanced facial recognition software.

"That's why it's perfect. I have access to Savanna, and the fires are literally happening in my backyard. I know how to use my resources." She winks. She scrolls through the application again on her phone.

The school bell rings. She stuffs her phone into her bag. "Okay. I'm going to try and go write this application so I don't have to worry about it after cheer today. I'll send it to you when I'm done. Thanks, Dyl."

"Yeah, no problem."

"Are you going to get some water?" she asks, pointing at the fountain.

"Oh, right." I nod. "Mhm." I bend over to get water, but I can't take my hand off the edge of the fountain to press the button because

I'll fly away. Kirsten stares at me. I mime drinking water and stick out my tongue to be funny, but Kirsten doesn't laugh.

"I'll see you later," she says slowly with wide eyes.

She races off down the empty hall. I slap my hands over my face. After my hands leave the fountain, I shoot through the air. My back bounces off the ceiling. I wish I went to St. Helena's now. Does this school have a chapel? Because I seriously need to go pray for my soul.

Kirsten does everything at 110 percent. I know she's not going to stop investigating these fires until she solves the case, wins that internship, and gets her work published in the *New York Times*. And solving it means finding out Jordan set the fires.

Someone just give me a sign that everything is going to be okay.

Sometimes, I like the idea of there being a higher power. It allows me to put the blame on them and avoid having to take any responsibility for my own actions. It really is a convenient way to deal with my issues.

Get too drunk and throw up in a bush outside Perry's house— that wasn't me. That was God teaching me a lesson.

Incessantly text a boy who doesn't respond—that wasn't creepy of me at all. That was God's plan for us not to be together.

Don't study for any tests and fail them all—that's God at work. He doesn't want me to go to Harvard and is simply guiding me along my path.

Forget my sister exists and leave her to sit by the sewers in the dark—that was God providing her with hard life experiences so she can grow up to be a strong woman.

Like the concept of love, the concept of a higher power is something else I don't understand. But that's a story for a different day.

My feet touch down. I collapse to the floor and lie across the tile, resting my face on the top of my hands.

The door to the faculty restroom beside me swings open. Dr. Brio emerges into the hall. I look up at him. He's tucking his shirt into his pants. I don't know why he couldn't finish getting dressed in the bathroom like a normal person. Across the hall, Savanna darts out of the admin offices and walks toward us. We make eye contact, then her eyes snap to the floor. She clutches her books to her chest.

This is my sign? I swallow. I have officially entered a simulation. Where is the abort button?

"Dylan, why are you not in class again?" Dr. Brio says. He hoists up his pants. "Please get up off the floor."

"The warning bell hasn't even rung yet—" I start. But the warning bell rings and cuts me off. I look up at the speaker next to the clock. Dr. Brio pulls his face inward. His chin merges with his neck. He peers at me through his glasses.

"I'm going," I say, standing. "A lot of people have been asking for life advice from me lately. I'm partly missing class because of them. It's not just me."

He chuckles. "That'll be the day," he says, waving his hand and walking back into his classroom. "That will be the day."

I roll my eyes.

I turn around to head to English class, but Savanna plows into me. I gasp. One of her binders stabs the area right below my nipples. I grab my chest, rubbing it to soothe the stinging skin. A few of her books fall from her arms to the floor. She grunts.

"Watch where you're going, Dylan," she snaps. "God, not only are you ugly and brainless, but you're blind too?"

"My back was to you. You should've seen me."

"Whatever."

I squat and pick up a few of her spilled papers. She frantically grabs at everything on the floor. Some of her hair is loose and not tied tightly back into her high ponytail as usual.

"Don't touch my stuff. I can get it."

I shrug. "Okay, fine. Just trying to be nice."

I hold out a few papers I already picked up. She glances down at the papers in my hands and her eyes bounce back to mine. Her lips are parted. The areas below her eyes are puffy and red. She rubs her brow three times. I look down at the papers and the top one is a handout for the National Suicide Prevention Lifeline.

She clears her throat. "Give me that," she says, ripping the papers from my hand.

"Sorry," I mutter, rubbing my forearm.

"What're you sorry about?"

She stands. We both take steps in the same direction and block each other's paths.

"Get out of my way!" she yells, and pushes me aside. She jogs swiftly down the hall. Her ponytail bounces with her strides, as perky as ever.

"Savanna," I call after her. "Are you okay?"

She looks back at me. Her lip curls. She disappears around the corner.

I chase after her. When I turn the corner of the hall, a door to the outside closes in front of my face. Through the glass, I can see a Blatt Builders truck is parked along the curb. Mr. Blatt stands in front of it with his arms crossed. When Savanna gets close, he grabs her bicep and thrusts her into the truck's passenger seat.

And now God is playing tricks on me. My problems seem irrelevant, and for the first time in my life, I'm worried about Savanna Blatt.

twenty-three

It turns out, Jordan was serious about doing something out-doorsy for one of our dates, because he's planned us a hike. It'll be no hike through the Colorado mountains, but I would walk down a dirt path through the local junkyard if it meant being with him, so I am excited.

At school the next day, he texts me a rapid-fire list of instructions after lunch. He might be looking forward to this hangout more than me, which is a welcome change.

Jordan

My iPhone says the sun sets at 5:30 p.m.

I get done with school at 2:45 p.m. and you're done at 2:15 p.m.

I know you have to take the bus home this week bc Perry and Kirsten have long practices but I think you said before you get home around 2:35 p.m. with the bus?

My bus takes forever so I'm just going to walk to the Starbucks down the street. I'll prob get there around 3 p.m.

Do you want to meet me there with your bike and then we can go to the park? There's this really cool trail at Ridley Creek State Park.

This would also all be so much easier if you had a car. Hurry up and get your license ☺. Okay there's a nun walking down the hall. Gotta go. See you after school! ♡

There's a lot of numbers there to process. I'm nervous I'm going to mess it up somehow. But what stands out to me the most is that he knows my schedule. He actually listens to me when I speak. I didn't even know what time he was done with school. Obviously I'm not going to admit that.

Waiting for cheerleading practice to be over would make me late, so I take the bus after school. The ride home worsens my ever-present nausea, and my body temperature is definitely up a few degrees. My throat thickens. I unzip my backpack and hold it on my lap in case I need to transform it into a barf bag. There are fifteen cackling freshmen in the seats in front of me. Their laughs pierce my eardrums. For the first time ever, I wish I would just float to the top of the bus. The looks on their faces would silence them for the rest of my ride. I rock back and forth until I get to my stop.

It's 2:40 p.m. when I get off the bus and all I know is that I'm supposed to be at the Starbucks at 3 p.m. I punch in our garage code and watch the garage door rattle its way open. I pull out a piece of gum from my bag, pop it in my mouth, and wheel my bike to the street.

The freezing air feels good on my face. It keeps my palms from getting too sweaty. The sun is setting, and the sky seems like it's getting dark fast. Hopefully, we can make the most of these two hours out in the wilderness. Plus, this could be the last time we hang out before seeing Dr. Ivan. I don't know if things will change after that visit. I don't know what our hangouts will be like. Knowing what to expect with this hike is comforting me.

But I can't keep this up. I feel like I could sleep for a week straight right now from the stress I've had thinking about the unknown. I want to see Dr. Ivan to feel better, but at the same time I don't. If I go to her, I'm admitting that these powers aren't going away.

I glide down the hill. My wheels click as they pick up speed. Jordan is standing on the sidewalk by the Starbucks drive-thru sign. He's wearing his long navy parka and the furry hood is pulled over his head. It isn't zipped all the way up and I can see his maroon tie and white collared dress shirt from school. My cheeks flush.

I pump the brakes, then take my feet off the pedals in front of him.

"Looking snazzy," I say, flipping my hair out of my eyes.

"You're looking pale," he says. "Are you still not feeling great?"

"Am I? Yeah, I'm not my best right now, to be honest. I think the stress from everything is just getting to me. I don't think it's the powers."

He frowns. "I'm going to fix this soon. We'll get to Dr. Ivan. She'll make you feel better. I promise." He steps toward me and pulls me into a hug. I'm still sitting on the bike, so my head rests perfectly against his chest. For a moment, I'm healed.

"We don't have to do this tonight," he says. "You should've told me."

"No, I want to do this. This is your thing. I'm still functioning, obviously."

"Are you sure? We can go watch a movie or paint." He sighs.

"It's just the way it's going to be for a little while until we figure out what's actually going on."

He rubs his jaw.

"What's wrong?" I ask.

He shrugs. "I'm just thinking. When this happened to me it was an accident...it wasn't controlled. But I did this to you."

"You're looking at it the wrong way. When it happened to me, it was an accident too. You had no idea this would happen. And neither did I. I'm not blaming you, so don't feel bad."

He nods, tugging his tie. "I don't want you to feel stuck with me."

I grab his shoulder. "I want to be with you now more than ever," I say. "I need you. You're the only person I have now."

"It's you and me."

I sniff. "You and me."

There's a pause.

"I also don't want to miss the opportunity to see you hike in your school uniform," I say.

He smiles. "I probably should've brought a change of clothes, but I forgot and I didn't want to waste time to go home and change."

"I'm glad you forgot. It's cute. It'll be the classiest hike Ridley Creek State Park has ever seen."

He laughs. "You're the best." He steps behind me to climb onto the pegs, but I grab his arm. "Do you mind driving to the park?" I ask. "My legs are tired."

"Yeah, of course."

We switch positions and I grip his shoulders. He's wearing fingerless gloves and wraps his hands around the handlebars. He kicks us forward, sending us rolling past the Starbucks. We leave the busy road with strip malls and gas stations to a more wooded, narrow street. There's no bike lane, and a few cars honk at us as they pass. I lean my body from side to side to avoid being clipped by a passing car's side mirror or overgrown tree branches.

It takes us about fifteen minutes to get to the park. We bike for as long as we can before the signs for trails start pointing into the woods and there's no more paved path to bike along. I dismount. Jordan locks my bike around a metal post that holds a dog poop bag dispenser. There are no cars in the parking lot or people at the entrance of the trail. I guess it's not so normal to go on a hike when it's thirty degrees outside. But I like the idea of it being just Jordan and me all alone in the woods. It's kind of how I feel in this relationship. There's this secret growing around us, and we're right in the center of it.

Jordan stops at the foot of the trail. He looks around, squinting into the distance.

"What?" I ask.

"Nothing," he says. "I'm just making sure we're not being followed."

I nod. We stand motionless. I listen to the area around us. The only noise I hear is the sound of winter silence.

"Do you think we're okay?" I ask.

"*Okay* is a complicated word in our case."

I sigh.

"I'm okay to go in here if you are," he says.

"I'm okay."

Jordan grabs my hand and locks his fingers with mine. "Ready?" he asks at the foot of the trail. There's white lettering painted onto the tree in front of us that says *Trail E*.

A shock runs up my arm. I squeeze his hand. "Yeah," I say. We're both grinning as we take our first steps into the woods.

My head cranes up. All the trees are bare. The branches create a ceiling above us and cut across the deep blue sky. A few crows caw in the distance. There's rustling of dried leaves. It's most likely squirrels, but hopefully a cute chipmunk will pop out if they're not hibernating or something.

The trail isn't paved. Instead, a bunch of stones are wedged about in the muddy snow. I walk carefully, avoiding the larger rocks and fallen tree branches so I don't twist an ankle.

"I miss hiking," Jordan says.

"Did you do it a lot in Arizona?"

"It's all I did."

"Really?"

"Yeah. When I said I grew up in a town in the desert with nothing around it, I meant it."

"Nothing?"

"Literally nothing."

"Except for that new Starbucks."

He smirks. "There was that. And much better hiking."

"Much better?"

"Um, yeah. This all looks like a horror movie with gray trees reaching ominously into the sky and dead leaves blowing across the street twenty-four seven. In Arizona there's red mountains and green cactuses and pink flowers and sun and rivers—"

"Rivers? I thought you didn't have water out there."

He laughs and punches my arm. "There's water. Actually, floating down the Salt River is one of the most fun things to do around my hometown."

"I'm just teasing," I say.

"I need to take you there sometime."

There's a fallen tree running along the side of the path. I let go of Jordan's hand and hop on top of the log. I extend my arms out to the side and place one foot in front of the other, slowly walking beside Jordan. Some of the dead bark crumbles beneath my feet.

"You can't walk on cactuses like you can trees," I say.

"Got me there."

"Just wait until summer. It gets a lot prettier. And when the weather gets warm, everyone runs out of their houses like they've never seen the sun before. I know of a river I can take you to."

"Sounds perfect."

He smiles up at me, closing his right eye as a thin ray of setting sun hits his face through the trees. His tan cheeks are red from the cold air. A summer with Jordan would be too perfect. Waking up to that smile every day with no school and the whole day ahead of us to do whatever we want sounds like a dream. There's no reason why it can't be my reality.

We'd eat endless Dairy Queen Blizzards for breakfast. I could introduce him to new flavor combinations besides the standard Oreo and vanilla ice cream. He's definitely a Brownie Batter kind of guy. After that we'd go on a perpetual hike through a green forest that doesn't need to be cut short by the darkness. We'd wash off our sweat in the nearby river, shirtless. Then we'd end the night in his basement with a successful make-out session and fall asleep watching a Netflix original crime documentary series. The make-out session would be successful because by then I'd be an experienced kissing expert.

We reach a fork in the path. To the left, it's a flat, even trail similar to the one we're on now. To the right, it's a steep, narrow climb up a hill. Jordan points to the right.

"You up for it?" he asks.

My mind is up for anything with Jordan. My body, not so much. I'm pretty sure my tonsils are swollen. I'll most likely need surgery soon. There's a constant flow of snot from my right nostril and my left one is completely clogged, stopping all airflow. Whenever I turn my head, it feels as though my neck bones are grinding against one another. There's a ten-pound weight in the front of my skull, weighing it down. The effects of my changing body are starting to be overwhelming.

"Let's do it," I say, because my heart is pounding toward the hill. My head can survive these symptoms. I don't know if my heart can survive letting down Jordan.

Wooden steps are built into the side of the hill—which I realize is more like a *mountain* as we inch closer to the top. We stomp up the makeshift stairs and use nearby tree branches to pull ourselves up the trail faster. I walk behind Jordan. A thin layer of slush forms along the bottom of his black dress shoes. I wipe my nose with my sleeve every other second. Luckily, the snot freezes on the fabric pretty quick once it hits the air, reducing the risk of webs of snot spreading across my body.

The trees begin to lose their shadows. I look back along the trail, and I can't see the fork in the road where we began our ascent.

"When should we head back?" I ask, my chest heaving. "It'd probably be, you know, a good idea not to walk back through the pitch-black."

"We're almost at the top," he says. "I can see where the stairs end. Come on." He waves me along.

I take a deep breath and lunge up the remaining stairs. My thighs are burning.

"I can't believe you've never been here before," he says. "It's so close to your house."

I scratch my head. I guess it is pretty wild that I dream of going to college in Colorado for the outdoors when I haven't even been to the outdoors around my own home. Truth is, I like my daily routine. It keeps me around the right people and protects me from the evil hands of people like the Blatts. It's also easy to follow and makes my days predictable.

But then a person like Jordan can come into your life and burn your daily routine to the ground—literally—and you find yourself hiking the trails of a state park in your backyard that you didn't even know existed. I might like my routine, but I'm starting to think my routine isn't good for me. It keeps me from meeting new people and doesn't let the right hands have a chance with me. Plus, who wants predictable when I could have never predicted Jordan coming into my life?

Jordan reaches the top first and places his hands on his hips. He turns to me, smiles, and then looks back over the horizon. I reach him a few seconds later, and we stand shoulder to shoulder.

"Oh, cool," I say. The sun falls through thin white clouds on the other side of the hill. Pink hues paint the sky. An old stone barn sits in a clearing at the bottom of the hill, surrounded by uncut grass dancing in the light breeze.

Jordan sinks to the ground beside me, and I follow his lead. The layer of snow freezes my butt, so I lock my arm with his for warmth.

He stares at the sunset, but I stare at the side of his face, wondering how he's real. The orange glow from the sky deepens the shadow cast beneath his thick brown eyebrows. His eyes are set back, in caves of fire and wonder. I kiss his cheek. He turns to me, smiles with closed lips, and kisses my cheek back.

"A good first hike, huh?" he says.

"A great one."

"Did you bring any water?" He takes a deep breath.

"No. Was I supposed to?"

He laughs. "I don't know. I didn't bring any either."

"Guess we're not as good at hiking as we think."

"Can you get dehydrated in the cold weather?"

"That's a good question. I mean, we're not, like, sweating profusely from the sun."

"True. I guess our bodies don't follow normal biological expectations anymore either."

I cough into my elbow and nod at the landscape in front of us. "See, it's pretty here. Like Arizona. But in a different way."

"I'm happy I'm here."

"Have you made any other friends yet?"

He shakes his head while picking at a strand of grass peeking out of the snow. "Not really. There's this one girl who's in, like, five of my classes. We talk all day, but I haven't seen her outside school yet. I don't know if we technically can be considered friends."

"Is she your orientation buddy?"

"Yeah, how did you know that?"

I shrug. "Just guessing. Can I ask you something?"

"Of course."

"I know you came here to get away from HydroPro, but are you planning on moving again? Like, after this semester."

He shakes his head. "I hope not. The last thing I want to do is start over again. If I can keep HydroPro out of my hair, I want to stay here as long as I can."

"Cool," I say, smiling. "Also, I wouldn't consider that girl your friend."

He laughs. "Plus, there's you." He grabs my knee. "You're my best friend here."

The stinging in my throat intensifies. I look up at the trees, and my eyes well with water. It might be from the cold, or it might be from the displaced liquid rising from my chest as it hollows. Is that all we are? Friends? I want it to be more so badly. I want *us* to be more. Maybe I'm moving too fast? Maybe he still thinks I'm scared of him? Maybe he wants me to bring it up first? I bite my lip, frustrated at myself for not knowing how this works. I look at the ground and the snow has melted around our bodies.

Our eyes meet and his flicker down to my lips.

"I know you're feeling down, but is it okay if I still kiss you?" he asks.

I sniff, then wipe my nose with my sleeve. "If you want. I'm kind of gross," I say, looking myself up and down.

"I want." He leans in and kisses me slowly.

His lips, we meet again. One of my favorite places to be.

He places his hand on my inner thigh. This kiss is wetter than usual. His breath scorches my chin.

I feel a slow drip of snot reaching the edge of my top lip. I pull away to wipe my face. He keeps his hand on my leg.

"You know what else I want?" he asks.

"What?" I inspect the booger on my sleeve.

"To be more than friends."

My skin tingles. Maybe I just got my answer as to how this works.

And maybe getting an answer rather than a question is actually kind of awkward. I don't know how to reply to this statement piece that just hopped off his lips. Is he asking me to be his boyfriend or is this something he's thinking about? Does he want to be more than friends now? Or is this his second body paragraph where's he's still building evidence and he's waiting to get to the conclusion before boyfriend status?

"Oh," I say. I start laughing, and I'm not sure why.

"What's so funny?" His face reddens and he rubs his chin.

I shake my head. I'm trying to say something, but words can't come out of my mouth because it won't relax into a non-smiling position.

I turn, looking into the trees to catch my breath. I pull my cheeks down to remove my perma-smile and swallow hard. I locate the nearest tree root in case I need to grab it to keep myself from floating to the sky.

I turn back to him. He's staring at me. "I was serious," he says. He throws a piece of grass in my face.

"I know." My giggling ends. "Can I ask you a question?" I ask. He nods.

"Do you want to be my boyfriend?"

"I want," he whispers, nodding like a puppy with his lips slightly parted.

We kiss again, and this time, I let the snot run over my top lip. No way am I pulling away from this.

I don't know how long we kiss. But when we stop it's nearly dark. I look at Jordan—I mean my boyfriend—and grin from ear to ear. I have a boyfriend now. And not just any boyfriend. The hottest superpowered boyfriend to ever exist.

"Speaking of being more than friends now," I say. "Kirsten is having a Nationals send-off party. You should come. It could be the perfect place to debut my new boyfriend." I grin.

"I can come under one condition," he says.

"What's that?"

"That I get to be by your side all night."

"Done!"

"Deal. Shall we, then?" he asks as he stands. He reaches out to me. I clasp his hand, and he hoists me to my feet. I brush off my butt and flick my hair from my face.

Over Jordan's shoulder, a shadowy figure darts behind a tree. My body stiffens. I squint to make out what I just saw. A twig snaps to our left, and Jordan jumps to my side. Every spark of joy that was inside my body dissipates.

"Jordan," I say, swallowing. "Is someone here?"

"I think we need to go," he says. His head swivels in all directions. His eyes are wide.

"Is it them? Is it HydroPro?"

"It must be. Let's go." He grabs my arm. I take one step, and my body immediately gets sucked toward the sky. With no ceiling to prevent me from floating infinitely away, I scream.

Jordan gasps. He squeezes my hand tighter and doesn't let go. His shoes lift an inch off the ground.

My body inverts. My feet point to the trees and my face to the ground. All my blood rushes to my skull. And it's hot blood. The temperature of my head feels close to 150 degrees. The pressure behind my eyes is going to push them from their sockets at any moment.

Jordan grips my arm with both of his hands. He pulls me to his body. His feet touch the dirt again.

His hands are on my forearm, then my elbow, then my biceps, and now they're under my armpit. I'm getting closer to earth.

"Relax," Jordan says through gritted teeth. "Help me out."

The weight of my head makes it impossible to think of anything else. I was just on such a high. I finally got a boyfriend and now he's going to be taken from me. Sweat seeps from my pores. The droplets travel in the reverse direction of gravity from my stomach to my chest, and from my neck to my forehead.

"I'm going to have to knock you out," Jordan says. "I don't know what else to do. They're going to see us!"

"Just do it," I mumble. Drool slides out of the corner of my mouth. "I'm in so much pain. Hurry and do it."

He bites his lip. He lets go of my arm and quickly places his hands on my shoulders before I float away. He closes his eyes.

A wave of heat explodes across my upper body like a bolt of lightning. There's a pop, and Jordan shoots off me and across the sky. His body plows through brush and smacks into a tree. Smoke fills the air between us. I fall and my stomach slams into the ground. Jordan settles a few feet away from me. He pushes himself up and tousles his hair.

I sit up and stare at him—not passed out, not blacked out, but... fully awake.

"Why didn't that work?" I ask. "I mean, it worked a little...I'm on the ground. But I'm still awake."

"I don't know," Jordan says quickly. He stands and brushes his hands together. "We need to see Dr. Ivan now. No more delaying. I don't know what's going on." His voice is panicked.

I stand and run to him. We embrace, then turn toward the trail home but freeze approaching the clearing. Six people stare at us, blocking the path. I recognize them all. They're the same people who have been following us. One has a gun on his hip. But the man with the long face is notably absent. I look at Jordan. In an instant, a thin ice-blue halo grows around his pupils. His eyes turn an orange-gold.

twenty-four

Unlike in my regular life before Jordan, everyone is staring at me. It's something I am still getting used to, but I'm positive that I don't like it.

Before I take a step, a smoke grenade lands at our feet. It pops, erupting gray smoke into the air. The plume forces its way into my throat, sending me into a coughing fit. Our surroundings become obscure.

I grab Jordan's hand and it's steaming hot. He kicks my feet, and we dart in the opposite direction.

We take a few strides, but in seconds, we reach the edge of the hill we were just gazing over. I peer down the steep drop. Broken tree branches, boulders, and piles of dead leaves are scattered across the ground. "Which way?" I ask. I turn and see that the gaggle of HydroPro stalkers are approaching through the clouds of smoke.

"The only way," Jordan responds. He takes off down the hill. I exhale and quickly follow.

"Are we going home?" I ask.

"They're coming for us. We can't go home yet."

"We didn't do anything wrong, though. And we're not sure what they saw." I smack a branch out of my face. "We should let them question us. They can't kidnap two kids. We'll call the cops."

He shakes his head. "We can't. It doesn't matter what the cops think. If we say anything about the flames and the floating and our bodies, the cops will think we're up to something. The people from HydroPro won't. They know it's real. They saw us using our powers just now when I tried to knock you out. They'll take me. And they'll take you. I escaped once before, but I don't know if I can do it again. This time, they could take us away from everything we know forever. We'll be experiments, not boyfriends. We need to get to Dr. Ivan."

Shouts burst in the night behind us. "Hurry!" Jordan says.

We sprint down the hill. The frozen ground helps us move quickly. HydroPro's flashlights brighten areas of the field in front of us. I duck whenever I feel a light on the back of my neck. I watch Jordan's feet as I follow his path. He pants.

"Head for those trees," he says, pointing into the distance.

"I'm trying."

Jordan makes a sharp turn. The ground is uneven as hell. My knees are shaking and my ankles are sore. Our bodies bounce up and down as we tear through the grass. Crunching leaves fill the night silence, and squirrels and birds scamper from us as we make our way to the trees.

Jordan cranes his neck back to glance at HydroPro. "They're not that close. Just keep going. Go in zigzags so we don't leave a trail in the grass."

We reach the wooded area. It gets darker as we lose the overhead light from the flashlights. But it's not a thick patch of trees. It only takes us a few seconds to run through it. On the other side is a highway.

Jordan abruptly stops. I slam into his back and grunt.

"Are you okay?" he asks.

"Over this way!" someone yells.

Jordan puts his finger over his lips.

Flashlight beams dance in the trees around us. We duck to the ground and crawl behind the biggest tree trunk we can find. Boots crunch across the ground at a quickening pace nearby.

"We're going to get caught," I whisper. "We look guilty of something now. We should've stayed."

Jordan peeks around the tree but jumps back beside me. His eyes are orange and blue. He's blinking rapidly. I grab his hand, then close my eyes. The heat against the insides of my eyelids warms my face. My breaths are shallow and quick.

A moment goes by, and my hand becomes heavy. Jordan pulls on it. I hear a familiar giggle from him, which forces me to open my eyes.

I'm taking in my surroundings from midair, halfway up the tree. My body is numb. Jordan smiles beneath me. I pull back on his hand.

"What the—"

"Shh," he whispers. "This is good. Keep going." His right hand clasps mine and his left arm hangs at his side.

I kick my legs through the air like I'm swimming as I try to steer us to a nearby branch. Most of the trees are dead, but there are some evergreens between them that can hopefully provide us with camouflage.

The voices of HydroPro grow louder as they near the tree line.

We're about thirty feet up when we reach the first sturdy branch. I wrap my legs around it to prevent us from floating any higher. I pull Jordan next to me. Together, we wedge ourselves between two branches.

"Go over there," he says, pointing to a branch that's surrounded by more leaves. We shinny across trees like Tarzan and Jane. We crouch, watching HydroPro search the ground beneath us. Our backs are against a center trunk. I cover my mouth to quiet my breathing.

"See them?" one asks.

"No. This is the end of the line too," another says. "The highway is on the other side. Unless they jumped into traffic."

Jordan's foot slips, and his shoe scratches the branch as it slides forward. He gasps at the sound, but then slaps his hand over his mouth. The people below us swivel their heads.

"Check the trees," one says.

They congregate beneath us, shooting their flashlight beams skyward. I let out a whimper as I watch the lights bounce along the leaves. A beam juts an inch from my hand, and I snap it to my chest. I squeeze my eyes closed. Jordan's body rises up and down against mine as he breathes.

"Let's circle back to the entrance of the park," another says. "We can check if there's any activity near their homes as well."

The others nod. They stomp out of the woods, leaving us alone in darkness.

I exhale as I drop my hands to my sides.

"Where's the closest Blatt construction site?" Jordan quickly says.

"What? I don't know. Why?"

"We're going to set a distraction."

"We're going to set a fire?"

Jordan nods. "Yes."

I grab his arm. "Jordan, we can't do that on purpose."

"We have to. You heard them. They know where we live. They know where *you* live." His voice cracks. "It doesn't sound like they're going to stop trying to kidnap us. Another fire will take the heat off us so we can get to Dr. Ivan."

"No pun intended?"

"No pun."

I huff. "This won't work."

"It will. Now float me down from this tree. We're wasting time."

I feel like Superman carrying Jordan in my arms through the air. It's as if he loses all his body weight when the hydrogen inside me takes over and floats me to where I need to be. My feet lightly touch the ground. We run along the highway sound wall, in the opposite direction of HydroPro.

We reach the new housing development on Liberty Pike, the place where Jordan set his first fire. Now, hopefully, it will be the place where he sets his last.

This development is big single-family homes. The model home—I guess they converted another one since Jordan burned down the first one—is lit up with multiple spotlights in the front yard. All the houses look the same except for the different colors of their shutters. A few of the completed homes have *Sold* signs by their curb. Piles of dirt and orange-plastic fencing are strewn about the street. We stop next to a parked bulldozer.

"Which one?" I ask, out of breath.

Jordan looks up and down the street. Some of the streetlights are working. Others just have wires sticking out of the top with no lightbulb.

"That one," he says, pointing to a house that's only wood planks and studs. It doesn't have siding or faux rock down the front.

"Are you sure about this?"

"Yes."

"But your powers? You're not supposed to use them like this."

"I won't tell if you don't." He stares at me blankly.

"Okay." I run my hands down my face. "Let's get this over with."

We walk to the back of our chosen house. There's a patch of trees behind us where we plan to make our getaway once the fire is lit. I look around to make sure no one is watching us. I listen for cars. Silence.

Jordan holds up his hand. His palm faces the house. I stand over his shoulder. He closes his eyes. The tips of his fingers start to shimmer. The air is sucked toward him. My hair blows across my forehead. He takes a deep breath before a flame blossoms in his hand.

Cracks of orange crawl up his arms. I take a step back. The flames growing from his hands spin like a tornado. The grimace on his face is an expression I've never seen before.

"Jordan, I think we should stop," I say. "I don't like this!" I grab his arm, trying to pull him away from the house. "There are other ways."

The light from his flames illuminates the entire neighborhood.

Trash blows across the street and the thin, newly planted trees are seconds away from snapping in half from wind force.

"We can't," he mutters with his eyes closed.

He pushes his hands forward, and the flames erupt, engulfing the house. The orange, blue, and yellow waves swallow everything in sight.

Jordan screams as he lets his arms fall. The fire on his hands dissipates. He collapses to his knees. He whimpers, clutching his chest.

"Jordan," I whisper. I run to his side, but when I touch him his skin burns me like never before. Black lines are etched onto his forearms where the flames lined his body, like they permanently charred him.

A piece of the house crumbles beside us. The crackling fire is as loud as fireworks on the Fourth of July.

"Okay, let's go see Dr. Ivan now." My voice is panicked. I shake him, but just for a second. It's the only amount of body contact I can tolerate. He moans.

An orchestra of police sirens and fire trucks plays in the distance. This plan is close to backfiring, and I can't let that happen. The day I get my first boyfriend is going to end well if it's up to me.

I grab Jordan to drag him to the trees. Every movement brings me pain. A sharp, shock-like sensation shoots down my spine. It knocks me to my knees. I press my hands against my temples. My lungs constrict. I can barely breathe. I grab him again and finish carrying him into the cover of the woods. We crumple.

Jordan pulls his phone from his pocket, then extends it to me.

"Call this number," he says.

"What?"

"Call it! We don't have much time. I overdid it." He gasps.

"Fine." I scramble forward and snatch the phone from his fingertips. "What am I saying?" I'm light-headed as I read the screen. The words are blurry.

"Just tell them you're with Jordan Ator and it's a code E nine."

"Is this Dr. Ivan?" I ask. I put the phone to my ear.

Jordan nods. He crawls to me and falls across my chest. He's shaking. He wraps his arms around my shoulders. He squeezes so tight the last remaining bit of air is pushed from my lungs.

"I'm sorry," he says.

"Why are you sorry?" I whisper. It's all I can manage.

"For everything. You're the best."

Someone picks up on the other end of the phone. "Hi?" I ask. "Yes, I'm with Jordan and it's a code E . . . crap, um . . ."

Jordan's neck goes limp. He's like a dead body on top of me.

"Oh, E nine. It's a code E nine. Please help us!"

twenty-five

I wake to the sound of beeping machines. I slowly open my eyes and the amount of light is unbearable. Everything in the room blurs for a moment. The floor and ceiling are white. The walls are clear glass. I'm the only one inside.

I move my hand to brush my hair from my face, but it's tugged back by a dozen colorful wires strapped to my arm. Cool air blows onto my bare feet from a ceiling vent. I don't remember how I got here. I'm wearing a white hospital gown. I feel my face, legs, and stomach. Nothing hurts.

A woman is sitting at a black desk outside my glass box. Her back is to me as she types something onto her computer. The rest of the outer room is empty and gray. It looks like a giant warehouse. Steel beams cut through the concrete floor to the ceiling.

I clear my throat. The woman jumps up and turns to me. She smiles slightly.

She walks to the glass, pulls a mask from a container outside the door, and puts it over her face. She ties the straps tight behind her head, then punches in a code on a keypad. A plate of glass slides open, allowing her to enter the room.

I sit up. "Are you Dr. Ivan?" I ask. My voice is raspy. "How did I get here?"

"I am," she says. She's wearing black pants and a striped button-up shirt with turquoise heels. Her long, wavy brown hair is pushed behind her shoulders.

"How are you feeling?" She clicks some buttons on a few of the machines. Their screens flash different numbers.

"I'd be better if I didn't keep blacking out. Where is Jordan?"

"The blackout was me. I had others from my team help move you. I couldn't let you see them." The mask muffles her voice.

"And Jordan?"

"He's not here right now."

"Not here? Where is he? Is he okay?"

"He's fine."

"Can I see him?"

"I'm afraid that isn't possible."

"What do you mean I can't? What did those people do to him?" I flail my arms. The machines move across the floor as I tug their cords. Their beeping intensifies. "He took me here to be safe and fix this. Did you leave him at the fire? Did you hurt him?"

Dr. Ivan resets a few of the machines. She sits on the edge of my bed. She grabs my arm. "Calm down, please. Dylan, you *are* safe. We didn't leave Jordan at the fire. We secured both of you."

My nostrils flare. "Then why isn't Jordan here too? Why aren't we both safe *here*?"

"He's safe too. But Jordan's case is more complicated than yours."

"How could that be possible when we both"—I wave my hand at my body—"are like this?"

She leans closer to me. "You're safe because no one knows you are living with the same condition. Jordan isn't so lucky. He was here. But then he decided to be moved."

"Moved?" My voice cracks. "To where? Away from HydroPro? They chased us through the woods. I know what they look like; I can help you find them."

She stands and walks to the other side of my bed. She switches an empty bag of fluid with a full one and hooks it up to my IV. I watch the clear liquid slide down the tube into my vein.

"I don't need to find them," she says. "I know who they are. I'm part of the faction that left after they . . . after they decided what they wanted to do with Jordan." She looks away.

I rub my nose. "Why won't they just let him go? He has nothing more for them. Didn't they test him enough?"

"You would think, but no. I'm afraid they'll never be satisfied. There are just too many possibilities—energy sources, heat therapy, medical advances—not to mention the monetary gain. It's unethical and it isn't right." She throws up her hands. "Jordan was affected from their own wrongdoing. They should let him be. But instead they designed several internal projects, simply based off the fact that he exists for them to use. I couldn't be a part of it." She rubs her forehead.

"He doesn't want all of this."

She twitches her head. "I know. I'm helping Jordan as best I can. I am keeping him healthy, extending his life, making sure the fires don't get traced back to him, giving him fireproof clothing, trying to keep his life as normal as possible. Hopefully, one day, he won't have to come see me anymore." She taps her fingers on her leg.

I turn my head to the side.

"You can trust me, Dylan. I'm going to do the same for you."

I look her up and down. "So they know Jordan is in Falcon Crest?"

"Who?"

"HydroPro. The people who want to take him."

"Yes. They do now. We've had to be cautious."

"And me?"

"We're not sure. It might have just been circumstantial that you were there whenever they were close to getting Jordan. They don't know you're with me now."

I nod. I observe the machines next to me. "Am I like Jordan now? Forever?" I scan my body.

She crosses her arms. "Well, your body chemistry has certainly changed. The tests show that. But I have no way to predict the future or how long the manifestations will last." She writes notes on a clipboard hanging from my bed.

"Do you think they will last forever?"

She shrugs while staring at me.

"Okay." I flick the blanket over my feet. I lay my head on a pillow and roll over on my side, facing the glass. "Just let me know when Jordan gets back."

Dr. Ivan sighs. "Dylan, I don't think you're understanding me. Jordan isn't here. He's not in this building. He's not in this city or state. He won't be back. We had to change his location."

My fingers wring the pillow. My hands tremble. "Well, for how long? He said we were going to figure this out together! He said he was..." I inhale. "He said he was dying. Am I going to see him before that?"

Dr. Ivan purses her lips. "Like I said, I can't predict the future." Her voice softens.

I grind my teeth. "Whatever. Can I be alone again?" I ask.

She nods and taps the edge of my bed. "Let me know if you need anything. I'll be just outside the glass."

I finally know where Jordan spent his Saturdays. I know Dr. Ivan. I'm learning more about HydroPro and what they've done to Jordan. I said I would be patient with him and let him reveal things on his own. But this isn't how I wanted to learn. Jordan said he would get me here and he did. I wish he hadn't. I didn't know it meant without him.

twenty-six

I toss and turn for a few hours in bed. I watch Dr. Ivan alternate between typing at her desk and walking along the windows of the warehouse. It's dark outside. I'm reading all the machines and monitoring equipment surrounding me, trying to understand what they're measuring.

Dr. Ivan notices I'm awake. She pulls a few things from a desk drawer before entering my glass chamber.

"Are you ready to go?" she asks.

"I guess I have to be."

She walks to my bedside. She touches my forehead and then nods. She unhooks all the wires from my arms and chest before removing my IV. I rub my wrists and bend my elbows, ensuring they still work. My mouth is dry.

Dr. Ivan pulls a little blue machine from a bag. It has a mouthpiece and long tube. She holds it out to me.

"This is an Elemental Balancer," she says. "Have you ever used an inhaler before?"

"No."

"It's taken the same way. Push on the top and breathe in from the bottom. This will temporarily change your hydrogen composition."

"Whoa, really?" I grab it from her hands and inspect the device. "No heat or floating?"

"No heat or floating. But use it sparingly. Once this canister is empty you can't have another. The back-and-forth is damaging to the body over time."

I sigh. "Kind of like how the air is eating Jordan?"

"Precisely." She hands me the bag. "And now you too. But I am trying to figure out the dynamics between the composition of the air and the composition of your bodies. Mindfulness is how you will conquer this over time. Find a space in your head that makes you feel comfortable and happy. Stay there, and the side effects should fade."

"But what if my happy place is Jordan?"

Dr. Ivan frowns as she writes a final set of notes on her clipboard. She recites an exit protocol for a few minutes that basically says don't mention her, this place, or anything that happened here to anyone.

"One more thing," she says. "I've been messaging your parents through your phone on your behalf—"

"What? You have?" My eyes go wide.

"They're not happy you had a sleepover on a school night at Kirsten's house."

"A sleepover? How long has it been?"

"A day."

I drop the Elemental Balancer on the bed and put my hands on my face. "My parents believed I had a sleepover with Kirsten?"

"Yes. It was for a school project." She says everything so deadpan I almost believe it's true.

"How do you know Kirsten and Perry?"

She checks off something on her paper, ignoring my comment.

"My number has been added to your phone," she continues. Her speech quickens. "I'm going to check in with you every so often. We'll set up another time for you to come in soon. Again, do not tell anyone about this."

"For how long? Do you know how hard that is?"

"No. But Jordan did." She raises an eyebrow.

My stomach sinks.

"There is a nightclub on the ground floor of this building. You're going to walk out through there and call your parents immediately to tell them you're on your way home. Do not text. Call them so they have voice confirmation. They've been asking you to call. Any questions?"

"Um, no?"

"Good. One more thing. Jordan left this for you." She holds out a thin piece of white paper. My heart skips a beat. I take the paper from her hands and unfold it so fast I rip one of the corners. "I think it will help with what I was trying to explain to you earlier."

"Why did he give this to you?"

"I'll be outside," she says, exiting the room.

I read.

Dylan,

If you're reading this, it means you're awake and I finally did something right. It also means you're mad as hell at me.

And you should be. I get it. I'm sorry. I lied to you and tricked you. Most of all, I'm sorry I had to leave you.

But I take back what I apologized for in your bathroom that other night. I'm not sorry I let you get to know me. I'm not sorry I had a crush on you and kissed you. It's because of those things that I had to leave you.

As soon as you got into this situation, I knew I had to get you out. Yesterday was too scary for me and I couldn't bear to see you get hurt . . . because of me. So leaving is the only way for me to fix this for now. Dr. Ivan is going to take care of you. She'll explain more.

I'm hoping I'm only gone for a little while. But don't wait for me. Everything is unpredictable and I can't say if I'll be back as long as HydroPro is still around.

I hate what HydroPro has done to me. Before my accident, I remember being a normal kid in Arizona and wanting everything in the world. But after the accident, I learned the truth about the world and then I wanted none of it. It's not fair what the accident taught me.

On the night you turned, I saw it in your eyes and knew you were scared. I knew then that the world changed for you too.

But in my heart I know that if it wasn't for HydroPro, we would be sitting here together, wanting the world.

Talk soon (hopefully).

Jordan

I cover my mouth with my hand as his words go blurry on the page. I blink, sending a few tears from my eyes. The water spreads the black ink across the paper. I sniff, crumple up the note, and toss it across the room. I slam my head on the pillow.

My mind flashes back to the hours before we got here.

All that time, he knew what he was doing. He knew those hours were possibly our final moments together. He knew he was going to leave. I wish I had known too.

I try to remember his final words, his final smile, how his hair fell on his head. I think of our final hug. I feel his arms over my shoulders and his chest against mine. I clutch my arms around my waist. That hug was different than the rest of our hugs. It was tighter, longer, and more meaningful. Now I realize why.

There were no words to describe the feelings I had for Jordan. I guess it's fitting that he left me in silence.

I follow Dr. Ivan's protocol down to the letter. I call Mom. She explains how she's upset that I not only had a sleepover on a school night but that I also missed family dinner—again. She tells me I'm not allowed to go out this weekend. She thinks my head has been all over the place and that I need a few days to collect myself. I couldn't agree more. In fact, I kind of think I'm grounded by the end of the call. But Mom describes it as more of a self-reflection event.

I take the train home from the city. I glide along the tracks past the lit city skyscrapers and home to the suburbs. Jordan is the only thing on my mind the whole way there.

I think about the fallout from the fire we set before he disappeared. I open Safari and search *Falcon Crest Arsons* to see if there are more news articles. And there's *a lot* of articles. Most are from local news stations and magazines. But one is from a Wilmington, Delaware, news station. Another is from New Jersey. My eyes scan for other cities to see how far the news is spreading.

I click on a video with the caption *String of arsons upsets quiet suburb of Falcon Crest.* A blond woman in a bright blue jacket walks toward the camera. I pop in my earbuds.

"Right now, I'm standing in what was supposed to be a secluded development of twenty luxury homes," she says. "But as you can see from the horrifying image behind me, those homes are now a pile of ash."

The camera cuts from the woman to charred wooden studs piled on the ground. I recognize everything.

"This unlucky site had already seen its model home go up in flames several weeks ago, but last night, another home under construction fell victim to arson."

A fireman appears on the screen. "We haven't seen a string of fires of this magnitude in the twenty years I've been with the department. It's really concerning. . . . Combined with the weather and low nighttime visibility, it made for a real mess. We're lucky none of these fires have been in a home that's currently occupied."

The screen cuts back to the woman. "Lucky indeed. With the arsonist's motive still unknown, residents have been on edge for the past few weeks. Police need your help in identifying two young males believed to have intentionally set one of the fires. All the arsons so far have taken place at one of two Blatt Builders–owned construction sites, and people are wondering what, if any, connection there is between Blatt and these fires."

I lock my phone and toss it in the open seat beside me. I put my hands over my face and let out a soft scream. I bang the back of my head against the seat. Not only is everything getting worse, but I have to deal with this all alone.

When I get home, I step up to the front door and put the Elemental Balancer to my mouth. I press the button at the top and inhale. The air or medicine or whatever burns as it goes down my throat. My vision blacks out, as if I stood up too quickly, and I brace myself against one of the front porch columns.

After a moment, I regain my sight. I shake off the dizziness and head inside.

Mom, Dad, and Cody are sitting on the couch in the living room. Cody is snuggled beneath Mom's arm. Everyone's plates are still on the kitchen table with a bowl of green beans. It's almost as if I've been gone for months.

I lie across them. The Balancer works. They hug me and touch me without getting burned. Cody smacks my butt. Mom gently massages my head with her fingertips. My hair falls forward and covers my face.

My eyes slowly close. I feel like I haven't slept in days even though I was apparently knocked out for an entire twenty-four hours. I leave them before I fall asleep. I don't know how long the Balancer lasts and I'm afraid if I pass out, I'll wake up to the screams of them being burned by my body.

twenty-seven

"Do you think it's a little much if I wear this cropped sweater in February?" Perry asks, spinning in front of the mirror.

"I think you're supposed to wear a shirt under that," Kirsten says.

"Yeah, but that's a little much."

"It could look cute with high-waisted jeans."

"Yeah, maybe. I don't know if I want to wear high-waisted jeans, though."

We're in the fitting room at H&M. It's huge and fits the three of us. I haven't heard anything from Jordan, so my only choice is to continue with life as normal—which includes going to Kirsten's party.

When I call him, the phone doesn't ring and it goes straight to voicemail. When I text him, I get a *Not delivered* message. And when I message him on social media, it never gets read. He has completely and totally cut me off and disappeared.

"Dylan, are you getting anything for the party?" Perry asks, pulling the sweater off over her head. There's an explosion of static shocks. She throws the sweater on a bench. Her hair sticks out in all directions.

"I have my party outfit," I say, tugging on my hoodie.

"You wore that all week."

"And?" My appearance hasn't been my top concern lately.

"I knew something smelled," Perry says.

"I can't show up to the party with a new boy and a new outfit," I say. "Unless you really want the attention to shift from the cheerleading squad to me."

"Oh shoot," Perry says, and puts her finger to her lip.

"Are you going to crack a smile at the party?" Kirsten asks. "Your morosity over the past month is starting to wear on me. We don't need this energy heading into our competition."

I pull my lips back to show all my teeth. "How's this?" I ask.

They laugh.

I'm really not a big drinker or a big partier in the first place. The parties themselves always remind me of when those bearded men in raincoats on the Discovery Channel dump a bin of fish on a boat and all the fish are flapping and floundering about—there's a lot of noise, it smells, people are wet, and everyone's eyes have the same hopeless look of desperation.

Truth is, I am going to Kirsten's party without a boy and a new outfit, so there won't be any attention on me. Which is for the best, if I'm being honest. I haven't told them that Jordan is gone because I don't know how to explain it. In their eyes, Jordan is a normal boy. There's no reason why he would leave me without warning other than him just being a mean person. They would hate him, and I don't want them to think that about him. Instead, I told them he has a family party and might come to Kirsten's house after if it finishes early enough.

But in the back of my mind, I can't help but think how I mentioned this party to Jordan before he disappeared, and he said he would come. I know it's not healthy, but I am heading into the party with the thought that he's going to show up. This was communicated before he left, so maybe his promise still stands. Maybe this is when he plans to return to me and make everything okay again.

"Did you invite Darlene?" I ask Kirsten as we leave the mall. I toss my coffee in a trash can.

"I don't have her number," she says. "Why?"

"I want to invite her to the party. I follow her on Instagram. Is it weird if I invite her on there?"

Inviting Darlene will give me some sort of purpose at this party. I'm thinking my first order of business in correcting my life post-Jordan is fixing my relationship with Darlene.

"Do you really think your fight was that bad that you need to invite her? Have you ever even hung out with her outside school?"

"No. But she was being so nice, and I was rude. I just feel bad."

"You might be the only person she knows at the party."

"I mean, she can bring a friend. She's definitely cooler than me, so I'm sure she has plenty. She did tell me not to talk to her, though."

"Oh, then definitely don't message her."

"What if it was code for *Please reach out*?"

"It wasn't," Perry says. "She wasn't flirting with you."

"Agreed," Kirsten says. "A few of the other cheerleaders came up to me yesterday at practice and asked if they could bring friends. I said any junior can come. If she wants to be there, she'll show. Otherwise, just give her space."

I grunt. "I hate playing games. This is why I don't interact with people."

"I have been texting Savanna, though," Kirsten says.

"What?" Perry and I ask in unison.

"For what purpose?" I press.

"For the party. Relax," Kirsten says.

"I thought you said you weren't going to invite her personally."

"Well, you're right about that. But I decided to use that as an icebreaker and then asked her if I could interview her dad for the news project."

"What did she say?" I ask.

"She said she would ask her dad. He was just with my parents the other night, so I can't imagine he would say no."

"Any leads yet on who is doing the fires?" I bite my fingers.

"A few." Kirsten smirks. "But I can't say anything yet. I don't want to spoil my article for you."

If Savanna shows up to the party, that could be another good thing. I can't believe I even thought that in my head. But ever since the Lifeline flyer fell from her arms, I've been thinking about what it means and what to do.

The Google takeaway is that I should talk to her about it and ask questions. I don't want to go to our school counselor or tell my parents because I'm not entirely sure she is actually suicidal. She might have been taking the brochure to someone else or doing her own research for a school project. Post-Jordan, I think it's better to not make assumptions about people. The last thing I want to do is put unnecessary pressure on her.

But I can't get the look in her eyes out of my head. I spoke its language. The way she looked at me when she saw the brochure in my hands was so familiar. It was begging me to bring something up that she couldn't bring up on her own. I don't need to have a conversation with her tonight. I just want her to know that the opportunity to talk to me is there. Everything Savanna Blatt does is calculated. If she was asking for help, I don't want to ignore her.

After the mall, we drive to Party City to get a few supplies. The party starts in two hours. Kirsten rushes us into the store. She decides we need to split up to get everything as quickly as possible. I'm tasked with paper products. Apparently, it's all I can manage. Perry is assigned snack foods and sodas, and Kirsten says she'll get some decorations.

I walk to the paper product aisle expecting to grab some red cups and white napkins, but it offers me so much more. My eyes go wide at all the options. I look up and down the shelves and there are all kinds of cups and plates with different themes I never knew I wanted to experience. I'm suddenly excited about this party, and the feeling is welcome.

A Day in Paris theme? Yes. How romantic. But Jordan isn't coming and I don't want to be reminded of love.

Floral Tea Party theme? Classy. The paper cups have little paper handles that fold out to make them look like teacups.

Black Light theme? Yikes. The cups are neon, and the packaging contains little plastic syringes that I guess you use to shoot liquor into your mouth. Screams *date rape* to me. Pass.

Princess theme? No. Kirsten needs to simmer down with that. I don't even want to present her with that option.

Mexican Fiesta theme? Could be fun. But I don't trust some of the degenerates of the junior class to not be racist.

I decide to go with the Floral Tea Party cups, napkins, and plates because why not. They match nicely, and I'm laughing at the thought of people drinking beer with the little teacup handles.

I shuffle to the registers with everything clutched in my arms. Perry and Kirsten stand in line at register four. Kirsten picks through a rack of key chains next to the candy.

"What are those?" Kirsten asks, grabbing the Floral Tea Party napkins from my arms. She flips them up and down to inspect both sides. "Is this all they had?"

"Yep!" I say. "And you're going to use them."

When we get back to Kirsten's house, she locks the front door and explains that everyone has to come and go through the basement. This is a strict no-main-house party. The girls go to Kirsten's room to get ready, and I head to the basement to set up all the decorations. I arrange twelve Floral Tea Party cups in beer-pong formation on a folding table.

I put all breakables, like candlesticks, vases, and fake potted plants, in a few cabinets underneath the TV. I step to the center of the room and look at the bare coffee table and shelves, placing my hands on my hips. I huff.

I realize I have no idea where all the decorations were in the first place. Mrs. Lush is going to sniff out the party the second she walks down here. If one item is out of place, she'll know.

Last summer, I slept over at Kirsten's house when her parents went to a wedding out of town. She wasn't allowed to have people over, so she decided we would just watch a movie. I lay on the three-cushion couch, and Kirsten lay on the two-cushion couch in her living room. I propped two pillows on the armrest during the movie, and the next day when Mrs. Lush came home, she asked Kirsten why the couch cushions on both couches were in "sleeping arrangements" and who she had over to the house. Kirsten better have had this basement decor memorized; otherwise, it's over tomorrow.

"We should cheers to something," Perry says. We're sitting in the basement before the party starts. She pours some alcohol and soda into three cups. I sniff the liquid and snarl. "Bleh."

"Cheers to..." Kirsten says. She tilts her head to the side and stares at the ceiling. "Oh, duh...cheers to Falcon Crest Explorers Varsity Cheerleading winning Nationals!" She beams.

"Winning? Ambitious cheers," I say.

"That's right!"

"My turn," Perry says.

"Oh, we're each doing a cheers?" I ask.

"Yes."

"Okay." I start thinking about all my cheers options in my head.

"Cheers to Dylan and Jordan having a lifelong relationship full of love and happiness."

I frown and lower my cup.

"Aw, Perry," Kirsten says. "That's sweet."

"Deep," I grunt. "But I doubt that's happening."

"Whoa," Kirsten says. "Why are you so miserable? You haven't been able to stop talking about Jordan for weeks, and now everything is doom and gloom."

"I'm sorry," I say. "Cheers." I raise my glass and gently tap their cups.

"Your turn," Perry says, turning to me. "Try not to be too depressing."

"I have one. I think there's a certain man from your past we should revisit with this cheers."

"Keaton?"

"Yes."

If I can't have love, I at least want my friends to have it.

"I think it's been festering," I say.

"Festering?"

"Bubbling underneath the surface. I think the love is still there. Plus, prom season is coming up. You have to position yourself now before everyone gets snatched up."

"What made you think of this?"

"I don't know. Just want my friends to be happy."

Kirsten laughs. "You get your first crush and now you're Cupid."

"I'm just saying." I hold my hands up. "Hear me out. Your hair is on point. He's going to be here tonight. If you do anything that ends up being awkward, you're gone all next week and won't have to see him. The stars are aligned for this one."

"I mean, fine," Perry says. "If we're going to be ambitious tonight, then cheers to Keaton being my boyfriend again, Ms. Gurbsterter getting out of my hair, and me not getting swallowed by a crocodile in Florida."

"Wooo!" we shout.

Cheers to Jordan coming back, cheers to Jordan coming back, cheers to Jordan coming back, cheers to Jordan coming back.

I repeat this in my head. We clink our glasses together.

Well, shocker of the century, but it turns out doing a cheers before taking a drink does absolutely nothing. This party took a turn toward out of control literally fifteen minutes after the senior cheerleading girls arrived and Jordan didn't come back. I don't know if I'm more pissed that I don't get to see him or that I spent my whole day prepping for this stupid party and now have no reason to be in attendance.

My teacups didn't work out well either. Which I'm disappointed about. The beer disintegrated the paper cups and they weren't very durable for beer pong. People started shouting and complaining about having paper residue on their fingers. How was I supposed to know that would happen? Some senior guy ran to Wawa to get red Solo cups and now the party has lost all its character.

I'm still in my original position at the bar. My feet haven't moved in two hours. It's nice to be in the corner of the room because no one can lurk behind me, and I have a really good view for Jordan-watching.

The basement is jam-packed. The crowd stretches from wall to wall. I guess that's one of the downsides of having a ginormous suburban basement—it can hold your entire student body and even have room for the junior classes from three neighboring high schools. Honestly, though, I don't recognize 75 percent of the people here.

Two girls with teal hair stand over a bowl of Doritos in front of me. They each pick up a chip every other minute and take little, gradual bites like squirrels. They don't say much to each other. Instead, they communicate via a mixture of nods and eye rolls.

Some tall skinny guy with a cigarette tucked behind his ear speedwalks back and forth through the basement. He's carrying a bottle of vodka. There's a chain hanging from his pocket and an alien-head patch ironed onto his jeans. He hasn't spoken to anyone here since he's arrived, so he's either lost or looking to beat somebody up.

There's a crash and a few shrieks by the coffee table. I jump. A shock runs down my body.

"Dammit," I mutter. The Jenga tower finally collapsed. I was mentally preparing myself for that but got distracted by this shady snake slithering through Kirsten's basement.

Perry emerges from the crowd and walks over to me. She ducks below a few sweaty arms. "Have you seen Kirsten?" she asks.

"No."

"I hope she's okay. I'm sure she's freaking out about this."

I take a drink even though I don't like what's in my cup.

"Keaton's on his way," she continues.

"Oh, yay! Cheers to that," I say. I smack my cup against hers. "Jordan isn't coming anymore." I pout.

"Aw, no." She puts her arm around me.

"It's okay. I'll live vicariously through you and Keaton. Your cheers for me didn't work, so it's up to you to keep superstitions alive for us."

"No pressure," she says, and takes a drink.

"None."

"Do you know these people here?"

"None."

"I know that girl doing a keg stand." She points to a girl with bleach-blond hair upside down in the air. Two boys hold up her legs and beer spews from her mouth. "She goes to St. Helena's. You should ask Jordan about her."

"I'll pass. How do you know her?"

"We had confirmation together in seventh grade. We both picked Saint Maria Goretti as our confirmation name, and she said I was a 'dumb, copycat, public-school bitch.'"

"Cute."

A tall, hot boy appears at the bottom of the basement steps. Keaton Cyrus has arrived. He's wearing black jeans and a forest-green quarter-zip. His hair is perfectly coiffed. Perry's face lights up, and it's too obvious she still likes him. He makes eye contact with us and waves. He slinks through the crowd in our direction. His head stays above most of the other bobbing bodies.

"Hey, guys," he says. He hugs Perry. He holds out a closed fist to me, and I pound it because we're bros.

"Are you the bartender, Dylan?" he asks.

"Um, I've been standing here all night, so I guess I might be. What can I get you?" I pick up a towel and throw it over my shoulder.

He laughs. "What is there?"

"A keg." We glance at the keg and it's surrounded by drunken couples rubbing each other and people licking the nozzle. "Which you probably don't want."

He laughs again.

"Put vodka in Coke for us," Perry says.

"Done!"

I line up the cups and pour. Keaton sings the Drake lyrics coming from the speaker under his breath. I slide Perry and Keaton their cups and grab my phone. I text Jordan that I miss him and ask if he is okay. The messages immediately bounce back with red exclamation points and say, *Not delivered*. I slurp my drink through a straw, and it's truly awful. I pat my tongue against the roof of my mouth.

Keaton starts coughing. I look up from my phone.

"Whoa, Dylan. How many shots did you put in this?" he asks.

"I don't know. Are you supposed to count?"

"Apparently not."

I hang with Perry and Keaton for a little while, but I feel myself shrinking into irrelevance beside the bar as the night goes on. Most of the time they're talking around me about memories that aren't mine, and I kind of get the sense I'm intruding. I chug the rest of my drink and toss my cup into the bar sink.

"I'm going to go look for Kirsten," I say. Which is partly a lie. I'm going to look for Jordan too. I know we just became boyfriends a couple days ago and I'm borderline obsessive tonight, but he told me I was dying, then left the state. That's a different level of ghosting I never even thought about, let alone prepared for.

I put my hand on Perry's back and take my first step of the night. My foot is so heavy.

Perry screams. "Ow, Dylan!" She lurches forward into Keaton's chest and tries to rub her back. "What did you just put on me? That hurt."

"Whoa," I say, and sidestep into the wall. "I'm sorry. Did I hurt you? I didn't do anything." I inspect my hands. There's an orange glow beneath my skin. I shove them in my pockets.

"Are you okay?" Keaton asks Perry.

"My back is on fire," she says.

"I'm going to go look for Kirsten," I repeat.

"Okay, well, text me when you find her," Perry says with a grimace.

I walk to the center of the basement and my knees are wobbly. I want to grab a random person to keep myself from falling over, but I'm afraid I'm too hot. I look at my hands again. The tips of my fingers are shimmering. I've never been drunk with my new body. What have I done?

Bad decisions by me. That drink was too strong. There must've been at least three shots in my cup, which means I've had, like, six shots altogether tonight. Oh my gosh. *Six.* I hold up my hand in front of my face. That's more than one shot for each finger. More than a hand's worth of shots.

"Dylan!" Perry shouts.

I spin around. "What? I didn't find her yet. Stop rushing me."

She rolls her eyes and holds out my phone. "You forgot this."

"Stop stealing my phone, girl. I need it." I grab it from her fingers.

"You're welcome," she says and pushes back into the crowd.

"I'm going to look for Kirsten," I say. I shove my phone in my pocket and rub my sweaty hands down my thighs. When I do, a small flame slowly grows along my finger from the friction.

"Ah!" I yell, and pat the flame out with my other hand. I spin my hands in front of my face and squint at the glowing layer of fire beneath my skin. I snap my fingers and another small flame shoots into the air.

"Whoa, man, sick trick," a guy next to me says. "You use a lighter for that?"

I ignore his question. Then I laugh. I keep making my way through the basement. I snap again and another flame erupts. A flash of light illuminates my face in the dark basement. This is reckless, but if there's one way to get Jordan's attention, it's by making my presence known.

With every snap of my fingers, a new set of faces looks at me. I'm waiting until one of them is Jordan's beautiful face.

Snap.

Snap.

Snap.

I reach the other end of the basement and I'm still alone. My vision is blurry from the heat in my face and the booze in my body. I decide to head to the kitchen and look upstairs.

At the bottom of the steps, my eyes lock onto a pair of black combat boots. Darlene Houchowitz glares down at me with the disdain that a peasant like me deserves. The light from the kitchen glows behind her.

"Darlene! You're here!"

She holds her chin in the air and her arms nonchalantly hang at her sides. "Yeah, who isn't?" she grunts.

"I'm so happy you're here. Like, so happy." I can't control my face. I'm beaming.

She rolls her eyes. "Save your fake sentiments for someone who cares. For the last time, I don't care that you didn't join the group."

Brenton Riley rounds the corner to the basement steps and my jaw drops.

"Well, if it isn't the whole GSA? Freshman at the party!" I shout. "Look at you."

"I thought you didn't know Brenton," Darlene says. She turns to Brenton and whispers loud enough that I can hear, "I wouldn't go near him. He's been acting weird lately."

I don't know Brenton. I've never seen the kid in person. I stalked his Instagram after I learned of his involvement with the GSA and had to see what this little JFK was about. His bio literally says *passionate about social change.* He has shaggy brown hair and thick black-rimmed glasses, which I think make him look smarter than he actually is.

"Are you Dylan Highmark?" he asks.

"The one and only." I poke his shoulder and he shudders.

"Don't touch him!" Darlene yells at me. "Come on." She grabs Brenton's hand and ushers him down the stairs.

"Hey, have you guys seen Savanna?" I yell after them.

"Are you serious? Get a life, Dylan."

Ugh. I run my hands through my hair. Probably not the best person to ask. I take a deep breath and collect myself at the top of the steps. I put my hands on my chest and try to sober up. I take another deep breath. Jordan is not here. Time to give up. I'm going to get a glass of water and then go sleep next to the sticker of Ariel.

There's a few stragglers upstairs who aren't supposed to be here, but it's still so much quieter. I close the basement door behind me.

My ears are ringing. I toss my phone on the kitchen island and pick up a glass from the sink. I fill it with water and chug.

Out of the corner of my eye, I spot a boy with a complexion similar to Jordan's and dark brown hair. I turn and speedwalk to him. I grab his shoulder and spin him around. "Jordan?" I ask.

But it's not him. The boy jumps from my grasp. "Dude, did you just burn me?" the guy asks. "Can I help you?" He looks at me like I am a freak—which I am. A floating, lonely freak with a body temperature of 110 degrees Fahrenheit who is going to die any second.

"I wish you could," I say. "I really wish you could." I don't know what comes over me, but my throat thickens, and tears start streaming down my face. I wipe my mouth and cover my face with my arm.

"Hey, are you okay?" the boy asks me. His voice softens.

"Should we help him?" another girl mutters.

I wave my hand at them. "No, I'm fine." I sniff. I reach for my glass of water, but I smack it off the counter and it shatters. It makes me cry even more, and then, without my usual warning from my body, I shoot to the kitchen ceiling. My back slams into the drywall and half of me goes through it. I fall back down through the air and land on the kitchen island. The countertop knocks the wind from my chest.

The others in the kitchen scream and run down to the basement and into other rooms. I slide off the counter and collapse on the floor. I stand and race upstairs before I can do anything else.

I get to Kirsten's room and slam the door behind me. I pull off my shoes and my hoodie and dive onto the bed. Kirsten's bedspread is a fluffy mess around me. The room is spinning, and my cheeks are hot.

My heart skips a few beats. I picture Jordan in the bed with me, positioned against my chest. I drape my arms over a pillow as if it's his shoulders and put my chin on the corner as if it's his curly brown hair. I cry again.

"Goodnight, Jordan. Wherever you are."

I'm asleep for 1.2 seconds before I'm being jostled awake by someone. "Dylan, wake up!" Perry screams.

I blink rapidly. My mouth is dry. My throat is scratchy when I swallow. "What's happening?" I ask. My head throbs. I think I'm already hungover. Keaton is next to her.

I look out the window. The sky is still black. I rub my eyes. The party music is off. There's a man shouting downstairs, and someone pounding on the other doors upstairs. I grab my phone and it's 1:48 a.m.

"The cops are here," Perry says.

"What? Are you serious?"

I jump out of bed. As I head for the light switch, Kirsten's bedroom door bursts open. A cop appears in the doorway and shines his flashlight back and forth among Perry, Keaton, and me. I freeze and hold up my hands.

"Out!" he yells, and thrusts his thumb over his shoulder, pointing back at the hall. "Mandatory evacuations."

I turn to Perry and she shrugs.

"Now! Let's go," the cop says. He leaves the doorway and searches the rest of the hall.

I grab my hoodie from the floor and slide it back over my body. I hop on one foot as I try to put on my shoes as quickly as possible.

"We got busted?" I ask.

"I don't know. I fell asleep too and just woke up when I heard the cops shouting," Perry says.

I rush into the hall and look over the banister into the foyer. Everyone from the party files out the front door. Some people still have cups in their hands. Two cops stand at the bottom of the steps. Kirsten cries beside them.

I walk downstairs.

"Hey," I say. My voice is raspy.

"Dylan!" Kirsten says. "Where have you been? Are you okay?" She hugs me.

"Of course I'm okay. What's happening?" I glance at the cops watching everyone leave.

"Another fire got us busted."

"What fire?" My body stiffens.

A few more kids shuffle through the front door. The last group includes the familiar ponytail of Savanna Blatt. We lock eyes. My mouth falls open a little. She made it after all. Her arms are folded, and her gaze doesn't leave mine until she goes through the door.

The line of partygoers comes to an end. Two more cops emerge from the basement. "All clear," one says.

The other cop walks down the stairs and pushes Keaton's back. "You all have to leave too," he says.

"Wait, Kirsten has to leave? This is her house," I say.

"We didn't get busted for the party, Dyl. They're evacuating the whole neighborhood. Go look outside," Kirsten says.

"What?"

"Miss, we'll address this later," a cop says to Kirsten. He's scribbling some notes on a pad. "We have bigger things to take care of tonight and just need to make sure everyone's safe. Let's go." He points out the door.

I run outside. Cop cars and fire trucks fill the street. Parents yell at their kids and push them into cars. Some people look at the sky with their hands over their mouths.

"Watch out!" a fireman yells, and runs past me pulling a long yellow hose. I spin to dodge him.

I turn around. The sky is bright orange. Flames billow among the woods behind Kirsten's house. Tree trunks split in half as they crash to the ground. Dozens of firemen are at the edge of the woods, spreading a white powder across the ground. I swallow.

"But...but...Jordan isn't here," I say to myself out loud. The sirens and shouts from parents drown out my concern. Unless... he is. A thought strikes me. What if Jordan set this fire as a signal to let me know he's back?

I take off down the street toward the burning site. But I only complete a few strides before grinding to a stop. My knees crack. HydroPro's silver cars pull up to Kirsten's house, skidding to a stop along the curb. I stare at the tall, slender man as he exits one of the vehicles and then close my eyes for a moment, hoping to make myself disappear.

When I open them, the tall man is power walking toward me and shows no sign of slowing.

"Dylan," he says. "Give me five minutes to speak with you." He reaches for my arm.

"Get away from me!" I yell. I turn and dart down the street.

Another fire truck drives past me. Its siren makes me cringe. Kirsten comes running outside, filming the scene with her phone. She dashes around from cop to firefighter and then to a different cop. She types notes as she speaks with them.

The commotion disappears behind me. The tall man stands still in the middle of the street, staring. His black eyes shrink in the distance.

If Jordan wanted to be at the party, he would have been here. But he chose to stay away for a reason. I'm not going to go after him and bring HydroPro with me. But if this fire wasn't him, then who was it?

I clutch my wrist and watch the night go up in familiar flames.

twenty-eight

I'm up extra early this morning to prove to my parents that I'm able to go to school. It's torture. They've been off my back, and I need to keep it that way.

After the party, I was so hungover the next day that I only moved from my bed to pee or get water. I tried to play *SimCity*, but I couldn't even do that because the screen was making me nauseous. I've mentally added *worsens hangovers* to the list of powers from my new body composition.

I could stay home today, but I need something to distract me from Jordan. When I am awake, I think about him. When I'm sleeping, I dream about him.

I shuffle through the hallway in an undershirt and shorts and plop into a seat at the kitchen table. I sigh. My eyes itch. My parents are already dressed in their work clothes. Dad is reading the news on his iPad, and Mom is cutting a cucumber at the kitchen counter.

"Feeling better?" Dad asks without looking up from his screen.

"Yeah, totally," I lie.

I steal a piece of toast from his plate and bite it. It's my favorite kind of toast, with butter and cinnamon and sugar sprinkled on top.

"You should drink something, Dylan," Mom says. She pulls orange juice from the fridge and pours me a glass. She walks it over to me and places it on the table.

I take a sip of juice.

"I just can't even believe Kirsten would throw a party like that," Mom says, shaking her head as she walks back to the counter. "She's always been the most responsible one of your friends."

Kirsten's parents called my parents when they got home from their trip on Sunday to apologize for the party. I think they made it seem like we were all snorting drugs off one another's stomachs or something.

Dad looks at me and closes the case on his iPad. "You're all lucky you got away with warnings," he says. "But I'm glad you can see this is not a good habit to get into. Look how it's impacted your day." He stands and packs his things into his messenger bag.

I stare at my orange juice. Lucky for me, apparently my parents don't believe in grounding us. They trust me to reflect on my decisions, learn from my mistakes, and make better decisions in the future. And lucky for them, I've had time to reflect all yesterday. After much deep thought, my only mistake from the past weekend was putting too many shots into my mixed drink. If I'd only used one shot, I wouldn't have been so drunk. I also should not have used my powers in the basement, or talked to Darlene, or burned Perry, or exploded through the kitchen ceiling. Other than that, the rest of my decisions that night were solid choices . . . if there were any other decisions I made.

Kirsten got grounded with no end date, and Perry's mom asked her how she could handle college, let alone cheering while in college. They were both allowed to go to Nationals, but with no phones. I haven't talked to them since Saturday. With our group chat dead and Jordan gone, I've only received one text the past few days, and it was from Cody.

"Was your friend at the party?" Mom asks. "How has he been feeling?"

I take another bite of toast. "He wasn't there."

"That's a shame. When will we get to meet him?" She wipes her hands on the kitchen towel.

"Never," I say, swallowing.

My parents exchange a glance.

"All right, I'm off," Dad announces. He pats me on the back and kisses Mom good-bye. "Have a good day, Dyl."

"Bye," I grunt.

"Remember, I'll be back late tonight. I'm finally having dinner with the CEO at my new company."

"Oh, yeah. How is that going?" I ask. With everything going on, I haven't paid the slightest bit of attention to Dad's career moves. He could be working at my school as the lunch guy for all I know.

He shrugs. "Same stuff but working for this new energy company. Lots of great benefits and stock options." He takes his phone from his bag and hands it to me. "Here. Look at this. Check out number three."

I grab his phone and watch an article load on the screen. The title reads "Top Five Philadelphia Companies to Watch this Year." I scroll and number three is HydroPro. My jaw drops open.

"Pretty neat, huh?"

"You're kidding me!" I shout.

My parents' heads snap in my direction. Mom drops the knife she's using to cut vegetables and it clatters on the counter.

"Kidding about what?" she asks, clutching her hand to her chest.

I lower my voice. "I thought you worked in finance?" I ask, turning to Dad.

"I do. Every company has a financial department," he says. "This is cool, Dyl. They have..."

He keeps talking, but it turns into a mumble as I tune him out. I toss his phone back to him and cross my arms. My feet tingle and I wrap my feet around the legs of the chair.

There goes my fantasy about bringing Jordan to my house for a spaghetti dinner with my family. I can't bring him here. Not like how he is. And not with who Dad is working for.

My parents always tried to assure me home is a safe space. But how can they keep it a safe space if they no longer know what's dangerous?

When the front door closes, Mom drops her salad ingredients and then walks to the table. She places her hands on the back of a chair, staring at me.

I stop eating my dad's toast and look up at her. "Um, yes?"

"Is everything okay, Dylan?"

I let out an awkward giggle. "Mom, you know I've been drunk before. I don't get why you're making such a big deal about this."

"It's not just the party—I mean, that's a big part of it. You've never been a 'partier.'" She uses air quotes when she says *partier*. "But the past few weeks I feel as though you've been a little out of sorts."

"I'm honestly as perfectly normal as I've always been." I stand to walk my dishes to the sink.

"See," she says, holding out her arm. "You're walking away from me. You've always been so comfortable talking to us before."

"I'm not walking away from you. I literally have to get ready for school. Now I feel awkward because you're analyzing my every move."

"There are a lot of lies happening these days and a lot going on with your friends . . . with the lake accident and this party and your new relationship. It can be overwhelming."

I rinse my plate and cup and put them in the dishwasher.

"Mom, I'm good. Trust me." I walk over to hug her but stop myself short in case I'm too hot.

"Well, if you're ever not good—"

"I will tell you. Yes."

"Good." She returns to rinsing cherry tomatoes. "Did you shower yesterday?"

I shake my head.

"Well, go take a cold shower. It'll help you feel better." She waves me toward the hall. "And I hate to say it, but you smell a little and your hair is very greasy."

"Well, okay. Thanks for the morning self-esteem boost."

"Do you want a salad for lunch?"

Should I tell her about HydroPro and what they're after? Should I tell her that what they're looking for is right here in their home? They don't care about Dad's job, or Philadelphia, or stock options. They only care about being close to Jordan. And maybe that's the one good thing to come from this news. If HydroPro is sticking around here, then Jordan might be closer than I think. Maybe they're keeping business open here because they know Jordan has something to come back for.

twenty-nine

School is quiet. Everyone is keeping a low profile since the party. Half the junior class is phoneless, grounded, or still hungover.

There's a heaviness hanging over our town like a morning fog now that there is someone running around trying to burn it down. I mean—I know Jordan started a few of the fires, but now that there's a copycat out there, even I'm a little freaked. The teachers' faces are painted with streaks of nerves, and they spasm every time they get a call from the front office. It doesn't help that news vans have been parked outside school all week, asking us to comment on the fires and the Blatts as we enter and leave the building.

Savanna came into school late. There are rumors floating around that her dad doesn't want her in school until the arson case is solved because he feels she isn't safe in public. Last week, I would've said that's a dumb excuse because the fires have nothing to do with the Blatts. But now I'm not so sure that's entirely true. There could be a deranged arsonist capitalizing off what Jordan started. Or worse, another boy Jordan passed his powers to. But I'm suppressing that thought.

I get to homeroom right before the bell rings and slide into my seat with my backpack over my shoulders. Darlene is a few rows over from me. I make sure to look everywhere but her eyes.

Brook Hempshire, our homeroom representative, walks to the front of the room with a stack of red-and-pink cards. She has strawberry-blond hair and her face and arms are covered in freckles.

"Hey, everyone," she says. "Today is the last day you can buy Valentine's Day 'grams for your friends. Does anyone want one?" She holds up the cards. A few people raise their hands and she delivers the cards to them.

I totally forgot about the upcoming holiday. I was so close to having a valentine this year for the first time ever. And I don't expect Jordan to come back before then. Is he actually still my boyfriend? What happens when your boyfriend disappears without a trace? Is there a time limit you give yourself until you're single again? One month? Two months? I'm not sure. I'll give myself a year, because I don't want to *not* be Jordan's boyfriend.

I raise my hand to purchase some 'grams. This could be my last Valentine's Day ever, so I might as well make the most of it. I keep my face forward because turning my head makes me nauseous. Brook arrives at my desk and stands beside me.

"How many do you want?" she asks.

"How much are they?"

"Fifty cents."

"Is it candy or something?"

"You can pick a red rose for love, a pink rose for a crush, and a white rose for friendship. They get delivered on Valentine's Day with your card."

I rummage through my backpack and pull out two crumpled dollars. "Can I have two white roses, please?"

She hands me two cards, and I give her a dollar. "Or wait, can I have another one too?"

She hands me a third card and I give her my other dollar. "Just give me those signed cards before the end of homeroom."

"Yeah."

I pull out a pen and tap it on my forehead as I think of what to write. After a minute, I start signing.

TO: *Perry Lillian Lyle*　　　　　**HOMEROOM:** *6C*

Roses are red, violets are blue,
You're my best friend, and I love you.
You're in Florida this week, it's no fun.
How am I supposed to function, when you're my sun?
Call me crazy, but I think it's true.
You've been my valentine since day one, wahoo.

FROM: *Dylan Emory Highmark*

TO: *Kirsten James Lush*   **HOMEROOM:** *6C*

Someone call 911.

What I'm about to say can't be outdone.

I got some breaking news.

Missing you is giving me the blues.

You're my favorite valentine.

Can't wait to see you on Dateline.

FROM: *Dylan Emory Highmark*

TO: *Savanna Blatt*   **HOMEROOM:** *1C*

FROM:

I run the cards to Brook, and she puts them in a brown paper bag. I walk back to my desk and there's a beep. The loudspeaker crackles on. Sadly, it's not Kirsten's voice.

"Will all homerooms please report to the auditorium. An assembly on fire safety will be taking place. Again, all homerooms please report to the auditorium for the assembly on fire safety. Thank you."

A collective sigh erupts across the room. Assemblies are usually annoying, but this could be good for me today. Hopefully, I can get in a back row and sleep through my lingering hangover. I stand and walk to the front of the room to get in line. My legs are wobbly. I wipe sweat from my forehead and tap my thigh, waiting for this line to get going. I'm getting nauseous standing up here for a few seconds.

Lunch is always awkward when Perry and Kirsten aren't here. I have no friends and the feeling of wanting to eat in a bathroom stall is real. I've never actually done that, though. And I never will. Partly because I don't care if people see me eating alone, but mostly because our school bathrooms are sewer-like places and would ruin any appetite I have whatsoever. Teen rom-com movies aren't based on facts because we know sweet movie-star Sally isn't eating her turkey-and-cheese sandwich with fart aroma leaking through the stall cracks.

Mom packed me a salad today, which is nice because I don't have to wait in the food line. But that means there are fewer people sitting at their seats. There are fewer people for me to choose to sit with and an increased risk of random people sitting with me after they get their food. Uncontrolled environments like this never work out in my favor.

I scan the tables and spot Keaton. As I walk over, one of his soccer friends sits in the open seat next to him. The closest open seat to him is, like, five people away. Five people I don't know. I don't want to be an awkward turtle at the end of the bench.

There's a commotion of chairs squeaking against the floor, and a crowd laughing behind me. I turn and survey a few more empty tables. I see Savanna sitting at the edge of one. She's alone. Everyone files into the cafeteria from the assembly. As they pass Savanna, they dump their fire safety materials in front of her. The pile of papers quickly grows into a mountain. A few people toss water bottles onto the table too. Savanna squints at them.

"Hey, Cruella, you can't just sic your dogs on the arsonist and end this BS?" someone asks. They roll their eyes.

I look at Keaton and then back to her. I take a step toward Savanna.

My new body must be starting to disrupt the chemicals in my brain, because I don't think I've willingly participated in an extended social interaction with Savanna Blatt since the eighth grade. I don't know what to expect. I don't know whether she's going to bite my head off or completely ignore me. But maybe since she's by herself she's in a different mood. Everything going on in our town right now can't be easy to handle, especially when you push every single person away from you like she does.

I'm literally being Mom right now.

I reach her end of the table and sit on the same side as her. I leave one open seat between us. The procession of students has ended. A few fire safety papers slide off the table onto the floor. I clear my throat and unzip my backpack to get my salad. Savanna turns to me and wipes her face with a napkin. Her lips are bare today, but her nails are pink.

"I think you're in the wrong seat," she says. Her tone is sharp as always.

I shake my head and pull the red lid off my salad container. "I'm aware of the seat I chose."

"Oh, right. Perry and Kirsten are away, so there's nowhere else for you to sit."

I ignore her comment and pour my dressing over my salad. I mix it up with my fork and shove some of the leaves in my mouth. I watch Savanna bite into a rice cake with peanut butter.

"I don't need you to feel bad for me," she says. "So just go away."

"Oh, I don't feel bad for you. I came over here looking for some information on fire safety." I smirk. I pick up one of the handouts and pretend to read it.

Savanna scoffs. "Everyone here is an asshole," she says.

"Including me?"

"Especially you."

"Were you in the assembly this morning?" I ask. A Craisin is stuck in my back molar, and I pick at it with my finger.

"No. Why would I go to that? So the entire school can stare at me the whole time?"

"I don't know."

"I came to school last period." She snaps off a piece of her rice cake and puts it gently in her mouth.

There's a minute of silence.

"Was the assembly informative?" she asks.

"The fire marshal was there. He told us what to do in a burning house."

"That's helpful, considering all the fires happen in empty houses under construction."

I shrug. "You never know."

"How is your boyfriend doing?" she asks, then laughs.

"Fine." I nod. "Why is that funny?"

"Just a shame Jimmy didn't work out. Can't imagine this new guy is any better. Kirsten mentioned at cheer that he was going to be introduced at her party. He wasn't there, though, obviously. So I wouldn't even be surprised if you're making him up."

"How did you hear about him, anyway?"

"I have my sources at St. Helena's."

"So you just decided to tell the whole school about it by making up that I paint weird portraits of him?"

"Well, I thought your relationship should be celebrated and spread widely, no? It seems like you can't decide whether you want to show him off at parties or keep him a secret. Which is it, Dylan?"

My body shakes after she finishes her sentence. Savanna puts her face in her phone. I squeeze my hands into fists below the table. If only she knew what I have been through the past few weeks, then she'd never think I'm making him up. I wrap my legs around the chair. I touch my finger to the pile of papers from the assembly. A small flame bursts unexpectedly from the tip, lighting the brochures on fire. The thin flames glide along the rectangular edges. I grab one of the nearby water bottles and pour the water over the flames until they're extinguished.

I make eye contact with a boy sitting alone at another table. A freshman, maybe. His jaw is slack. I scowl and spin my finger at him, gesturing to look away.

I lean closer to Savanna. "What you did was mean," I say.

She looks up at me as if surprised to see me. "What was?" she asks.

It doesn't shock me that she can't remember which moment I'm talking about. There's just so many to choose from.

"The fake Instagram."

"Oh, that?" She waves her hand. "That was hilarious. I actually forgot I had that account. I should post—"

"Just stop!" I raise my voice. Savanna jumps. "Just because it's funny to you doesn't mean it's funny to everyone else." My voice cracks.

"It was a prank," Savanna says softly.

"It was cruel."

She sighs. "Okay...well, I guess, like, maybe I shouldn't have done it."

I shake my head and then rest it in my hand.

Savanna and I eat our lunches while we scroll through social media. No one else sits with us. We get a few stink eyes that basically say, *What are those two doing together?* Which I agree with 100 percent.

I'm waiting for my apology, but I realize it's never going to come. After what feels like years, I take a deep breath and turn toward her.

"Hey, Savanna?"

She locks her phone, then faces me. Her ponytail drapes over her right shoulder. Her eyebrows are raised, waiting for me to continue. She blinks.

"I know you're not my biggest fan, but, like, if you ever need someone to talk to...you can talk to me or something." I rub my hands down my thighs.

She licks her lips and stares back at the table. She scratches the hair in front of her headband.

I nod and tap the empty seat between us. "Right." I blow air through my lips.

I don't know why I attempted this. She doesn't even deserve this from me. Hell, she was one of the reasons I was almost suicidal. I stand.

"Do you not like tomatoes?" she asks.

My head twitches. "What?"

"Your salad. You didn't eat any of the tomatoes." She points at it.

I look at my salad container. It's empty except for a layer of uneaten cherry tomatoes at the bottom.

"Oh...I usually do. But I'm not feeling too well today, and the texture was making me gag. For once, I'm not in the mood for some balls in my mouth."

She laughs and bites her lip. She looks unfamiliar with a smile. "God, Dylan. You're so disgusting," she says, rolling her eyes.

I think it might be her way of saying *okay*.

"Would you like one?" I ask.

She scans the tomatoes for thirty seconds before plucking one with her fork and taking a bite.

The class bell rings shortly after. I watch everyone trudge out of the cafeteria. I'm staring at the backs of their heads. It's a sea of brown, black, blond, and red circles bobbing along with the current, the same current that takes me from class to class and from school to home. I don't need to see their faces to recognize the flow. Every day, the thousands of attendees of Falcon Crest High awaken at the same time. Every time we switch on our lights in the morning, it sends a ping to my consciousness. Like how the moon is connected to the tides, we're all connected to the same push and pull that emits from this building.

And after this past weekend's fire, I'm realizing Jordan and I are becoming intrinsically linked in similar ways. It's not the symmetry of his teeth or the definition of his stomach alone that pulls me toward him, but the extraordinary composition of our lives that makes us fit together. The extreme is our normal, and no one else's. My Ghosters of Christmas Past might have nice physical features, but no one looks at me, holds my hand with the same warmth, or brings a smile to my face as quickly as Jordan does. And none are made of fire. None could understand if last weekend was a signal, which is why I'm going to respond. We're dying. And time is running out.

The cafeteria is empty. I wait until the food service staff close the metal dividers between the seating and food preparation areas before moving. I scoop the pile of brochures into my arms and carry them across the room. I drop them at the base of a long row of vending machines right below the fire alarm. My eyes scan the cafeteria again to make sure it's still empty so no one gets hurt.

It's not hard to get a fire going with the level of agitation coursing through my veins. The laminated brochures act as a perfect source of kindling, igniting a fire in seconds. I know one of the rules is not to use my powers on purpose, but communicating with Jordan must be one of the exceptions.

I race away from the growing plume of smoke. When I'm halfway down the hall, there's a quick succession of explosions as each vending machine catches fire. I jump into the closest classroom and slide into a desk, tapping my chin as teachers race by me toward the blaze.

If there's a chance Jordan set the last fire to let me know he's still here, I want him to know I'm still here too, wanting the world.

thirty

Next Saturday, I'm back with Dr. Ivan.

When I arrive, she makes me fill out a twenty-page form to document everything that has happened to me since my last visit. It asks me about the powers that have manifested, my physical reactions to the Balancer, situations when my powers are most active, and everyday things like how my sleeping and eating patterns have changed. There is even a question about my "libido and ejaculatory history post body-composition change." I leave that line blank.

Now she has me back in the glass box, which has been cleared of the bed and all furniture. I'm shirtless and barefoot, wearing only shorts. Wires are attached to my chest. They hook up to a dozen machines pushed up against the glass. Overhead lights shine down on me from all sides of the box. My hands rest on my hips, waiting for directions.

"Have you heard anything from Jordan?" I ask her. She's typing on a computer.

"I have not," she says. Her head moves slightly from one end of her screen to the other as she reads.

"I thought you were supposed to be taking care of him."

"It's not just me on the team. I'm tasked with you now. I have other partners looking after Jordan."

I blow air from my nose.

"There were a couple other fires this week. I'm thinking Jordan might still be around." I pick at one of the wires on my chest, watching for her reaction. She looks up from her screen and stares at me, expressionless. Then she returns to typing.

"Those weren't him," she says. "Like I told you before, he's not around here anymore."

"How can you be so sure?"

She raises an eyebrow. "I'm sure."

She stands and walks to the edge of the glass box. She pulls an access card from her pocket, puts it against the glass door, and enters. The form I completed earlier is attached to a clipboard in her hands. She flicks through the pages, nodding as she reads. "You seem to be handling everything relatively fine." She tightens a few of the cords on my chest. Goose bumps cover my skin.

"That's what you got from that? I'd hate to see what handling things badly looks like."

"We should be good to go." She exits the box and tosses the clipboard aside. "Can you run for me?"

I look around with my eyebrows raised. "Like, right here?"

"Yes, in place." She crosses her arms.

"I guess." I start to jog. Dr. Ivan walks around the glass box with her arms crossed. She watches numbers change on the machines surrounding me.

"Faster," she says.

I pump my arms and move my legs at a quickening pace. The machines start beeping rapidly. "What is this for?" I ask between heavy breaths.

"Very good. Jumping jacks." She ignores me.

I squint at her. "Are you serious?"

"Yes. I'm watching how your body reacts.... Looking at your heart rate variability, body temperature, and other things." She circles her hand in the air. "Keep going. Jumping jacks."

I stop running and huff. I lift my arms, then wave them in the air. I sync my lower body with my upper body, bringing my limbs together and then pushing them apart. Some of the cords get in the way of my movements, slowing me down. My heart pounds against the inside of my rib cage.

"Push-ups," Dr. Ivan blurts.

I roll my eyes and drop to the floor. I can't remember the last time I did a push-up. My arms are sore after five reps. Sweat drips off my nose onto the floor.

"Stand up and jump as high as you can."

"Just jump?" I ask, panting. My shoulders rise and fall as I breathe. The muscles over my stomach contract.

"As high as you can." She nods at the ceiling.

I jump.

"Again," she says.

I jump.

Again and again and again. We repeat the cycle of running, jumping jacks, push-ups, and high jumps several times.

My hands are covered in sweat by the fifth round. They slip along the concrete floor as I attempt more push-ups. My hair is drenched and falls into my eyes.

"Jump," she says, and raises her hand to the sky.

I quickly stand and jump. When I land, my foot slides on the sweat-covered floor, and I fall. My arms flail as I land on my back. The back of my head smacks against the floor.

"Jump," she repeats.

I clench my teeth and slam my fist into the ground. I stand, but I don't jump.

"No!" I shout. Spit flies from my mouth. "Screw you!" I point at her and charge the glass. I smack my hand against the wall right in front of her face. She doesn't flinch. It leaves a sweaty handprint. "I hate you! I don't know why I'm doing this. I don't know you. You suck at helping Jordan and you suck at helping me. You're all pieces of shit. Every one of you at HydroPro. Just because you left the company doesn't mean you're not responsible. You did this." I tap hard against my bare chest. "To me and to Jordan and to his parents. You're not a good person. You say you are. You *think* you are." I bite my lip and shake my head. "You don't know what I need." I step back to the center of the room. "I'll do this myself." I tug at the cords on my body. "I'll get Jordan back. You'll see. You'll see." The cords pull at my skin. "Dammit. How do you get these things off?"

I throw my hands to the side and then suddenly shoot to the ceiling of the box. The machines go wild, like a dozen fire alarms blaring at high volume. Dr. Ivan grabs her clipboard and takes notes.

I spin through the air. The wires tug me to the right and to the left. When I float too high, they tug me closer to the ground.

As I watch Dr. Ivan scribble on her paper, I realize this is probably what she wanted. Sure, she was testing my heart rate and temperature during the exercises. But she was causing me stress on purpose to get me to float and see my manifestations. I know it's to help me, but I don't want to give her the satisfaction. When Jordan complied with her, it got him nowhere.

I think about what they've done to him, and my future without him. I flex my arms and scream. A fireball grows in my stomach. My eyes blur and my vision goes black. Then I explode. Just as Jordan did on the lake. It feels like when hot coffee travels down my esophagus, but all over my body.

The machines go silent. The glass walls shatter around me. I fall through the air until my bare skin smacks against the concrete. The fire dissipates, and I'm left bent over on the ground surrounded by a circle of black ash.

Dr. Ivan swallows and takes a step back. "I think that's enough for tonight," she says.

I stare at her.

Dr. Ivan forces me to stay with her for another hour while I calm down. I shower, then sit beside her desk and drink a glass of water. My hair is wet. Water drips from my head to my knees. She's typing notes on the computer.

"Can I go?" I ask, biting my fingernails.

"Are you feeling better?" she asks.

"No. I have a chronic fever and debilitating anxiety from my potentially near future death. Am I ever supposed to feel better?"

She sighs. "I'll see you next Saturday." She pulls a paper from a drawer and puts it in my lap. "Use this to track your manifestations this week." Her hand brushes her brow.

The paper has a table composed of columns for each day of the week and rows for each hour of the day. Across the top, there is a heading with random numbers and the words *Special Projects*. I stand and tear it in half.

Dr. Ivan's eyes go wide, her mouth agape. "What are you doing, Dylan?"

"I'm not coming back again," I say, shrugging. "I'm not your little project. This is my life. I don't feel better when I come here. I'm going to find Jordan and let this play out. And if it means dying together, then so be it." I throw the shredded paper. The pieces dance through the air as they fall to the ground.

"Dylan, you have to come back."

I turn and walk to the door.

"Dylan!" I hear Dr. Ivan's chair slide against the floor as she stands. "Dylan!" She slams her hand against the desk.

I stop walking. My body goes rigid.

"There's a . . . a potential cure," she says. Her voice is softer. "An antidote . . . of some kind."

My hand grips the doorknob. "A what?" I ask, my back facing her. I squeeze the knob. My hand shakes.

She exhales. "There's a technology that might be able to reverse the course of your changing body."

My hand instantly heats up. My fingers melt into the doorknob, leaving an impression of my prints. As I turn, the knob is ripped out of the door. I toss it across the room before it liquefies in my palm. It clinks along the concrete floor until it stops near the remnants of the glass box. I power walk toward Dr. Ivan.

"A cure? Do you have it?"

She holds up her hands as she walks backward. "No. It's in development by HydroPro. I've heard about it from a few of my remaining connections. It's a result of some of their original experiments with Jordan. That's why I still need you. . . . To get a way in—"

I slam my hands on her desk. "Does Jordan know about this?"

She shakes her head. "I didn't want to give you two false hope."

I laugh. "That would be better than what you're giving us now. How are you going to get the antidote from them?"

"I'm formulating a plan with some other partners from my team and—"

"So you don't have a plan?" I nod and dart back to the door.

"Dylan, please wait!"

"I don't have time to wait! Jordan could be out there putting himself in danger for no reason."

Like I've said before, waiting around has never done me any favors. Jordan left because he thought it was going to save me. He thought the best thing for us was to live separately. But now I know what the best thing is for us—it's finding this antidote and bringing us back together.

thirty-one

My body trembles on the train ride home as I google HydroPro's address again and look at the building from every angle on Street View. Within minutes, I locate several doors, garages, and windows I could infiltrate. Getting into HydroPro won't be an issue. My powers make that part simple. I could float to the roof, melt a lock, or fly through an open window. It's finding the antidote that's going to be complicated.

But one thing I know for sure is that HydroPro is obsessed with Jordan. There's bound to be crumbs of information scattered about the facility. I'm hoping once inside, all hallways lead to Jordan.

I pull up the news article about Jordan's accident and jot down his parents' names and other details I can look for once inside HydroPro. I open Twitter and search for tweets about the company. There's nothing that seems useful.

There's a tweet from Kara Bynum saying the cheerleading squad is back in Philly. I click her account and scroll through her tweets. There's no mention of them winning any competitions. I think it's safe to assume a national championship for Falcon Crest Cheer Squad wasn't in the cards this year. I scroll farther down and find the real trophy.

Kara tweeted a picture of Ms. Gurbsterter and Perry on Wednesday. Ms. Gurbsterter is wearing Mickey Mouse ears on her head and a fanny pack around her waist. If she's trying to stay lean, someone should tell her a fanny pack doesn't accentuate the hips in the best places. She's beaming and has her arm draped around Perry's shoulder. Perry's staring at the camera, completely deadpan. But I can tell she's about to vomit from the odor that's most likely leaking from Ms. Gurbsterter's armpit in the Florida heat. I hope the torture Perry is going through becomes worth it in the end, because that girl needs a win.

Speaking of, seconds later I swipe away an influx of messages from Perry and Kirsten asking me to hang out and call them. They are definitely back in town and it looks like they got their phones from their parents. They sent me pictures of their completed spring paintings. Mine still only has a couple shades of blue.

I exit the app and lock my phone without responding. I have nothing to say to them because I don't want to lie. Continuing to ignore them sucks, but it's less risky. I don't trust myself enough to keep track of the lies I would need to tell them to explain my and Jordan's whereabouts.

Not only will this antidote cure Jordan and me, but it will also fix the messed-up relationships I currently have with my best friends and family. I'll be able to be myself again. Who would've thought I'd want to revert back to ordinary Dylan so quickly?

The train drops me off at Liberty Pike Station. I unlock my bike from the fence and pedal down the desolate road toward HydroPro. I pass the Blatt development of new homes on Liberty Pike. I stare at the ghostly houses, thinking of when Jordan told me he burned one of them to the ground on his first night in Falcon Crest. I frown, thinking of the loneliness he felt when he moved here. It hurts even more to think how he's probably feeling that same way again right now. I hope I eased the isolation for him during the brief time we were together. I know he did for me.

In the corner of my eye, an orange spark flashes in the sky. I slam my pedals backward, my tires skidding along the pavement to a stop. I turn, watching the housing development for any sporadic bursts of light. It remains dark.

Then there's a thud, like a door slamming closed. Goose bumps erupt on my arms. It's Saturday night, so there is no way construction is currently happening. This site should be empty. But it's not. The sounds are either Jordan or another arsonist. My heart flutters at the thought of Jordan being close to me again. But if it's the other arsonist, I need to shut them down. Jordan can't come back to Falcon Crest if HydroPro still thinks he's too dangerous for normal life. If someone other than Jordan is running around setting fires and making the town unsettled, it isn't fair. And I'm tired of things not being fair.

I drop my bike at the curb and walk into the construction site. I creep along the mud between two half-finished homes, my hand gliding along the prickly plywood. In the mud are two sets of footprints. I bend down to inspect them. I place my right foot next to the prints and it's significantly larger than both.

Suddenly, there's another sound. This time louder, like a shampoo bottle hitting the shower floor. I whip my head up from staring at the ground. My body stiffens, and I retreat against the nearest house. I press my back against a wall as I try to calm my breathing.

A murmur of whispers erupts in the night. There's a giggle. My face wrinkles. *Who is this?*

I slowly slide down the wall to my knees, then crawl along the frozen ground toward the sounds. I reach the freshly paved driveway and I spring up. My eyes lock onto a small set of flames burning on the side of another house farther down the street.

"No way," I say to myself. I start running to the home. The fire outlines two window frames. It quickly climbs to the roof. The gray smoke grows thick. It contrasts against the black sky.

Two hooded figures jump from the doorless front entryway of the burning home. My breath catches in my throat. I halt in the middle of the street. My shoes scrape against the concrete.

The figures wear black pants, black shoes, black gloves, and black hoodies. One has a black bag draped over their shoulder and juggles a bottle of something between their hands. They walk casually across the front lawn of the house. When they reach the curb, they wrap their arms around each other.

They must not know I'm here. They can't know I'm here. I inspect them. I take a step back. Then I take a step forward. It can't be him.

"Jordan!" I yell.

The figures freeze. They push themselves apart and slowly turn their heads to look down the street. When they see me, they bolt.

A shock travels down my body. I throw my head back and break into a sprint. My arms flail. I don't really have a choice. I came here looking for something and I found something. I can't stay here alone either. This house is about to be covered in flames in 2.4 seconds, and the cops would love to find someone to arrest for the arsons at this point. HydroPro infiltration is temporarily on hold.

"Hey!" I yell. "I'm not looking for trouble! I just have some questions."

They don't stop, or even look back at me. The figures jump over a curb and disappear between two homes. I hang a sharp left off the street and copy their trail.

They head down a grassy hill. One falls to their knees. They quickly jump back to their feet and run into the street. A car skids to a stop. Its horn blares. I cringe at the sight. The headlights shine directly on them. Their bodies keep moving across the pavement. They vanish into a wooded area.

I sidestep down the hill, watching every move I make so I don't trip like them and fall into the street. After all this, getting run over by a car would be too anticlimactic. I didn't become a freaking part-time superhero to get killed by a grandpa on his way home from purchasing lottery tickets. I watch the lone car glide down the road and take with it the last remaining bit of light, then I cross.

I enter the trees. But I quickly realize I'm running after nothing. I stop. It's silent. I listen for a sound. The trees creak back and forth with the wind. The burning house crackles in the distance.

A twig snaps, followed by nonstop crunching leaves. I take off after it. I shoot a flame into the air and the arsonists appear in the brief flash of light. They stumble, shuddering from the sudden burst of heat. I run alongside them.

I know I'm not supposed to voluntarily use these powers, but I need to use them. For Jordan. He used them to save me, and I am doing the same. I jump over a rock and blast another flame through my path.

I don't see the arsonists. I shoot another burst of light and there's nothing. I'm losing them.

I shake my hands at my sides and then jump into the air mid-run. I go maybe a foot above the ground, but then gravity pulls me right back down. My ankles twist. I jump again and again and again. I go nowhere. I suddenly want to do this stuff and it's not happening. Just my luck. I grab a branch and hoist myself up into a tree. Maybe a higher starting point will do something for me.

A siren goes off in the distance. I look back toward the Liberty Pike development. Red-and-blue lights flash between the trees.

A pain shoots across my chest. I let go of the tree, and my body flies through the sky as if I'm shot out of a cannon.

Mortal peril always seems to do the trick.

I grab a branch and secure my footing on the tree. I'm partly swinging, partly jumping from branch to branch. Every time I falter and fall through the air, my body bounces back to the tree canopy as if there's a perpetual trampoline beneath me. I shoot sporadic flames and follow the lit path. The arsonists come back into my view. From my vantage point, I'm about ten yards from the fleeing shadows.

"Hey!" I shout when I finally catch up to them. They're directly beneath me. "Who are you?"

They don't look up. Instead, they make a sharp turn and dash in another direction. I grunt. I jump onto a tree branch and fling myself backward to change course. There's a crack. The branch splits from the trunk and spins through the air before it smashes into the ground. A thud echoes through the woods.

I cover more ground—or air—faster than they can. I watch them dodge tree trunks and rocks and falter as they trip through holes. The tree canopies are dead and leafless. I have a clear path.

I've nearly caught up to them again. They're breathing heavily.

"Stop!" I yell. Their heads twitch. They investigate the area behind them. I see their chins. Strands of long hair blow out from their hoods. The rest of their faces are covered in shadow. "Where is that coming from?" one of them calls.

Frustrated, I shoot my biggest flame yet at a tree just ahead of them. The woods transform into a fireball. The tree trunk blasts upward from the ground like a volcanic eruption, its roots tearing the dirt. It comes crashing down and cuts off the arsonists' path. Their hands fly out to their sides as they stop running. One of them attempts to climb over the fallen tree, but they yelp when they touch the scorched bark and fall back.

I'm crouched on a branch. My eyes bounce between them.

I let go of the tree, then zoom to the ground. My feet hit the dirt and leaves swirl into the air around me. My legs are weak. My feet tingle. The arsonists turn and face me. They gasp for air.

I take a step forward. They jump back and grab each other.

"I'm not here to hurt you," I say.

"Then leave us alone," one of them says.

"I just want you to stop. Why are you doing this? You're messing up other people's lives."

"You don't know the first thing about it." They reach for their hood.

"Don't!" the other arsonist says. The voice is familiar.

But they don't listen. They pull down their hood. It's a girl. She has short, curly brown hair. Huge round eyes inspect me. Her lips are tight.

The other arsonist grunts. They drop their bag and grab the girl's arm, stepping in front of her.

"You're more of a freak than I originally thought, Dylan," they say. Chills erupt across every inch of my body. The other arsonist flicks back their hood.

And there she is. High ponytail and all. Savanna Blatt stares at me, expressionless.

thirty-two

Sometimes I get the strangest urges throughout the day and I wonder if I'm the only one who experiences these feelings. Like, I'll be sitting in Dr. Brio's Chemistry class and randomly get the urge to scream at the top of my lungs. Or I'll be cutting cucumbers for my salad with Mom, and I'll want to chop off one of my fingers to see what her reaction would be. Or I'll be in the passenger seat with Kirsten and want to grab the steering wheel to send us spinning through the air. I don't actually want to do these things, it's more of a what-if situation.

But right now, I have a very real urge to strangle someone. It's not a what-if situation but more of a when-can-I.

"You!" I scream, and charge at Savanna. "What the hell are you doing here?" My voice cracks.

She throws up her hands at me. "What the hell are *you* doing here is the question."

"Freaking chasing after you. . . . I don't know." I turn around and put my hands on the back of my head.

She steps closer to me. "Are you trying to torch me with a flame-thrower? You're a psychopath."

"I don't have a flamethrower. But that's none of your business. Why are you burning down your dad's houses and then blaming everyone else? First you ruin my life with that stupid prank you pulled and now you're trying to ruin my boyfriend's life."

She laughs. "If that prank ruined your life, then you didn't have a life in the first place. And how am I ruining your boyfriend's life? Every time something goes bad for you, you blame it on me. Maybe you should start thinking less about what I'm doing and more about yourself. Then maybe you'd actually accomplish something."

"Shut up, Savanna. You're the last person who needs to be giving life advice." I cross my arms. "And who is your friend?" I nod at the other girl.

"None of your business," Savanna says.

"You know him?" the girl asks.

"Unfortunately." Savanna rolls her eyes.

"Is he the other arsonist?" the girl asks. She points at me.

"I don't know. Wait." Savanna raises her eyebrows. "Why were you at Liberty Pike?" she asks.

I stare at her in silence.

"Are you the one setting the other fires?"

"No!" I yell.

"You're lying! You were at the houses with some sort of equipment to set fires. I just saw you."

"I don't have time for you."

"I don't care if you are, obviously. I'm one of them too. I'm not going to rat you out. Just tell me."

"Like I am going to trust you. Were you setting fires so people could obsess over you more? This makes no sense."

"Quite the opposite actually. And it's been working fine until you decided to show up."

"What?"

"Are you the other arsonist?" she repeats.

"It could be his boyfriend," the other girl says.

My eyes flick toward her and my face flushes.

"It is, isn't it?" Savanna asks. "Is that how I am ruining his life?"

"Who's out there?" a man yells.

Savanna's eyes go wide and her mouth falls open. "Dad?"

"Uh-oh," I mutter.

Savanna sprints away from me to her bag. She pulls a lighter from her pocket and shoves it inside, zipping the bag closed. She thrusts the bag into the other girl's arms. "Take this and run," she says.

"What? No," the other girl says. "I'm not going to leave you here with this guy."

"I know him. It's fine. I'm not going to let my dad find out about us this way. Just go."

"You're sure?"

"Hello!" her dad yells again.

A flashlight beam hits the branches above us. A dog barks.

"Yes," Savanna says. "Go!" Her voice is panicked. She runs her hand through her ponytail, then pushes the girl farther into the woods.

Savanna turns to me. "Not a word."

"About which freaking part?" I ask.

"Don't play stupid with me, Highmark." She grips my bicep. Her long nails dig into my skin. "Please. Just not tonight."

I look to the rustling leaves where the other girl disappeared. I don't know who she is, but Savanna must care about her deeply. Savanna has never begged in front of me, and I don't think she ever would unless the situation was dire. These days, I know about dire situations and I know about caring for someone. I'd want her to do the same for Jordan if the roles were switched.

"If my secrets are safe with you, then your secrets are safe with me," I say.

She nods. "Of course."

I turn, and a flashlight is on my face. The light blinds me, and I wobble to keep balance. Everything is out of focus.

"Savanna?" her dad asks. He scratches his head. Two of her brothers and a cop are at his side. Or at least, I think that's who it is. They're more like blurry figures. The cop grips a dog leash. A large German shepherd sniffs frantically at the air.

"Dad," she says, breathing heavily.

"What are you doing out here? It's not safe. Who are you with?"

All four flashlights shine on my body. I look down, grabbing the light on my stomach.

"No one. I mean, yes. It's Dylan Highmark. But just him. You've met before. We're...um...We were..." She swallows and looks to me.

"We're working with Kirsten Lush on her intern project about the arsons," I say. "She interviewed you before. We heard there was a fire and came looking for details."

Savanna's chest deflates, dropping her shoulders.

"This isn't some fun little project," one of her brothers says, stepping forward.

"Enough, Miles," her dad says. "Savanna, get home, please. Let Kirsten do her own work from now on. And I don't want you around Dylan any longer. Understood?"

There's a quick series of snapping sticks in the distance. Everyone freezes. Miles raises his eyebrows. I stop breathing. It's the other girl. I bite down on the inside of my cheek. Mr. Blatt's eyes slide to the side. The dog's ears perk up.

The silence is broken by a symphony of police and fire truck sirens. The Blatts turn back to the street.

"We should go," Miles says.

"Savanna, you heard me," Mr. Blatt says.

She nods.

He turns and runs back to the street with his sons, the cop close behind.

"Thanks for that," Savanna says.

"Yeah, whatever." I place my hand on my forehead. I take a step, but the corners of my eyes go black. My vision blurs. My feet slide against a tree root and I stumble.

"Dylan," Savanna mutters.

My mouth opens, but I can't form words. The thud of my heartbeat pounds in my ears.

"Are you okay? What's happening?"

The world turns sideways, and my head smacks against the dirt.

thirty-three

I wake up later that night to someone knocking on glass near my head. The thud rings back and forth between my ears. My eyes snap open. I'm lying across the back seat of a car. Through the window, a middle-aged blond woman waves at me.

"Excuse me," she says. Her voice is muffled. Annoyance is painted across her face.

"What?" I ask, rubbing my head. I push against the seat and slowly sit up. My back aches. Savanna is passed out in the front seat, her head against the steering wheel. "Savanna!" I yell, and kick the back of the driver's seat.

Her body spasms and she jolts awake. "What?" she yelps. She's still in all black—black pants, hoodie, and shoes. But her hood is down, and she's ditched the black gloves. Her eyes are puffy.

"Hey," the woman says. "You're in the parking spot for charging electrical vehicles. There's only one of these. This isn't for napping."

Savanna looks back at me and slides her fingers through her ponytail. She cracks the window and turns to the woman. "Hi. We were just moving. Thanks." A fog spreads across the glass as she speaks. The woman presses her eyebrows together and nods. She clutches her purse with one hand and directs our car from the spot with the other.

"God, this woman is annoying," Savanna says while waving at her. She reverses out of the parking spot and moves us across the lot.

"Where'd you take me?" I ask, straightening out my clothes.

"Relax," she snaps. "You passed out in the woods. I had to get you out of there."

"Oh, now you're helping me?"

She crosses her arms and lets out an intense breath. I roll my eyes. She taps her fingers along her arm. "I think we need to talk," she says.

I sigh. She is the last person I want to talk to right now. I check my phone, and I have three missed calls from Perry.

"Fine," I say. I look around the parking lot and spot a Whole Foods at the corner of the shopping center. "Can we talk in there at least?" I ask, pointing at the grocery store. "I'm starving. Plus, that woman is still staring at us."

The blond woman sits in a Tesla in the next row of parking spaces. She's on the phone. I don't know who she is calling, but we definitely don't need another guest to explain things to if she's calling her husband or someone.

My pulse picks up the second we walk into the store. The Whole Foods buffet is amazing. Where else can you get Thai food, pizza, mac 'n' cheese, and tomato bisque together without questions?

I grab a brown container and load it with veggie spring rolls, some chicken and rice entree, and a random potato salad that looks good. Savanna gets a slice of white pizza, and we sit at the table in the farthest corner of the dining area.

"So, what do you want to talk about?" I ask. I'm going to let her lead this conversation. I know we both want to ask each other what the hell is going on, but she owes me. I'm hoping this is going to be an extended apology over the fake Instagram, or an apology for trying to set me up with Jimmy, or an apology for tormenting me across the span of my childhood, or a reasonable explanation for being an arsonist, or all four. I bite into my veggie spring roll.

Savanna picks at her pizza crust and gingerly places tiny pieces into her mouth but doesn't take any bites. There's a whoosh of air from a vent above us. A janitor sweeps trash from underneath a table nearby.

"Dylan . . . I just wanted to say I'm sorry. I didn't know you were going through all this." She looks around the empty seating area.

I choke on the flaky crust of my spring roll. I pound my fist into my chest. Did she just utter the word *sorry*?

That's not how I was expecting this conversation to start. I mean, I was hoping it would. But my expectations for something going my way for once were about as high as I could float off the ground before assuming my powers—aka nonexistent.

I swallow the last bit of food in my mouth and think before responding. There's no point in being bitter. We all do shitty things to each other. It's not like she was setting the fires on purpose to get Jordan caught too or mess with me and get me in trouble. How was she supposed to know? How was anyone supposed to know?

I take a deep breath and stare at her blankly. "It's fine," I say.

She sits back in her chair and crosses her legs. Her hands are folded in her lap.

"To be fair, I think we're both going through something," I say.

"You got that right."

She looks to the side. Her white hair looks an even brighter shade of white against her black ensemble.

I put down my fork and wipe my mouth with a napkin. "When we ran into each other in the hall that day and I saw the suicide flyer...Is it okay that I bring that up?"

She nods.

"I thought it was because of the fires. I thought maybe they were stressing you out. But you were setting them yourself. I'm just confused." I flip my hands on the table. "I don't get how that prank would make you feel better."

She shrugs. Her eyes glaze over. "I'm not here to talk about the prank."

"Huh?" I raise my eyebrows. "What are we talking about, then?"

"The fires," she presses. "They were freeing me."

"Freeing you? What? Now I'm confused."

"Over the past two months, I have been able to be more me than ever before in my life. My parents...my brothers...no one was paying attention to me. They were so busy. Since someone else was setting the other fires, I thought no one would know. I thought I could get away with it to keep it going for as long as possible."

"You love attention. What are you talking about? And, not to be rude, but don't you think that's a little extreme? Couldn't you have just talked to your family if something was going on?"

"It wasn't extreme!" she snaps. Her nostrils flare. "You don't know me or my family."

I hold up my hands. "Sorry. I didn't mean to assume."

The buffet area is dead silent. Savanna's voice echoes whenever she speaks.

"Don't you think your boyfriend could've talked to someone?" she counters.

I'm silent.

"See," she says. "It's not that easy."

I nod.

"It was him. Wasn't it?" she asks. "I heard you yelling his name back there at Liberty Pike. You thought the fire was being set by him and you were looking for him, weren't you?"

"Yeah," I say.

"Why?"

I take a deep breath. "I can't really tell you. But you know how you thought I had a flamethrower back in the woods?" She nods. "Well, I didn't. I was shooting the flames with my hands. And Jordan is the same."

Her eyes bulge. She looks at me the same way I look at every Chemistry test—with disgust and confusion.

"Wait, what?" she asks. She stands from her seat.

"Sit back down," I order, looking around the buffet area. I said it casually because there's really no right way to warn someone about this.

She throws her head back and laughs. "You really have no low, do you? There might be a few different ways to handle this, but making up absurd lies isn't one of them." She slowly sits again. "I was trying to be serious with you. My life has been affected. This isn't a joke."

"I am being serious with you, Savanna."

"I don't believe you. Shoot a flame, then." Her shoulders bounce.

"I can't just do that here. Are you not listening? I can't bring attention to myself. Jordan is missing because of it. There are people after him, and the fires make it obvious where he is."

"Missing? Like, kidnapped?"

I fill her in on HydroPro's pursuit of Jordan. I leave out my eventual demise.

"That doesn't make sense," she says.

"To be fair, neither does your explanation. So I guess we're even. That's all I can disclose for now." I lean back.

"So I'm just supposed to believe you make fire from nothing?"

"Yeah." I shrug. "I can float too, if that piques your interest a little more."

She shakes her head. "You really are like a rat in a lab, Highmark."

I stand. "Well, we've spoken enough about the fires. I'm glad you told me whatever it was that you told me. Good-bye, Savanna." I take a step, but she grabs my arm.

"I didn't tell you yet," she says. Her lip quivers. "There's more to explain. The truth is..." Her voice is shaky. "I've been wanting to tell you something for a while now. Well, for years really. But I guess you know what that is now."

After everything that's happened the past two months, I'm smarter than letting myself make assumptions about people. "Oh, yeah? What's that?"

She spins her thumbs in her lap. "I don't know. We're more alike than you think."

I chuckle. "I'm sure you have some great qualities somewhere in there. But I highly doubt that."

She bites her lip. "This isn't supposed to be funny."

"Well, tell me. I don't understand."

"I'm..." She takes a deep breath and then hangs her head.

"You're...?"

"I'm..."

"You're what?" I press.

"I can't say it."

"Well, that's not going to help me understand."

"Dylan..."

She puts her hand on the table. It's shaking. I furrow my brows and inspect her body movements. I quickly reflect over the events of the past couple hours to try and figure out why Savanna is acting this way. The one thing that's different is the presence of that girl. Suddenly, the only thing I can picture in my head is their constant touching at the fire, in the woods, and before the girl's escape. There's no way. But also, there kind of is a way. In fact, Savanna's behaviors—practicing attention-diverting tactics; assuming an uncrackable, icy demeanor; pursuing the focused sabotage of Dylan Highmark—pave the way.

"Wait. Are you...?" I ask, sitting back in my seat.

She half nods, then shakes her head.

"How do I know we're thinking the same thing?"

"I don't know."

"You're gay?" I ask.

"Yes! And I don't know what to do about it."

Her face contorts and then explodes. Her cheeks are covered in tears within seconds. My mouth hangs slightly ajar. But I quickly snap it shut.

Part of me wants to jump across the table and hug her. The other part of me wants to throw my potato salad in her face. I thought I would be better at something like this. I want to be happy for her, but I'm having trouble forgetting the level of shitty she's been to me since middle school.

"Like..." I start. But I have no clue what to say.

She wipes her mouth with her sleeve.

"You don't have to say anything," she says. "I'm not looking for you to be my friend. I know I suck. I'm so sorry for the way I treated you."

"Why did you?"

"Why did I what?"

"Treat me like that."

She inhales. "I honestly don't know. It, like, always seemed so easy for you. It came so naturally. I felt stupid around you."

"Are you kidding? Nothing about my coming out was easy. It's still not easy. And you and your family were some of the people making it so hard. You hurt my feelings...a lot." My voice falters.

"I know. When you sat with me at lunch the other week I thought—"

"I thought you were in trouble."

"I was! And I am. These past two months...I just lost it."

"What do you want from me?"

"Nothing. I just wanted you to know so this all made a little more sense."

"It doesn't. This whole thing is wack. And I don't mean you. I mean you, and me, and Jordan, and everything."

Savanna sniffs and looks at the ground. "Really wack," she says.

"Am I the only person who knows?" I ask.

"Yeah." She tugs at her ponytail.

"Are you going to tell other people?"

"I'm going to try. Not my family, though . . . at least not yet."

"Yeah, they don't seem to be the most approachable."

I push around my food. I know right now Savanna is so nauseated she's about to puke. Her mouth is probably numb. She's squeezing her fingers to stop her hands from shaking.

"I don't know if I accept your apology, but I'm really proud of you and happy for you. I know it isn't easy. I feel like in most coming-out moments this is when I am supposed to say this doesn't change anything between us, but in our case, I hope this does change things between us."

She laughs. "Thanks, Dylan."

"Are you dating that girl from the woods? You know I need the scoop now."

She laughs again. "I guess you could say that."

"She's pretty."

Savanna's face turns red. "Her name is Devon. She goes to St. Helena's. She was actually at Kirsten's party."

"Ah. A Helena Ho. Seems like all the hot gay people go there."

She shrugs. "I wouldn't say that."

"You're right. We're hotter."

Savanna smiles. I reach out my hand and spread my fingers. She puts her hand on mine. "This is weird," she says.

"I guess we can both be 'woe is me, we're the only gay people in school' together now," I say.

She hums. "I guess so."

Out of the corner of my eye, I notice a familiar head of long blond hair standing next to the pizza counter. I turn to get a better look. It's either Perry or an identical twin. Kirsten emerges from an aisle holding two drinks and stands beside her. The massive key chain hanging on her fingers gives it away.

"Oh no," I mutter.

"What?" Savanna asks.

"Kirsten and Perry are here. I've been ignoring them. They're going to freak if they see me."

"Where?"

"By the pizza."

I place my elbow on the table and hide my face in my palm. I twist my body away from their direction and stare at the wall.

"Let me know if they're coming," I say.

"They're coming," Savanna says.

"What? Already?"

"Dylan!" Perry shouts.

I sit up and our eyes meet. She's grinning from ear to ear. They both look tan. She places her pizza on a table and runs in my direction. Her arms are outstretched for a hug.

"Where have you been? I've missed you! I loved your Valentine's card at school."

I look at Savanna as I feel my body heating up. Orange light glows beneath my fingernails. I dig through my pockets and realize I don't have my Balancer. This is bad. Not only have I ignored them, but I'm here with Savanna, the one person I claim to despise. So many questions are about to be launched at me. How do I explain? *Think, Dylan. Think.*

Before Perry reaches us, I stand and extend my arm in front of me. My chair crashes to the floor on its side.

"Wait, stop!" I yell.

Perry comes to a halt an inch from me. "What's wrong?" she asks.

"I...I'm sick. I don't want to give it to you."

Savanna winces. My body is steaming. I know if I hug Perry, she'll get burned.

"That makes no sense," Perry says, rolling her eyes. "I think I'll take my chances." She takes a step. I jump back.

"I'm serious," I say. I push my palm through the air at her chest. "Just not right now."

She squints at me. "You're being really weird." Her eyes dart to Savanna for a second and then back to me. She mutters, "What?" under her breath and fixes her bag hanging over her shoulder.

Kirsten reaches us. "Fancy meeting you two here. What's the occasion?" No one says anything. Savanna has yet to say a word. It's as if she's transformed into a different person after coming out.

"Let's go, Kirsten," Perry says. "I think we're interrupting. Dylan doesn't want to talk to us." Perry grabs Kirsten's arm.

"What do you mean?" Kirsten asks, wiping her lips with her arm.

"I didn't say I didn't want to talk to you," I say. "I just can't hug you now. I'm still sick." I sigh. "I'm sorry. How are you?" I try to fix the conversation.

"You seem fine to me," Perry blurts out.

"Why haven't you been answering our messages? We've been asking you to get dinner with us for days." She nods at Savanna. "No offense."

Savanna shakes her head.

"I thought you were grounded," I say.

"We just lost our phone privileges while we were away. We're allowed to leave the house."

"Oh."

Kirsten crosses her arms. My skin tingles, like my whole body is asleep. I grab my chair from the floor and bring it right side up. I sit down and dig my feet underneath the table legs, knowing what's about to come.

"Okay, well . . . can we hang out tomorrow?" Kirsten asks. "Your lack of response kind of makes it hard to plan."

"Um . . ." I start. I look at Savanna as if she can help me. Her eyes glaze over. I have to go to HydroPro tomorrow. It's my last chance to find Jordan. I have to fix everything. Even though it was worthwhile, this Savanna diversion delayed my plans enough. Time is running out.

My feet lift off the floor. I grip the edge of the table and push myself downward. I exhale hard.

"Come on, Kirsten," Perry says, pulling Kirsten's shoulder. "You got your answer."

"Dylan, you've been acting strange lately and it's obvious," Kirsten says sternly. "You said before no secrets between us. What is up with you?" Kirsten tries to tap my arm, but I dodge it.

I'm biting my tongue, trying to keep myself from floating to the ceiling and my skin from bursting into flames.

Perry shakes her head. "Did Jordan do something to you?"

I unclench my teeth. "It's not like that!" I yell, and smack my hand against the table.

Everyone jumps. Perry's and Kirsten's faces are scrunched. Perry's fingers tighten around Kirsten's arm.

Savanna puts her two fingers over her eyes and mouths the word *eyes* to me. Panic rips through me. I pick up my phone and look at my reflection in the black screen. The ice-blue halo shimmers around my pupils. I look to the wall.

Kirsten and Perry take a step away. "Well, gosh, Dylan. Enjoy your night," Perry says.

Kirsten looks me up and down. "We've done what we can here," she says. "Let's go." They pick up their pizza and leave the store.

My hands are shaking so hard the table rattles between me and Savanna.

"Dylan, calm down," she says.

"I don't... I don't feel well," I say. A lump forms in the back of my throat. A sharp pain radiates from my spine and shoots across the sides of my body. I don't think I've ever had a fight with Perry or Kirsten, let alone both at the same time. If I don't have them, then I have no one.

I lurch over the table and vomit. Most of the brown liquid makes it into my food container. A few chunks splatter across the table. Savanna screams. She grabs a fistful of napkins and wipes up my vomit. She tosses the soaked napkins into the container and then runs away to throw everything into the garbage.

A text from Kirsten pops up on my phone. It says, *Way to go. Perry is crying.*

Maybe they're right. Maybe Jordan has done something to me. But his life is on the line, and I don't know how to make decisions when the stakes are that high. Lying to protect him seems like the right call. He's fighting for his life, and I'm just a boy with a crush and some friend drama. Somehow I've become the keeper of everyone's secrets. But they're not keeping me together; they're tearing me apart.

I cough. No more liquid comes out. My normal body wouldn't know how to handle this. But my new body seems to think it does, and apparently, it's by killing me.

thirty-four

On Monday, Mom changes around her work schedule so she can personally drop me off at school. I took one too many puffs of the Elemental Balancer after the Whole Foods incident and slept the entire weekend. I've been gone from the house at so many random times these days my parents no longer trust me enough to take the bus to school alone, which is fine. Getting a ride to school is far superior to taking the bus with the driver who blasts country music and fifty snoring freshmen.

This is the first time I've been grounded, and I don't think my parents quite know how it works. I don't have time to add *handing out grounding tips* to my to-do list, so I'm just sitting back and enjoying the ride.

Mom grabs my shoulder as I'm getting out of the car.

"Have a good day, Dylan," she says softly. She forces a smile.

I nod. "Thanks. I'll try."

"Maybe we can do dinner sometime this week?"

"What? We eat dinner every night?"

She shakes her head. "You know what I mean. Out to dinner . . . just you and me. You can tell me about the boy you're seeing."

I run my finger along the door handle. "Dinner could be nice."

She rubs my arm. "Please let me know if you need anything . . . anything at all."

I sigh. "Mom."

She holds up her finger. Her eyes are glassy. "Dylan, don't."

I clear my throat. "Thanks for the ride. I'll see you after school." I exit the car and slam the door shut. I take a deep breath and look up at the morning sun reflecting off the school windows.

Savanna is sitting on a bench by the main entrance. She's staring at me. She slowly brings her hand up and waves. I walk to her.

"Hey," I say.

"Hey," she says. Her cheeks are rosy, and her lips are a deep shade of red. She's wearing a navy cable-knit headband, a green puffy coat, and navy gloves. "How are you feeling?"

I sit next to her. "I've been better," I say. I crush a stone into the sidewalk with my boot.

"Have you heard from your boyfriend at all?"

"No. I don't think I'm supposed to be expecting to either."

"He might come back."

"Yeah, well . . . a lot of things might happen. How are you feeling?"

"About what?"

I chuckle. "About how you're going to walk through these doors and be yourself for the first time?" I nudge her with my elbow.

"To one person."

"One is better than none. You know I'm here for you, right? If you ever need someone to talk to, like, in real life . . . I got you."

She nods. "Thanks, Dylan. You don't have to worry. I never called that Lifeline . . . you just caught me at a low point." She adjusts her headband.

"I don't care if you did or didn't. It just helps to talk about this stuff out loud."

"You're the expert, aren't you?"

"Just speaking from experience."

Savanna wipes her nose with her glove. "I've been a lot better since I told you. But to be honest, I don't want to leave this bench. I feel like everyone is staring at me already."

"No one is staring at you, Savanna. I'm the only person who knows. Everyone still thinks you're heartless."

She smirks and slaps my arm. "Am I going to get that from you for the rest of my life?"

"No." I smile. "Maybe just half of your life." I lean into her.

"Fair." She purses her lips.

"Just think, I've been out since freshman year and who cares about my life?"

She crosses her arms.

"I'll answer for you," I say. "Since I know you're trying out this new 'being nice' thing—and that was a great start, by the way—but the answer is no one."

"I think I messed things up for too long." She sniffs.

"Everyone is going to love the real Savanna. In fact, I'm personally very interested in getting to know her. That old girl you thought you needed to be? She's gone."

"I hate her."

"Tell her!"

"I hate her!"

"Okay, not that loud. People already think we're out of our minds."

I scan the parking lot for Perry or Kirsten. For the first time in a while, my body is cold.

Mom hasn't moved. Her car is parked in the same spot where she dropped me off. We make eye contact through the windshield. She throws up her hands. She points toward school and mouths, *Get inside.*

"We should probably go," I say. "Before my mom requests to follow me through school all day."

"Okay," Savanna says.

I stand and take a few steps. Savanna stays planted on the bench. I extend my hand to her. She clasps it and stands.

"This is your secret to share," I say. "You don't have to tell anyone today or for the rest of the school year if you don't want to. Just be you."

"Yeah, I mean, I'm not going to announce it from the loudspeakers like you did."

I shake my head. I pull out my magical inhaler from my pocket and take a few puffs. I don't think I even need it, though. The thoughts of everyone I'm missing are weighing me down.

thirty-five

Savanna and I split up at the first hallway, and rather than going to history class, I go somewhere that actually matters.

I reach Dr. Brio's classroom and knock on his door. He's sitting on one of the lab stools and grading tests. He licks his finger, picks up a paper, and glances at me out of the corner of his eye.

"Mr. Highmark." He sighs.

"I know. I should be in class right now."

He takes off his glasses and places them on the black countertop. "You have been in and out of school a lot lately. Is everything all right?"

I nod. "Can I come in?"

He extends his hand to one of the open stools. "What can I do for you?"

I pull the stool farther out from the lab bench and sit on it.

"Can humans breathe hydrogen?" I ask.

He sighs. "No. Humans need oxygen to live. There are very, very small amounts of hydrogen in the earth's atmosphere. But nothing substantial that we could live from."

"Right. But what if we we're made of hydrogen? Like, I know we have carbon, nitrogen...mostly oxygen in us. But what if we were all hydrogen? Remember that picture in our textbook with the diagram of the guy, and he was filled with the different percentages of human body elements?"

He smiles. "Yes. I remember the diagram. I'm glad you're looking at your book."

"Yeah. Sometimes it's informative."

"But I don't understand your question. The human body composition is the human body composition. If it was something else, it wouldn't be human."

My eyes drift to the ceiling. "Interesting," I mutter.

Does that mean I'm not human anymore?

I pull out my phone and text Jordan, *I miss you*. It bounces back with the error, *Not delivered*. It floats beneath three other messages in the feed that also failed to deliver.

Dr. Brio slashes a red mark across a paper and moves it from one pile of tests to another pile.

"Any other questions?" he asks.

"Yes, one more. What are your thoughts on gay rights?"

He laughs and drops his pen. "Wasn't expecting that question, but an easy answer at that. Fully support."

"Great!" I stand. "Then you would be interested in being the faculty sponsor of the Gay–Straight Alliance?"

He cocks his head back.

"I'm in the group and we're in need of a sponsor," I continue. "Otherwise the group is going to disband after this year."

Dr. Brio stands, picks up his stack of tests, and shuffles to his desk. I follow him, hoisting my backpack tighter over my shoulders.

"Mr. Highmark, I would be happy to be a part of any extracurricular activity that you are doing. I'm honored you would ask me to sponsor. Just let me know when and where."

"Thank you! There's a meeting today after school in the library."

"I'll be there."

"Amazing. I can't wait to tell Darlene." I head for the door. Hopefully, I can mend things with at least one person today.

"Dylan?" Dr. Brio asks.

"Yeah?"

"Do you have the paperwork for me to sign?"

"There's paperwork?"

He shakes his head and waves me out the door. "I'll take care of it. Just get to class, please."

I pass Kirsten's locker on my way to history class. She's switching out her books. I watch her delicately stack her textbooks into a perfectly organized pyramid. She swaps a blue pen for a black pen from an *ABC News* coffee mug. Two vertical rows of sticky notes hang on the inside of her locker door. The top one says *To Do*. I read her to-do list, and the third note down says *Find out if Dylan is okay*. My heart breaks even more than I thought it could.

With Jordan gone, I realize how much I've neglected Kirsten and

Perry the past couple weeks. I was so obsessed with someone new that I forgot about the people I've known forever. Kirsten and Perry don't want to listen to a word I say now. I wouldn't want to talk to me after the way I treated them at Whole Foods. But getting Jordan back would mean nothing if I lose them. They deserve my trust as much as Jordan does.

I approach her.

"Hello," I say.

She jumps. "Jeez," she says, brushing her hair behind her ear. "You're the last person I expected to sneak up on me."

It's silent for ten seconds.

"How are you?" I ask.

"I've been better. I finished writing up the article about the fires, though. So that's good."

My body doesn't react to the word *fire*. I'm over it. I'm sick of reacting. I'm tired of hearing the word *fire* and getting nervous, and lying to my friends, and pushing everyone away.

"Oh . . . that's great. I can read it over if you want someone else to take a look sometime."

"Yeah, maybe."

My jaw tightens. I want to tell her things. But I don't know how.

"Okay, well, I need to go," she says flatly. "I fell behind on my usual homework trying to finish the news article."

"What? That's it?"

"What do you mean that's it?"

"You're going to walk away?"

"Yeah, Dylan. You've been ignoring me ever since I got back

from Nationals. You don't get to talk to me whenever it's convenient for you."

"I haven't been ignoring you."

"Oh yeah? What would you call it, then, when you're trying to talk to someone and they never respond? I texted you after Whole Foods because Perry was crying, and you still didn't respond. I saw you had your phone."

I don't say anything.

"Yeah, thought so," she says. "Listen, I'm happy you're okay and had a fun night with Savanna. Maybe you needed it or something. I don't know. But I'll see you around this week."

My breath catches.

"Kirsten..."

She shrugs. "Maybe text me sometime when it fits into your schedule."

She takes a step. I run my hand through my hair. "Wait," I say. "Wait. Just wait." I lick my lips. "Remember when I said I couldn't tell you stuff?"

"Yeah, obviously. That's why I'm upset with you. We've always told each other everything for ten years."

I nod. "Well, I'm going to tell you now and you can't tell anyone. This isn't like everything we've told each other before. Promise?"

Kirsten nods. She looks over her shoulder. "Yes. I promise."

I grab her arm and pull her into the closest janitor's closet.

"What are we doing?" she asks.

I hold out my open palm, close my eyes, and tighten the muscles in my face. I know a fireball erupts from my hand when Kirsten screams.

"Oh my god!" Kirsten says, pushing me away. Her books crash to the floor. "What the—" she shouts. She tumbles back and trips over a mop bucket, falling on her butt. Her mouth is agape. "What was that? What have you done?"

I knew she was going to have to see it to believe it.

"Shhh." I help her to her feet. "Remember when I first met Jordan and I said he was both hot to look at and hot to touch? That's what I meant."

"It wasn't a firecracker?"

I tell her all of it—the first Dairy Queen fiasco, the night in the tub, the pond, the fires, the chase at the park, the hydrogen chamber, Jordan's disappearance . . . all of it. Except I leave out Savanna setting the other fires.

Kirsten's eyes dart back and forth as she connects the dots. Her hand is stuck over her mouth.

"You didn't believe me the first time," I say. "But I need you to believe me now. I couldn't tell you things before because I had to protect Jordan. But I need you and Perry."

"This is purely an oversight on my part. I should've seen the evidence. It was right here in front of me the whole time. The two men in that video setting the fire . . . it's you and Jordan. How did I not recognize you?"

"I—"

"I knew there was no logical way I survived falling into the ice. But of course I wasn't going to question it. I'm still alive, thankfully. Now I see how the ice melted. Come to think of it, I remember seeing an explosion above me while I was underwater. Jordan kept me warm, didn't he? This totally throws off my article. I thought it was those men in the silver cars. I was just about to solve where they're from. I'll have to rewrite—"

I grab her shoulders. "Kirsten, relax. I need you to edit that article. I don't know what's in it, and it might be too dangerous for Jordan . . . and me."

"Forget the article for a second. So he's not here anymore?"

"I don't know where he is."

"And those people from HydroPro? They're after you?" She hugs me but then quickly pulls away. "Oh, I forgot already. You're burning up."

I laugh. But my smile quickly fades. Is this what it's going to be like from now on? Am I only going to get short hugs because people can't bear to touch me?

"But I have a plan to help bring him back."

"How?" Kirsten asks.

"The doctor I am seeing mentioned that HydroPro is creating some sort of medicine or antidote that can fix Jordan or help him stay alive . . . and me. Jordan doesn't know about it. If I can get my hands on it or prove to Jordan it's real . . . he can come back. He left because he thought he was killing me, but he's not."

"How are you going to get it?" Kirsten asks.

"I'm going to find a way inside HydroPro."

She gasps. "Is that safe? What if they capture you and you don't get back out?"

"What is safe anymore?"

A group of people walks by the janitor's closet. We pause and wait for them to pass before speaking again.

"I'm sorry you had to go through this alone," Kirsten says.

My vision begins to blur, and I look to the ground. "It's okay . . .
I think. If I have you back, I'll be okay."

"Of course you do."

"I'm going to need your help, though."

"What's it involve?"

"Well, I've been doing some investigative work of my own. I
know I said you can't publish the article as is, but you can publish it
a different way. I have some evidence to share with you. Then I need
you to broadcast it to the public. It involves you being center stage."

"Say no more."

I pull out my phone from my pocket.

"Piece of evidence number one," I say. I show her the picture I
took of the silver cars at the first fire.

"Hm," she hums. "The silver cars. I know this."

"Yes, but I know who they are."

"Who?"

"HydroPro."

"HydroPro?"

"Yes."

"I need more."

I slide through my camera roll. "Piece of evidence number two."
I open the video she sent of Jordan and me hopping over the fence
into the town house development, except I cut out the first half of
the video with us. The second half films the brigade of silver cars
arriving at the scene.

"I'm intrigued," Kirsten says.

"Evidence pieces numbers three, four, and five should be the
other videos you have of HydroPro pulling up to the other fires."

Kirsten smiles.

"Now pull up the pictures you took of the scene after your party."

She follows my instructions and puts her phone in my face.

"Look here...here...and here." I point to the backgrounds of different pictures, all of which have the silver cars in the street.

"They didn't actually set these fires, did they?"

"Not exactly...but where Jordan was, HydroPro was. It's circumstantial, but who says we can't get out in front of them? And here's the final piece of evidence." I show her screenshots of the cars outside the HydroPro facility.

Kirsten taps her chin. "This, my friend, is what we call a case."

thirty-six

I run to the library after school. I scan the computer stations and tables in the center of the room. There are a few lone people studying and a girl painting her nails at one of the computers. But there's no Darlene.

I walk to the librarian's desk.

"Hi," I whisper. The librarian looks up at me from her seat. "Where is the GSA meeting?"

She moves her mouse to wake up her black computer screen and gives it a few clicks.

"It looks like it's scheduled in meeting room C," she whispers to me, then points down the hall.

"Okay, thanks," I whisper.

I speedwalk down the silent hall and spot Darlene through the windows of meeting room C. It's at the end of the bookshelves. Her glasses are orange and her skirt is yellow. She pulls a case of markers from her backpack and places them on a long table. She's alone. I open the door and walk inside.

She looks up. Her body goes rigid.

"Dylan," she says. Her feet shuffle back a couple steps.

"Hey," I say.

"We have a meeting in here. It's closed for studying."

"I know. I'm joining the meeting."

She sighs, and her shoulders drop. "You don't have to do this. I don't need sympathy participation."

"I want to be in this group."

There's silence.

"Since when?" she asks.

"Since today."

She crosses her arms.

"I'm serious," I continue. "I kind of didn't realize until this weekend how much I wanted to be here."

"Are you okay, Dylan?" She taps a pink marker against her finger. "I remember the last time we talked you said you were going through a lot. Then all that weird stuff happened to you in the hallway and I ignored you. I didn't mean to."

"What do you mean? You invited me into this group. You were there for me."

She smiles. "I'm glad you're here . . . at least for the final meetings. There's really not much left to do. Just a couple more events through the spring, then we're done." She places a few papers on the table.

"Not final." I hold up my finger. "I got us a sponsor."

"What? Who?"

"Dr. Brio!"

"Chemistry Dr. Brio?"

"Yes!"

"I thought he sponsored, like, five clubs already? The sophomore Bio teacher, Mrs. McClane, told me a teacher couldn't sponsor more than two, so I didn't even bother asking him."

I shrug. "I don't know. I just asked him. She must not have been an ally."

"Clearly. She was trying to sabotage us."

"Glad we're weeding them out early."

Shortly after, Dr. Brio walks into the room followed by Maddie Leostopoulos and Brenton Riley. Maddie has a Greek flag patch sewn onto her backpack. Brenton carries a thin black leather binder clutched to his chest with golden initials emblazoned on the front. Everyone takes a seat around the table. I tap my fingers on the armrest as I scan everyone from head to toe. I avoid eye contact with Brenton, hoping he somehow forgot the events that occurred at Kirsten's party.

"So," Darlene starts. "This is an exciting meeting because we have a new member and a new sponsor joining us!"

Maddie claps.

"Since there are some new folks here, I thought we could begin by going around the table and saying your name, pronouns, a little bit about yourself, and maybe a fun fact."

Everyone nods.

"I'll go first. My name is Darlene Houchowitz. She/her. I'm a junior here, obviously. My fun fact is that my three middle toes were webbed together when I was born but as I grew older, they separated. And I identify as an ally."

"That sounds like it hurt," I say. "That couldn't have been fun."

"True. Maybe it's more of a, like, a unique fact. Maddie, your turn."

Maddie waves. "You all know my name," she says, laughing. "I think everyone was at my sweet sixteen party last year. Except for you, Dr. Brio. That would've been weird. No offense." She turns. "Oh, and I guess you weren't there either, Brenton. You were still in the eighth grade. So, maybe just Dylan and Lena were there. But you still all probably know me."

Dr. Brio shakes his head.

"My fun fact is that I go to Greece every summer with my family, and this year I'm going for the month of July. I'm also an ally."

"Yay," Darlene says.

We turn to Brenton.

"Hi. I'm Brenton. My pronouns are he/him/his. Freshman. I've been to all the Smithsonian art galleries and museums in DC."

"Oh, impressive. Any favorites?" Darlene asks.

"Probably the National Museum of the American Indian."

"A classic."

Dr. Brio clears his throat as he sits up in his chair. "I'm your favorite Chemistry teacher, Dr. Brio. I go by male pronouns. I'm happy to be here to support this important group. And I've been teaching high school chemistry for more years than all of you have been alive."

We throw our heads back and laugh.

"Probably combined," Maddie adds.

He chuckles.

Everyone swivels their chairs to look at me.

"Hello," I say. "I'm Dylan Highmark. He/him." I wonder what I should say as my fun fact. I don't have a shortage of those to choose from these days. I shoot flames? I can float to the sky? I'm no longer human, according to Dr. Brio? But then I remember that my life was cool and fun before the powers. I think of a good one. "My fun fact is that I have had the same best friends for a decade." I smack the table at the end of my sentence.

Maddie grabs my knee. "You're also the only gay person in the junior class," she says, smiling. "That totally should have been your fun fact. Especially here."

"Uh, you're right," I say. "Next time I will *totally* use that one."

Darlene smiles. "Okay, then! We're happy you're here, Dylan," she says. "You too, Dr. Brio." She pulls a folder from her bag and takes out a few packets of papers. "So let's move on and talk about our springtime advocacy events—"

The meeting room's door handle jiggles, and the door is gently pushed open. Darlene stops speaking. Everyone snaps their heads toward it.

I turn and watch Savanna slither through the doorway. Darlene looks at me and frowns. I nod at her, then wave Savanna inside. She sits next to me.

"Can we help you?" Darlene asks. "We're having a meeting. This room is closed for studying."

"Hi, everyone," Savanna says softly. "This is room C, right? I'm here for the meeting." She's staring at the table and doesn't make eye contact with anyone. Her back is slouched. She repeatedly runs her hand through her ponytail.

Darlene looks at me, then at Savanna, then back to me.

I shrug.

Darlene clears her throat. She leans forward. "We were going around introducing ourselves. But before we move forward, I would like to reiterate that this is a safe space. Does anyone need an explanation of what that is?" She's staring at Savanna.

The room is silent.

"Good," Darlene says with a nod. "Would you like to go, Savanna? Everyone else already went."

"Yeah, sure," Savanna says. She turns to me. "What do I say?"

"Just, like, our names, pronouns, a fun fact, and anything else you'd like to share with the group," I instruct her, tapping my fingers on the table.

"Oh . . . okay, cool," Savanna says. Her voice shakes. "I'm Savanna Blatt. Um, a fun fact for me is . . . I don't know. This is boring, but I have three older brothers." She grimaces. "Sorry."

"You don't have to apologize for your fun fact," I say.

"Right." She smiles slightly. "So, that's me." She sighs.

"You forgot your pronouns," I whisper.

"She?" Savanna asks.

"Great," Darlene says, exhaling. She re-collects her papers. "Well, I am so happy everyone is here. We've grown quickly! Back to our calendar of events."

"And maybe just one more thing," Savanna says. She's sliding a ring off and on her finger. Her nails are lime green. She glances at me.

I nod.

Savanna leans forward. "I'm happy too. But if any of you tell anyone I'm here, *happy* will be the last emotion you feel."

Everyone's smiles disappear from their faces. The room goes

quiet. Maddie's jaw drops. Darlene freezes in her seat. Brenton pushes his glasses farther up his nose. Dr. Brio's face reddens.

Ah, forever a charmer. That wasn't the glorious coming-out moment I was expecting, but I swear it was on the tip of her tongue. I shoot Savanna a look, shaking my head.

She shrugs.

Darlene swallows. "Um, okay," she says.

There's a minute of silence. Suddenly, Darlene bursts into laughter. Her head falls back as her mouth opens. I look at the sneer painted across Savanna's face, then start giggling. After a few moments, the whole table laughs, including Savanna.

"Whatever, Savanna," Darlene says. "This is just the most ridiculous group of people I've ever seen." Tears of laughter stream down her cheeks. She slides everyone some papers. "We're happy you're here."

I feel like I'm floating, but I'm still in my seat. I study Savanna, and my mind skips over its usual string of first thoughts. Rather than seeing the level of neon on her fingertips, shade of her lips, scowl on her face, or height of her heels, I envision her in her bedroom. I think of all the nights we were awake together staring at the ceiling, less alone than we thought.

I'm grateful she kept me in her orbit through the years, even though sometimes it involved my demise. For someone who used to break my heart on the daily, she's doing a great job of patching it back together.

The solitude of my bedroom used to provide me comfort—just as Savanna's meanness, I'm assuming, acted as her own security blanket. But being here is showing me how good moments passed me by while I was keeping the same four walls around me. And we've all lost out on what it's like to be around a happy Savanna.

No matter the past events that occurred among us, or the future that is yet to unfold, the laughter currently around this table makes for a moment that can't be missed between two people who've spent too much time wishing they'd be overlooked.

thirty-seven

A few days later in Chemistry class, the back of my neck is on fire. But not from my own internal body temperature. My ability to tolerate Perry's silent, hot breath blowing down my spine has reached its limit. Fixing things with her is the last piece of my life-correcting plan before I infiltrate HydroPro this week. If something bad happens to me there, I don't want to leave my friendship with Perry on a bad note. If I disappear, I want her recent memories of us to be good ones.

I watch the red line on my iPhone clock make its way to the twelve. My pencil spins between my fingers. The wood begins to get flimsy. I look down and drop it before it melts into a pile of ash on my notebook.

The clock hand finally reaches the top of the hour, and the class bell rings. I spin around in my seat.

We make eye contact for one second before Perry pulls her books to her chest and jumps from her desk.

"Perry, wait," I say, shuffling after her.

She keeps walking through the classroom. She's wearing her cheerleading uniform. Her hair is in a wavy ponytail with a white ribbon tied at the top.

I dart in front of her and block the doorway before she can leave. She steps to the right to squeeze by me, but I sidestep to block her. Then she bends down to duck under my arm, but I lower my hand against the door frame, and her forehead smacks into my forearm.

"Would you stop?" she says, stomping her right foot. "What do you want?"

"Can we hang out soon?"

"You're kidding." She shakes her head.

"I am, actually. I understand you're mad. I get it. But I think all the silent treatment has been enough. Don't you?"

"No." She smiles. "You gave me and Kirsten the silent treatment for, like, two and a half weeks. I think it's only fair you get the same treatment."

"You can't be serious. You were grounded for half of that time."

"As serious as Ms. Gurbsterter is with her Lean Cuisines." She squints.

I sigh. "Perry, I'm sorry. I really am."

"Are you? Or are you just sorry we caught you keeping secrets?"

"What? Not at all. I haven't even thought of it like that."

"Well, I have. Maybe I shouldn't have tried so hard to find you a boyfriend. I didn't know you were going to forget about me. You're going to date a lot of people throughout life and if your way of getting into a relationship is to stop talking to all your friends, then good luck."

I huff and rub my hands over my face. "Can you cut that? Seriously, I haven't forgotten about you."

"Where would you be this weekend if you weren't dating Jordan?"

"What?"

"What would you be doing?"

"Um..."

She sighs. "Well, Kirsten and I are cheering at the basketball game tonight. Come hang out."

"That's what I'm asking about!"

"Good. It's the varsity boys' championship game. If they win this, then they go to States. That's why I'm wearing my uniform. There are banners all over the hallways. Are you not paying attention to anything?"

"Not lately."

"Okay, well, then my case has been made."

She walks out the doorway and into the hallway. Her cheerleading skirt sways side to side.

I chase after her. "I'll be there."

"We'll see. Oh, and I think your best friend is waiting for you to go home together." She nods to the other end of the hallway.

I turn around, and Savanna is leaning against a row of lockers, staring. She waves with two fingers. Perry disappears around a corner.

"Hey," I say, exhaling.

"Hey," Savanna says. "Is she still mad?"

I nod and wipe my hands down my thighs.

"Any word from Jordan?" she asks.

I check my phone. "No. What are you doing tonight?"

"Going to the basketball game with the rest of town. How 'bout you?"

"Okay, cool. Same. Can we go together?"

"Yeah, of course."

"The whole town is going to be there?"

Savanna nods.

A lightbulb goes off in my head.

The game starts at seven p.m. and I am standing in my driveway at seven p.m. waiting for Mom to come outside. I'm still grounded, but apparently, I can go out as long as she or Dad drives me. It makes no sense, and my parents are horrible disciplinarians. I wish I could get legit grounded at least once. All the cool stuff happens to kids in the movies when they get grounded—they find a trapdoor in their closet; an alien communicates with them and they're so bored they respond; a long-lost lover returns to their window in the middle of the night and they have to secretly sneak out onto the roof. Maybe Jordan will come back and throw rocks against my window if I'm trapped in my bedroom.

Mom walks out the front door and drives me to where I want to go without question.

We pull up to Savanna's house, and two cop cars are parked along the curb. Their lights blink without noise. Savanna walks out from her garage and slides into the back seat. We greet each other with a nod.

"Did you tip off the news?" she asks in a whisper.

"Kirsten did," I say. The shadows of passing cars move across Savanna's face as Mom drives us to school.

"The cops came over asking a bunch of questions . . . trying to get ahead of it."

"She's going to do the press conference right after the game and tell everyone how HydroPro set the fires. Apparently, her contact at the station was able to set it up. The police will find out soon enough. The town's attention will be on the press conference. It will give me some cover when I try to get into HydroPro after the game."

She grabs my arm. "Are you sure you want to do it this way?"

I jerk my head back. "Yeah, this makes the most sense. Kirsten is all about it too."

"I can just admit to what I did."

"You're not confessing. Your parents are assholes. Why would you take the blame? We have pictures and videos of HydroPro at every arson scene. At the end of the day, they're the ones who started this mess. They should take the fall."

Ten minutes later, Savanna and I walk into Falcon Crest's gymnasium. I never knew it could hold a crowd this large. The bleachers are full, and people are lined up against every wall, watching the game.

The first quarter is over already, so maybe this won't be as painfully long as I thought. Who knew another side effect of Jordan was that I would become an active member of the school community? I'm in the GSA, I'm attending sporting events on the weekends . . . I might as well run for class president at this point. Or better yet, vice president. It still has the glitz without all the responsibility.

I lock eyes with Darlene in the bleachers and she waves. I push Savanna in her direction. We climb the rickety wooden stairs to the second-to-last row and squeeze past a group of people. Brenton is sitting next to her. His legs are crossed.

"Hey!" Darlene shouts over the cheering crowd. "I didn't know you were coming."

"Yeah. I'm actually here to cheer for Perry and Kirsten more than the basketball team."

"Cheering on the cheerleaders. I like it."

The Falcon Crest cheer squad is beneath the basket by the scoreboard. They're jumping around with perma-smiles. Kara Bynum is thrown into the air. She doesn't fall after three tosses, so maybe her balance is improving after Kirsten and Perry expressed their frustration with her ankle strength. The team is winning 22–18.

I stay standing, so I'm easily visible. Kirsten spots me first. She waves. Perry taps Kirsten on the shoulder and then whispers something into her ear, holding her pom-poms over their faces. Perry does a cheer routine and her eyes don't leave me.

Someone makes a three-point shot, and the crowd erupts in cheers. The bleachers quake. The boys run back and forth across the court so quickly that my head is going to swivel off my neck as I try to follow.

"When are you going to tell Perry about everything?" Savanna asks.

I glance at the scoreboard, and there are ten seconds left in the second quarter. I watch the clock tick to zero until the buzzer rings.

"Now. And I need you."

"What? Dylan." Savanna grabs my arm. Her fingers tighten around my bicep. "You can't say anything about me . . . or the fires. I'm doing that on my own terms."

"I would never out you. I'm talking about Jordan. And what we are. That's all. I promise. We're going to discuss the plan for tonight and you're involved."

She nods, swallowing. "Okay." She tightens her ponytail.

We race down the bleacher steps before the crowd filters from their seats.

The cheer squad makes its way to the locker room. I dart across the court and grab Kirsten's and Perry's arms.

"Can we talk to you?"

"Now?" Perry asks. "And what do you mean *we*?" She looks at Savanna. Her eyes are wide. "We have the halftime routine in, like, five minutes." Perry pulls her arm from my grasp.

"All I need is five minutes."

"Oh, we're doing this now?" Kirsten asks. "Okay."

"Doing what?" Perry asks.

I usher them into the weight room next to the gymnasium. The change in noise level is drastic. I can hear them breathing. I keep the lights off. Perry crosses her arms, still holding her golden pompoms. I stare at them. Savanna stands next to me.

"Well, talk," Perry says.

"I have to tell you something."

"This is a new concept." She glances at Kirsten.

"Just listen," Kirsten instructs her.

"I know I've been terrible and I'm sorry."

"Okay, good. Go on."

"And I know my answer as to why I've been terrible is equally terrible, but there's been a lot of stuff happening in my life the past couple weeks that I couldn't talk about with you until now. I haven't been ignoring you. I just didn't know what to say."

"Are you two, like, dating or something?" she asks, looking between Savanna and me. "I really don't get why the four of us are here. Kirsten, do you get this?"

Kirsten nods rapidly. "Yeah, I do actually." Her face is red.

I spill.

At the end of my rant, Perry stares at me with pursed lips. She puts one of her pom-poms to her chest. "I thought I was surprised when you came out, but this is next level. I know I responded to that in the best way, so let me think of how I want to respond to this secret."

I shake my head. "I don't even know how to react to this, so I'm not expecting any type of response," I say.

"I think our takeaway is that studying science has clearly been a complete waste of our time since it doesn't even hold up in the real world."

"Perr, be serious," Kirsten says.

"I am serious," she says. "No, but seriously, this is bizarre and more ludicrous than the time in Florida when I tried to push Ms. Gurbsterter off the boat and into the Everglades. I'm mostly annoyed you told me last."

"The truth just kind of came out," I say. "I didn't pick how."

"But wait," Perry says. "This organization is deadly and wants to cut off your limbs to test them as a car engine and you want to go inside their headquarters?"

"Yes, right after the game once my mom picks me up."

"Well, I'll meet you at your house." She adjusts her bow.

Kirsten shoots her a look.

"What?" I ask. "No. I'm not going to risk you getting taken too." I slice the air with my hand. "I just wanted you to know about me in case I never come back. I didn't want you to think I was ignoring you for any other reason."

"I'm not going to let myself be left out of this even more," Perry says. "Kirsten is giving the press conference and Savanna . . . I actually still don't know why Savanna is here."

"She caught Jordan and me setting a fire," I lie. "You three are the only other people that know."

"Yeah, and I helped bring Dylan to safety," Savanna says, turning to Perry. "You could just say thank—" She pulls her lips inward, stopping the upcoming insult before it leaves her mouth. Her eyes travel to the floor.

"Okay, whatever," Perry says. "I basically put you and Jordan together. I should be there to reunite you."

"How did you put us together?"

"I forced you to stalk him."

"Actually," Kirsten interrupts. "I think I forced him to stalk Jordan's house. I gave the license plate suggestion first."

Perry waves her hand. "We both put you and Jordan together, and the three of us are going to work together to get him back, like we always do. We've missed you and can't lose you again." She smiles.

I tap her perfectly white sneaker with my foot, blushing.

"Maybe we'll get some powers out of this tonight too," Perry says, grinning. "This life is a bore. You can't have all the fun."

I cross my arms and fake a laugh. "You don't want any. Trust me."

"I wish you guys weren't so casual about this," Kirsten says. "You know trespassing and lying to the press are crimes, right? You are about to break into a serious facility. Lots of things can go wrong. You could get arrested, Perry."

"You honestly don't have to do this, Kirsten," I say. "I swear I won't be mad."

"I don't back out of my commitments. I'm just saying we should proceed with a little more caution."

"I'm coming too!" Savanna blurts.

We freeze.

"To where?" I ask.

"HydroPro...tonight...I owe you."

"What?" Perry groans. "Oh, come on. Owe him for what?"

"More people might just bring more attention," Kirsten says.

I nod. "It's fine," I say. Savanna doesn't need to out herself to Perry and Kirsten to prove why she wants to be there. My chest tightens. I'm somehow out of breath. "The more help there is, the better the chance we get Jordan back."

An announcer comes on a microphone and introduces the cheerleading team for their halftime show.

"Text us after the game," Kirsten says. "We'll be ready."

"I will. I love you guys."

They nod and walk backward to the gym door. They exit the room and join the other cheerleaders as they walk from the locker room.

They run to the center of the court. Their music blasts from the speaker, and the crowd echoes their cheers. Kirsten and Perry move with blank expressions across their faces. Perry is paler than she was five minutes ago. She glances in my direction, but I don't think she can see me in the darkness.

I slowly walk back to the bleachers and watch life unfold around me, unsure of the chaos I may have just released.

thirty-eight

Mom texts me about her arrival at the beginning of the fourth quarter because she doesn't want to deal with the traffic at the end of the night. The game clock ticks below eight minutes. I stand and head for the parking lot. I rub my sweaty hands against my thighs. My knees wobble. The buzzer rings, sending my heart toward the ceiling. Two substitute players switch with two guys already on the court. I scurry across the front row and burst through the gym doors, out of breath.

Savanna stays behind with Perry to watch Kirsten's press conference. If the plan goes right, it will grab the attention of all Falcon Crest and HydroPro and keep them out of my hair as we infiltrate the building.

We are winning by ten points, so I think there will be more games, meaning everyone will be in a good mood tonight. Maybe at the next game Savanna can bring her girlfriend. Then at the game after that Jordan will return and we'll be together again, and we'll all be friends at the State Championship, and we win life. Boom. Positive vibes only heading into tonight.

Three news vans are outside. Someone has placed a small podium nearby with six microphones on it. Camera crews set up their tripods while two news anchors tap their heels against the concrete. I cover my face as I dart past them.

When I get home, I run straight to the basement. I scroll through Twitter, reading tweets about the upcoming press conference, until I hear my parents go to bed. I tiptoe up the stairs and into Dad's office. His HydroPro ID badge sits on his closed laptop, its lanyard wrapped tightly around it. I shove it in my pocket. I collapse into his leather chair and spin in circles as I wait for Perry's call.

Five minutes pass. Then ten . . . then fifteen. There are no updates on Twitter. I bring my fingers to my mouth and chomp on my nails. Then Perry's face appears on my phone screen. I spit a fingernail from my tongue and answer her FaceTime.

"There you are," I say. "I was getting nervous the press conference was canceled."

"Oh no," Perry says. "It's more than on. I'm going to flip you."

She flips her screen from her face to the parking lot in front of the school. It looks as if the entire audience from the game moved from the bleachers to the area in front of the podium.

"Where are you guys?"

"We're at Kirsten's car. I tried to park as close as I could. Can you see? Oh, wait. Here she comes!"

Kirsten steps up to the podium. Her head pops into the air about two feet higher than the sea of onlookers. Her hair is no longer tied in its cheerleading ponytail. She delicately brushes it behind her shoulders, then grips the sides of the podium. She flashes the crowd a tight-lipped smile.

"Oh my god, she's loving this," Perry says.

I laugh.

The news lights are so bright I can barely make out her expression. The faces of the people in the crowd are black silhouettes. She clears her throat.

"Hello," she says in her announcer voice. It's slightly shaky. This is probably her biggest career moment. She clears her throat again. Cameras click around her. "I would like to thank you all for coming here and taking the time to listen to me. Especially after such a great win by our boys. Go, Explorers!" She pauses. A few scattered claps come from the crowd. "I will be short and will be taking questions after I finish my statement." She runs her fingers over her right ear.

"Is she going to get on with it?" I ask.

"Shhh," Perry says.

"My name is Kirsten Lush. I am currently participating in Six ABC's investigative journalism competition that started last month. And while our final articles aren't due for another month, I feel the evidence I have collected on the recent scourge of fires is too strong to keep to myself and continue to leave Falcon Crest, my home, in danger. As most of you are aware, a series of fires has destroyed many of the beautiful new homes being constructed throughout our town. The police have categorized this as an arson case, and I am here to tell you that they are correct."

"Wow, she's killing this," Perry says.

"I have identified a group of suspects from video surveillance, witness testimony, and trace evidence. If you focus your attention on exhibit A." She extends her arm to the side. Someone props up a white screen beside her. She plays the crowd the video of the silver cars at each of the scenes, displays quotes from witnesses putting them outside each fire, and shares photos of them at the scenes.

"These cars, and our suspects, belong to one of our newest neighbors. And it turns out, they're not so friendly. HydroPro." She switches the photo to one of the silver cars outside HydroPro's facility.

The crowd erupts in gasps. The reporters push themselves closer to Kirsten. The clicking cameras intensify. Flashes blast across the screen, and I'm seeing blue and yellow dots. I shake my head.

"This is the new headquarters they completed constructing this winter, just as the fires began ravaging our hometown. This corporation interrupted our businesses, public safety, and peace of mind for no other reason than its own self-interest. With this new information, we expect law enforcement to investigate the full extent of HydroPro's presence at the sites of these arsons and determine this company's true intentions. Without purposeful action, I am afraid we may never return to the Falcon Crest we once knew. I'll take your questions now," Kirsten says. She smiles and bounces her shoulders.

The crowd starts yelling.

"Kirsten!"

"Any evidence on the motive?"

"Why would they do such a thing?"

"Where are the videos from?"

"Kirsten!"

"Can you name suspects?"

Perry flips the camera back to her face.

"Okay!" I say. "Let's go."

Perry hangs up without saying a word.

I slip out of my house through the basement door. I stand at the stop sign at the end of my street for fifteen minutes before they arrive.

The go-kart pulls up to the corner. Perry rolls down the window. She's wearing sunglasses. The white turtleneck underneath her cheer uniform is pulled up over her chin.

"Get in," she says with a smoky voice, nodding. "It's go time."

I laugh as I get into the back seat.

"We were the only car leaving the lot," Savanna says.

"Perfect." I look Perry up and down. "Did you bring a change of clothes, by chance?" I ask. She's still in her maroon-and-gold cheerleading outfit with a shimmering white ribbon tied on her head. She might as well be wearing one of those highlighter vests bikers wear at night. She's asking to be seen.

"Oh no. I left my robbery outfit at home when I was leaving for the game," Perry says.

I roll my eyes and hold up my hands. "I get it," I say.

In a couple of minutes, we arrive at HydroPro's complex. There's a large white sign with the company logo at the entrance. It's illuminated by a series of in-ground lights. We turn down the entrance road, and Perry pauses the music on her phone. There are no streetlights, and the glow from the main road dissipates as we get closer to the building. A heavy border of trees surrounds the complex.

The entrance road goes on for what feels like a mile. The ride is also lengthened by the fact that Perry is driving at two miles per hour as if a herd of deer is going to jump into the road at any second.

The building finally appears in the distance. I look to the right and to the left and can't see where it ends on either side of the horizon. Parts of the structure are all glass.

A hundred yards before the building is a guardhouse. A gate is attached to it and lowered in front of us, blocking the road.

"Uhh, did anyone plan for the fact that maybe we can't go through the main entrance?" Perry asks.

"I was just following Dylan's directions," Savanna says.

"My apologies. I've never infiltrated a high-tech energy company before. I didn't know there would be security checkpoints," I say.

"Maybe we should turn around," Savanna says.

"Wait!" I yell. The gate on the left side of the guardhouse rises. A line of silver cars zoom through the opening and exit the campus, heading in the opposite direction of us. "Get low," I say. Perry puts the car in park, and we sink down into our seats. I peek outside through the bottom of the window. I watch five silver cars drive past us. I quickly pull my phone from my pocket and open Twitter. I check the news, and they're tweeting about Kirsten's press conference. It's started. HydroPro is on the run. It's our time to move.

"Um, Dylan. We're being summoned," Perry says.

"What?" I sit up in my seat. Through the front windshield, the security guard waves us forward.

"Do I go or high-speed reverse out of here?" Perry asks. Her hand clutches the gear shift.

"Um . . ." I swallow and look around the road.

"You have one more second before I make an executive decision."

I take a deep breath. "Go forward. I can make it work. I'll make something up about my dad." I can also torch the guardhouse as a distraction if things get too bad. I keep forgetting I have other skills now besides being silent and awkward.

We slowly approach the guard.

"Oh my gosh, I know him," Perry says.

"You do?" I ask.

"It's Kara Bynum's dad . . . from cheer. Play it cool. Play it cool."

He stands in the middle of the road with his hands on his hips until we're a few feet away. The headlights shine on his black uniform. He circles the car and taps on Perry's window. She lowers it. Her face is tense.

The guard leans closer to the car.

"Mr. Bynum?" Perry asks. Her voice rises five octaves. She flashes a huge smile. Her red lipstick from cheer makes her teeth look abnormally white tonight.

"Perry?" he asks.

"Hi, Mr. Bynum," Perry says, inching closer to the window. She waves. He chuckles.

"What's happening?" I ask aloud.

"I didn't know you worked at . . ." Perry starts, but then taps her chin, searching for the word.

"HydroPro," Savanna whispers.

". . . HydroPro?"

He smiles and shrugs. "I mean, why would you?"

"You're right. Why would I?" Perry lets out a fake laugh. She scratches her head.

"Are you girls already done cheering at the game? Kara must be done, then, too."

"Yup!" Perry says. "We just finished up. The boys won. It was a great game." She nods her head.

"Oh, that's good to hear. Did you do the Nationals routine at halftime? You know, I still have that music mix stuck in my head."

He raises his arms and sings. He throws in a few beats here and there. His hips move side to side, and he dances in front of the guardhouse. Perry and Savanna bop their heads along. I stare blankly.

Mr. Bynum stops dancing and laughs. "I miss being in Florida with you girls. That was a great trip."

"It was, minus the fact we didn't win," Perry says, shrugging.

"Oh, no need for that attitude." He waves his hand. "We'll get 'em next year." He sniffs. "Wait a second." He puts his hands against the car. "What are you doing out here? Shouldn't you be out celebrating with the team after the big win?"

"Um . . ." Perry mumbles something to herself. She pulls her lips in and looks at me. I pop my head out from the back of the car in between the two front seats.

"Hi," I say. "I'm Dylan Highmark. I don't think we've met before. I don't really know Kara, so that's why you probably don't know me. But I know of her because we go to the same school. I have talked to her a few times here and there, though. I saw her tonight at the game, but I didn't talk to her because she was on the court cheering. Obviously. Perry knows her through cheerleading. I'm best friends with Perry, so I know of Kara through her also."

Perry and Savanna stare at me without blinking.

"Okay," Mr. Bynum says slowly. "That still doesn't tell me why you're here."

"Right . . . right." I lick my lips. "My dad actually works here too. Cameron Highmark? I don't know if you've heard of him."

He nods, then steps into the guardhouse. He types something on the computer.

Perry turns to me. "Did you forget how to form a sentence?" Her words are sharp.

"Oh, shut up. I'm doing my best here." I shoot her a look. "I'm stopping by to give him something," I yell out the window.

Savanna cringes.

"He works in the finance department?" Mr. Bynum asks.

"Yeah. He just got hired too, so that's why he's working a little late."

"Okay. I see him in the system." Mr. Bynum prints a small white slip and throws it on Perry's dashboard. He points down the road. "That big brick side of the building to the right is all manufacturing, so don't go there. You want to make a left at the next turn. Administrative offices like finance and research are to the left."

"Research?" I blurt.

He nods. "Yes, but you want finance. First floor on the left wing."

"Okay, thank you! Bye!" Perry says. She quickly puts up the window and hits the gas. "I think I'm going to pass out." She exhales.

I collapse and slam my body against the back seat. I rub my neck. "That was not as smooth as I pictured it," I say.

"You think?" Perry asks. "You're lucky I decided to come. My hands are so clammy." She slides her hands up and down the steering wheel. I look through the rear window and watch the gate lower behind us.

"Cross perimeter . . . check!" Perry says, holding her finger in the air. "What's step two?"

"Turn left," I say.

Fortunately, the left side of the building is all glass and we can see through the exterior walls. The lobby is empty, and no one is sitting at the front desk. I pull my dad's ID card from my pocket and put it against a black box next to the door. A green light flashes. The door clicks. We enter.

"There's a directory," Savanna says, pointing at a sign between elevators. We jog to it. I read the map and room labels. *Human Resources, Finance, Quality Improvement*, blah, blah, blah. All are on the first floor like Mr. Bynum said. The map of the second floor reveals five different research sections. Section E says *Special Projects*, just like the paper Dr. Ivan gave me. I put my finger on it.

"That one," I say. "This is where we're going."

thirty-nine

We reach Section E. The double doors reveal a long hallway with several offices on either side. Pendant lights hang from the ceiling, shining circles onto the white floor. It's quiet.

"I guess we start at door number one," Perry says, shrugging. I nod. She walks over to the first door. My body tenses up. She grabs the doorknob. Hopefully, door number one reveals the grand prize, the cure for Jordan and me sitting in a lit glass box, and this doesn't turn into a sad daytime game show, where the doors reveal random objects like lawn mowers and lamps.

"Behind door number one is . . ." She closes her eyes and swings it open. A gush of air poofs my hair to the side. We peer inside. The room is dark.

I slowly walk through the doorway. A large wooden table is in the middle with maybe twenty chairs around it. It's a conference room. Perry reaches for the light. "Don't," I say, extending my hand. "Leave it off. The wall is all glass. Someone will see us."

"Over here," Savanna says. She walks toward an open door at the far end of the room. On the other side is another space with four gray cubicles. A cubicle is constructed in each corner. A long, skinny table runs down the middle of the room. Rolled-up papers and drawings of various machines are strewn across its surface. Every cubicle is in disarray. Multiple coffee cups sit at each desk. Files and folders are stacked in towers on the chairs. Open notebooks sit with pens lying on the page as if someone stopped writing mid-sentence. According to a name tag, the first cubicle belongs to Dr. Peter Roland.

"Everyone pick a cube and see what we can find," I instruct. Perry and Savanna nod. Perry walks into Dr. Roland's cube and opens a drawer. Savanna enters the next-closest cube. It belongs to someone named Dr. Micha Stalling. I head for the one in the far-left corner. I freeze when I see the name tag. It says *Dr. Maria Ivan*. I gasp. A heavy feeling grows in my stomach.

"Guys!" I shout.

"Shhh!" Perry hushes.

"Sorry," I say, lowering my voice. "But this is the person I've been seeing." I point to the name tag. "And who Jordan saw. She said she's on *our* side and not with HydroPro anymore."

Perry leaves her cube and walks to me. "Maybe she did leave the company and they haven't changed her desk yet?" she suggests.

"No, that wouldn't make sense," I say. "She said she left a while ago." I slap my hand over my forehead. "Oh my gosh. This can't be happening."

Perry inspects the space. "Is that her?" She points to a picture of Dr. Ivan and a little girl.

"Yes," I say, swallowing. I grab a paper on her desk. It has last week's date on the top. Dr. Ivan's signature is etched on the bottom. I show Perry.

"Okay, maybe she's lying to you?" she questions again. Savanna watches us from her cube. Her brow is furrowed.

"Everyone search faster," I say. "I don't like the feeling of this."

I sort through every paper on her desk. I search for the words *Jordan, Ator, antidote, flames, fire, 110 degrees,* and anything else related to Jordan's case that crosses my mind. The sound of metal drawers opening and closing fills the room. I flop into Dr. Ivan's chair and attempt to log on to her computer. My fake passwords are rejected three times in a row. I read through a stack of sticky notes. But the notes are written in sloppy cursive, and I can't make out most of what they're saying.

"Hold up," Perry shouts. I jump from my seat. My breath quickens. She raises a paper into the air and shakes it. Savanna and I jog over.

"Look," Perry says. She points at the top of the paper. "It says *Experiment 1066-11C.* Then below it, it says *Section E, Laboratory Three.* We're in Section E."

"Okay?" Savanna asks. "What is experiment 1066-11C?"

"I don't know," Perry says. "But look at this column."

The paper lists numbers and calculations in multiple columns. I don't know what they mean. But in the fourth column, the word *Ator* appears seven times.

"Jordan's last name," I say. My eyes go wide. "Thank you, Peter Roland. Where's laboratory three?"

We dart out of the room, racing down the hall.

"Laboratory one," Savanna says, pointing at a sign. "Keep going."

We pass laboratory two, then slow to a jog. We approach the door for laboratory three cautiously. It's partly ajar. I lean closer to the opening and hear a conversation. I put my finger to my lips. I push the door a little farther open. Then the three of us slither inside through the crack. We tiptoe down a short hallway, which eventually turns into a large open space. The ceiling must be four stories high. I peer around the corner of the wall. My eyes lock onto two figures. I jump back to shield myself. My breath catches in my throat.

"What's wrong?" Savanna mouths.

"It's her," I whisper.

"Who?"

"Dr. Ivan."

Savanna and Perry shake their heads. "We should leave," Savanna says. She grabs my arm and pulls me to the door. "She's obviously not trying to help you. She can't be trusted. The police can handle this."

"No. Not yet. We have to try. Jordan is counting on us."

I look back at the scene. A man with gray-and-black hair is sitting at a desk. Dr. Ivan stands over him. Her hands are on her hips. I was so focused on her that my mind didn't register the long, oval face and thin, skeletal frame of the man. It's him. The one who's been following me. Why didn't he leave for Falcon with the others when we got here?

A glass chamber, just like the one at Dr. Ivan's office, is built across from them. It's empty inside.

"What would you like me to do, Pete?" Dr. Ivan says to the man. Her face is tight. "He's not going to come tomorrow like he is supposed to, and I certainly can't kidnap a kid." She throws her hands into the air and then rubs her forehead.

"You have to find a way," Pete says. His tone is sharp. "Or the experiment isn't going to be valid. There can't be these large gaps of time in the research. You and your team have already ruined the experiment with Jordan. Don't mess this one up too."

"You're not listening to me." Dr. Ivan makes a fist. Her hands shake. "The boy is frustrated, and rightfully so. We have to give him time to cool off, and then we can restart the experiment."

"Well, maybe if you hadn't told him there was some ridiculous antidote to fix him, he wouldn't be so comfortable running around town and skipping his visits! That was the whole point. Scaring him so he would come back to us." Pete swipes a pile of papers from his desk. "This isn't some science-fiction movie." He shakes his head. "Antidote . . . You've got to be kidding me." He crosses his arms.

"Oh, really?" Dr. Ivan paces. "I had to make up something. He was about to blow up the lab and run away for good. In my opinion, if he thinks there is an antidote, he will keep coming back."

"And what do you suppose happens when he keeps pressing you about the antidote, and then finds out that he isn't dying and there is no need for your fake antidote? Have you thought that through?"

Dr. Ivan cocks her head. "Did you think through the possibility that your first subject could pass on his powers to someone else? And did you think through that maybe if that were the case, it would most likely be someone they were close with? Did you think through how that would affect your experiment?" Her head falls into her hands.

"Hey!" a man's voice shouts from behind us. "Who are you?"

Savanna gasps. I snap my head in the direction of the sound so fast my neck cracks in three places. Two men are standing over us. One of them grabs Perry's arm and pulls her to his chest. Perry screams. She kicks her legs into the air. I stand, stepping out from behind the wall. Savanna jumps behind me.

"Let go of her!" I yell.

"What's going on over there?" Pete asks. Dr. Ivan's heels clack against the floor as she walks toward us.

"Wait, wait, wait," she says. "That boy is much more powerful than you think. Back away from him." She points at us.

"How long have they been there?" Pete asks. He stands and slides his chair across the floor.

"I said let her go," I say to the man holding Perry. Dr. Ivan is right. I am much more powerful than they think. She told me not to use my powers for my health, but maybe she was really saying that to keep herself safe. There's no reason to hold back. It was another lie.

I step forward. The man takes a step back. He squeezes his arm around Perry's neck. Her fingers pry at his wrist. Her face scrunches and reddens.

The man next to him pulls a gun from his waist and points it at me. "Back off, kid," he says.

My body heats up.

"Do not shoot him," Dr. Ivan says.

"Who are they?" the man asks.

"The boy is part of the Ator experiment. I know who he is. Just let me talk to him."

"You don't get to talk to me!" I yell. I turn and stare her down.

"Dylan . . . let me explain." She slowly creeps forward with her hands in the air.

"You had your chance to explain. Instead you chose to lie."

"It may seem like that—"

"It is like that. Are Jordan and I dying?" I ask one final time.

"It's complicated."

"Are we?!"

"No! You're not." She hangs her head.

I take a deep breath. I put my hand in the air, palm facing toward her as if I am about to blast a series of flames her way. She stops walking and whimpers.

"Don't come any closer," I say. She nods, biting her lip. "Tell him to let go of Perry."

She looks past me to Perry. "Let go of the girl," she says. Her voice is uneven.

The man only tightens his grip. Perry chokes. He glances at his partner next to him.

Suddenly, an alarm booms from an overhead speaker. A red light flashes from glass boxes haphazardly spread along the walls. My body shudders. Savanna covers her ears. I look across the room. Pete reaches for a phone in the wall next to his desk. His other hand presses an alarm.

"We need extra security to laboratory three in Section E!" he says. "Right now!" He slams the phone down.

I don't hesitate. I lunge toward the man holding Perry and press my hands into his arm as hard as I can. He screams. His arm goes limp. My red handprints are etched into his skin from the heat. Perry falls to the floor, gasping for air. She clutches her neck. The man with the gun turns and runs for the door. My heart is racing like never before. I jump and float through the air after him. I squeeze my muscles to zoom faster.

I reach the door in a few seconds and land in front of it before the man has a chance of escaping. I hold up my hand. He's unable to stop his momentum, and it collides with his chest. The collision knocks him backward. His face instantly turns a deep shade of red. He collapses to his knees. His limbs jerk three times before he passes out with his mouth agape. I grab the gun from his hand and shove it in my waistband. The alarm still rings.

Savanna holds Perry and rubs her back. Dr. Ivan comes up behind them and shakes Savanna's shoulders.

"Girls, I am here to help him," she says as I get closer. "Let me help. Speak some sense into him."

"Get away from them," I say. I snap my fingers, causing small flames to erupt from their tips. I pull out the gun. Dr. Ivan stands and runs from us toward Peter. I raise the gun and point it in her direction, but I'm not aiming for her.

I fire at the experimental glass box. Everyone freezes. I fire again. The shots are louder than the alarm. The glass box cracks and spiderwebs around the bullet holes. I fire at every corner of the box until I'm out of bullets. I throw the gun at the glass and scream.

"No more experiments!" I shout. "No more." I look at Dr. Ivan as I say the words.

I turn to Savanna and Perry. "Guys, help me load everything inside."

"What do you mean?" Savanna asks.

"The files and papers and all their equipment. I'm going to burn it."

They nod and run to the file cabinets, shelves, and boxes lining the walls of the laboratory. We pile everything next to the crumbling glass box. As I dump a drawer full of papers from Peter's desk, I kick one of the walls of the glass box. Half of it shatters to the floor. Dr. Ivan watches in horror, shaking her head.

I stand over the pile of Jordan's misery and HydroPro's secrets. I shoot a flame from my hands for what I hope is the last time. The papers catch fire first, followed by the computer equipment. Savanna gives Peter's desk a push, and it rolls into the flames. The added fuel sends the fire spinning toward the ceiling. The glass box slowly disintegrates into nothing as the heat intensifies.

"Stop!" Dr. Ivan yells. She grabs a large broken piece of glass from the floor and charges me. "You're destroying everything that will help you."

The extra security guards enter the room. Dr. Ivan waves them after us. "Stop them! Detain them!"

"Run for it!" I yell to Perry and Savanna.

I turn my open palm toward Dr. Ivan, preparing to knock her out with flames, but I freeze.

Peter walks up behind her, cocking a gun and pointing it at the back of her head.

"No," he says flatly.

Dr. Ivan slowly raises her arms. Her chin trembles. "Peter... what... what are you doing?" The whites of her eyes show as she strains to look at him. "Shoot them, not me. Them!"

"We've had about enough of your disgraceful experiment."

"My experiment? It's...it's ours." Dr. Ivan spins to face Peter. He tightens his grip on the gun. Flame light flickers along the sides of their faces. "We've been working on this for almost a year. What are you doing? We came here for—"

"I've been here for the Ators...to protect their son...and now protect Dylan. That's it." He nods in my direction.

I swallow. Perry grabs my wrist.

Dr. Ivan's mouth falls open. "What?" She gasps for air. Her eyes bounce between Peter and me. "But...why? How?" She clutches her chest.

"Greg and Jen were the best people at this company. They were trying to do good for the world. I wasn't going to leave you to your own devices here and destroy what they built. Guards, escort her out, please."

"No!" she shouts. She makes a run for it, but the guards, who outnumber her by five, trap her within moments. They lock their arms around her and drag her toward the door.

"Save my notes from the office! Don't let this be a waste!" Her legs flail as she's pulled from the room. She loses a shoe as they turn down the hall. The sound of her voice becomes muffled by the crackling fire.

I step toward Peter. His brow is clammy. "You?" I ask. He puts his gun back on his waistband.

"What about me?" he asks. He wipes sweat from his lips.

"You weren't trying to kidnap me...or Jordan?"

He shakes his head. "Jordan wasn't as alone as you think. How were my undercover skills?" He winks. "If you would've let me talk to you earlier, I could've explained and avoided this mess."

The flames climb the walls, reaching the ceiling. Pieces of debris begin falling to the floor.

"You knew his parents?" I ask.

"For decades. Came to know Greg when we started at HydroPro together as junior engineers."

"You're from Arizona?"

He nods. Sparks shoot from the burning pile of broken glass and equipment. They whiz past my head. "Kid, you're going to die in here if you keep asking questions. And that would end up being a hell of a waste of my time." He puts his hand on my back and pushes me forward toward the exit. Perry and Savanna follow with glazed eyes.

We run through the same halls from earlier. Red emergency lights guide us back to the main entrance. The deafening fire alarms continue to reverberate in my chest.

"Does this mean you saved Jordan?" I ask, running to Peter's side.

"No. I wasn't aware of that emergency number he had for Ivan. He ran from her, and I don't know where he is." He stops us at an intersection. He peers around the corner, then waves us onward. "When you and Jordan were in Ridley Creek State Park, I threw that smoke grenade to divert HydroPro, but I lost you guys too."

"That was you?"

He nods. I choke on my breath, thinking of how Kirsten sent his picture to the police when we should have sent Dr. Ivan's.

"Where can I look for him?" I ask.

"Your guess is as good as mine."

He's running as fast as my thoughts are racing through my mind. When we reach the lobby, a horde of police cars and fire trucks are parked outside. I spot Kirsten talking among a group of reporters.

"You can't go out there!" I yell to Pete. Before anyone sees us, I push Perry and Savanna behind the front desk. We dive to the floor and crawl into a front office.

Pete huffs as he spins to change course. He follows us into hiding.

I push my back against a wall.

"They here for me?" he asks. "You really should've let me talk to you earlier."

"I'm sorry," I say, breathing heavily. "If I knew you were on my side, I wouldn't have ratted you out."

Pete nods. "You did what you had to do. I'll figure something out."

A bang erupts in the lobby. "Falcon Crest Police!" someone shouts. "Come out from that office now!"

"You're going to be on your own now, Dylan," he says. My face wavers when my name leaves his lips. "I've done all I can. The rest is up to you." He gives me his gun.

"Wait, what?"

Pete jumps out of the room and back into the lobby with his hands up. "I'm here."

"Hands up! Put your hands up!" the police shout.

"They're up," Pete says. "Everyone calm down."

Metal handcuffs grind and click into place around Pete's wrists. Boots squeak along the tile floor until the lobby is silent again.

Perry shakes me from my daze. "Dylan! We have to get out of here."

I nod. I lift a chair and chuck it through one of the office windows. I wrap my arms around Savanna and Perry, and we float through the broken glass to safety. We sprint across a grassy field for about a hundred yards. Before we enter a wooded area, I turn back to look at HydroPro. An orange glow flickers in each window.

This experiment ends just as it started, by erupting in flames.

forty

HydroPro is the only topic covered in the news over the next few days. The Philadelphia facility is permanently shuttered, partly from the investigation and partly because it's halfway burned to the ground. Even if nothing comes of the inquiry from Kirsten's reporting, at least Falcon Crest knows them for their arsons and crimes rather than their hydrogen-fueled vehicles and machines.

I've blocked Dr. Ivan's phone number. I have no interest in devoting any more of my mental capacity to her. Each day, I bring my paint-by-numbers canvas onto my front porch to paint and watch for silver cars. But there's always nothing. Today, I've finally finished my spring painting of the blue flowers.

Kirsten's press conference is making national news. It started off local, but then someone retweeted the original video and another person retweeted it, and then it was viral. She's been doing a different interview for a blog or website every day. She's basically famous. I want some credit eventually, but I am letting her have her moment for now.

I'm in Kirsten's room standing next to her desk. Kirsten is sitting in the middle across from Savanna. Professional ring lights shine on their faces. A camera is set up on a tripod on her desk, recording one of her interviews. My hand hovers over it.

"Why did you feel like it was finally time to come forward and tell your story?" Savanna asks. She's holding a small notecard over her crossed legs. For once, the roles are switched. Kirsten is an interviewee.

"For me, I think the turning point was when I realized how much the fires were affecting other people," Kirsten says. Her hands are folded in her lap. "I was frustrated with the pace of the investigation, especially since I was seeing firsthand the burden that it was placing on my fellow classmates. It became more than a contest for me." She shrugs. "In the end, the public was in danger, and I had a responsibility to share what I knew."

Savanna nods. Then Kirsten turns to me. "Okay, hit Stop," she says.

I push a button and stop the recording.

"How was that?" she asks. "Was that better?"

I nod. "Much." That was the third time we filmed that segment of her interview with Savanna.

"Awesome." Kirsten gets up and plucks the camera from the tripod. "Thanks again, Savanna. I'm getting so many questions through Instagram and Twitter too. We're going to have to film a few more of these Q and As for fans."

Savanna smiles. "Of course. Anything to help set some of this straight."

"So, did you win the contest?" I ask.

"I think I technically disqualified myself," Kirsten says. "But who even cares anymore. I'm getting more internship offers than if I won the contest. I don't know how I am going to decide which offer to take." She clicks through her camera roll. "I'll have to edit this fast. Do you want to stay and help me edit, Savanna? You can tell me if any angles are bad for you."

"I think my angles are the least of my concerns now, but I can definitely help." Savanna clicks off the ring light.

"What's on your agenda, Dylan? Do you want to stay?" Kirsten asks.

I shake my head. "I think I am going to go for a walk." I look out the window. The ground is covered with snow.

Kirsten sighs and walks toward me. "Are you sure you're okay, Dyl?" She gently massages my arm.

I throw up my hands, then rub my forehead. "I'm trying to be."

"Nothing from him?"

"Nope."

Kirsten gives me a hug. "I still think there's a chance he'll come back."

"I hope you're right." I lift my backpack from the floor.

"I'm sorry, Dylan," Savanna says.

"Thanks, guys."

"How is your dad holding up?" Kirsten asks.

"He's fine," I say. "His old company took him back right away. It just makes things harder because I can't talk to him about what happened. He goes on and on about HydroPro . . . but he barely knows half of it."

She nods. "Well, we're here."

"I know. And I love you guys for it." I grab a stack of paper from Kirsten's desk. "Can I take some of this?"

There's only one method of communicating with Jordan I haven't tried yet, and that is the old-fashioned US mail. I decide to respond to the letter he wrote that Dr. Ivan gave me.

I leave Kirsten's house and walk to the woods. Snow falls gently from the sky, the ground is frozen, and my phone says it's twenty-one degrees, but I'm not cold. I clear the wintry mix from a stump and take a seat. I rest the paper on my knee, tapping a pen against my chin. I don't make an outline in the Notes app on my phone or think about what to say. I word-vomit on the page the first things that come to mind.

I thank Jordan for wanting to keep me safe. I write about the butterflies in my stomach on the night we met. I share the feeling of the pit in my stomach on the first night without him. I recall our bike rides through Falcon Crest, and how his steady hands on my shoulders were nothing short of subtle magic. I tell him that I am sitting here wanting the world. But a world with him in it. Lastly, I disclose the details about the experiment, HydroPro's lies, Peter, and that he's not dying—and neither am I.

There's a reason to come out from hiding and come back home. I hope this letter convinces him.

It ends up being six pages long. I stuff them into an envelope, write my return address in the top left corner, and put Jordan's name in the center with no delivery address beneath it. I don't know where to send it, but I know of a good place from where it could be delivered. I stand and head for Jordan's aunt's house.

Gray clouds cover the sky. Snow continues to lightly fall, just as it has the past three days. Everyone is hibernating, so Jordan's neighborhood is silent. I knock on the front door of his house. Someone opens it in seconds.

A woman looks me up and down. "Can I help you?" she asks. She's tall and thin, with short black hair that ends above her shoulders. It's the same color as Jordan's hair.

"Hello," I say, smiling. "Are you Jordan Ator's aunt?"

She nods. "Yes, I am. Are you a friend of Jordan's?" She clutches her arms and rubs them. The light reflecting off the snow brightens her face.

My throat gets thick and my bottom lip quivers. I turn to the side and press my hands against my eyes to keep them from tearing up.

"I am." I sniff. "You and I have never met, but I've been hanging out with Jordan for a while."

"That's nice to hear. I'm glad he had a friend while he was in town." She opens the door wider. "Are you cold? Would you like to come inside?"

"No, thank you. I was wondering if you knew where Jordan was. I miss him and would like to see him."

She frowns. "I miss him too. But the last update I received was that he was back in Arizona with some other members of our family. I haven't heard anything in a couple weeks, though. Ever since the accident, Jordan hasn't been the best communicator. But we try." She shrugs.

I nod and look at her feet. I shift and my boots crunch into the snow on the front porch.

"Do you know if he's okay, at least?"

"As far as I know . . . yes."

"Okay." I dig into my pocket and pull out the letter. "Well, if you ever see him or find out where he is, could you give this to him? Or mail it?"

"Of course. What is it?"

Over her shoulder, a familiar face pops on the television screen in the living room. It's Peter. I listen to the news anchor. "Now we turn to the ongoing investigation into the HydroPro corporation and their involvement in the Falcon Crest arsons. One of the employees taken into custody from the fiery inferno that shuttered the building is speaking out against the corporation. Dr. Peter Roland has apparently struck a deal with law enforcement officials to lessen any charges potentially brought against him. The transcript remains sealed for now—"

"Are you okay?" Jordan's aunt asks.

I shake my head and refocus my eyes on her. "Yes, I'm fine," I say. "Sorry, what did you ask?"

"The letter." She points at my hand. "What does it say?"

I hold out the letter to her. "Just something I think he should know."

She takes the envelope. She turns it over in her hands and inspects it. "I'll be sure to do my best, then"—she looks at the return address on the envelope—"Dylan." She smiles.

"Thank you. Have a nice day."

"You too. Safe ride home." She waves and shuts the door. Snow slides off the door frame and lands beside my feet. I stare at the door for a moment. I'm hoping she opens it again and insists on bringing me inside for tea or coffee. I want to sit with her and talk about Jordan through the night. She's the last connection I have to him.

But nothing happens. I take a deep breath and turn for the street. I mount my bike.

Before I was in a relationship, I always thought people were so dramatic when they got upset about breaking up with their boyfriend or girlfriend they were only dating for a short period of time. I cringe now at the advice I gave Perry to "just get over" Keaton and my contempt for the other couples at my school who cried after a split at the school dance, or whined in the cafeteria about wanting to get back together with their crush.

I don't know why we mock people who want to be with the person they love. We say things like, "Doubt it will last" and "It's cute for now." But I think when it's real, it will always last—whether you are together or not. Even if it just lasts as a memory. It's still something.

Your partner literally becomes a part of you. I never thought about the word *partner* until now. I like it.

And when a piece of you is missing, you do your best to get it back. If you lose your phone, laptop, favorite pair of jeans, or other parts of your identity—you look for it until it's found. And no one gives you crap about it. We don't label someone as desperate, lonely, and pathetic when they're searching for their lost thousand-dollar iPhone. If Kirsten told me she lost her car, my first thought wouldn't be to say, *I'm sorry. There are plenty of cars out there for you.* We would scour every inch of Falcon Crest until we found the car. In the past when someone lost their laptop at school, the administration literally put up posters and made announcements about it over the loudspeaker. When a relationship ends, it's whispered about until it fades away.

Then again, maybe everyone helps you search for those types of material things because they know what to look for. They're tangible items everyone has held at one point. They can't help you look for love or tell you how to get your boyfriend back because they haven't seen the pieces. They weren't a part of it. They didn't feel it. They never held Jordan.

Jordan and I were each part of a story, a hug, a kiss, and a friendship. None of those things can exist without the other part. When you lose that many parts of yourself, it hurts. And when you realize those parts are irreplaceable, you become lost too.

forty-one

"Ugh, finally," I say, picking up an empty Blizzard cup I dropped on the floor. Two last customers leave Dairy Queen after an unexpected rush. I shoot the cup into the trash can like it's a basketball. Then I wipe up the candies I spilled all over the counter while trying to juggle three Blizzards and an ice-cream sundae at the same time.

"You're getting so busy now," Savanna says. She's sitting at a table with Kirsten. Our normal isn't what it used to be, but we're all enjoying it. It's nice to have someone new around, and throughout this whole ordeal I've learned that I've always had more people in my corner than I thought. "We're going to have to stop coming."

"Oh no," Kirsten says, laughing and waving her finger. "One thing you should know is that we never stop coming. No matter how busy it gets."

It's March and people think it's time for ice cream. But it's not. Society has tricked us into thinking March is a spring month when it's actually a winter month. Spring break is in March. The first day of spring is in March. All the calendars have grassy and flower pictures for the month of March. But in all my lifetime, I don't think I've ever experienced a pleasant March in Pennsylvania. It snows, the sky is gray, there's black slush everywhere, and people wear flip-flops when it reaches fifty degrees outside. And we know their toes aren't ready for that exposure this time of the year.

It's been almost one month since there was a fire in Falcon Crest, Pennsylvania. Meaning it's been over one month since I last spoke to Jordan. I've checked my mailbox every day and my letter hasn't been returned by the post office. It's somewhere out in the world. Maybe it's in his hands. Maybe it isn't.

I've picked up a few extra shifts at Dairy Queen during the week to keep myself busy. Or at least that's the reason I've told my parents. In all honesty, I'm trying to be here for Jordan. He knows I'll be here. But I still don't know if he's coming back.

It's been two weeks since my last incident with my powers. I melted a few pencils at school after a particularly stressful test. But I've learned how to stay calm in most situations. I'm able to work again and touch ice cream. Dairy Queen also isn't the most stimulating environment for me, so I'm not afraid of any unexpected situations that'll cause me to blow up the soft-serve machines.

My only change in practice is that I don't flip the Blizzards upside down when I serve them to customers. I'm afraid my hot fingertips are enough to cause it to slide out from the cup. Customers are supposed to get the Blizzard for free if we don't flip it upside down. Most people don't know that, though. So I can get away with it. A few brats do, and I give it to them. It's better than trying to flip it, having the ice cream spill all over the floor, embarrassing myself, and then remaking it in shame while everyone watches.

Plus, spilled ice cream all over the counter might trigger a memory of the first night I met Jordan, and I'm trying not to think of that. Or him.

The door opens and the bell above it rings. I toss my rag on the counter. "We're closed—" I start. But then I see Perry sashaying through the doorway. She's wearing her all-star cheerleading uniform, which is like the Falcon Crest uniform but multiplied by a thousand in intensity level. It's turquoise and bedazzled. Her hair is puffed six inches above her head. Her eyelids are blue, and her eyelashes are longer than normal by a few inches.

"Ladies and Dylan," she says as she enters. "I am pleased to say that as of today, I am Falcon Crest's newest cheer captain." She brings her arms skyward and then does a cartwheel. We clap.

"Ms. Gurbsterter is letting you do it next year?" I ask.

"She is! All thanks to this one over here." Perry nods at Kirsten. She pulls out a seat at the table and sits with them.

"I didn't do anything," Kirsten says, blushing.

"You did, though. Gurbsterter has not shut up about your press conference. She claims she hasn't seen things so bad in this town since George H. W. Bush lost the election to Bill Clinton in the nineties. She said we need a win at Nationals next year to raise the spirit of the town, and I'm one of the best cheerleaders she has. It's kind of annoying that I've been telling her that for years, and she decides to listen now because of you and not me. But it worked, so I really don't care."

"Snaps for Kirsten's influence," Savanna says.

We snap our fingers.

"We should all celebrate with ice cream!" I exclaim. "What do you want before I finish cleaning up?"

"Vanilla ice cream with rainbow sprinkles," Savanna says.

I stare her down. "Now you're just trolling. You get that every time."

"So? I like it. You think I'm getting it because it's rainbow. Stop judging."

The door clicks open again.

"We're closed," I yell louder than last time. I lift a spoonful of rainbow sprinkles and shake them over Savanna's cup of vanilla ice cream.

Kirsten and Perry scream. The spoon twitches in my hand.

I spin around, suspecting a masked murderer has entered.

"Are you still open?" Jordan says.

My eyes go wide. A jolt of heat travels from my head to my fingers, and the cup of ice cream explodes in my face. But I'm unfazed. It's him. It's really him. He's standing in the center of the store. In real life. He's wearing his red hoodie.

Who am I kidding? I was always thinking about Jordan.

And in this moment, I'm almost positive love can't be routine when it's with someone who excites you. His presence hits me like when a favorite memory you forgot comes rushing back and you experience it all over again.

I run out from behind the counter and into his arms. His hug is just as I remember. And this one leaves a new, better imprint on my chest. I kiss his lips, and they taste the same. His hair is messy. He's warm but not burning hot. He's just right. He's perfect.

He pulls out a crumpled piece of paper from his pocket and places it in my hand.

"What is this?" I ask.

He smiles. "I wrote you back."

I unfold the paper and flatten it on the service counter. My letter is on one side, but I flip it over and scan some sort of colorful drawing on the other side. I quickly realize what it is.

It's a drawing of a city. The layout is like the game *SimCity*. The name of the city is in the bottom left corner. It's called St. Dylan. The population of the city is two. The mayor approval rating is 100 percent.

It looks like he chose to start the city by the train tracks—such a wise decision. Some argue that starting the city by the water is better, but the train brings in more revenue.

A street winds through the buildings in the shape of a heart. At the bottom of the road is an assemblage of Dairy Queens and Starbucks. There's a wooded section beyond the city limits. There are hiking trails and ponds. A few sketched homes are scattered among the trees. It's labeled *M. Night Shyamalan's Village*.

There's a residential section with a few burning houses. Beside it are fire trucks and cop cars. An Italian restaurant serving eggplant lasagna stands in the city center. At the bottom of the paper is the list of icons that designate what your Sims need, like electricity, water, and trash removal. There's a new one with the label O_2 and a corresponding bubble that says *In need of oxygen*.

Two Sims stand at each end of the city. There's a circle around their feet and a bubble above their heads, like they've been selected. I read the first Sim's label. It's Dylan Highmark. The description reads: *Came from Pennsylvania. Hot hair. Floats. Looking for Chemistry cheat sheets.*

My eyes jump across the page to the second Sim. It's Jordan Ator.

The description reads: *Came from Arizona. Hot temperature. Might go up in flames soon. In love with Dylan Highmark.*

I swallow. My hands start shaking. I stare at the paper. For some reason, I'm scared to look up.

I reach across the counter, open a drawer, and pull out a pencil. I extend Dylan Highmark's bubble and write, *In love with Jordan Ator.*

This piece of art is better than anything that's featured at the galleries or hanging in my room. I don't have to search for a relatable message or envy the people in the picture. This one is for me.

I roll the paper back up and throw it at Jordan. It swirls through the air and dives to his feet. He leans over, picks up the paper, and unrolls it.

A smile grows across his face as he reads. He tosses the city over his shoulder and runs to me. He squeezes me so tight it will be impossible to let go. I don't care where he's been or how long he's been gone. Things like this don't happen twice without reason.

"I was afraid to come back here after the first night we met because I didn't want to get to know you and then leave . . . or die," Jordan says. His hot breath envelops my face. "But tonight I couldn't get here fast enough. Because now we have a chance at forever."

I kiss him again. We still have our powers and life will be different. But no one can take forever away from us.

There's no complex explanation for love, like I thought. It happens unexpectedly, just like how Jordan walked into Dairy Queen tonight. You're never ready for it. You can't be. There's no way to see it coming.

Jordan and I saw the same spark. Like fire, we couldn't look away. And then at some point, the magical switch happened that took us to a place of love. I can't pick out the moment or the hour. It moved at warp speed. We flew from one scene to the next. The force knocked me out and gave me life. Jordan's touch was an energy I never felt before. In times of need, we read each other's minds and supported each other with super strength. Looking back, I now accept that forming a relationship with a stranger is supernatural. Flames and floating are pretty cool, but there's no superpower more profound than being yourself and making someone fall in love with you.

Who needs an Elemental Balancer when Jordan Ator is all the balance I need? He wipes vanilla ice cream from my lips, kisses me, and we float to the ceiling.

acknowledgments

The publication of this book has been nearly a decade in the making. From working on my craft to finding representation, several groups of people have helped me persevere and achieve this dream. I would like to thank:

My family—Mom, Dad, Augie, Alexandra, Joe, and Jules—who have provided me with unwavering support throughout my personal, professional, and academic trials. I have always felt you were behind me. Thank you for loving me as I am and helping me along my path. The space you create for me got these words on the page.

Liz Parker, my literary agent, and everyone at Verve who helped sell this book! I can't believe my novel gets to debut with the Disney Publishing Group. You made this crazy dream of mine into a reality. Thank you for finding me in the email slush, connecting with my characters, and believing in this story before I even knew what it would become.

Augusta Harris and Brittany Rubiano, my fantastic editors, who made this book into something truly special. It was a joy to work with both of you throughout this process. Every single edit you proposed made this book a more enchanting story. I could not have asked for better advocates to lead me through publication.

The extraordinary team at Hyperion. Phil Buchanan, my designer, and Patrick Leger, the cover artist. This book looks better than anything I imagined. I will be forever swooning at the interlocked hands over Jordan's heart on the cover. Sara Liebling, my managing editor, who deftly liaised my novel through departments at Hyperion and beyond. Guy Cunningham, copy chief, who made sure every detail of this book made sense for the readers. Dina Sherman, Danielle DiMartino, Andrew Sansone, Holly Nagel, Elke Villa, and Seale Ballenger, the marketing and publicity team for Dylan and Jordan. So appreciative of your work in spreading the word and making sure this story not only existed but was seen, read, and heard.

Kelly Brightwell, Lexie Gregor, Sarah Hawksworth, Marissa Lawlor, and Brittany Spear. Thank you for being the best group of friends I could have ever asked to grow up with. We've experienced life's most important moments together and I could not have done it without you. Even on my loneliest days, I always knew I had you by my side. Many of the laughs, memories, and relationships in this story are inspired by our adventures. I can't wait to see what's next for us.

Nicole Matteucci, my favorite and forever inspiration. Thank you for pushing me to always be the best version of myself, being a steadfast listener, and helping me realize my goals. Life knew I needed you, and I'm so glad we both arrived early to class on the first day of graduate school.

Hannah Ellis and Rachael Riley, my hype crew, who let me skip happy hours to type in my room and finish this book. You provide me with so much happiness that I just had to sprinkle some of our best moments together throughout this story. I'm grateful I met you when I did, and even more grateful for our adventures together that have yet to come.

Nyssa Entrekin, Michelle Gross, Grigorios Papadourakis, Reed Rickards, Matthew Rigsby, and Khalida Sethi, who were the very first readers and champions of *The Temperature of Me and You*. Thank you for your willingness to see an early draft of this story. Your feedback and enthusiasm pushed me forward to believe in myself, finish this book, and make it what it is today.

You, the reader. This is the beginning of my author journey and I'm so grateful you're here at the start. Thank you for choosing to spend your precious time with these characters. Your readership is what it's all about and will help me bring more stories to life. For your dedication, love, excitement, and support, I sincerely thank you.